The Gre

Michael Cisco

Foreword
By Rhys Hughes

Chômu Press

The Great Lover

by Michael Cisco

Published by Chômu Press, MMXI

Published in April 2011 by Chômu Press.

by arrangement with the author.

All rights reserved by the author.

ISBN: 978-1-907681-06-6

First Edition

Design and layout by: Bigeyebrow and Chômu Press

Cover illustration by: Torso Vertical

E-mail: info@chomupress.com

Internet: chomupress.com

The Great Lover

For Autumn

Contents

Foreword
by Rhys Hughes

Is it possible to say anything at all about a perfect work of art? I ask this question not merely for rhetorical effect, but because I genuinely want to know the answer. I'm fairly sure the answer is "no" but I'm willing to be corrected on this point. Certainly the idea of writing about music has been ridiculed, not least by Wittgenstein, who argued that it is fundamentally absurd to describe one language in terms of another.

Michael Cisco's work, *The Great Lover*, is prose rather than music and thus should be a valid construct to write about. Yet because of its special rhythmic force and dark energy, the way it inhabits its own length exactly but does so by propelling itself constantly forward like the purest melody, it seems to me to be the closest any example of writing can get to being music without producing audible sound. I know of almost no other writer who can do this. So does Cisco's sublime use of language in this manner position his book beyond critical discussion?

I say "almost" no other writer, for there are a small number who also know the secret. Cisco is not an entirely isolated author but certainly he belongs to an extremely rarefied group. Last year I discovered a book entitled *The Blind Owl*, a short novel, almost a cosmic horror prose poem, by an author previously unknown to me, Sadegh Hedayat. The theme of Hedayat's remarkable book is partly the effect of isolation on the creative mind. It is heady stuff indeed, blackly rapturous.

When I was younger I remember feeling a particular kind of shudder at the sheer strangeness of certain passages in Michel Leiris' *Aurora*: the clarity of the oddness was awful but also somehow ecstatic. In Leiris it comes in waves; in Hedayat the effect is constant. *The Blind Owl* is a deeply disturbing book and one feels there is a malignant intelligence about it that is independent of its author; that once it has been read one may never escape from its influence. It is difficult for me to explain this feeling rationally, because by definition it is a *feeling* rather than an analysis. On some level I believe this book has planted a seed in my soul and I don't know what sort of nourishment the growth will take from me, nor what sort its fruit may eventually provide.

Cisco's work is powerful in precisely the same way and has the same effect on me. In terms of narrative drive, dynamic form and force, *The Great Lover* is radically different from *The Blind Owl*, but it haunts the waking mind with equal conviction and bittersweet dread. It therefore comes as little surprise that Cisco is an expert on Hedayat; but it doesn't seem that the Persian writer, who committed suicide in 1951, is a direct influence on the contemporary voice of Cisco: rather it is a case of two great and odd minds inventing authentic forms of mystical terror that despite many cultural differences have also a few parallels, or perhaps meta-parallels, utter originality being one of them and an ability to root itself into a reader's soul being another.

The conclusion is slightly worrying, for it implies that there is more to the printed page than the end product of playing with patterns, shuffling conventions, the mechanical games of sentence structure. A cluster of monkeys bashing on anachronistic typewriters might eventually recreate the books of, say, Anatole France or Olaf Stapledon, two writers I admire enormously, but one feels they could never properly replicate Hedayat or Cisco. Even if an infinity of years was available to those poor primates and the inevitability of eternal randomness meant that Cisco's exact *words* were reproduced in perfect order, there still lurks the mysterious suspicion that the *nous* would be missing.

Wittgenstein once postulated a magical pill that could fill the man who swallowed it with the same feelings, to the same degree of intensity, as if he had just listened to a Bach fugue. He asked us to consider whether the existence of the magical pill would make the fugue superfluous. His own answer was that the pill could never be a substitute, because a fugue, both in idea and reality, is more than its final effect. It is a process in time and space, and the process is the thing itself.

Those teeth are like fence pickets. I touch the oily lapels and collar. Their grit clings to my palms like wet sand. I throw my arms around his neck — it's so thick my hands don't meet... I climb up onto him and press against the unyielding surface, with my cheek to the pebbly pig-iron of his bulging, bull-like neck... Now it's turning into skin, the metal is changing, and begins to yield. It softens — it yields. The statue is turning its face to me, turning into a human being.

The ultimate value of *The Great Lover* is not merely in the sensations generated by its resolution, which are more than the sum of the sensations created in the reader during the reading itself, but the peculiar fact that during the reading one begins to feel the text really is alive, transforming itself into something human too. That is *its* process, or life cycle. Cisco doesn't rely on horror props to manipulate the reader's reactions in this regard. He has created an organism rather than a machine, and the resultant entity, this book, seeks to engage with its reader on a basis that is still, for me at least, unclear. Symbiosis or predation?

Although that sounds rather fanciful, this impression is tangible, not purely lyrical or symbolic. Perhaps it is the sheer wealth of imagery and multitude of concepts that achieve this daunting effect. *The Great Lover* is full of clever conceits, tangential ideas that fly off, twist and re-root themselves back into the main body of the text. It is a densely layered work consisting of so many strata of meaning that its dynamic has the appearance of accelerated geology, passages rising, enveloping, drifting into new configurations like the continents of an unknown world buried beneath our own, rather than merely queuing up and waiting their turn to perform, as passages in the vast majority of novels do.

"Given the proper conditions," declares the character Ptarmagant, "life could arise spontaneously again, as it did at first. Nothing prevents this. It could happen… anywhere. New, unevolved organisms, living by wholly other principles." One wonders if what is possible for life might also be feasible for works of fiction. The works of Cisco, Hedayat, a precious few others, *do* give the impression they belong to a separate tree of existence, growing in parallel with the more familiar trunk of mainstream weird writers, perhaps even in pre-established harmony with it, but not dependent upon its shade or support.

As for Michael Cisco himself: I know very little about him. In fact I have deliberately avoided researching the man. Bizarrely, it feels almost sacrilegious to do so; better by far to preserve the riddle. I received a copy of *The Divinity Student* through the mail several years ago and was excited to discover a writer who cared about philosophy and used it in a way that was beguiling and dreamlike, but also highly controlled and assured. In my mind, Cisco forms an unholy trinity with Hedayat and Ligotti as the chthonic gods of existential horror.

The subterranean mindscape of *The Great Lover* is a cosmos entirely unto itself, a mysterious, reeking, unutterably strange, hazardous, fecund and carnivalesque digestion of events, ideas, opportunities, revelations and mutations. Cisco's imagination is the most monumentally Tartarean of any dark fantasy writer currently writing. In this endlessly unfolding network of cavities and situations, nothing at all is predictable. Cisco, after all, is the man who dared dream not only of invasion of the celestial realms by the denizens of hell, but a counter invasion of hell by those of heaven, for the sake of a perverse balance.

In one of my own forthcoming books there is a scene in a tavern where are gathered a selection of notable modern authors. Michael Cisco is the first of them to be introduced by a guide to the narrator, with the words, "He's a writer of elegantly dark philosophic fantasy but one who is often overlooked — he's philosophical about everything except that fact." This is making an assumption about Cisco's attitude that has no basis in reality; I don't really know how he regards himself. Yet I suspect the time is coming when to overlook him will be still to see him, for if anyone has the ability to bend light it is surely Michael

Cisco.

To sum up briefly, *The Great Lover* is a disturbing and enormously powerful work, a valuable addition to Cisco's impressive bibliography. Among other things it creates a perfect equilibrium, by compression, between external and internal reality. Never before have I laboured so helplessly over writing a foreword to a novel. Immediately after reading it, I realised I had nothing much to say. It's a perfect work of art.

THE GREAT LOVER

The birds suddenly leap into the air from the grass and from the trees, come together and rise in a palpitating clot, then disperse to the horizon... each one black against the darkening blue sky. The wind leaps from the grass and trees, it rises and grows stronger, more alarming. Over my grave the turf is ruffled, the dry flowers knock against my stone battering their petals away. The world is filled with energy; these minute events each impart another twist to this or that hidden coil, and behind our earthen walls decay rifles our bodies like hot wind — we feel it, too. The wind rises and flickers through our sere, pompous grave clothes. At its far extremity a woman in a costume raises her veiled head and howls softly at the sky. She is turning into a coyote with a light heart, though her appearance stays the same.

Though I can turn my head neither to the left or right and so am unable to look at my neighbors in the earth, our nerves have grown and penetrate our caskets. They wove a nervous lace through the solid rock. Batteries of memory in random series — we are there wherever wind blows fire burns water laps dirt melts because there are memories of yours in all these things, memory to heal or harm. In the *story* the weapons of memory cross with the present's weapons; in the world, no one ever tells a story in which we have *no* part. The line passes through us, and we can feel every train go by. We can feel every word on every train going by.

My coffin is suddenly ablaze with light. A luminous vapor appears with a pop like a cloud in a cloud chamber directly above me and my coffin glows like a fluorescent tube. I can see myself, all withered. The ridgy skin is stretched taut over my deflated eyesockets; my eyes appear to be open but cast down; and it is this modest, still face that I bring to you. My lips have dried and stretched themselves over my teeth in a flattened ellipse, and it is through this crooning aperture that my voice passes out to you by way of those subterranean vibrations I mentioned by way of those subterranean vibrations. Now off to the left, I see

Michael Cisco

another coffin, lit from within, transparent, its tenant bows her head. One by one, in some cases two at a time, like the lights of a theatre marquee, coffins around me burst alight with pale, blonde flame, tenuous as mist; the light is absolute. Irresistible commands drift horizontally through space and through matter like flakes of marine snow, evenly spreading on their own. Whenever one collides with a secret germ of happiness inside, it joins itself to it ardently, becomes it, so that it is a joy to obey. The turning of a page, an irresistible command.

The pale road presses out from between my lips, the anonymous skull voice. In the dark, we are hanging together on the billowing canopy our nerves made, a diamond of eight coffins trailing long nervous manes. We hang in fertile flesh-eating graveyard earth. Its spray flecks my skin with bright cinders, and lying here I experience the onset of spring, a warm elongation of limbs, of gently rising sap, the distention of lungs as they greedily fill themselves with the fragrance of new flowers.

A thrill of suspense draws us taught on nerve-lanyards. Something is happening. Our nerves rise like weary hands and clasp together, forming mercurial connections sealed with white coagulant. Dry and brittle as straw, they creak as they lean toward each other; as they knit, they become humid and supple. Now they gleam with perspiration, a salt mist gathers around an elastic web of thickening white cables. I feel a draught in my skull, sly jets and whistles of air — we eight are no longer strangers. Above us jaws open wide even blacker on the inside — now one by one our jaws also drop open. We will unhurriedly draw this light into our desiccated bodies. It will consume us and alchemize us, and when we are done, we will die again. Our frail bodies shudder, vibrate with strain. Our voices burn together into one voice, like rising from a terrible fire a ball of black smoke that is our voice speaking loud enough for you to hear. We are the undergrounders.

You can hear my words, but you cannot hear the wild gaiety with which I speak them. I am the voice from the midst of eight golden coffins.

"hic locus est ubi mors gaudet succurrere vitae"
"this is the place where death rejoices to teach those who live"
—motto from an autopsy room

CHAPTER ONE

The morning raises the city's tide so you feel the whole city wobble, climbing up round your belt like weightless gelatin. (This is the map just breaking in to remind you to keep a look out for me.) On into the afternoon here it is again, the staggered city struts along tripping but never less full of itself than in the hours leading up to quitting time and sunset. The wind slaps a man going along the pavement full in the chest with a windblown leaflet. He peels it back and looks at the big black words without scanning them, only taking the whole sheet in at once shallowly; it says "Respect to the Skeletons of the Robbery Victims, To the Bones Red Without Blood, To the creeping Grins of Ghouls and Gibbons with Eyes like Full Moons, To all Nocturnal Animals that have not yet been mastered, To Sardonic Teeth, the Of of Of and the And The And The and To the destructive detriment of all thrones of every nation and the steady development of all astonishing disintegrations and transformations in and throughout all the Cardinal and Ordinal Worlds, and in All Spaces and Times, This Goes Out to Trim Hand and the two Stolen Skeletons, This Goes Out to Laughing Eyes, This Goes Out to You Here, This is a Four Noble Truths: Life is Joy — Desire is Life — Lose Desire and You Are DEAD — Strong Desire willing and desiring are one dance move the Very Biggest, distribute in and through your bodies with perfect ease and effortlessness." — The *Preta Sa Terma* [70 B.C.E. (M.T.A/c.m.a.p.)] All right fine I drop the paper in a can and cross the street. Swivelling my head and shoulders around to look for cars I don't see the open manhole. Falling in, I crack my head on the metal rim — knocked unconscious. A splash down there — only a whisper, unnoticed on the street.

Down below the streets, he is going to die. He floats face down, a bubble of air inside his coat makes a glistening hump in the brown water. A few viscous bubbles rattle in grey-brown froth around his ears and temples. The current carries him beneath slimy brick arches smooth as intestines, past a spacious concrete platform bristling with iron rods.

Here the tunnel is larger, the water thick and clotted; a thin bow wave ridge of scum rides before his brow. Brick tubes open on the main, admitting dim patches of sallow light on the rolling water. He is syphoned deeper, down a sloping ramp with a rustling cape of sewage, into pitchy tunnels. He turns this and that way in the stream like a tossing sleeper — his arms make weak, formless gestures. An evil slurrying sound is rising out of the darkness ahead. The current grows rapid, the water is disturbed, his body turns and flails against the oozing brick of the tunnel walls, feet and hands smack against the bricks, and a moment later are swinging in open water. The noise suddenly becomes a roar, edged with a hiss, resounding in a large, enclosed space. Still with his face in the water, the man begins an accelerating spin, one leg is sucked downward and his body is now fitfully exposed to the air, tumbling in the shallow bowl of a whirlpool. The drain batters his body against its edges for a few seconds, his puckered face white streaked with brown upturned as he goes down feet-first. The coiling water closes black over his face...

-o◦o-o◦-

Morning egg white of the sun, light instantly frosting the sky in gold white and pink layers. A crumpled-up form is lying on concrete made dazzling by light on the water. Sewage steams in oblong tanks sunk into the platform, and flakes of sunlight throb on the surface of the river beside the treatment plant. I am lying in a puddle of dark brown water, on a water-marbled strip between two of the tanks. I can't see any of this, because I rest on my face, shoulders pushed forward, palms up at my sides. I spread my arms a little thoughtlessly push myself up onto my forehead, chin down on my chest. Pain stiffens my arms or stiffness pains my arms... my hands grope distractedly at either side of my head.

The Great Lover puts my palms to the ground and pushes himself up. I stand slowly, tilting one vertebra on top of the last until he is more or less erect, though his knees are still bent. Sewage streams from my clothes and a cloud of flies dithers around me. His face is white as wax, my glasses are mashed out of alignment but the lenses are clean, the silver frames still gleam. I can feel their misfocus like a knot inside each eye. His face is coated with a grainy film of dried brown sewage laced with an arabesque of livid white cracks, and his lips are powdery and wan.

I tilt his head and shoulders back, staring transformed at the sun. Its warmth is welcome, but I'm cold inside. Seagulls are suddenly wailing all around me wailing, climbing on slow-rising ribbons of heat reradiated by the concrete. I stand in the center of their fat, up-spiralling column. I hunch a little, standing with head bowed because it's heavy, with a sagging mouth, drooping shoulders, knees bent, arms hanging, surrounded by the darting forms of swift gulls and brown flies.

—o—o—o—

Street rumble is only just starting to grow, still somewhere far off, and the downtown streets are nearly deserted. You can see him coming slowly from the direction of the river, walking bowlegged with sewage slopping from his pant cuffs. I walk with his hands pressed to his chest; soft morning air flows over, full of invisible birds with brilliant metallic plumage, the street is lined with shining invisible skulls. Dawn light on a dull red rail trestle bathes it with honey, then changes it to the rich hue of arterial blood...

What happened?

The sky has turned white, clouds are pale irregular prominences and fat pillars blending with the white of the sky so that only their outlines are visible.

What happened?

The trees—

What hit me?

The trees are just closing, branches steeple over my head. Who is that? — And what's it?

That is what's that. Who doesn't know the answer and asks?

The trees sparkle with bright new leaves. The lanes in the park are still empty. He walks slowly, pink afterimages dancing in his dazzled eyes. Did something happen? Something happened *to me*. What's the matter?

Now he stops on top of a low ridge overlooking a vast meadow the grass breathing a milky haze; he is looking at a single tree far off across the meadow, standing a bit out from the rest, a towering corona of green on a mammoth black trunk. My knees go slack and I drop onto them, staring in astonishment at the tree that stands in the milky haze of the calm meadow like a god.

I hear a bird's voice ring out clearly close by — and now I see: there is a single, enormous flame superimposed on the tree, no it's inside the tree. A blonde flame extending from the roots nearly to the topmost branches. It is not an image: it burns but is not consuming the tree. It is still and perfect, like a candle flame in a closed room. And now I can see with eyes hot and brimming the flame is many flames, a small flame at the tip of each branch standing straight up like brilliant jewels. A gradual wind sets the branches nodding and the flames serenely rise and fall without changing their shape, or flickering, the bird is singing and the branches tenderly knead the air each with its serenely undisturbed flame.

He is gazing at the tree as though it were the first thing he had ever seen. Tears drip from his eyes, and soak into the shit on his face.

—◦—◦—

I peer at a warped reflection in the steel seeing dark whorls all through my face that seem to float between my face and the steel like they can't make up their minds where they are. Fingers smudging the buttons brown I tap out a phone number I remember. He has a blind need to try to tell someone what happened. A few numbers in, he hangs up and fumbles out a brown slimy coin that oozes into the slot leaving ridges of pale brown filth to either side of the opening. Dials again, ring purrs repeatedly down the long tube of the line, then the receiver out there picks up with a snap and a voice like irritable smoke is instantly drowned out by a loud disgusting slopping sound like vomiting underwater.

I hang up and stagger out of the booth — the sound is what's left of my voice. I try a few test words and the sound so horrifies him that he pulls out a pocket sewing kit threads the needle and sews his lips together, thread rustling through punctures in flesh like numb dough, cinched tight.

The jive of the city is growing with the gathering day and people are starting to blunder out into the air, startle the daylight. Dream panic of being seen cracks — he looks around, sees a manhole, lifts it and darts down closing it behind him. For a while he hold on to the rungs, his face an inch away from the underside of manhole cover, listening to feet tramp on it.

A patch of irregular light on scrolling brown water, a brick edge. The light casts a foggy reflection on the ledge. A rat is looking diagonally in his direction. Its eye is perfectly round and black as a pool of oil, with a shapeless gleam. Although it is surely filthy, its coat catches the dim light like a shirt of glinting mail. With only vaguely-coordinated, spasmodic movements, it begins to dance this way and that, lifting its muzzle, flicking its whiskers and ardently sniffing the air. For a moment, it seems to look directly at him, clutching the brick edge with its naked, mummy hands. Then, as if yanked by a string attached to its nose, it turns and vanishes. His left hand is trailing in the sewage, the rest of him sprawls on a spacious stone ledge. I'm in a domed atrium at the upper end of a long vertical shaft. The chamber is round, about eight feet high at the apex of the dome and twelve across, with a circular ledge around the top of the shaft. Sewage fills the shaft to within a dozen or so inches of the ledge, and I had to break through thick scum at the surface. Its tatters cling to me still, lending him a certain excremental majesty.

The walls are made of bricks, fitting together into a smooth fabric of black rectangles and livid mortar lines. The bricks are smooth like partially digested and acid-eaten. One side of the chamber opens out into a low-roofed platform with a broad, curved, apse-like area, walls and floor coated in a dingy layer of whitewash and guano from the tropical birds that live down here instead of alligators. There is also, at a right angle to this, a truncated rectangular passage, looking to be an unfinished, high crawlway, ten feet long, whitewashed, with a number of deep, roughly cylindrical alcoves bored horizontally into its stone walls.

I droop onto the ledge; what ensues is something deeper than sleep.

Now he rises stiffly, brushing aside a toucan, and begins to grope along the walls. Cool air slides through a crusty grate high up, also admits feeble light. It's been a long time, and abstractly I notice I feel no hunger or thirst. But something is tickling far up in my nose; it makes me sniff, and sniffing makes it stronger.

He crosses the ledge in two steps and drops face-first into the water. There is a slight upward current. He crawls like Dracula along the curved wall of the shaft, head downward, then turns to descend into the transverse tunnel at its base feet-first. The current is strong, but it takes him in the direction of the summoning smell. He rides at the surface his body limp his face exposed, eyes craned along his nose. When ledges appear framing the swift but still current, he grabs the stone and hauls himself clumsily out of the water, shit streaming off him like a hood flung back. Now he walks, bent slightly forward and sniffing ardently. There is an anemic light here, faint from manhole covers and storm drains, but the hum of the sliding water, and the crinkling and sucking it makes on the stones, cancels street noise.

The passage opens out to form an irregular cavern, floor littered with rubble and trash, cone of light from a circle in the ceiling. Brown iron rungs run up the wall to the opening, but the scent doesn't come from up there.

He cuts into a subway tunnel — the lights of a station, blocks away, jab my eyes. Shadows of indistinct people interrupt the lights. They fascinate me.

Shrill warble of a train somewhere, and a gush of wind that pushes the smell over me. I walk toward the platform, blocking its light with his hand the better to see his dim surroundings. A form, the smell's source, lies near the wall. On approach it proves to be a dead boy, lying on his stomach, tousled muddy-blonde hair, little hand up near his face. The Great Lover stands over him — his hand reaches down, taking the boy's shoulder firmly in his long fingers, and he gently turns the boy onto his back. The eyes are dark and flattened, the nose pushed to one side, the mouth droops, a black and wine-colored bruised band around his throat where he was strangled. The Great Lover squats down, dark and enormous over the brightly-colored boy; he takes the back of the boy's head in his large right hand and scoops him off the ground with his left. He rises to his feet, the boy's body lying along his left forearm, and head cradled against his right shoulder. Remote train shrieks come along the passage, and a low rumble.

I take the boy with me back to the sewer. The current is against me in several places. Completely submerged, I hold the boy by the arm, trailing behind me, and brace myself against the tunnel walls with my feet, pulling myself forward with his right hand. The quiet, implacable current presses like an invisible palm, soft clots buffet face and body.

Here's the chimney. I put the boy on the ledge and haul myself out of the water. I know exactly what to do; he carries the boy into the apse and lays him carefully next to the wall. He'll need to find a pillow or something; for now he will rest the boy's head on a pair of bricks. He overlaps the boy's hands on his solar plexus and carefully sets his feet side by side, wipes the muck from the boy's face with his fingers. I sprinkle the boy all over with powdered stone, until he's all white.

Those who know how to look will find uncharted bodies lost or hidden everywhere in a city of this size. Between the massive, pyramidal foundations of towering buildings, in vaults and passages steam tunnels and drains, bones bursting from the black earth beneath parks and from former potters' fields, the roots of the hanging tree. When I smell them, a pang of love and grief hurts me, a distinct pang for each one, as though each one were emitting his or her own proper grief, and the feeling burns there painfully in my otherwise numb and lifeless breast until I go do something about it. Here I follow a smell to a smashed shanty in another subway tunnel, walls of corrugated metal bolted to a heavy wooden frame now lie mostly flat on a heap of rubble, mounded over with spectral clear plastic tarp that had been the roof. Pull back the tarp, seize one of the heavy walls by its edge flipping it aside with one hand as though it were light as foam and shifting the stones this way and that I uncover the glassy dead gaze of a lean, dark-skinned woman. Now she lies beside the boy, shrouded in condensed milk powder I pour from a can. As I arrange her limbs, the pain runs out of me like water out of a jar.

Someone has made off with a woman's golden chain; at sight of transit police the thief drops it on the platform, walks past the police and boards the next train. I take it, leaving a smear on the dirty tiles, and put it around the boy's neck, the heart-shaped bauble over his folded hands. The fire in me changes shape, and a small fragment of the pain becomes a sharp rueful little satisfaction as I do this.

Now there are five bodies lying side by side in the apse. Clawing in the dirt where crumbled walls have fallen away he has uncovered numerous human bones and skulls. He homes in on them lying tangled in the roots of trees or where they have come streaming from a shattered coffin. One of the far-flung tunnels leads to a grouping of antique cisterns — the stone walls there are bulging and tearing, and in one place gave way entirely — tarry dirt had poured through the gap to form a ragged conical mound, studded with coffins. Over several days I carefully cover the intact coffins, and remove the skeletons from the destroyed coffins. Disassociated bones go in the alcoves of the crawlway, long bones lengthwise knobbed ends facing outward, flat and small bones at the backs of the alcoves, and skulls rest on top.

I collect empty bottles and melt the glass on my gas ring, moulding the soft, glowing glass between his hands, making cloudy eggs and diamond-shaped ornaments clear or green or filmy brown. While they are still hot, I press the ornaments into the walls around the ossuary alcoves. The cooled glass eggs he gently pushes between the lips of the bodies in the apse. Using a piece of thin copper piping I can also blow glass bulbs and filmy intestines of thin glass.

Gills of rich carmine fungus grow up the architrave's ridges. The smaller birds like to perch on them. Some of these gills produce luminous bulbs, from which I make a thick phosphorescent ink. He sleeps in the atrium, either on the ledge or floating in the water. I don't need the rest — I need the dreams, in particular, the memories that creep into them. Binding a lock of the dead boy's hair to a bit of rusty metal, I make a brush, and write what I can remember on the walls of the atrium, using the glowing ink. In addition to being luminescent, it is also weakly caustic, so that the words are not only painted but shallowly engraved on the wall.

An idea appear in his mind as though through glancing contact of an astral nerve. I blow some glass vessels including a sizeable alembic. Foraging in basements he finds some fittings he can use to string together copper pipes, and screws, and a roll of wire. He strips the insulation from the wire and uses it to hang the alembic, the glass tubes, and other vessels from the ceiling of the atrium; the copper tubing he uses to expand his gas ring, adding several new fires. After numerous tests involving heating and cooling, distillation and reactivity and so on, he identifies several varieties of sewage and gathers large samples of the more promising types.

Now, after repeated reductions, homogenization and liquefaction, he has extracted a thick, black-ochre concentrate, volatile but still fluid. Steam and rank smoke from the vessels and burners braids into a single plume which escapes through the leftmost slot in the ventilation grate, while the other slots continue to admit relatively fresher air. The Great Lover produces a skull from one of the crawlway alcoves and lays it, upside-down, in a specially-constructed copper frame above a tiny radiating device dull red with flameless heat. There is a small opening at the skull's base, into which he pours the steaming concentrate. Then he inserts a paper cone into the hole and sifts in a carefully-measured mixture of powdered metal he has rendered from the stones. He removes the cone and gently agitates the mixture by tipping the skull back and forth in its housing. Swiftly, he produces the golden earrings and places them in the skull's eyesockets.

Over the next few days I watch the skull, now and then idly tipping it a little. In the meantime, I spread dust on the stone ledge and draw the same figures in it with his finger, groupings of threes and fours on a diagonal axis, arrangements of triangles. When I run out of room I smear the dust smooth and start again. This is not idleness, this is part of the procedure. I see each phase in flashes that come with a poignant feeling, like longing over a familiar landscape. I think they come from the dead bodies, as a repayment.

A click inside, a warm light chest and buoyant head. The air grows lighter and fresher as though it were dropping straight from a dense canopy of new leaves. I pluck up the skull and upturn it. The mandible drops open and something pops out, striking the stone ledge with a clink. The Great Lover gently puts down the skull and takes up the fallen object: an irregular lump of shining gold.

—◦◦—◦—

Observing the passers-by from a drain, I stand ankle deep in a noisy flow of running-off rainwater. At this angle, I see mostly criss-crossing feet, but a steady enough stream of faces intently dart back and forth. I feel stupid, numb-minded. What is it about them that makes thinking so difficult? The street overhead is completely filled with them, their thought word and breath. There is enough room there, where somehow he impossibly used to walk every day, too hopeless to see. This person is now too flimsy, the mantle of weariness, soft and heavy, that used to lie like a yoke across his neck and shoulders, is gone and nothing is weighing me down anymore. Whether or not one could say it is easier, he is a site for the passing of time, like a landmark in the weather, and not yet an actor. I'm still hesitating. This has all the attributes of a dulling force, strange and tender like magnetic repulsion.

—◦◦—◦—

First the bodies — then the spirits. Pausing to frisk through a heap of refuse, it would suddenly become sad remains. He would hang his head at once, his hands would drop to his sides, as if I knew and grieved the passing of whatever bygone thing they had once been or belonged to. Elsewhere, a steadily-developing chill sensation, like a steady draft, comes over me, and at its most intense a blue-white snow-reflected light dazzles my eyes, making me squint, although I see no light. After a few moments, the impression becomes a little tentative, and I get back up, uncertainly looking to follow it, trying to encourage it. The feeling recedes — now it's gone. I'm all giddy, pitching at random against the walls, all the wind knocked out of my brains.

He's walking now his right foot seems to grow heavy as he puts it down and once flat on the ledge it simply stops like it were glued there. My forward momentum lifts from my body, lighter and lighter, thinner and thinner. The sewer water is petrified in the channel solid as wrinkled brown glass — I start to giggle inanely for no reason, like cold fingers tickling my insides make me do it.

A figure, silhouetted against the shaft — outline of an ear, a few strands of hair, the edge of the shoulder. The voice comes through the figure, which is a three dimensional aperture to space resounding with disembodied speech. The impalpable blast of this voice dapples my giggling face, and the front of my body, with points of searing cold. It is pronouncing its words slowly and with vehement precision, but they are garbled by their own echoes and I can't hear too well through the inner pressure of laughing. For an instant I see a drooping figure, a face, a wan blue sky, grey transparent sun above, the water a gravel drive, the walls are golden ivy.

There are apprentice-spirits who learn their business by teaching you. The foundations of the city of sex between the ice at the surface and the sea floor are gargantuan buttresses of swooping girders, shaped like the roots of cypress trees.

"What?" I'm chortling, "What's that?"

Voice travelling, somewhere in the black-radiant tunnels, billowing along the walls — inaudible, just an intentional tremble in the air... buzz in the walls. Dream images come over so rapidly they just dart by like scintillating fish. Something has been set in motion, a powerful machine gears up around me. This is some dream; there's something I need to do, but by now I'm lightheaded and still laughing, feeling drunk.

In an unfamiliar apartment an hour before sunset comes a beam of sunlight from a pale sky, through winter steam. It scans the floor and then up the wall, the door, and stops on an old-fashioned brass doorknob. I go over to it, bend to inspect it. There is the room bent round, no sign of me, but, deep and far off inside the reflection, Cassiopea on its side. I grab the doorknob, which is now protruding only from the wall, and peer at it directly. The constellation shines through the mist that the reflection is made out of; it looks warm. The wind tugs me to and fro, and enveloped within it there's a heatless wind from space pushing me off the earth. All around are cloudy depths, clear grey ectoplasmic seams in the wind and deadly rags of black air scud by. Now it's like I'm looking through a greasy glass; clear grey jelly condenses cold-burning on my sore face and minute filaments from the air lace my eyes, hot and painful. My skull aches down the middle as if it were split with a crack. With all this pain, the truth can't be far away. I feel three light puffs, like three eruptions across his chest, and start awake clutching at my shirt in confusion.

—○○—○—

As they shrink the red lights of the train begin to shimmer, and an unrelated wind disturbs frosty smoke oozing along the tracks where I cross them, slip edgewise through the gap in a row of sooty concrete panels. I rub his jaw; the threads binding the lips have stretched a bit, and sunk in, so I can move my mouth pretty easily. Still, I leave them there. I like the weird feeling.

No trains are in sight, but coattails still pull to one side, rise and fall, and bits of trash flit past in the air. A streak of light like a shooting star draws my gaze to where a tiny rod of light hovers in a pile of litter, dotted over with delicate, snowy little mushrooms. A soft mesh of distant frog songs rises from them; their white caps make Cassiopea's cold fires gleam from the tunnel floor. The rod of light is the reflecting sharp edge of a knife lying there, on its back. I have to tug it loose, there's a slight resistance as though he were detaching a powerful magnet from a metal surface. I turn it, holding point toward me, flat of the blade resting on the fingers of his left hand. One creamy silver edge, a notch by the small gilded hand guard and then a sweeping curve, a thick flat spine, the handle is wrapped in a black leather ribbon and topped with a round steel cap.

I put the point of the blade through a teepeed newspaper — it cuts easily, with a quiet rasp. I slash the paper and it folds open exposing the writing on the reverse of the page. It's sharp all right. I rise from my crouch holding the knife and turning it this way and that, point toward my chest as I pivot and collide with a steel post I forgot was there and accidentally stab myself in the heart. My vision slides down the post as I float back on the rebound, my hand falls from the handle but the knife stays where it is, held in place by my chest. I look at it with a complicated feeling, only the top layer of which is intense chagrin the blade cold in my stopped heart.

I start counting. He keeps restarting without knowing what number I'm counting to or whether I should count up or down. I take the handle in both hands in amazement at my stupidity — my hands are like images. My legs are film. Arms catch me as I pitch backwards, my head flops to one side and I'm face to white face with the dead boy I found.

"Hey, bubby!" he trills happily, batting me twice on the cheek with his free hand. "Don't panic!"

Blurry underwater white figures float up around me to the deep sonorities of a distant harp — my body can't be felt, just maybe a cold outline. Two skeletons dance out of the gloom of the tunnel toward me, their knees laced together in a glacial jig; they wear whackily-grinning paper maché skull masks and tinselled headdresses with wiggling parts, and they dance in a halo of heatless crystal flames, like the skeletons of fires. My eyes die. I feel myself slump and crash forward onto my face. The handle of the knife bangs against the ground, and the cold blade pushes muscle apart and slice heart — thud. I'm sliding forward with a tickle in my throat, like the weakest giggling imaginable; I feel my nose push against a mushroom, snapping the cap from its tender stalk.

Now I'm watching from where you are, while here on the page I'm sagging like a stick of melting butter that plops out of me in mouthfulls, and the puddle's edge advances jerkily. A train whirrs somewhere a few blocks away; its wind raises little hackles on the surface of the puddle, and I giggle idiotically like a drain unglugging. The blood butter has stopped spreading. The bulging edge of the pool catches lights and they rise along the curve. It swells, flaps up clumsily and in on itself, flows back in a coiling bundle, rises into the air, an opaque sail of fascinating red, curving away from him. Its upper hem makes a hood — then a globe, flat where it rests on the ground. As it swells, taking the last of his blood, it reels itself in toward the wound, wobbling like a belly dancer. A dead rat emerges at the base and its maggots stand on end do a belly dance and spell THE GREAT LOVER across its red surface. Air crash of a passing train blows them all away in a puff of oily white smoke. My body turns slowly onto its left side as the globe wriggles under it. Now I'm on my back, the knife engulfed in the globe, as it settles over the wound.

The blood reaches in through the wound making a ventriloquist dummy of my body with the opening on the wrong side. The globe of blood rolls up as I jerk onto my feet again and surrounds my head. Crystal fire breaks out again. I don't see anything, I don't know where I am, if I'm still there with you or what.

Nothing to see; I feel like I'm falling. The horizon shimmers with fury. In the subway tunnel, but as vast as a planet all bloody. I start to laugh and thick plummy blood backs up into my nose and down into my lungs making me cough and splutter, tears running down my cheeks but my diaphragm won't stop squeezing hiccupping and giggling. I can see through the thinning red that I stand on a sandy sheet of iron straight to horizon. The air reverberates with shrill blows in a rapid, unhurried rhythm, a trench of molten metal all the way along the horizon. Silhouetted against its light there's a colossal kneeling figure, holding what looks like a spear, point down against the iron, and the crashing blows are coming from him. Light from the trench creeps around the back of the figure, dimly outlining a lot of naked muscularity under thin skin. Now I make out the legs of the others; a ring of giants. The spear is a long metal stylus; the crouching figure holds its point against the iron and the flattened end aloft, the others strike with chiming long-handled sledges one after another with perfect syncopation.

In black ice below my feet I see a ring of white figures from above their arms flung up to me swaying like seaweed. They wriggle together then fall, spelling out PLOT SUMMARY with their bodies. I start sliding along the surface as I bend to look at them, like there's no friction. They're spelling out other things or saying them I think but this glide is taking us away. A ribbon of gold-white fire is pouring into the trench from a vessel deep above in the dark, and as the trough begins to fill its glare intensifies. Naked giants show legs braced, body flexing back, arms fully extended, their hammers' heads nearly scrape the ground behind them and then fly like lightning never missing the end of the stylus, ring against its metal, scatter a flock of sparks. Their flanks sequined with perspiration they swing the hammers weightlessly back and forth. The moment one hammer lands it rebounds up and the next instant the hammer of the one next clockwise strikes and rebounds. The one holding the stylus draws it smoothly back and forth in curves and crosses, the others adjusting their blows with uncanny skill to its constantly altering position. Tense concentration, pain, exasperation, rage, and fear on their faces, and I'm still sliding along on imaginary skis giggling and choking. One by one, rosy streaks drop from sky vessels into the trench and now, overhead and between them, in the dark a vast pointing hand. The finger moves and points, and without looking up the kneeling figure moves the stylus to and fro, and the hammers follow with unbroken rhythm — the finger points, the stylus is moved, and the rhythmic hammers follow.

I pick up speed and leave the ground. Just in time, as the channel overflows its banks and thrashing metal froth boils into the cuts of the stylus. The updraft gives me a boost and I look on curiously. Blazing liquid fills the grooves tracing a subway map. The air is igniting, burning billows flare against me in soft pulses of parching heat. Blood drains bitter and dirty into my mouth nose eyes ears and down the thick arm into my chest — the knife is gone but my body sense comes back with unbearable pain like a many-angled diamond-hard object wedged in my chest. My laughing and choking turns to hacking cries of distress and bewilderment that I hear from somewhere else. Bubbling plumes of fire orange and white flash over him too fast yet to ignite his clothes, running in subway tunnels — if you look, you can see a dot there moving on the map, leaving a thinning streak of red. The sky is strung like a harp with cables of liquid iron or white-hot nerves.

I am leaping up the steps from the tunnel to the platform edge, a filthy tramp, comically rushing for the train — running for the first car, pinwheeling his arms, uttering shouts of alarm, the conductor shakes his head as he passes seeing blinding letters on black iron. I board the first car, dancing in place with my hands clapped to my eyes yelling "Ow! Ow! Ow!" — With two tones the doors clamp together, I double over blinded as the car begins to roll — passengers start back in alarm. I can't hear them over the noise of smashing hammers and the steel wheels of the subway car gnash as it changes tracks with a burst of azure sparks. The shifting of the stylus tracks the massive veer of the car right to left as it changes tracks with clattering wheels like crashing hammers — distracted I turn and crash into a stream of molten steel I forgot was there, my clothes catch fire and fire stitches into my chest wound, gold-white fire crawls in my veins and belly-dances on my nerves. I panic and flail and claw, fall screaming to the floor of the subway car — sealed in white flames — passengers jump from their seats, the train operator thrusts his head through the door of his compartment to see... Now my eyes are whiting out — a white searing blank — I hear a voice like the roar of a monster fire and then the PA droning out station stops, buzzing in my throat. That's my voice, isn't it? The fire cleared my throat.

CHAPTER TWO

Transit police are shouting at me and trying to herd me off the car with their flashlights. That is, they yell through their hands, faces screwed against my stink. I sit up at once and smile at them; I want to seem affable. I get up stiffly and the less sportsmanlike of the two takes a swing at me, so, when I'm erect not to say stable I toss my maggoty dead rat to him. It splats against his chest, breaking his morale. He runs away with loud ejaculations of revulsion. The other, seeing my sudden movement, had lunged a little toward me, but watched fascinated and disgusted as I threw my rat, reversed his movement, turned a little as his partner fled, and now he doesn't know what to do. The car is being held in the station, and a crowd is eyeing us both from the platform. I bend angularly to retrieve my rat, then run for the stairway, moving faster than I imagined I could. Barrelling through the turnstile with a terrific racket, in a flash (I guess) I am up the steps in autumn air.

Over broad stone wall into the park, slope is steep and I fall clumsily forwards off my feet flinging his hands before me into the bracken. Now I dart along the slope, find a rocky hollow where the earth has subsided beneath the roots of an enormous tree, and squeeze myself laboriously into it. While the compression is brutal, I stay there for some time, my nose thrust into a little heap of down — a cat had made a meal of a bird here some time, maybe. Puddles sliding in the wind color of weak milky coffee, the wind has whipped it into a fine yellow froth at the edges; soil like coffee grounds pressed into a paste.

Waking up is a succession of many lifting veils. I've been staring out at the weakening daylight, without really wanting to take it in. A mouse scoots out from under a bush and stops, looking at me. Taking this as a sign that there's no one threatening around, I quit my hole and gingerly unkink my spine. There are yellow, eye-shaped leaves scattered all over the ground, and like cupped palms they have caught brilliant rainwater. I find a brown human femur without meaning to. I unhastily clean and pocket it, amble on in the direction of a shallow stream that flows beneath a stone bridge.

The dashing stream, piebald with rags of light... fade to light shining on the faces of the busy street, water furling in the gutter and him walking oblivious there by the curb. The water bunches before my shoes. As night falls I'm noticing more love coming out, like fireflies. There are other Great Lovers here, of both sexes, suavely dressed, clean, with gold around their necks. Here's a paved, triangular park with trees in planters, really a glorified traffic island; I drop onto one of the benches and unobtrusively observe the habits of "my kind." They ripple along the edges of the pavement or hover in deep doorways, peer out from windows, from passing cars. Their lukewarm eyes probe the crowds with a soft insistent gaze, and some have invisible sea wasp feelers that stretch out in cigarette smoke, billow over a bar or a restaurant like limp piano-playing hands feeling for availabilities like reading braille. They select and ease alongside with a light touch and a light word and a smile like a white seam in a dark cloud, and an aerial spiral of a haunting fragrance... the transaction clicks in hardened shadows against a sky like orange cream.

Walter Benjamin observed that the city is where you find love at *last* sight: the Great Lovers are the hyena-jawed scavengers who retrieve the lost objects of ardent glances. They are at once more and less alive than I am, like vividly-colored picked flowers already wilting. They are faint and vague, and avoid each other resentfully. These Great Lovers home in on people who have unwittingly been charged with the longing of others, soaked with it like static electricity, and this is their food. So the more they feed the more they attract, but leave them alone a while and they clabber, shrink, grow hard and crack open in places like a dried-up piece of cheese. In an attic somewhere you may come across some unidentifiable piece of something, a pale hard adipocere thing of no particular shape or smell, fuzzed all over with dead mold — you're looking at the belle of the ball, wasted and gone these many years. Pull away the mold, and see the intaglio broach, put your ear down by it and hear the ticking of a jewelled watch embedded deep inside. I may be a caricature of that caricature, the comic-book version, but it's not so bad. What was I before? I don't remember. What does it matter? What good would remembering do me now, anyway? I look with longing at forgetfulness. Never mind. Life goes on. I'll wait to do my summarizing later, when I've had time to digest what I've seen.

Medical science tells us that red haired persons exhibit greater sensitivity to pain and pleasure. I have spent my time trudging between the lights, camouflaging myself as a sack of garbage on the curb, or huddled on benches. The other homeless here all seem dazed; their attention steams out of them in a diffuse broadcast, unless they are actually begging. Otherwise they're waiting to beg or building up their strength to try again. I am building up my strength to borrow, since I'm not interested in money, and what I want is not something any amount of begging will get me. Medical science tells us... and a striking red-haired woman has just gone by.

At once, I follow, doing math in my head. My motions seem more robotic than amorous, but looking at her I am bursting with desire all at once, as though a second me had been jammed into the first like a foot into a tight stocking stretched at the seams. Desire bellows in me like droning music. Now she is waiting for the light, and I creep up near, desire reaching through my ribcage toward her like prisoner's arms thrust out between bars. I have to mind the wind so she doesn't smell me. At most she might think there's a sewer grate somewhere near. A prisoner might half-dislocate his shoulder reaching out from his cell window just to feel daylight touch his hand. I chew my lower lip through the threads from left to right. Whisk! I spin one floating strand of her hair round my index finger hold it there, letting her pluck it loose as she steps into the street, turning away the moment it is free.

In the alley peer at it burning like a red wire on my foul finger, still alive with her life and my yearning makes it glow so bright I blink and blink.

—∘◦—∘—

The Great Lover sits in his atrium, chin in hand, finger tapping his cheek knocks off little puffs of powdered sewage. He is lost in a brown study of the hair, which sits spotlit on a satin pillow beneath a glass bell. The white satin on which it lies glimmers with its magic fawn glow.

I have a noisy neighbor inside my skull, thumping up and down and clattering pots and pans, which is what passes with me for thinking. Thinking has snared me and now I can't stop. Shit, gold, water, and combinations of elements in general bring life about, this is my crotchet, and this thought has attached itself with an intolerably intense and sustained meaningful look in my direction to the feeling of pity and animal reverence I feel for these cadavers and body parts I've assembled and cubbyholed here in my den. All right all right — the amber gleam, the clue is there in the livid heat of that hair's light. Gold. Red, rubies and blood. My buttery gold blood on the ruddy gilded guard of the knife, and right about then the boy caught me didn't he? Yellow teeth in red lips, in a white face, in a color code. I clatter in my pots and pans; I can make gold. I know how, I think perhaps because I may have seen the trick go by in the flurry of my first death agony, as I flew, flowed, along in streams of golden turds.

I excavate the wall at a strong point and hollow out a space, fill it with fuel and stoke it to kiln heat. The Great Lover, wearing a lady's fur coat and pearls against the intense heat, and with a welding mask over his face, thrusts a skull-shaped crucible into the open hearth. His feet work a treadle-bellows. White-gold light shines in the vessel, illuminating a mosaic subway map taking shape on the wall. An amber drop glinting like sunlight congealed in honey drops into the harelipped leer of a maggoty rat — it spins and curls in on itself, turning into a perfect, seamless sphere of warm skin about the size of an orange. Too strong, and that's a bit creepy, I think, edging the ball into the sewage with my toe.

I dilute my elixir carefully and now it looks like scintillating black and gold quicksand. Fresh out of maggoty rats, I wildly dispense it to my collection of bodies. They stir and titter, begin to move. With a blaring wheeze of triumph, I take a long draught from the crucible and shiver across the brink — the flames reach out and try to grapple me — perspiration bursts out all over my body and my nose rebels at the stink. I want an antidote — but by mistake I take another drink from the crucible! I spit out most of it, my mouth is flashing hot and cold, and the stuff seems to want to sprout a cock's comb from my chin where it dribbled from my lips. Taking out my shears, I trim the comb back aggressively, but I tend to bleed now my heart's beating again. I'd become accustomed to its absence — it restarts, and I blow up like a balloon, or so it feels. White figures, blurry and moving with galvanic spasms, are roaming the atrium, chirping like birds and lowing like cows.

Recovery was a slow and tedious affair, but steady, and I had help from the gnomes I call them that on account of they *gnow* things. Observe — I stop one of them, the zombie of a twelve-year-old with longish blonde hair and a rabbity mouth, powdered from head to foot like the rest of them.

"Hey, you!" I call, "What's six plus two?"

"Nine!"

"—See?" All kinda little friends.

He becomes blurry, and knucklewalks off.

The Great Lover settles back in his fur coat. Countless pairs of reading glasses, bifocals and half-moon glasses hang on lanyards around his neck running down to his waistcoat. A pair of specs is perched high on his filthy brow, and at the moment he has a monocle screwed into each eye. The spavined stool he sits on shimmies and creaks under his weight. He gazes in rapture at the red hair under glass, presses both fists to his chest, elbows up, and shivers in transports of desire. It is a ruby circle of glory!

Now he takes up a scraper and a bucket and, walking in a crouch, stalks awkwardly after one of the gnomes. After a few near misses, he corners one and begins vigorously scraping it with the scraper, catching white shavings in the bucket. The creature whimpers — he's not taking off any flesh, just the white coating. Finally the gnome slithers bonelessly out from his confinement and the Great Lover runs his fingers through the contents of the bucket. Then he puts it next to a hastily improvised gauge and the little lights tap on, indicating the presence of ionized matter: soap. The Great Lover grins with satisfaction and dumps the shavings into a bubbling vat scavenged from a brewery. It has a spigot at the bottom; when turned, a tube of hot white soap drops from the faucet into a mold. The Great Lover pulls back a curtain revealing shelves of fuming corpse soap. Selecting a ripe-looking cake, he steps into a clawfooted bathtub and scrubs himself vigorously without undressing, his many pairs of glasses whipping this way and that as he turns himself into an abominable latherman. He pulls a chain and the water comes crashing down over him with the sound of a toilet flushing. A passing gnome accidentally hands him a huge bath towel streaked and brown; he dries himself thoroughly and then dives into the sewer headfirst.

He comes out a manhole and makes his way along the tunnel, shit gushing from his clothes. Pausing briefly for a breath spray — now he struts from one end of the subway platform to the other making eyes at female commuters, who flee in dismay clutching their noses or reel to the edge and puke noisily onto the tracks. Not seeming to notice he bends forward a bit to scan the seats of the subway car — an appealing haunch flashes past and he follows, swinging his right arm almost to the ground.

Fast as a gazelle she has disappeared down a flight of stairs to a lower platform — no don't let her go yet! He swings round the banister on one arm and leaps down the steps, landing with a slam of feet and a splatter of sewage in all directions from his clothes. Commuters scatter like roaches.

The oblivious haunch flits into a subway car. She is an exotic fish, rare and beautiful, shimmering with color so vibrant it croons to him a long-noted female song. A moray eel pops from his fly and snaps the air in galvanisms of thrills. He scoots along the silver flanks of the steel reef — in the future: the subway car topples from a barge into the sea to form an artificial reef... fish move like ghosts among the seats, take turns bubbling through the intercom...

The doors close behind me and everyone in the car reels away with groans of revulsion. Now where did she go? Hard to tell in this rout...

—○○—○—

I'm restless and it's not just because of the gnomes who seem never to sit still, but amble around bumping into me constantly as I lie on the shelf — my eye stubbornly returns to that red ring under the glass. I notice. I go cold inside, get up and go over to the glass and take out the ring.

Abandoned buildings, formerly a hospital complex; four tall lean buildings with stone walls, little white-sashed windows, steep slate sleep state roofs, situated around a courtyard with dead trees. My fumes turn into eight fanciful golden coffins, rummaging like tiny birds in the branches, giant spinning diamonds behind the teeth in their skulls.

He picks a spot at one end of a gallery hallway just two stories from the top, and draws a circle on the tiles with a thick grease pencil he'd found in a garbage can. Within the circle, he draws an oval, representing her, and a triangle, representing him, then unwinds the hair from his finger, laces it between his lips to straighten it with spit, then presses one end into the grease margin of the triangle, then presses the other end into the grease margin of the oval... leans forward with his palms on the ground, so that the two symbols are in the angles formed by his thumbs and hands. One by one, candle flames without candles descend through the ceiling and stop, hovering about a foot from the floor, forming a ring round him. He does not look up. With no plan at all in mind, he runs the tip of his finger along the length of the hair from the triangle to the oval, again and again, always in the same direction, from him to her.

She is sleeping.

In time, her dream appears: a small clapboard house on a tufted grassy plain or marsh stretching off to a distant, mercury-colored beach. A waxy sky, a massive wooden picnic table with benches, laundry drying on lines strung from the house to a pair of tall bushes; weak wind pilfering everywhere. She is sitting at the table with scrapbooks of poems and drawings in a heap, most of them on butcher's paper or brown newsprint. She is wearing a tweed skirt and a sort of tight khaki jacket, buttoned up, her hair gathered at the nape. She's dreaming her face is darkened by incurable, mortal illness, and she draws, using small stones to hold the paper flat; her sketch is only just begun, he can't make out what it will be. He can see another, pinned down against the wind with what looks like a wooden iron; a still life involving a bundle of flowers against a dark background — the flowers are luxuriant, and a little grotesque. He notes one in particular, which has long wavering petals, yellow spotted with black like ripened bananas, and there in the shadows just left of center is her face, hidden in among the flowers, shadowed and drawn, downcast, intolerably sad.

Some time later he sees her again. She had somehow been caught naked far off down the beach, and was running awkwardly back to the house over the uneven ground, her pale arms raised a little like wings, her hair not dishevilled at all but still pinned up neatly. She is uncanny without her clothes, like a figure in a painting. He is struck by the wind from her body, and it evokes in him a ghostly love, not for her, but for everything.

"I love," he says flatly, his lips not far from the floor. The words are soaked up by the wood and deadened. "I love," complete in the intransitive, like "I go." He can't hear himself say it. If he could have heard it, he would have turned himself into a cartoon again.

She dashes into the dark house. He finds her upstairs in a shift, trying to open the window. The sash won't rise evenly, and keeps jamming against the sill, requiring her to jostle it and pull it down again and again, trying to raise it level.

When he fills his palms with her warm shoulders she stops slowly and sways back against him familiarly. Then she turns abruptly and flings her arms around his neck, kissing a face that is, for her, perfectly featureless and clean. This is not his body, as it crouches on the tile in the hospital, tapping away at the little tiles with letters on them; she embraces a puppet she improvised just now. He in turn possesses the puppet, without really choosing to. Now that they are alone together in this room, her intimacy draws me in like water running down the sides of a bowl to the middle.

When she presses herself against his icy body he can tell the puppet is death at the same time, frightening but not threatening her. The puppet isn't death it's a harbinger of death drawn by her mortal illness, something like that. She is going to bribe him with her love, or that's what this is turning into. She accepts his anonymous weight and freezing hands, pressing her down into the yielding mattress, and in time the walls become grainy with gathering dark and the windows have faded to pale blue smudges in the air. Her dream is agonizingly slow to fade, and her bed has become a hard tile floor under her back. There is a ring of candles, or candle flames, burning around her, and somehow a terrible smell — weird to smell something strongly in a dream. Death has cheated her, and she is at her funeral — in the morgue itself not even in a chapel — lying in her coffin, without even a single mourner in sight. She bitterly reproaches her friends in a sharp voice that simply appears around her without compelling her to move her lips. Still death's weight freezes and immobilizes her, and still death seems to enjoy her, more and more. I am inside her and her dummy, in the overlap. Suddenly she shies away from the sensation, horribly cold and empty, spirals away in anger and disappointment toward her friends; she starts awake, fumbles for the light, and gazes woozily at her furniture, which rushes forward from the recesses of her apartment to reassure her.

Everywhere an even radiation of pearly light direct on the gritted nerves. Unmoored, he drifts down the gallery, seeing through the windows the courtyard, the tree whose upper branches are lost in the gloom, the tall brick façades, and a confusion of colored lights and clustered reflections of lights, orange and violet. His reflection seems faceless at first, but this is the blur in his vision which is sharpening slowly. The windows flash by. He wafts against an azure streak of windows, spotted with lights.

––◦━◦––

He lives in the sewers, insulated by the water and the dirt suspended in this water — long wool sleeves down over fingers trailing in puddles — and in the black world between stations: black and pumpkin lights — snow bank stations — the trains shrilly call to one another blind and massive in the dark — black rushing silence, rent by screaming trains... Like the hideous angler fish of the ocean's deepest places, he is an otherworldly scavenger drifting in currents heavier than avalanches, slow as glaciers, a sea wasp with a bridal train of tingling nerves that drift in the sewage time and again tangling in women's dreams. He doesn't resist, but the effort involved is always too much. It isn't necessary to make the effort, but then the dream engulfs him anyway dragging him by the nerves and that is by far the greater ordeal. So when the undertow of her godlike whim draws at him, he must go, and make the effort. It is comparable to improvising a complex piece of contrapuntal music in coordination with other musicians who know what they're doing and who are extremely precise doing it... the pull on the nerves wrenches him with a strong gentle sway into his core, they are meanwhile reaching out to fondle and garland the dream like limp braille-reading fingers.

An irresistible impulse drives him to pick from among the crowds on the subways, eyes gleaming with water through the rind of dirt, a shiny hard varnish on his face. Constant practice has given him total control over his stench; he can contain it on the subway cars using olefactory camouflage, then release it in a concentrated invisible attack if necessary, closing it around his victim like a suffocating cloak.

Black hair, neat as a pin, stylish. When she got off the train I felt hurt, as though a long, comfortable acquaintance were suddenly interrupted; as though she and I were already sweetly old and familiar to each other. I was always too late. She had me following her from room to room. Now at last we are in the room together, briefly. She touches a lamp standing by the door.

"This would break up the lines of the room," she says, and vanishes in the blackness of a huge window, leaving me alone.

I look around. The dream is still going. I put my hands in my pockets, glancing without great interest at the walls and ceiling, which billow a little, like projections on screens. They are even slightly out of focus. Or my eyes are. No, I see the lines in the floor clearly. Uncertain what to do next, I lightly kick the lamp and in her voice it says, "This would break up the lines of the room."

I kick it again.

In her voice it says, "This would break up the lines of the room."

—◦◦—◦—

The glowing amber-ivory blonde, fine-featured, gazing soulfully out the train window. An invisible jet of time or space or something like that streams from her eyes, and in exactly the same way a jet of water introduced into a pool induces the rest of the pool to flow with it or through it, I feel myself begin to flow and stream repeatedly through her eyes.

That night, in sleep, she watches a viscous tendril of smoke stretching across a shaft of pale sunlight, expanding to form a transparent canopy of grains too fine to see. This smoke — from a snuffed cigar or an incense stick or a snuffed candle's wick — sinks toward the floor, seems to touch and sense it. There are dim white heaps of warm, crumpled linen in the hut's shadowy corner.

The whitewashed hut stands in a little clearing of tall grass, surrounded on two sides by spellbound trees; nothing stirs among these ancient, shaggy boughs, and the gloom about their trunks is perfect. Overhead the warm, crumpled clouds race across the sky, infinitely deep and high and remote.

Half in the pale shadow of a tree by the path, she is standing in a colorless dress flowing to the ground, her hands resting on the skirts at her hips. The light of the sun slants across the lens of her unshaded right eye, illuminating the separate fibres of the iris, bleaching its green to grey. Her vehement face is dappled by freckles, and the shadows of leaves. She is transfixed by a thought, and stares as though it had appeared before her like a ghost out of the sunlight.

She looks up, past the hut, to the treeless slope above. High against the horizon, looming up like a tower, is the shapeless peak of naked rock. The slopes above the treeline are criss-crossed by wooden fences.

Michael Cisco

Standing, by a fence below and beside the peak, interrupting the horizon, her lover faces her and the valley. He is wearing a nankeen vest, and has a fowling-piece cracked and resting on his right arm. His straw hat is pushed back above his brow, and his dog sits in the grass, just as still. He looks down, or rather back, to where he'd just been, using eyes not proper to him — they're my eyes. These two are not looking directly at each other, but at some midpoint in the landscape which receives and relays the gaze of each to the other. His face, free and impassive, calm and happy like a god's; her face, tense with a savage joy and expectation.

—○○—○—

Young Katherine Hepburn type; from a distance she looked like a slight old woman. *Pale* skin, like wax paper, pink and red around the eyes — not from crying, could simply be from looking. Lean, wise-seeming face, precociously knowing. Swingy shoulder-length nearly grey-silver blonde hair in an old-fashioned style, a windbreaker over her dress. The man with her is the father, I suppose. They are conversing properly. She is cheery, but not bubbly or ebullient. Almost certainly very thoughtful. A hard-to-fool woman — ergo, less than perfectly happy. Mature, and resigned.

That night I feel the tug. It's like the initial motion of the train, as it overpowers the *vis inertiae*. I speak this scrap of Latin to myself in the way I might dawdle a little on the threshold or stop to look for something I already know the whereabouts of, a way of jerking back or pausing for a moment when my will is split between wanting to go on and not wanting to go on. I suppose I'm under the impression that a bit of erudition might encloister me, putting me beyond her reach, so I wouldn't have to go with her.

With a soft, tearing sensation, like the parting of lips, my nerves tug me and I go with her.

Spacious, limpid air resounding with outpouring sunlight of the hypnotic day, twinkling leaves in the trees and a glare shimmering on wet grass dark green as seaweed. A woman's voice winds everywhere over the headstones, calling to her lover with a moaning song, luxurious

32

and yearning. The love song comes out from a grave beneath a tree: the turf grows transparent and then vanishes, layers of earth underneath disappear like onion peels. In the pit, now, there is a shadowy coffin. The lid disappears; the pale violet radiance of her gauzy dress wanly mingles with her skin's greys and blues, eyes sunken and head thrown back on the satin pillow, mouth slack. Faded hair the color of sun-bleached grass and tenuous as cobwebs streams back from her brow. Her song is still audibly emerging from her memory.

—Beneath a tree, on a green hill, a hypnotic day with a view of a valley checkered with ponderous shadows of clouds, all frothing grass below the mountains, which blaze like scattered mirrors filled with giant sunbeams. They are alone, on a striped blanket, in the effortless shade of a widespread tree. There's one moment in particular, when there was a feeling of tipping equilibrium, and somehow she had rolled onto her back bearing him in her arms partially on top of her.

—Another memory is intruding, a painless, disembodied memory: she rolls into tiled room. His hands tug at her dress and she is kneading handfuls of his thick sweater, her body is unceremoniously lifted and dumped onto the table, a triangular rubber wedge under the small of her back. She thrusts her hands into his hair. The coroner plunges the bread knife into her abdomen and saws up to her sternum, then up in a Y shape across her chest. She raises herself slightly as he pulls her dress down, bringing her arms to her sides to help him slide it off, not looking into eyes she wouldn't have remembered at all. Her hands are greedily rubbing the skin of his broad back, and the bone saw cuts through her ribs and the muscles around the sternum. The entire assembly is removed like the top of a pumpkin, tossed aside, exposing the heart. In her grave the memories can't be divided, she is sighing. He covers her throat with kisses. The coroner tosses her flaccid heart into the tray of the grocer's scale and speaks its weight to the recorder. Her back arches and her cries are briefer and briefer — swifter and swifter the coroner looping her intestines over his hand in a dripping brown bundle — my cries open out again and become desperate — her back arches as he thrusts his red arm up to the elbow into my body cavity to draw out the lungs. She wakes with stifled cries still seeming to feel the regular tug of the stitches sewing shut my empty corpse.

Dr. Thefarie checks his watch without seeing the time; it is a tic. He is waiting on an elevated platform, pacing back and forth a few steps every now and then. Strange hypnotized day. The cars passing under the elevated platform, odd variability of perspective as they come, pass, and drive away down streets visible to the end. Above him, a silver blemish in the sky, a sore spot, surrounded with eyelashes or scars.

The platform sways slightly, like the deck of a ship, and the train comes banging in. Dr. Thefarie boards the train, sitting by the window with his knees clamped in his fingers.

"Man near me is making a pointless attempt to open his clandestine beer bottle with his house keys. Once we're moving, every vista no sooner glimpsed than cut off by sailing buildings. The sun hits the scratches in the windows from a high angle and they shine like new wire. From the gaps opening and closing in the rattling doors, a breath of tarpits, gasoline, stagnant pipes and lights. Now look at this man self-importantly eating his plastic tray of vegetables, as though he'd thought of it all on his own. Paper in disarray on the floor of the train driver's compartment, door swings a little to and fro. The exposed headline reads '—or be gone!'

"We're under ground. The tunnel lights appear vertically flattened, throwing off vertical lines of light, slanted like distinct Vs; these lines diminish in number as the source draws near. Rows of light bulbs like yucca plants are spaced out along the line. This interminable subway ride will break you down like an interrogation. Nothing is worse than a good-looking woman who doesn't know how to dress herself—"

In a characteristic gesture, he taps the breast pocket of his tweed jacket, to feel the tube of pills there.

Brown horsey girl with plump feet, black and white clothes, and this small prim blonde with a ski jump nose, but the *real* vision, she's coming through the turnstile. (Dr. Thefarie makes his transfer and leaves the scene — now we can be alone). Black hair medium-length and straight, fair, with glasses and red lips, lovely white dress with red blossoms. Her proportions are breathtaking. I want her and me pressed tight as Inca masonry.

Her dream is a silent film. She is a pale waif like Mary Pickford in a virginal frock. She will marry both of these high-stepping suitors, one dark one fair, both with stirrup trousers, snug-vested floating weightlessly together arm in arm through the door on pointed toes...

Years later they have become cowering old men with beards down past their waists. She comes home from work, grown into an enormous harridan of a woman, her hair in a kerchief and wearing an apron for some reason, her small feet in their dark practical hard shoes convey an impression of compact power and danger like horses' hooves. The husbands wait helplessly afraid in the parlor of a huge dilapidated house. They fling their arms around each other shaking violently, knees knocking, their cheeks pressed together, staring at the front door. She storms through, swinging her heavy lunch pail, bellowing curses at them and brandishing her gargantuan arms in pantomime rage as strings of silent firecrackers go off in the corners. The husbands cower and wince, seem to shrink.

But now they have laid a cunning trap for her: one of these two husbands has released a little petted mouse into the room. She catches sight of it scurrying along the bottom of the walls and her eyes light up. She pounces, scooping the mouse up with one deft swoop she has it in both hands and tears it in her fierce teeth, blood dribbling down her chin, eyes shining like starlit water. The two husbands have taken advantage of this distraction and advance on her from behind carrying a huge portrait of her as a younger woman. Pulling the canvas free of its wooden frame they wrap her in it, now toss over her a massive and costly Persian rug so heavy it knocks her flat. In a twinkling, they've rolled her up inside and bound her with two lengths of twine. Her kicking feet protrude from one end of the bundle, but her head is inside. The two husbands clasp left hands and dance jubilantly around each other in a circle, wagging their right index fingers in the air. In their transports they hop over her, turn, and hop back, in perfect time, back and forth, in opposition.

Their children, legions of boys and girls in sailor suits, file into the cavernous kitchen below, in the basement. Chopping blocks stand there in rows, like schoolroom desks. The floor is inundated with pecking chickens. Each child goes to a block and takes up a meat cleaver. In exact synchronicity with their fathers' little bounds, the children seize up chickens from the flagstone floor, slap them down on the blocks, and whack their heads off with a single chop. The husbands hop, the children chop, the husbands hop, the children chop...

Inside the carpet, she stares in horror as the mouse in her hand transforms into a little naked man in white fibrous wadding — he'd been one in disguise, and now he's dead and can only return to his former shape, not his former size. His body is whole, but he looks as though he'd fallen from a great height, lying there in her palm. Her heart swells with pity and sadness. But now it occurs to her that she might be able, for some reason she can't be bothered to acknowledge at the moment, to restore him. No means present themselves. She lies back and imagines what would be nice if he were to join her there, at his proper size. He would see leeches of fire adhering to the raw nerve — flames sucking like leeches on a web of throbbing nerves...

This woman's monotonous speech like rattling chain, ghosts stand clear the doors. There's a metal plate on the floor, a circle with three concentric rings and four screws. A brown-skinned man with a devilish face, moustache, benign expression, his ears barely attached to his head sits opposite Dr. Thefarie. Also a nodding man who squints at everything. Look along the car to all the bobbing knees — doors open — Spargens, a big, boxheaded man with crumpled features, graying hair, huge glasses, points across the platform at a vagrant type hunched in the handicapped seat of the car on the parallel track. The vagrant is filthy, his head is nearly hidden in a chaotic profusion of clothing, and his eyes peer out with electric brightness like the beast in the jungle.

Dr. Thefarie nods almost imperceptibly, and Spargens shambles onto the vagrant's car. Those electric eyes are fixed on a woman with dark, nape-gathered hair gathered at nape, white armless top, pale glasses, monkey-like expressions faintly traverse her fine-featured enchanting face.

I want to give her a long bath... she dreamt she stood naked before a huge audience and sang to them from the end of a long spotlight that breathed and sighed and caressed her.

━━∞━∞━

Lovely bookish type, pale face, and shoulder-length straight black hair. The foggy mystery of her naked body takes shape in my mind. I see her sweet, inadvertently tranquil features. A memory dream... I think of her heavy bangs... white and death... stiff feelers rattle like dead boughs... I press my lips to her cold cheek, sticky with jam... cold child ghost Victorian...

She is borne away from me on the ghost train, where she rides with another man in a vampire cape. The cars roll off into the distance, pulled by a tiny locomotive trailing smoke against the mountains. I've left the track.

I pass a dead tree made from painted foam rubber and draped with paper maché spanish moss. I'm kicking through heaps of foam rocks. A huge cobweb, stretching from one dead tree to another, gets in my mouth and tangles in with my laces. Bit like cotton candy. These rocks hurt my feet, and I nearly fall. Wind rattles dead branches. I can hear an owl hooting. The soot and silver sky still seems as close as the backdrop had been. Clouds bisected by the horizon move swiftly by.

All the light from above goes out; only a wan glow from the phosphorescent ground mist remains, shining up on blue tombstones. Shrill cries come from the graves. Surrounded by a heap of brittle black wreaths is a stately bier, on which a glass coffin rests. A woman lies on her side within it, dressed in white lace, white stockings, black shoes. One hand lies on her hip, the other under her cheek. Low, funereal music rises from her — an organ, sounds like — and a woman's voice quietly recites an elegy to its accompaniment.

I must see her face!

Her abundant black hair radiates from her head like a sheet of rippling water, and her face has been painted silver-blue, even her eyebrows and lashes. I notice that she is breathing peacefully and it shocks me like a physical blow makes his insides tremble. He strokes the glass tenderly, gazing in awe at her tranquil, sideways face. A weblike cloud of nerves curtains him its tendrils rub the coffin longingly. Somber voice, resignedly beautiful music, go on eternally in the ceremonial gloom here. But when he wakes up — I can't remember it! I never saw her before! Who is she? I want to go back!

Old wives, if there are any left, will tell you that, if someone stares through a window persistently enough, that person's image will faintly remain in the glass. Her face in my memory is just like that, I imagine. Only her expression stays with me, of which the music, and the voice if not so much the words, are a part. I want to go back!

—○—○—

Elfin woman, lean as a rail, poised, tasteful, a little extravagant, bewitching texture of her skin as the light from the candle on the table makes it glow, in the V of her shirt where her skin is stretched over the bone. I forget himself. His behavior becomes artificial, painfully self-conscious. Picking up a paper he isn't interested in reading, he holds it before his face at an unnatural angle, moving his head ostentatiously back and forth, screwing up his mouth with apelike concentration as though he were devouring every word. Meanwhile he keeps looking back in her direction in a way so flamboyantly concealed as to become only more obvious, reeking with embarrassment. Pretending to search his pockets, his stinking clothes flabby as wet sacks, for some elusive personal item gives him a painfully transparent pretext to turn his head in her direction. The dear knife is gradually stabbed into me, through my eyes. The icy shit of strangers runs down my legs and pools at my feet.

Love at last sight, half-formed phantom of desire mechanically snuffed out by shuffling feet, subway doors, time tables, the phone company. Life, élan vital complete with foul smells and slimes, invisible beneath layers of muck in me, somehow sticks through to me, urging me on to collect and shelter all those stillborn phantoms as it did the cadavers I rescued from being forgotten.

He won't fight I, it. The night in that place gathered together like a sheaf of wheat and was cut in half by the bow-shaped ruby edge of her upper lip, hard and elastic. I sit on the fire escape and tiny cherries adorn the branches — I have only to move my hand to pick them. They sprout directly from the branch, long tubes with brilliant red bulbs at the end. Eating these cherries would be like plucking off bits of rash; they would tear free with a soft rip, a relief for the sighing tree. I look in through the window, into her bedroom. She is somewhere in the remoter parts of the apartment, arranging something. There is a table by the sill, and on it there is a folded map with

CITY OF SEX

in a white panel. Like the City of Destruction, or the City of Commerce.

Some severe-looking models with sad, scrawny bodies, are sitting by the door and ducky is a lean young woman with big glasses — mannerisms of a dowager professor, also of a girl raised entirely among adult WASPs probably already middle-aged when she was born. Her smile is apologetic, but she is lit up with happiness now, who knows why, and bright clean neatness. Walks past me holding her body lightly. She dresses the way I imagine people do on yachts — her mouth as she passed was a compressed vermillion diamond. I can hear how she would say hello, with a dying fall and commiserative expression, much looking down, downcast eyes. Her eyes would rise and fall like sparkling waves.

Ducky's models rattle together like the contents of an umbrella stand and swing their long hair. I follow her out the door into peachflesh flames and creamy webs of blue fire with golden tips.

His planchette unaccountably begins to move, he sees the bridge's graceful arch is of interlocking metal beams... Very little commerce in the City of Sex, which is all shining steel and glass like the Crystal Pavilion, and situated exactly under this city, in the hollow earth. Those galleries there are lined with private homes, and business is

Michael Cisco

often conducted in living rooms and kitchens. The natives come in two basic varieties, the tall dark-skinned Day People of the long gestures wafting hands and slow willowy grace, and the rubbery semi-aquatic Night People pale as flounders with bodies like translucent rubber. Here she is on the beach filling out a crossword puzzle with wry sadness, her mouth twisted to one side. She brushes one of his nerves from her face like a lock of hair. With one stroke of his hand he smooths her white summer dress away and sun bounces from honey skin. The northern lights tenderly part their veils to me and I sink beneath her skirts, a pink-tipped violet flame curls up her milky leg.

—∞—○—

Staring at the clouds until they turn pink with my eyes' blood: indigo shadows and pink crusts, a familiar, always new landscape, a sort of homeland. I know that is where I am going or someplace like. Clouds are mesas and rafts, icebergs, a great plume spreading out like volcanic smoke... The shadows are blue, and the land beneath — mountains and sphinxes...

Two hawks fly near me: nearly motionless in the sluicing wind, they hold their places with jerks and flows and adjustments, seesaw describing invisible U's in the air. A gaze is emitted from them. Wire spokes flash in my eyes, I see wheelchairs.

—∞—○—

Young woman talking to her friend outside the cafe, they've just come out, finished dinner saying goodbye. Pleasing bright features, creamy blonde. A spontaneous performer, every moment of the narration she is giving (that I can't hear) she illustrates with a vivacious gesture. Warm attentive face, listens to her friend's story with rapid nods, little frowns and grins as she eagerly sympathizes. What generosity! Luminous eyes (they really are!) whose light spills out and over the curved tops of her cheeks, a surprisingly unexaggerated smile. Twice she flings out her arms to clasp her friend warmly, all unabashed. Nothing comes from her without a flourish. Compact, warmly effusive, generous. At least from a distance — through glass. But even from here, I can't take my eyes from her; she has me, and though I stay hunkered down where I

40

am, by the dumpster, I go with her, like the flu. Take me with you, my heart wails, and she takes me along as heedless of me as an updraft is of the newspaper it carries soaring into the air.

She unfolds into a huge creamy blonde world. I am breaking into the old weather station in the park. Formerly the guest house of an estate that had passed to the parks department, the station is a two-story Victorian gingerbread, sealed like a mummy in rubbery institutional paint. Soft warm night, with air like fine sand.

There is an empty corner room on the ground floor, with dead leaves in the corners. He kneels on bare boards, carefully places his notebook closed on the floor in front of him, and draws his grease pencil ring around himself. A draft stirs the leaves. He recites the "universal monochord" and thick sewage flows out from beneath his coat, its circle, brown and black, spreads uniformly and stops at the grease boundary. In his mind already he sees the downy breast of her dream, an incandescent fog of caressing pink and gold light: the elegant summer dusk, the cordial house, the family.

Here she is, her syrupy hair sheds a heated little glow over her face, her fluffy white body. Her lover, a blonde dream-boy dressed for the moment in a powder-blue prom outfit, is just offstage, shuffling his feet. He's waiting nervously to be introduced to the parents, hefts the bouquet, clears his throat and checks his breath in cupped hand. In the weather station, I drop forward in the circle, head down, and thrust out my hands. These appear behind young Lochinvar, reach slowly out for him, then whisk! He is yanked backwards into the shadows. A frenzied cascade of arms and legs. The dream-boy flops about in wild convulsions, stuttering and grabbing at his face. His eyes sink into the sockets, his eyelids sag inwards, gape open on an inner abyss into which his eyes are tumbling. In the front room of the abandoned weather station, there I rock back and forth; my arms behind him, I lean back, and my eyes disappear into my head. My face gleams mother-of-pearl. My notebook rises in the air, flips open with a pop, and dream-boy's eyes appear on its pages, staring incredulously into each other with a moral expression of helpless terror. Meanwhile, my eyes are in her dream.

A desperate struggle ensues: dream boy's eye sockets bulge out grotesquely as his face wrestles with my eyes. The whites glimmer between the shuddering lashes, and now his lids are forced apart — wildly misaligned livid eyes fairly exploding from between them. Dream boy's feeble will subsides. The Great Lover awkwardly raises his body from the floor, doggedly adjusting the necktie as the legs kick out, give way, stick straight out again.

She is waiting, beginning to get impatient. His cue still hangs unheeded in the air. The dream lists uneasily, but the Great Lover's nerve-projection is firming up swiftly. Now the rosy-cheeked young man strides onstage leading with his forehead, louring up through his eyebrows, dragging the bouquet on the floor behind him — walk like the boy! Suddenly he straightens up with a winning grin and comes on stepping high, quick offer of the flowers.

The dream settles again, she beautifully returns his smile. He pulls his blazer around to hide the huge satyr-play erection bulging down his pant leg to the knee. Turns his head to cough into his fist, clandestinely yanks his tongue and the erection retracts. This is her father in his cardigan and her mother in hers... her pimply brother who assembles model airplanes in his spare time... how do you do?... the cousins... the minister. The smiles the extended hands the welcoming sounds the melting walls and ceilings, the extended leisurely dinner dissolving with exquisite slowness finally to the primeval bedroom beneath the rafters... sinking for a long time into her gossamer bed and slow-warming body. In my circle I bend forwards and backwards, swinging my face up to the ceiling and down to the floor emitting barks and growls through lips crisp hard and shimmering every hue, like mother of pearl streaked now with tan bile while, in her dream, her lover's body arches over her and then descends like a pallid sail.

She coos and sighs and spreads her hands on his waxy shoulder blades, his lean hairless body is clean and gentle and soothing, she melts in pink and blonde clouds and sunshafts. I am rocking frantically now, the sewage pool contracts and expands in regular intervals, and inside me somewhere are two parentheses facing each other, glowing with warmth, full with alien pleasure. A vast black bow regularly sweeps the sky as though the shadow of a gargantuan windmill were interposed between this dream and the sun, the dark arm of a machine the size of space. She is becoming abandoned, stopped wanting clouds: she grips and gets urgent, and the two parentheses in him are warmer and warmer without ever becoming hot. They only radiate a vilely delectable warmth. Her clouds rumble together like boulders, she is poised to fall in among them, and when she does the Great Lover's body shudders and contracts, his nerves lash the ceiling like a whip. I vomit across the floorboards, spatter the dead leaves — my mouth stretches against the laces, my pearly features bulge, I heave thick spurts of fawn bile on the floor.

...She is lazily recoagulating herself in her dream. The clouds are back pink and gold, steaming with milk and honey and butter. In the dark of the room, I shiver and strain with the deepest-churning retchings, black pitch-thick dregs drop from my gaping mouth, hang from wrenched lips like threads of tar. I list forwards. My eyeless face lands on the sloppy boards with a splat, the notebook snaps shut and drops to the floor. Dream boy's head rises woozily from her shoulder and he gazes down at her with his own stunned eyes.

"Did I come?" he falteringly asks. She wakes up laughing.

...My eyes roll uncouthly, now back in their own sockets. Through the window, I see the metallic, deep-indigo sky like fragments of mirror. In among the branches I can make out something else: a large pair of perfectly round eyes. An owl is looking at me. Or is it a man?

A big, slovenly gray-haired man with thick glasses?

CHAPTER THREE

At the far end of the subway platform there is a jagged cloud of smoke turning its cheeks in the stale air. It forms sagging, many-jointed fingers that point in the direction of a solitary man standing at the far edge of the platform, gazing into the obscurity of the tunnel. Two twill legs project from his short raincoat, and there is a narrow-brimmed old man hat on his head. This is Armand Hulferde; he's a *scientist*.

He looks old; a hollow-chested, slack-shouldered man. His big, flaccid hands, dangling at his sides, look like gardener's gloves; he has a long toneless face just beginning to drop jowls, and sagging red eyelids. His features were birdlike once, now melting in time. Inside his raincoat his shirt fits loosely on his spare frame, the collar cinched with no necktie, pants belted up over his stomach. There's a peculiar manner — how to put it — not pleasant to understand about him; more than detachment, he has the affectless air of an appraiser, veins full of smoke. Lately he has spent a great deal of time standing at the far ends of subway platforms, staring deep into the tunnels — and now he finally sees what he wants: a humped shape scuttling along the tunnel wall, an incongruent way of moving, like a suave crab.

Hulferde starts waving at it, trying unobtrusively to get its attention, restricting the movement of his arm so that his body will screen it from view should anyone be watching behind him. His embarrassed gestures don't match the expression on his face. Hulferde peers into the dark for a few seconds, then waves vehemently at something to come to him out of the shadows. The ember at the end of his cigarette traces a lingering zig-zag in the gloom. The figure pauses, the head rises up against a blue light. Hulferde leans forward and waves his dry floppy hand at the sodden, spiky head. The shape glides toward him and then stops fifteen feet from the platform edge. Hulferde resolutely steps down to the purple gravel of the tunnel floor and crunches a few feet into the shade.

It's late; there are no trains. The tunnels are eerily still. The dense air sliding over them both smells of ammonia, graphite, and rust, which smells like cold blood. The Great Lover is standing there by a heap of trash, his arms hanging down, returning Hulferde's gaze with a slack, stupid look, eyes glistening like mercury in a face masked in grime. He's wearing a hat that fits like a skull cap; the brim is folded back and stands upright, the fabric cut into regular triangles all the way around, like a crown of dingy black felt. He sports a very sophisticated-looking silk cravat around his neck.

"I've been looking everywhere for you," Hulferde tells him peevishly.

"—Well?" His voice is cloggy, like he's got a wad of hair stuck in his throat.

"The others told me about you." Hulferde has been interviewing Great Lovers for weeks — fleetingly he remembers talking to one, a male with a flat golden chain around his turtleneck... "Oh that — *that one*... I'd say he knows more about nerve projection than any of us. I mean it is his entire technique." The fragrant man had made a dusting gesture with his middle ring and pinky fingers, indicating panache.

In the present, Hulferde looks squarely at me. "You died."

"That's right."

"...How did you come back?" This is off the subject, but Hulferde is curious.

I shrug. "I don't know."

"Did you do it yourself, or was it done to you?"

"I don't know..." I'm tired, suddenly irritated. I don't like being made to talk. "Stop asking about it."

"Well, I have something else I want to ask you about. My name is Hulferde." He has the wary formal demeanor of someone who doesn't deal often or well with people, and whose chief concern in a conversation is to avoid contamination.

Nothing in the Great Lover's appearance changes, and he does not answer.

"Would you be so kind as to give me yours?"

The Great Lover's behavior is a weird mix of weariness and

punctilious exactness, like an uncertain performance. "I have none to give. You must refer to me in the second person."

A mounting self-consciousness is making Hulferde uncharacteristically hesitant, dilatory. "You... abide down here?"

"Here, and in the sewers."

"And... what do you do, when you are not above ground?"

"I collect specimens."

"...Of what?"

"Of whatever."

"—In this filth?"

"My condition is not noticed here."

"You seduce women in their dreams — is my information correct?"

"No."

He looks annoyed. "I don't believe I've made a mistake."

I wave my hand a little. "Close enough."

"But you never pursue a physical consummation."

"I am not presently able to do so."

"You're saying you're impotent?" Hulferde asks.

"You," I say without really understanding what I'm saying, "and others of your kind are unable to touch me because I am below your level."

"You were human once..."

"I was demoted."

"What are you now?"

He gazes directly at Hulferde smiles for the first time and says through his threads, *"I am a character in a book."*

"Don't say that! Don't say that! Don't say that!"

Hulferde flaps up and down the length of the platform in stroboscopic bursts of light and noise.

"Forget that I said it."

Hulferde really forgets, continuing to look expectantly at me, as though his question had not yet been answered.

"I am like a demon, or a mischievous ghost."

"...I don't normally discuss personal matters with others, so I may express myself a little awkwardly."

The Great Lover's outline alters slightly — what could this preamble possibly signify?

"...I have a problem that might interest you."

"I'll listen to what you have to say."

"Bluntly speaking, my problem is sexual." He folds his arms on his chest and lowers his head. "Frankly, I don't like women, never have."

"...And why indeed should a man in your position feel any different?"

"—I don't want women around me — I don't want to be more attractive to them. I want to be released from these *ridiculous urges*, so I can do my work without this constant distraction."

"You have a strong drive, keeps interrupting."

"Yes. Exactly. I have been actively seeking a solution to this difficulty for some time, and to this end I have contacted and interviewed some of, well of your kind." He looks up. I do nothing. "—An ordinary seducer is of no use to me, but your talent for nerve projection, as they call it, presents me with an intriguing possibility. If I may explain?"

"I'm not doing anything."

Hulferde begins to lecture. He speaks quickly, with his chin down.

"Civilization removes us from the immediate exigencies of evolution. As Freud explained, the life-energies arise in the libido, and it is only by sublimation that they become available for uses unrelated to reproduction. This requires discipline, for, however thoroughly this redirection is accomplished, the energies in question always retain the essential character of their origin in the sex drive. Maintaining the divorce between drive and goal therefore cannot be achieved without a constant, enervating effort. Among those with weaker libidos this effort is correspondingly less, but so is the productivity of the individual in question. It's my bad luck that I have a very powerful libido. While this means that I possess considerable vital energy, quite above average, there is a roughly equivalent claim on my self-discipline."

Hulferde shruggingly indicates himself.

"I have no illusions about my appearance. The trouble and

expense intercourse entails seems excessive to me. In every conceivable arrangement, given present conditions, waste is indicated. I have been trying to discover some way to put an end to this waste, and to place all my energies at the disposal of my work. Naturally, I at first considered the possibility of a libidinal suppressant: a drug, or perhaps a simple surgical procedure. However, since the libido is so to speak the 'engine,' if mine were to be eliminated or reduced in force, there would necessarily be a corresponding attenuation of my energies overall. I would derive no benefit from these measures.

"But then it occurred to me," and now something faintly glimmers in Hulferde's eyes, a clammy excitement, "that a prosthesis might be better; I mean a device which would have and suppress my sexual thoughts for me, while transferring their neutered force to me. I could then separate myself from my libido while continuing to derive from it the full streamlined might of my own proper vital principle. And because the negative effects of sex deprivation are a consequence of the stagnation or misflow of the sexual energies from the drive, once the drive is displaced, these negative effects would not be of any concern."

He pauses to look at the Great Lover. Hulferde is an intelligent, unfeeling man, but he is not cagey or manipulative.

"I needed to understand more about sex transfer, which is why I spoke to the others. But they mentioned you, and your 'nerve projection.' This is precisely what I must learn, as I hope you already see?"

The Great Lover lists to and fro on his feet, mouth slack, like a man on a meat hook.

"My prosthetic device would have to be equipped with a telepathy axon for the transmission of neutered vital force. Already, I have constructed two different prototypes, and yet I find I cannot make them work. Could you help me?"

This last question is uttered with such tensely embarrassed flatness that it sounds like a statement. The Great Lover audibly inhales through his nostrils.

"I infer from your gestures" (Hulferde waved his hands about vaguely while describing his device) "that you fashioned it in the form of a receptacle?"

"That's right."

"That's wrong," my voice sounds muffled and sleepy, and the words seem to pass through me without being assembled by me, as though I'd memorized them under hypnosis. I feel a tingling sensation at the top of my neck, and an acidic trickle or rasp at the back of my throat.

"The sex drive is expressed in every nerve of the body," I go on. "It is not restricted to a proprietary brain structure, nor is it a variety of thought. If you are to induce it to migrate, you must give it an environment recognizeable to it. You must construct your prosthetic in such a way that it corresponds in every particular to the dimensions of your own body. It needn't be your double in every detail, but the volume and form must be identical. It must have your proportions exactly."

"—Yes, that sounds quite correct," Hulferde says with thoughtful ardor. "I will assemble it as you say, but — while I am confident I can manage the task alone, it would take, I'm sure, far less time, with your guidance. I am at present working on a new variety of nerve gas, and my deadline is very tight." Hulferde is getting excited; he is already designing a figure in his mind. "Will you help me build this device?"

My head wavers; I have trouble coordinating my gestures. They are fragmented over the several parts of his body at different times and out of order.

"Yes, I'll help you," and that yes is squeezed out of me. Am I sleeping? "Where do you live?"

Hulferde immediately steps forward extending his card. I take it in thumb and forefinger and crush it into his pocket, turning to go.

"I'll be at your home in two days' time," the demon in me says.

—o—o—o—

That night, Hulferde dreams: "I am levitating over a city at night. Also a black carpet covered with flowers in pale colors. The lights and blossoms mingle on a dark field, then pour down in two opposed parabolas behind the face of the sewerman. I am seeing this face from an angle, just above and to the left of the left temple. The lips of the mask open and a dense brown fluid gushes out."

Ding-dong. Hulferde opens his front door and immediately locks eyes with the sewerman.

"Come in."

He doesn't move. My home is a converted stone coach house with a deeply-recessed front alcove. The sewerman stands in dazzling sunlight, reflecting from the wet street behind him.

"I've come for our appointment," he says.

"Yes. Well, come in," I say, a little nervous. The sewerman doesn't move. The sun reflecting from the wet street shines into my eyes, which are not adjusted, my having only just come from the gloom of the interior of the house, and so he is partially obscured by a sort of a blot.

"Why don't you come in?" I ask.

"You must ask me three times."

"Why?"

He doesn't answer me.

"Come in, then."

He enters. I notice no smell coming from him, despite his filthy appearance, and there are suds clinging to his clothes.

"Happy Valentine's Day," he groans.

I hadn't realized that.

(Hulferde's house is neatly organized, but dingy, with dust piled in the corners and a sort of rabbit-cage odor. Passing the open bathroom door, even from the hallway I could smell the towels. — GL)

We spend the first day taking some rather embarrassing and intrusive measurements; the sewerman handles me as callously as he would a piece of pig meat, but his manner satisfies me he knows what he's doing. After the measurements are taken, we must make a precise map showing exactly where all of my nerve centers are in my body, as these will be the positions for the electrical "joints" of the armature of the Prosthetic Libido.

Into the early morning we work to create a full-scale drawing on butcher's paper, which we tape to a table. Glass eggs are laid on the schematic to show where the most important systems will be placed. The most important of all will be the lumbar-area fusion pile, which I have already started to design; the Prosthetic Libido's mechalogical processes are to be powered by a device that will produce and decay enormously heavy artificial particles. While this will be very expensive, I do not anticipate any difficulty in financing this project, because I hold numerous patents and military contracts, and I supplement this with money from clients who are addicted to my nerve gases, which they use in small doses recreationally.

"Your consciousness is an expression of your entire nervous system and not this or that part of it. I should have thought that would be obvious."

He is showing me a schematic of nerve tissue, made in three layers and spun out into filaments and fine membranes. I notice his voice changes depending on what kind of thing he is saying. For example, his manner is now very clinical.

"Any part of the body can be erogenized. Here we must do even more than reproduce exactly the distribution of your coordinate nerve points in space; we must give them far more sensitivity, both to the usual sort of stimuli and to altogether new stimuli, and make sure there is no interference."

"What interference?"

"If they are not well aligned with each other, the nerve centers may jam each other. They must also be shielded against environmental interferences."

"Do you mean electric fields?"

"All manner of interferences. The human nervous system is vulnerable at many points, especially to confusion of signals as a consequence of overlapping, contradiction, and vague multi-registration; with the Prosthetic Libido, we have the opportunity to introduce a new and superior efficiency. Its experiences will be totally lucid. This will permit near-perfect concentration, for both of you."

"Wait — you, you say it will think?"

Michael Cisco

The sewerman looks intently at me, "You said you wanted something that would have your sexual thoughts for you."

"I meant a receptacle for my thoughts, not a distinct thinking mind."

"I have already explained to you that no such receptacle is possible. The Prosthetic Libido has to have consciousness, and a personality, because otherwise it will not be able to suppress the sexual energy it embodies. Otherwise, suppression would remain your responsibility, and you would gain nothing by the transference but a complicated extension. I am sure you will be able to control the behavior of the device — we need only build in certain safeguards."

"I'll get to work on them at once," I say, with misgivings.

—◦◦◦—

The sewerman puts on his rubber gloves and injects me with a local anaesthetic, then he makes an incision, exposing one of the nerves in my arm.

Applying a compound we have prepared to the nerve, he leans over it and I think mumbles some incantation, which did not at all please me. He places the end of a narrow tube against the treated nerve and closes the wound, leaving the other end of the tube exposed. The exposed end is pressed to an adhesive patch on the skin. This he now covers with a very flat plastic cup, firmly taped to my arm.

After a few hours, a small white dot can be seen just starting to emerge from the tube end. Within twenty-four hours, the dome is completely filled with an opaque white substance, roughly a gram. The sewerman takes off the dome and pulls the tube out. I find I can't resist the temptation to touch the white material.

"It feels like a fingernail."

"It's human plastic, nerve-resin."

From this sample the entire nervous system of the Prosthetic Libido will be cultured. The nerves are cultivated like vines, on frames made of amber and suspended in a solution of electrolytes and some other chemicals.

The brain itself must be grown like a plant also, very slowly, a

52

single micro-layer at a time, and, as he insists, completely in the dark.

"Memory endless and integral, accumulating its own things."

I am required to sleep in the room with the brain incubator, because my proximity will sensitize the tissue and make it more receptive to my nerve patterns. The sewerman insists that my unconscious brain activity will produce this telepathic harmony on its own.

Questions over the skeleton caused us nearly to fall out with each other. It had to be made out of a metal, but whenever I brought samples to him, he always found some pretext to reject each one.

"None of these is shiny enough."

"What does it matter how shiny they are?!" I cry in exasperation, after many attempts. "They are metal, and strong — so what if they aren't shiny?"

He would simply repeat himself until I left to find another sample. This kind of behavior raises serious doubts in me about him. I have noticed he seems to suppress himself, and he especially seems to struggle to keep a straight face when he talks with me. Despite this, we are making real progress, and his ideas always seem to be right.

Finally he is satisfied with a titanium-platinum alloy, which will be reinforced with microfilaments of carbon. This reinforcement was extremely difficult, since it could only be accomplished in a furnace capable of producing extraordinarily great heat.

Assembling the remainder of the body is easier, since I have been synthesizing artificial gem stones in my own lab for many years. The Prosthetic Libido will have muscles made from flexible diamond, the skin and the soft tissues will be made of flexible opal, and the entire body will be given a clear enamel casing designed by me to be as durable as possible. The connective tissues will be made from petroleum colloids.

While I prepare these elements, the sewerman sculpts the face. First, he asks me whether I want the Prosthetic Libido to have a likeness of my own face or not, and, when he assures me that the appearance of the face would have no bearing on the efficiency of the machine, I say, "No, in that case. I would rather it looked nothing at all like me."

He seems to be basing it on an unrealistic portrait etching of Percy Shelley; I think the face is too feminine, but this is plainly the way he intended it to look all along. Again, I wonder if this machine is going to do anything for me, or if he is simply using me to advance a project entirely for himself. I study the material we have assembled once again with a fresh eye, and I can find no reason to believe he is deceiving me.

Following his directions, the tongue of the Prosthetic Libido is woven of strong silk, with glands that produce a saliva infused with cocaine and a slight fragrance at either side of its base. The eyes are meteoric glass with irises of emerald; I bleach clear spots in the center of each iris to form the pupils. While I am occupied with this, he starts to create the hair. Although by now I know it is pointless to argue with him, I can't keep silent about this. I tell him there is absolutely no reason to go to the considerable difficulty and expense of providing the machine with hair, but as usual he overrules me.

"I assure you," he says, and again, even though he is completely serious, I get the feeling he may explode at any moment, perhaps laughing wildly in my face, "the hair is crucial for sexual innocence, the absence of which will strangle the libido as the transplant takes place. The Prosthetic must be wide open, at least to begin with."

After several trials, he decided to give it a scalp of thick copal wires and pearl fibres. The copal is a pale orange color I dislike. In fact, I find this hair the least pleasing aspect of the Prosthetic Libido.

Because he is always talking in riddles, or performing as I have described, communication is strained between us, with the result that much time is wasted and I am constantly confused. For example, with considerable effort I produce a suite of artificial organs made from dense clay, exactly the size and weight of the organs they duplicate. When I show them to the sewerman, he sweeps them angrily to the floor, seizes me by my collar, and screams,

"Simulations and make-weights will not do — the heart must beat the lungs must breathe — *it must live!*"

Then he releases me, points at my table and says, "Start over."

"This is how you help me?!"

He looks back at me from the door with an enormous smile, and then, without a word, runs away down the hall, laughing like a madman.

I restrict myself to developing the systems and the mechanical infrastructure, while he does the modelling. The genitals of course had to be put together thoughtfully and with a great deal of care. The glans is made of enamel; the shaft has three collapsing chambers which can be erected by an inflow of silica beads that are finer than sand. These three chambers surround the pseudourethra like the points of an inverted triangle, giving the entire structure a broad flat upper surface and tapering sides. The entire structure is wrapped in a web of nerves, twice as dense at the tip and along the ante-dorsal ridge; then it is sheathed in a sensitive integuement of overlapping rings made from fossil beeswax, reinforced with flexible loops of diamond wire. There are two layers of these rings, one within another. As the member grows erect, the upper ring segments are pulled apart, and the lower segments rise up between them.

The scrotum is a pouch of flexible opal lined with silk floss. I had thought that a pair of glass eggs would be good enough substitutes for testicles, but he vehemently disagrees with me and says the testes must have "functionality." This term he has tried to explain to me many times but I still fail to understand at all what he means by it. The Prosthetic Libido will not be able to reproduce and there is no allowance in its mechanology for hormones, so what function is there for the testes to have?

He makes them by himself, in his own lab, and then brings them to my home in a plastic bag full of almond oil. They resemble small brains the size of turtle eggs. When I look at them closely, I see miniature gold cogs and gears between the folds, and once briefly I caught a glimpse of a light, like a star, deep inside one of them.

I try once more to oppose the sewerman when he says the Prosthetic Libido must have an anus.

"There must be digital access to the pneumatoprostate."

He holds in his hand, already made, the glands that will produce cocainated lubricants.

"All right, but why can't we do that with a pad at the base of the spine, for example? It will not evacuate. Digital access to the pneumatoprostate does not seem like a sufficient reason to create an entirely new structure."

"No, in this case the anus will be exclusively a pleasure organ."

"I don't see the need."

"Anal stage critical to repression."

He is screwing his face around trying not to mock me to my face. I become fed up.

"You may dislike me or find me ridiculous—"

(He smells like wet concrete. — (heart with smily face in it) GL)

"but are you toying with me?"

He points to the Prosthetic Libido — "Not me, him!"

—◦◦—◦—

Oh brothers and sisters, the labor is hard and the hours are long. Hulferde nods off on a chair, his head falling forward he is reading a book called *Drugs and the Ocean*, a passage describing a man hooked on panic: lying sleepless in his bed, nausea, tachycardia, shivers, the bed clothes soaked in cold perspiration... That was a good one, gleaming in memory like precious stones in the sun, and the bitter acidic grey of the steel wing, gagging on the acrid mustard of diesel jet fuel as the plane hurtles wildly down the runway his knuckles white as snow on the armrests...

...A man gives a woman a diamond ring. She pops it into her mouth and bites down, gnashes her teeth on it — blood jets from her gums cheeks as she screeches "I want to feel it cut my mouth!! I want to feel it cut my mouth!!"

—A woman speaking Spanish nearby, her eyes suddenly flicker like fluorescent tubes and her jaws, tongue and lips accelerate like a rabbit's, picking up speed until her jaws rip clear of her face and splinter apart, teeth blasting all over creation like bullets. A truck's back-up beeper starts with a drawling first note: the driver reclines smiling in his seat, the two beeper horns close around his head screaming the note into his vibrating ears — he sighs with pleasure as his eardrums are smashed and blood streams down his neck.

Pigging down fistfulls of cashews from a birdbath, a pair of idiots in grimy tweed suits are playing a *weltspiel* (world-game) on a stone table; each pair of tiles removed from the board is a pair of lovers who will never meet: the goal of the game is to *remove them all.*

An evil image... an Edwardian parlour... noon... light slants in acutely... There is — this is not one of my dreams, is it? It feels like memory, but I have no such memories — there is an upright piano in the middle of the room... a voluptuous, woozy woman in a very sheer dress leans over the back of it while a small boy practices at the keys... from time to time she takes a candy from a dish and pops it gracefully into his red mouth...

I am red mouth light crick in neck being dragged by the collar, I am awake — the sewerman has me by the collar and is pulling me through the door — I stumble and grope for words to complain. I see stars and bare branches. We are going to a stone outbuilding I don't recognize — I still dream. On a stone table the Prosthetic Libido is lying in a box packed with cashews. Glancing into the arch of the ribcage a balmy summer day, milky haze over the grass, already with thee, tender is the night...

While the transplant will take only a single operation, he says it is advisable to record some libidinal material in advance. During live transplant, the libidinal wire recordings will be played back to supplement my own spontaneous libidinal activity, and this will imprint my libido more strongly on the artificial nerves of the prosthetic. He explains to me, again with that annoying look of hidden mockery I am starting to hate, that the playback through the nerves creates a so-called "phantom patterning" which itself acts as a microreceptacle for the sex drive.

I must stimulate my libido in order to make this recording. I have some pornographic films here, but he refuses to permit their use, saying, "You'll have to buy new ones. The unfamiliar material will be more arousing and, ideally, produce an occasional shock response. The closer you can get to your limit the better the readings will be."

"Perhaps — a living woman?"

"That would not be appropriate."

"Why not? The response would be more natural…"

"It is no less in our nature to love images. I am able to make communication across dream-membranes by means of this principle."

—◦◦—◦—

Hulferde watches blue movies while I read the ticker tape, and record the nervous response on a specially-made device. This all takes place in the basement. Hulferde sits in a chair with a jumbo umbrella over it, his privacy protected by a curtain on rings. Beneath his bathrobe he wears a number of sensitive measuring devices like delicate little propellers. I sit behind him. The recorder is the size of a freezer, open on top with a pair of upright needles that occasionally spark across. They write the ganglial information on wire that spools on steel bobbins. The recording "head" is an array of tone arms not unlike the mystifying bundle of feelers around a lobster's mouth, engraving the entire surface of the wire as it passes.

We run tests using some of Hulferde's old favorites, in order to calibrate the sensors.

"These aren't sensitive enough."

Hulferde fidgets and snorts in frustration.

"If you want this to work you will need more sensitive equipment. You buy cheap tin receiver modules at the five and dime don't expect sound results."

When everything is ready Hulferde breaks out the new movies — no pretext of a narrative and so brutally unadorned as to be almost abstract, like nature films shot by extraterrestrials. Passion-exasperated cries rattle in the plastic coping of the projector's one speaker with the volume turned all the way up. I grease the pins and knock bolts of blank wire into place with a mallet, start with flat readings. Hulferde must prolong his excitement steadily, without starts and stops, and, when orgasm is eventually permitted, he must be careful to permit total relaxation afterwards so the whole sequence may be recorded complete.

"At this point I'm going to have to ask you to start stimulating yourself," I tell the curtain. "Avoid climax, please."

A horizon of grey mountains and a wan, sulfur-colored sunset appears behind my back, and a wind with a slightly bitter taste to it brushes over me with its ringlets. The earth rumbles beneath me, as though a train were rushing beneath my feet, but the sound and the vibration seem to go down into the earth toward the City of Sex.

The first hour or so is completely wasted; Hulferde is too inhibited. But eventually after some impatient throat-clearing from me he hits his stride and the recorder starts getting good signal; the wires levitate off the spindle floating on recorded lust bands, and the lead motes swirl up out of the neck of the bulb. The curtain surrounding Hulferde shivers. The machine is whirring and clanking; far from distracting him, the sound of heavy equipment seems to encourage Hulferde. When the high stimulation begins to register I dip my finger in a pot of ink and slash it across the paper tape to mark the time. The recorder demands constant attention; I have to keep spitting on the valves to keep them from sticking. The fumes make my nose run, mucus cool on my upper lip.

Brief flashes — keep jerking to see who's there in the corner of my eye — ectoplasm is gleaming on the console and dribbles down the curtain. Ectoplasm cool on my upper lip — a voice might be saying "'cause we like it so much" amid many other voices words equivocal sounds rise from the floor or topple in from the walls.

A silhouette rushes toward me flinging up its arms and vanishing... a woman stands beneath a tree in white haze on the bank, he can make out the white dress with green embroidered flowerets *como hielos* or icing I mean, tapioca pearls on her gown and *pelo de humo*, eyes drip lecherous milk onto glazed hands... the ribbon around her neck is crowded with microscopic embers for scales, and it creeps slowly from left to right across her white throat, saying *ma gorge est pleine de chevaux* or at least he smells like he's been rolling in pungent grass, anyway her face is swinging to and fro like a peephole cover, and her long black bangs tattoo her twitching eyelids and lashes... her mouth is shaped like a diamond on its side and her lips are thin and dark almost like a cat's (say *I own you* or maybe *I won you*). The lips are open and hide the teeth, the inside of her mouth is dark. Her lips are fairly dripping with saliva as clear as glass, and they don't keep the same shape from one moment to the next. I can feel and smell her creamy breath... though she breathes it in my face, I feel it hit my lap...

The movie has broken into its high-calorie phase. I really got to ride the oil pressure control, which is a garden hose faucet — lean forward to spit on the hissing valves, little puffs of steam slither out of the open chassis. I can't stop sniffing. I can feel the worm oozing down from my nose and pressing against the rim of my upper lip. The focus just went out — I fix that, damp the motor a bit more, check the gas pressure, re-key the foot pedal again, wipe condensation from gauges, spit on the valves starting to glow hot, goose the current a bit more.

The room rocks and booms. There are rows of straight glass ribs between the valves, each one ends in a bulb filled with shuddering mercury. As the experiment continues the room fills with a musty smell of hot grease, like the inside of a typewriter. A chorus of voices lacing through the noise, on the screen a hydraulic struggle is playing out in a series of unedifying close-ups, the soundtrack gargles and whines out the speaker. The machine is churning, dark curling red flames sputter around the wires as they pass through the guide-holes to the spools, the magnetic filings shoot to the top of their bulb and hang there vibrating, a desperate commotion ripples across the machine, the tone arms blur together with a sound like a whole string section playing pizzicato and a forest of bare arms are lifted on all sides... the machine thumps the floor and falls still. The end of the film pops off the rear spool slap slap slap slap slap...

—o—o—

My name is Vera. I am not a *character*. I won't explain, but I will tell you where I am now... on the platform, of course... there is cold wind, there is trash on the curb I can smell. It stinks like death.

My father says now is the only time when anything can happen, which is naturally why now writes as it does. I repeat these things to myself feeling I understand them perfectly, but without being able to explain them at all.

Let's be alert again. Now nothing has changed, the rags still blow around the tree, whose branches rattle with a barren sound, and the earth holding its roots is pounding like a drum. I hear it, and it makes a hot spot of excitement in my chest. The rays of the sun lie flat against the ground and warm my face, and I imagine the earth whirling gaily around the sun, and the earth throbs like a drum... No amount of lies can separate me from this scene — or that remains to be seen. I can't see their lies, so they don't affect me so much. My father says I'm lucky — why should I argue? I let it go.

I play with words so they won't remain exactly but stay alive in their own way, or so I feel them living. The lies I feel all around are different; they're not playing. I visualize an arch crisscrossed with wires, sky a perfect crescent of blonde gold, blonde air golden — brass fumes and copper smoke. Is the word I want "blonde," like a blonde word? It must be smooth, smooth and groovy. From this image all the rest proceeds. The arch, arching back to my parents and my ancestors. Wherever they came from, my ancestors all gave me exactly the same things: heart, bone, brains, silly eyes, gristle, muscle, appetite, nerves, hair, teeth, malice, spirit, and love, and breath — no I take it back, the breath is mine, my happiness. They gave me this language and these color words I hear without knowing what they mean. Everyone is confused when I use color words or I speak about brightness and darkness. I think about color incessantly.

On the train one may observe these people whose lives are an endless rustling and rummaging in bags, eternally taking out and putting away, forever management of parcels of surrogate foods carefully wrapped and unwrapped like morsels of precious gold, like Etruscan artifacts. Bags within bags, systems of bags, hours, *whole nights* of bags; the world's silence fumbled away in the flames of thousands of tireless fingers rustling in bags.

My hand: fat pink yarns threaded with green, so I'm told. Color is as close to me as the vein in my neck. It's here in my hand, actually in it, not even so far as to be in contact with it. Color is a secret property of me. It's as weird as if I had a halo or an intangible tail. A spot on my wrist where something poked me. I have nothing to do. My guitar bag strap squeezes my shoulder. I try to picture the scribble described by this bottle here, rolling this way and that on the floor of the car. What if it drew something?

Lifting my head, I rest its crown on the poster behind me and forget the bottle. The tunnel crashes around us. I want to be a murderer stalking at night, I want to feel seared by malice and murderous hate, and I want to disappear into thin air when the sun rises... Or the sun's light transforms me into a plant, a wind, a cloud — I could rejoin my brother and sister sunbeams, shine on the earth all day stately and calm as a god, and then, as night falls and the light turns blood-red, I revert, am restored to the night's real pleasures of nakedness and swift stealth.

Wake to the sound of french horns imitating hunting horns, as they do in certain picturesque operas and symphonies. A woman sitting close by, talking on her mobile phone. She is listening; now she grins. Someone is gazing amorously at it, because it's complex and baroque, glistening with venom — a grin he wants to suck on like hard candy — a jaw-breaker. The same radiant fire that animates the leaves is there, what must be its own unique color in her. But who is he? Why do I shake as I wonder that?

<hr>

We insert the *in vitro* nerves, threading them down the spine and through the limbs, then leave them to develop the finer fibers within the tissues. The brain is fitted with resinous apertures through which we will draw the wires of the recorders. The top of the Prosthetic Libido's skull can be removed easily during this phase of its assembly. Later, when it is operating independently, the sewerman says the skull will fuse on its own.

"This was an excellent opportunity to experiment with independent recapitulatory formation. The diffuse mechabolism will monitor material autostatus and supplement the loss of any element by synthesizing new molecules directly. In most cases, the prosthetic will not even have to provide itself with any matter for use as raw material. Whatever is ingested will be processed at above ninety-eight percent efficiency, and, when there is waste, it will be evacuated in atomized exhaust from the mouth. He should be completely self-sustaining, over any length of time. Nearly indestructible, even in cases of significant injury."

"It will outlive me? What will happen to it when I die?"

"I don't know," he says offhandedly.

The Prosthetic Libido is my size and shape. When I die, it will go on. This thought strikes me with terrifying force as I look down at the table where it lies. I begin to imagine it has replaced me already.

"Is it necessary to make it so independent?"

"It must live!"

"But that's not what I wanted! I don't want some living machine to be responsible for, I just want some relief—"

He bursts out laughing — It is sometimes shocking, his reckless laughter, as if any moment he will have no face — only a wild mouth and light reflecting in his eyes with no gaze.

"Look, you want this or not? If you want this to work, you have to do it my way."

"I never wanted to make some life — that always was your idea! I think you are appropriating this experiment for your own purposes!"

"Of course what did you expect? I'm doing this all for charity — for your sole benefit?" His smile is wide and fierce, his whole face livid like steel, as I see it through the crumbling shit mask. "Of course I'm going to make life! Why else dude?!"

—∘—∘—

Now it is time to bring the prosthetic to "half-start," which is a special coma it will remain in until after the transplant of my libido into it. In order to establish protomechanostasis, the reactor must be idling, like a car engine. The Prosthetic Libido has a contact pad under the skin of its solar plexus. I begin the half-start procedure by connecting this pad to an external reactor monitor by means of an adhesive electrode.

The sewerman says, "It will not live without fire... tissue is solid fire, spirit is breath vibrating with word." I don't have any idea what he is getting at with that.

"Can't you be serious?" I ask.

He smiles at me and says nothing, going to examine the prosthetic. This he had left on the workbench, so that sunlight can shine on it through a kaleidoscope device he made and attached to the window. Rings containing colored glass slowly spin, and the rings all together also spin, not always in superimposition but moving in and out of different overlapping arrangements to create a variety of patterns, which are projected onto the prosthetic's body. This steady stimulation is supposed to promote the development of the nervous system *in situ*. For the same reason, he has brought in a device modelled on a marimba, consisting of metal keys tuned to different notes, which are played by a machine that also generates random patterns.

"Now I must give him the breath of life!" he says. His manner is becoming completely theatrical, and I am losing patience with him. He puts his face up to the prosthetic's face. "Be ready to start the reactor."

Though I begin to believe there is no point in putting such questions to him, I ask, "Shouldn't the breath — assuming it is necessary at all, which is not something you have adequately shown me — should I be the one to breathe into it, and not you?"

"My breath is cleaner," he says in a final way. "Please be ready to start the reactor."

(This is not an exaggeration; while the rest of me, I admit to my shame, stinks horribly, I do have odorless cold antiseptic breath, like an alpine blast. — GL)

He nicks his left wrist with a small knife. His blood has a strange appearance. I can't see it well from here, but it looks nearly blue.

He pinches his blood and holds it up to his mouth, drawing a long breath through it. Holding his breath, he carefully parts the Prosthetic Libido's lips. He closes its nostrils with his right hand and holds the chin down with the first two fingers of his left, presses his lips to the Prosthetic Libido's lips, and breathes out. The Prosthetic Libido's throat and chest expand and his body takes on a pink appearance, like a pink flush. At this sign, I start the reactor of the Prosthetic Libido going. The activity of the reactor is registered by the position of a copper bead on a horizontal indicator I have in front of me. The equipment around us makes no sound, with the exception of a small fan inside my console. The sewerman is striking poses by the bench like he is shooting arrows from an imaginary bow at the Prosthetic Libido. He does this so persistently that I wonder exactly what he thinks he is doing.

In no more than a minute, the bead begins to move, and within another thirty seconds it has reached 6.22, which is the idling point.

I say, "Half-start." The reactor of the Prosthetic Libido from this point is operating at the minimum level necessary to sustain its independent production of energy.

The Prosthetic Libido's chest rises and falls, very gently. The skin has also changed; I have no other description for it but to say it acquires a life-like quality it did not formerly have. As expected, with the arrival at half-start, the total-loss surface lubrication system starts working, and the micropores of the skin begin to produce a layer of odorless mineral oil, making the entire body surface slick.

When the sewerman sighs, I think I see an orange flame against the roof of his mouth, and when he speaks he appears to spit small pieces of the fire. The impression lasts only a few moments.

"This confluence of elements has already engendered a larval spirit."

"In that?"

"Yes."

"How do you know this?"

"The odor."

He leaves the room without elaborating.

—o—o—

The recordings have been edited and the operating theatre — a lumber room — is ready. The Prosthetic Libido lies on a table, its brain exposed pink and grey like a cloud above the rising sun. A heavy black curtain divides the room into two sections. The stretcher on which Hulferde will rest is head-to-head with the table, on the other side of the curtain, and it stands on an enormous wooden spool of metal cable.

Now to bring the prosthetic up to full start. After several misconnections finally they throw the switches. For a moment there is total darkness and a silence in which everything stops. Now a dim glow can be seen. The light gradually returns, with a lazy stirring in its — his — genitals and extremities. Life always just trickles in at first.

The breathing deepens... an expression of dreamy relish creeps over his features, his eyes open to two fringed slits, and mineral oil perspiration sequins his sides steaming with musk. Life rises and ebbs, rises higher and ebbs higher, higher still each time, like the swelling breast of a symphony, the Prosthetic Libido's life trembles on the verge and then spills over, becomes self-perpetuating. It draws deep and pleasurable breaths. The folds of its membranes soft as if they were just made of sky like silky wads of dusk about a disk of blue wands, spokes from an off-center opening in the base. They shiver, then it's as if they'd never moved, shiver again. A ribbon of pressure comes into existence nearly encircling the aperture from the outside. Its shadow is faintly visible on the interior canopy. At roughly regular intervals more such ribbons appear until the canopy is striped with spinning shadows, and now the lighter bands between them become shiny, a pink lambence makes them sparkle with heat mounting in gentle intensity as the instants develop them. The ribbons tenderly squeeze the canopy from outside, without deforming it, and the wands flex as a formation bows them outward. The off-center opening is sealed with a brittle film of some mineral like abalone lining—

—now it buckles before a gush of light, frothing in the wands and against aperture walls. In channels of soapy metal it sluices away into the body, bubbling up white and volatile where it touches the sides of the channels, shedding and reabsorbing thin shells of intense, pure hues on top, the color of the streams are pastels lit from inside that throw off striped fans and strobing marquees. The light thickens at the edges, then pulls apart in strings. The Prosthetic Libido sighs and shimmers a profusion of colors which, as I move to and fro, fitfully takes on the luster of sunlight — a hum of a hundred men I feel tremble in my throat and chest, then open out to a great and joyous cry I don't hear but that runs a hot river down my body to the floor.

The Great Lover gets the machinery running while Hulferde attaches contacts to himself, unable to see the machine through the sable curtain. He lies down on the stretcher in his street clothes, face down; there's a padded ring into which he inserts his head to keep his spine straight. The Great Lover dons rubber gloves and applies a topical anaesthetic to the skin at the base of Hulferde's skull. With one expert shove he drives home the point of an awl-like cutting instrument with an adjustable barrier around the base to prevent it cutting too deep. A brief sound of surprise issues from Hulferde, he jerks once, then goes limp. Only a drop or two of blood.

The Great Lover presses a release at the end of the cutter's handle; he extracts the device from the wound, leaving behind a small metal tube, angling up through the spinal aperture at the skull's base. Through this tube, the Great Lover introduces a number of wires one at a time, expertly twisting them so as to position the end of each wire in the proper brain area, finishing with the spinal cord. The other nerve impulses will be drawn out through the skin contacts, which are rounded domes, modifications of the cupping method. There will be a feedback arrangement, employing the recordings made earlier, which will be played back on Hulferde's nervous system and the Prosthetic Libido's in exact sync, reproducing the arousal state and greatly augmenting it. When fully engaged, the faculty of arousal will commit itself completely, and may then be extracted *in toto* with the application of an external vacuum. The principle is to induce flow by creating adjacent zones of high and low pressure.

In response to a question from the Great Lover, Hulferde mumbles he is ready to proceed. The Great Lover takes up a position perpendicular to the curtain, from which he is able to observe both Hulferde and the prosthetic. The machine controls, for the most part large iron wheels with protruding metal handles, surround him. At once, the Great Lover is setting gauges and turning cranks. The recorded wires emerge from a spindle box bolted to the floor and pass like harp strings through holes in a steel ring around Hulferde's head. From there they are drawn eight feet up to pulleys hanging from the ceiling, and go down again on the other side of the curtain. They feed, one by one, into the resinous apertures in the Prosthetic Libido's exposed brain.

As Hulferde responds to the recordings, the spool beneath his stretcher turns counterclockwise and the three-inch-thick cable unwinds, pulled into the Heavy Recorder against the wall opposite the Great Lover. The HR is triggered with a terrible sound, engraving Hulferde's libido itself on the cable with massive hydraulic rams that thunder like locomotive pistons, deafening in this not over-large room. A smell of motor oil issues from the machine. The erections of the two subjects rise in sync.

The cable runs parallel to the floor and enters a second machine which thrusts the end of the cable against a bore-headed bladed drill bit. The bit pares the cable's individual metal threads apart neatly like a slow-turning star, and each thread is drawn into the Prosthetic Libido's brain. Hidden wheels deep in its head draw the wires and respool them in that intimately dark spot; the wires are drawn at different rates and, after editing, are different lengths — one after another they suddenly pull loose from the spindlebox and with a violent spin of the prosthetic's wheels the wires snap free and whip through the room, whizzing into the Prosthetic Libido's brain with a sharp whine. Click — the wire vanishes — the resinous aperture closes; the Prosthetic Libido's brain begins to hum, a tone which is modified with each closure. He will be animated in Virgo. A distant music is audible, like harp notes scattered in a cave.

Now the gauges, which have been edging over steadily and at different times, all swerve at once to the line: transfer instant. The Great Lover spins his wheels and pulls levers. The cup-contacts attached to Hulferde's body all puff and sigh at once, like cloud chambers; wisps of white vapor appear in them. The hydraulic rams batter at the cable like the pistons of a gargantuan engine and then with a single abrupt motion the cable spool stops rotating and the HR's chopper severs the cable. The tail end feeds through the rams, and they fall silent as it is drawn into the separator drill. As the wires drop from the pulleys and slither across the floor into the prosthetic's brain, Hulferde begins to laugh — a giddy bubbling mirth spilling from his mouth — the Great Lover catches it, begins chuckling horribly, his sharky mouth stretches and smuts of fire jet out... and now the Prosthetic Libido is laughing too, a high clear fluting note. A laughing chorus billows around the room and chimes ring out.

Hulferde confusedly thinks the sewerman is ringing a bell — I can't see where he has it.

(Unlike me, Hulferde is unable to see that a small liberty bell has appeared just above the Great Lover's head, masturbating crazily its clapper whanging the inner surface of... The Prosthetic Libido hears it clearly. —The Author.)

—the Prosthetic Libido raises his torso, flexing at the waist, raises its arms elbows curled hands bending back at the wrists, as though the laughing and the music were buoying him up — his face is transported, his body sways and twines itself up the air — he is singing out with passionate joy—

The Great Lover capers up and down the room roaring with laughter, like a toe-dancing bull cavorting around the equipment, his tangled choker of spectacles rattling like a shamanic instrument. He thrusts his face, hard with fierce satisfaction, within an inch of the Prosthetic's dazzled eyes gloating and cackling, the bell above his head crashes and whips against itself as though a hurricane were driving it. He turns and dances out of Hulferde's house.

—o—o—

Hulferde gingerly removes the metal tube and the wires from his head; there is no sensation. He bandages his wound carefully and extricates himself from the contacts and devices. Not yet fully able to appreciate the change he sits on the stretcher a moment, rubbing his face.

Hulferde stands, and crosses the room, pulling the curtain aside. The Prosthetic Libido lies on its table, masturbating blinking and sighing — he turns his glorious eyes on Hulferde in astonishment and pleasure. Sunlight vibrates from his skin.

Hulferde looks at his creation with sour distaste — finally throws a cloth over it and wheels it into the storeroom. As he locks the door, he is already thinking only of the work that waits for him. He turns away preoccupied, a benzene ring in his mind.

CHAPTER FOUR

The earth is hollow — and I can prove it to you! (goes down steps to subway station)

...

I need love like I'm a plant in a cave but now there's no Love at all to be found, nothing like it anywhere, aynewerhe, wheneraye — I kick around in the trash feeling — I'm just sighing and pining. I clutter together among the other objects at the dark end of the platform, past the reach of the sodium lights that turn the mist into a blizzard of orange motes. I look out at a switching yard filled with broken furniture and tufted bracken, dark iron trestle bars the sky. The platform trembles, but I don't see the train for a long time. There is something at work below the trestle, right down deep into the earth, that is shaking the platform.

The train pulls in with rain rilling down its sides and I take a seat in the first car. It's empty. I close my eyes and I open my eyes and I see needles of light reflected in the polished steel pole. I close my eyes and open my eyes and I see tan floor streaked cream and plum. The train creaks through black space upon which lights and illuminated surfaces have been scattered. The distant skyline is stationary and the intervening buildings hurtle past and fall back into the cavernous night. A building stands there, crowned with an amber cone. Dead trees whisk along scribbling on the lights. Gleaming steel and fluorescent lights in the excessively bright car like a mobile morgue, a ghostly, transient feeling, like visiting a hospital.

Travel has an erosive effect on what is called sanity; the further one goes, the more uncompressed and irrelevant become the thoughts. The train dives into the ground and suddenly the fluorescents overhead go out; in rushing darkness I hear the door at the end of the car snap open, bang from the jam, slide back and clap shut. When the lights dazedly blink on again, there is a large shambolic man in a shapeless sweater sitting opposite me, writing something on a sheet of paper against his leg. Brow knotted against the upper rims of his thick glasses and crazy grey hair sticking out all over, his lips protrude to form a rigid bow-shaped funnel. Over the sweater he wears a burgundy vinyl jacket that's too small for him and a broad rock-and-roll belt with two parallel rows of metal-rimmed eyelets on crooked across his hips.

Suddenly he thrusts the paper at me, with a chewed-up pencil under his planklike thumb. There are three algebra problems written out on it. "Show your work," it says. Subway stations and tunnels pass like illuminated shipwrecks on the other side of the express brackets. I finish doing the problems and hand the paper back. The man runs the pencil down the page, making marks and checks. As the train stops, he gets to his feet swaying nearly off balance, hands the page back, and blunders out the door without a word.

In a circle at the top it says:

"A-

—this would have been a B+, but I'll give you extra credit for factoring the problem so thoroughly."

He's added this at the bottom of the paper:

"I am the first leper corpse and I lead a leper corpse." Train rolls through the station and for an instant I'm eye to eye with the head of a black man hanging in the window.

Riding on the undertaker in love withdrawal some days later — the passengers thin out in the mid-afternoon and you can feel the daylight energy of the sun just overhead. I'm sandwiched between that warmth and the icy entrails of the planet under me. So now we've just left the station and we're rolling steadily into the dark. I'm alone in the last car. An unfamiliar voice comes over the PA and says, after announcing the next stop and the transfers, in a tone so level and quiet I wonder if I *am* hearing it:

"Through the interstices of impersonal indifference hovers over the city like devil wings, not the indifference of one soul or another, but a property of the indifferent air and the hard blank canvases of the pavement the buildings. Like the ether of early astronomy it is infinitely rigid and permeates everything, a hard canvas the painted figures can feel unyielding behind them."

I get up and make my way through the cars to the one with the conductor. He is coffined up behind his steel door, speaking over the PA. At the next stop, I get off quickly and rush round to peer in his window. No one there. I look along the train and see a head drawn in as the doors close and the train pulls away from me.

Riding the train you discover the other chronics — there are those who, this or that or no reason, lose interest in work, in daily affairs, in food, in sleep, and take to riding the subways, settling on the trains like marine snow on the sea bottom. Overwhelmed and drained by the vampiric demands of bills and mail, haircuts, laundry, rent, they begin to fill up with a desire for complete quiescence, and this desire adds to their inertia. They don't want to die, to sleep — they want to forget and to meditate. They want to fall out of their sconces and stop working so hard to resemble this or that. No one is anything when they travel, or travel tends to rub identity.

...Vera swings a little against her father. On the subway, bodies shudder and tilt with the motion of the train like empty sacks. The communication of this movement makes the car into a big soup of partially-blended, partially-independent people. Most of them don't notice how loose their edges get when they ride, because they get on at an important stop and get off at an important stop. The trip in between is only an interruption the ample business of their lives immediately reabsorbs...

I can pick out the ones who ride all the time — they let it happen. The encroaching anonymity is turning into a new person. It cuts right through me like a knife — it's a horrible sound: I want you to watch me die, I want to be cut open and bleeding to death, and I want you to *watch me* bleed to death: it would be a tender, an intimate scene — the head goes pale and the lips droop — the face slowly drops with beautiful, celestial musi—

The petrified subway tunnel landscape: pencil-shaped stalactites, scurfy black scales, mineral ooze hardened like charcoal scum on the tunnel walls, dirty ink of puddles and leaks, flat blots of old fossil chewing gum... lichenous rust adhering to steel columns in modestly fantastic shapes, like gills of fungus... girders filmed with a thin layer of gelatinous metal, or sheathed in an elastic integument of thick paint like flexible amber. The lights in the tunnel, the pearly gates hanging in beaded lines... the corky crud between the rails, like chipped bark... thick flakes of congealed muck the size of rats' heads and matchbooks... hoses and wires, painted-over half-moon lightbulbs... alarmingly bright dry orange stain on the ground at the base of one of the pillars... thick black dust on the tiled wall opposite, something intimate and cloistered there like a familiar closet under the stairs, a boy's fortress as empty now as a rotted-out tortoise shell... steel button-box marooned high on the wall, where only the operator can reach it from the window of his compartment... serrations in the lower edge of the tiled wall like the outline of an inverted battlement... the motto "Don't Piss Here" spray-painted in pale yellow on concrete piling out on the railed cement pier past the no-entry sign. Smell of urine, heaps of tools, bags of metal. Rumble of trains is like ventriloquism, hard to place the source until you see the lights, or hear them angrily rampaging overhead, and often you never know where they are. Messages everywhere, almost all of them impossible to read correctly at first sight. Soiled feeling of old iron, old painted metal, just solid soil.

Sitting on the train we're subdued, watchful. To young thugs and religious old ladies on the train: you are wasting your time. This one here is so self-contained he absorbs light: his reserve is hostile most likely without meaning to be. My weird reflection in onyx window like the Cup of the Ptolemies, my grin warps out to the window's edges, my eyes like twinkling black pits. My face asks: *so what do you want to do today?* — What are you asking me for? I look at the advertisements. There's everything to read, but none of it makes sense, or the sense it makes is accidental. Silent and unconscious signs are also transmitted and received: I will stand here in the coveted spot by the door, I am just letting you on, I will move back to my spot by the door. Decay's alchemy makes these tunnels more and more like living things or to speak more precisely and not using anything as crude as metaphor or similie the distinction between the tunnels and platforms on the one hand and the decomposing remains of once living things on the other hand is to be made with a difficulty that can only be relied on to increase steadily.

Passengers break away like spores from a single dark cloudy mass of cavernous night, bobbing heads lightly pour in through the doors without the slightest displacement of air. Tidal forces pull passengers on and off the platforms... and here and there people reel or spin or sway a little in the eddies of these tides you sometimes feel roll along you — or you may rock with the motion of this inorganic train.

Sitting and hurtling through space in my seat, looking at my counterpart there in the glass, because it's underground that you meet yourself, and he says, "Oh Master I say : stay a journeyman" I tell him so that he nods agreement as the train pivots changing tracks. Watching from cover of an invisibility only the homeless can possess I make the whole system into my terrarium picking out the damned accommodationists from the typeless types I'm looking to contact. They eye me and I them and we make uncertain gestures testing testing 1 2 3.

Clean-shaven middle-eastern man in wool jacket and wool vest with a tote bag with "meadowlab" stitched on it; a shambling old man with a struggly beard, the pockets of his dirty down jacket stuffed with envelopes; woman in a kerchief and circles under her eyes surreptitiously picks a pornographic Spanish cartoon book from the seat beside her and, having concealed it in the plastic bag in her lap, pages through it poker-faced; drawn-featured black kid draped over a seat, head in a cave, his eyes scan crystal subways and amber subways, soapstone cars ride amber rails — roll on static cushions... I see his friends blast through the station on their skateboards and he glides out to meet them hands at his sides. The skinheads want you to see them as soldiers polices and racketeers, congregating in the last cars of each train hooked on nerve gas: they stow the canisters in their too-big-camouflage-jackets and dose themselves with modified inhalers. You catch a zap when the doors open and your whole face is wrenched around, your nostrils and sinuses burn like flaring embers...

The more you see the more you will see — stopped between stations and there's a dimly-lit brick passageway plunging into the dark directly before me. Someone is walking there, away from me. She turns and looks in my direction — a middle-aged woman with a ruddy face, a brimless hat perched on the head's crown, green wool coat. Her features are like a man's just slightly feminized and saturated with a weird charisma, as though behind that face a hand held something rare and precious together in a gently firm grip. She turns and walks away swinging a censor of black iron triangles and trapezoids. The feathers of incense rub up against her shoulders and then stretch themselves like nerves, reach for the walls and muffle the exposed bulbs. The train reels a little forward, then accelerates in earnest, taking away the woman. On the elevated line at sunset, I moved my head so as to bring my shadow over the man's eyes opposite me, shield the man's eyes with my shadow from the glare of the setting sun — I had no sympathy for the man himself, but I had sympathy for his eyes. What I did, I seemed to do for her, as though I wanted her to see me do it and approve. I get the feeling she's just died. I crack my hold on things in general fall into destabilizing gales, blow a tangle of clumsy, sincere nerves making cloud segments that fly away in every direction.

...Dr. Thefarie points out the Great Lover to me. Yes, he is clearly visible through the safety glass of the partition doors, alone in the car ahead — a filthy beggar, still in perfect possession of his faculties and yet he does not perform for the crowd. I do not believe he is — he is not oblivious to the crowds, on the contrary it is plain he attends to them closely, but he is observing them, and by that I mean he is scrutinizing them. That he is sensitive, and charged with a mercurial vitality which makes itself felt even across this distance, is as obvious as the raw and naked feeling he does nothing to conceal. His cheeks are wet with tears.

"I see: he will slump exhausted finally in his seat... and then, becoming transparent, he will turn and tilt slowly backwards, penetrating as he does so the wall of the car. His body will undulate as if it were forming a chrysalis, causing him to unravel into the wall like a spool of thread. No he will slide into the wall of the car in circular sections like a piece of flesh being cut by a deli slicer, his body rotating parallel to the cutting plane and paring in a continuous spiral shaving through the wall and down into the concrete of the platform. His fingertips will spin into the wall, dwindling to dirty pink buttons, then to dots, and then vanish altogether, followed by the legs, the shoe treads, all into the wall, and, from there, down into the station's concrete, where he will lie under multicolored layers of sediment accumulating over millions of years...

"On the surface above, wind, lightning, water, ice, and wildfire will rend the earth with their talons, claw at it with a slow patient fury like the diurnal vultures clawing Prometheus, until a slough of black, oleaginous muck is exposed, steaming in the sun, a putrescence concentrated and gelatinized into sizzling immortal slime. Then he shall emerge from this slime, in which decomposition has metamorphosized him into a hideous landbound merman, his legs smashed into a paddle-like tail. He will push his torso upright on his palms and waddle, dragging his useless hindquarters; his flesh will have become a ridged mass, like ropes of wax mashed together, and long strands of livid fungus will dangle about his head and shoulders like streaming tresses of white hair. Two apple-sized craters will be his eyes, their pits lined with a thickly-veined membrane the color of rust and quivering receptive to sensation; the mouth will be a lipless cavity with rigid edges, turned down like the mouth of a Greek tragedian's mask. With his emaciated, blind sockets bent back to the leprous sun, he shall survey from a flat stone the transformed landscape of primordial salt flats and pulverized metal that once was this wicked city, oozing shadows and boiling mud belching viscous clouds of grey protein slivered with magenta flames. Over a century of liberated carbon will revive, after a period of time in the ground, into new and violent organic compounds. A sadness dense as a suffocating dream billows from him now—"

Dr. Thefarie seizes Father Ptarmagant's shoulders as the older man sighs and slumps over nearly fainting, tosses a brightly colored afghan around them.

"Contact him," the voice returns quietly, pressing his hand to his brow. A Saami woman in native dress sprinkles camphor on a handkerchief and hands it to him, turns then resuming her game of darts.

———o○o—o———

The odor of the wind from the tunnels is always changing — now, a clammy, buttery smell. Slovenly, sitting with his legs up on the seat, usual drab shapeless clothes, staccato words alternating only two vowels his teeth capped with fountain pen nibs. The shuttle of the subway car makes a loom out of the city. He gets off at the next station. The subway map is eyeing me. The brown line is swelling in one place, where I am — the pigment sprouts out in a bead that breaks and runs like a tear down to the metal frame, where it collects again like a beady eye, watching me. The doors open and two almost identical young men in suits, beards neatly trimmed, roll through in wheelchairs, side by side. They watch me in silence. The one on my right is holding a hat box with a slot cut in the side.

"Nice weather we're having, wouldn't you say?" I ask, jumping up from my seat. I switch glasses, this prescription grabbed at random blurs my vision drastically so that I barely avoid tackling them both. Not able to see whether the one on the right has jostled the hat box or did hat box move by itself? "Don't I know you from somewhere?"

I toss heart-shaped boxes of candy into their laps and switch glasses again. The doors open and, with knowing smiles at me, they unlock their wheels and elbow out. A weak, muffled voice can be heard speaking with an accent: "Keeping secrets can become a habit, and you may find yourself harboring irrelevant or indifferent secrets." They kept the chocolates, though.

———o○o—o———

The police are sweeping the stations for panhandlers and I head for the tunnels the express booming into the station. Craning my head to look behind me I face front again just as my left shoulder clips a beam — I lose my balance spin round with a sickening shotput in the stomach and fall in front of the express. It hits me before I make it to the ground and bats me forward—

According to the map, he tumbles spinning across his width like a lathe, catches sight of the tracks flashing up towards him and dextrously pushes off them with a lightning fast touch of his palms. He is thrust back into the air where the train rams him again, sets him spinning again, and he spins, swinging his left leg directly out in front of him it jolts as it lands square between the rails and tosses him up again.

Now for blocks this goes on with the Great Lover tumbling like a porpoise riding a bow wave before the implacable steel brow of this despotic train, keeping himself in the air and off the mangling tracks with hands and feet elbows and knees and once, finding all these too far elevated to be within call, he drops down on the crown of his head and pogosticks himself up with his neck muscles — his right leg swings out awkwardly and brushes the third rail his body cracks like a whip and steam belches from his coat — he shouts in pain and dismay like the bray of the subway horn, narrowly missing the ground and the slashing silver rims. He waves frantically at the TO when the opportunity presents itself but the city spins past like a tornado in darkness made of pillars platforms tracks and the spray of rusty brown slime—

The train shunts wildly onto the local track and according to the map the Great Lover hurtles fifty feet down the express track — the train thunders out of sight up a ramp and the Great Lover lies where he stopped his head hovering off the ground and body bent like a warped LP. The train's noise fades, somewhere far off bellowing once... the sound spreads and thins out. The two men in wheelchairs are sitting on the tracks a few dozen feet up the tunnel from where he lies, looking at him, evidently waiting for him to notice them. They are both holding storm lanterns in their laps, and paperbacks into which they've stuck their thumbs. Somewhere in the distance at the end of his arm his hand is being shaken with energetic cordiality — the vibration of a congratulatory voice I can't really hear is dragging over me. My body is flushed with cold like a tube of wind, the intermittent sound I now hear is being made apparently by me as my body moans with shock and dismay and my mind just onlooks in confusion. The two men are rolling away from me with their lamps, in a trembling envelope of buttery light. There's a button I've never seen before pinned to the rotting fabric of my lapel that says "8.8" on it, in small numerals just off center. Oh how well is this I fall back to lie still and a rat is licking my hand rapturously like a faithful dog.

—○○—○—

Studying a water-damaged station map more than half of it blurred out and bleached making it more like an image of time, localized, than of the whole transit system. A dry, hollow-voiced wind brushes past like a gigantic ghost... I go to the edge, where a rat forages in the shallow water between the rails. Its nervous movements are made visible by the vibration of the water, as though its energy shimmered around it in black circles. Suddenly it is gone. It seems as though all the air in the station were leaking out into space in an ever-intensifying silence as every station light goes out at once.

I fling myself from the edge, retreating uncertainly until I feel the wall behind me. Thud of my feet, and then the tile cool through the back of my coat. From the depths of the station comes the faint sound of an exhaled breath that shivers in the air. Ammonia smell and a single clink of metal.

A few fluorescents click back on the far side of the empty platform. A two-car train with Not In Service signs stands there. The door rolls back and there's backlit Algebra waving me aboard with a floppy hand; the whites of his eyes burn in the gloom. Door drops to behind me and the station falls away in screens of passages and truant lights tunnels and catwalks.

I follow Algebra. The next car is full of shot glass candles and hanging paper lanterns, chairs cabinets a sink and a table, no windows.

The two men in wheelchairs flank the door, and a remotely familiar Arab man is there among a group of strange faces, all different but all subway types. Right in front me, seated behind the table, sits a big white man looking at me with his head thrown back.

"You should join us," he says in a voice that's thready and weak, but rebounds in his deep chest a bit like a pipe organ. "You belong with us — that is, I think you—"

He seems to be fumbling to say certain things instead of other things that might come more naturally, "—you would do well for yourself to choose to work with us."

"Uh-huh I get it," I grin. "You want—"

"Well don't assume too much. We can offer you something, things you don't know about yourself."

White shirt suspenders and pants, black shoes; his shoulders, though sloping, are at least a yard across, he must stand well over six feet. Huge hands splayed out on his thighs. The short white bristles of his beard show red-pink skin beneath like a smear of bloody snow, all the way down to his collar. The whiteness makes his thin lips seem redder. High pink forehead with a single unicorn-lock of white hair drooping forward. He wears big sunglasses like a pair of captured dusks that come down his face nearly as far as the tip of his nose.

"You want my special thing, like the ole man," I say.

"We need a demon to get things done," he says. Cold point in the hollow of my chest every eye here is fixed on me like I might do anything at any moment. Those gazes all burn in cold on me like focussed starlight. I see set mouths.

"And, well — what do —"

"We'll never work out anything without demon energy," he says to me.

All those eyes close bore into me; it's stuffy and cold at once.

"It's the most serious thing we're missing. The world uncoils one spring and that coils another, back and forth in an energy economy of give and play, but nothing big is ever launched in the world without great play and a concomitant release of forces from the tensions that ordinarily restrain them."

No motion, except the rocking of the train. The white man isn't groping around for words now, he's reading something back. I bubble out a stifled laugh.

"This is crazy," feeling weirdly happy.

The white man had left his mouth open, and now it flexes slightly upward.

"That's exactly what I mean," he says with a minute nod, and the rest of them seem almost to bend in a little, as though they were warming themselves off me.

"What are you talking to me about a demon for anyway?"

Still steady with that open-mouth smile, "You have him. He's down in there."

He pumps his pointing hand at me once.

"Sorry, friend. I'm not — I'm not a demon."

"I assure you you are."

<hr/>

This is Father Ptarmagant, formerly head of the department of ancient languages at the seminary called Meadowlab. When a close friend committed suicide, he left the school without a word. Then, on the first anniversary of his friend's death, students were surprised to hear he was preparing to deliver a lecture in one of the school's many old lumber rooms.

Here they find he has constructed a precise mock-up of his friend's apartment. Dressed all in white, his mouth set as hard as a line cut in stone, Ptarmagant sets forth the unusual points of the lesson plan. Producing a white dummy on wheels, apparently a modified dressmaker's model, and then an enormous Manurhin revolver at which the class gasps and a few start from their seats — the scent of its grease is detectable at the back of the room — Ptarmagant stands on the stage, gun hanging down in his right hand, commanding silence and attention with his eyes. He then begins to explain, in a booming voice, how his friend had returned home on this day one year ago at such and such a time, had washed, and changed his clothes, wrote the brief and hasty note... how he paced the room — and now Ptarmagant brusquely seizes the dummy by the back of the neck and wheels it to and fro.

"He paced the room for a quarter of an hour."

Ptarmagant stomps up and down, the dummy's wheels squeaking.

"A neighbor reported seeing him criss-crossing in front of the window."

He points to the window.

"She did not see him load the gun. Nor could she see it in his hand, as it was below the level of the sill."

Indicating relative position of gun hand and sill.

He moves the dummy in fits and starts.

"He's trying to nerve himself to do it."

He shoves the dummy down toward the floor at one end of the stage, by a low bookshelf.

"He kneels here and shoots."

Ptarmagant fires directly into the dummy's left side with a deafening crack jolting the whole room — the students scramble away from the stage shouting in alarm. Blood sprays from squibs planted in the dummy's body spattering the wall and floor. Hot iron reek fills the room mingling with the powder smoke: real blood.

"But he's only wounded himself," Ptarmagant bellows. "He's only managed to wound himself."

He puppets the dummy into an upright position, making it move like an injured man, then wheels it erratically into the center of the room.

"He's dazed and uncertain what to do next," Ptarmagant roars, his eyes starting from his head.

"He shoots himself again, perhaps by mistake, and falls."

Another explosion crashes in the room as Ptarmagant fires up into the left shoulder, flying blood streaking his shirt, the white floor.

Ptarmagant manhandles the dummy onto the floor.

"Now he wants to finish himself, but his right arm is pinned under his body and he cannot move it." The anger is draining out of his voice. A helpless sorrow is replacing it.

"He fires at himself from the floor."

The pistol erupts again tearing the top of the dummy's head in half, tufts of white stuffing spin in the air and blood spills out onto the floor.

Ptarmagant releases the body and stands, leaving the gun on the floor by the figure's side. His white clothing and the floor are stained with red.

—o—o—

Now he speaks with the desolate serenity of a man who has had to learn to console himself— "It was a cruel thing to do."

They dismissed him. He left town on foot one morning in the fog. The dream shows me.

Homeless, Ptarmagant walks on the margin of the road, leading by hand— Vera. No one knew her mother; Ptarmagant might as well have emanated her from his own mountainous person. She could have stepped fully formed out from behind an armchair standing in a dim corner in a quiet room, in the empty old house, on a breathless day. She doesn't yet stand as tall as his shoulder: a grinning mannikin— is it even human?— her eyes rolling incessantly, her lips pulled back in a wet smile that makes her look a little crazy. No one ever told her to keep her eyes closed.

That face— that face... I'm afraid of it— I'm excited by it! I feel like I'm dying— I'm dying, I'm in heaven... I want her— I don't know how I want I want... to be inside her I want her to be my home. How beautifully terrible she is and no one sees it, no one sees it but me— to everyone else she's always been just a stupid blind girl when you, you don't see yourself *you're blind*, she's you're

don't you see you're in the presence of ------------? I love it I love it my language is breaking so I can barely talk even around what I mean— then push push *break it all*— you're in the presence of

—everything —life... life... makes me smile... I feel it on my face it's her smile I wear. I'm not wearing it. I'm smiling it.

—o—o—

"I am not a character."

Have you guessed my secret yet? You're far out ahead of me if you have. It's there.

His reputation destroyed, he sank steadily losing everything a piece at a time and ended up riding the subway day and night, with only his daughter to look after him. Then he began to speak, specifically to prophesy to the cars; he would sit and boom out his prophesies for days at a time without moving eating or drinking, and began to attract a following especially among the others who had come loose, drifted and settled down here in the underground. His words and teachings rumble beneath the streets, along tunnels and across the sunless switching yards, transmitted and rehearsed back and forth making a web of living words in subterranean calligraphy. The cars are classrooms, students healed heads bent lips moving as they read and take notes, and he will at times address them, his disembodied voice ventriloquizes from no direction and hums with hypnotic power, but not sermonizing.

"You've probably always had him — you wouldn't remember the first moment..." Ptarmagant leans forward slightly, a big gesture coming from him.

"We need your help, and you need something to do. We've already initiated you this far."

"Help with what?"

"With the cult."

"Cult of the subway?"

"Cult of the subway."

The Great Lover first saw Vera Ptarmagant on the subway platform. Her left arm was linked in her father's right arm, and they were walking together along the downtown side.

They boarded their train, and sat next to each other in a seat facing the rear of the car.

Unnoticed, the Great Lover stood on the uptown side.

Vera had been concealed by her father's bulk — he towered over her. The Great Lover only had a few moments', as they were boarding the train, uninterrupted view of Vera's face, which was also a brilliant light. Vera's face transfixing lights to drown this moment, this moment, this moment...

As her face floods the world, I transform into a ten year old boy, with his hands pressed against his breast and his elbows raised awkwardly as though he'd been shot and were clutching at the wound, were being propelled backward off his feet, his eyes wide, and his tender red mouth slack, his face frozen in an expression of shock, and a vast enough stupidity admitting unbearably sweet, warm, spirited light.

After this, nominally, there's all sorts of stuff, moving around, talking, listening, day sky, night sky, indoors, outdoors, being alone and not, but whatever he appears to be doing is untrue, because he hasn't budged from Vera Ptarmagant's face, which is both hovering at her father's side as they board their train, and visible through the windows of the car as they sit together, and emitting a lighthouse beam that washes over him again and again from across the city.

—○○—○—

At first sight Vera Ptarmagant seems to be making comical faces, but this impression immediately gives way, not without a twinge of shame, to the discovery that she's blind, of course. She is walking on her father's arm, with her head tipped up and chin forward, her braid hanging straight down her back, its tufted end knocks against the base of her spine with each step. Now they board the train and sit beside each other; for one of what you will come to recognize as her suite of characteristic gestures, she strokes her spittly chin clean with her middle and ring fingers.

Vera was born blind, but, when she sleeps, she can see in her dreams. As a teenager, when her father was still at Meadowlab, she had been through certain trials, in which a boy was involved, difficult to explain, that had resulted in her extraction from school. After that, she had vomited stones everyone had to assume she'd swallowed flat and smooth like stream pebbles; some of these were inscribed with unintelligible, heterogeneous writing, and it was around then, although not for that reason, that she first began to see things in her dreams.

"This was how I learned to visualize people; it is like picking a familiar voice out of a crowd — first the sudden touch of attention, then the gathering in, then naming. I think I am more precise about it than sighted people are. I've asked people about it, and it seems they have trouble with other things pushing in on them.

"I have run my fingers over my father's face, and over the features of old boyfriends, girlfriends, but I find a tactile portrait is usually just an incoherent composite, with the features and textures all in a heap like a drawer full of stockings. The eyes are vibrating brushes with a wildly excitable energy. I have of course inspected my own useless eyes and found the slit there, the rolling ball; I've touched the ball itself, as I have no need to fear I'll hurt them, and felt them shiver with restless, electric power, all dammed up.

"Darkness was the first thing I saw and recognized. When I tried to see in my dreams my own eyes, I felt fluttering clumps of sinewy wire in my face, and then I saw them, scribbling lights.

"Eyebrows seem to be very high above the eyes and I never think of them unless someone mentions them. I feel my own, I suppose, embedded in my skin, but they just seem to go with the scalp and the wild ubiquitous material of hair. I have to remember the hair is connected to the head and not just hovering around it like a brambly background.

"I can see my father's head nestled in its hair. The nose is a flexible column with two slopes, standing upright on two intermittent legs of air. The skin's bumpiness appears as a satiny quality; the mouth is a cushion on a shelf, the teeth and tongue float there behind mounds of chin and cheeks with triangular indentations on top of the cheeks, jutting rectangular brow like a fuse box. The speech is also a part of the face — of course I know the mouth moves, but I tend to see only the sound, in a procession of dusky complicated shapes... Each different voice is a kind of whorled canister, pouring out triangular streams of dark-colored sound with the texture like thin clay, sometimes soft, sometimes baked or even glazed.

"When I have enough time to give, I can visualize people entirely. Sitting beside my father, I can feel heavy ruminative waves undulating from him. I don't know what colors are, except that they are to seeing what different pitches or timbres are in music. If I could see my father's waves, they would be the groaning color of a double bass or the boom of the lower notes of a guitar. When he appears to me, I see a jellyfish, or a space station: a no-color gourd floating in the dark, not quite upright, with thick sections, like pineapple rings, at intervals. The flat edges of the rings have regularly-spaced circular openings, from which protrude three or four feelers. Father rotates majestically in place, inside the shell of his sad and angry song."

She has a dancing face and body, like she could dance away melt into air—

That holy word "her."

Vera wears her thick hair in a frizzy black braid. She has a long neck, broad shoulders, an elastic body, her hands are long and a little oversized. She is wearing a shapeless, sacklike dress of dark material with tiny flowers sparsely embroidered on it. About thirty, seems younger.

What do I see in her I see spacious innocence perversity, she's really free, untethered. She's fairylike, but there's heat in her, too. There is an earthy ground in there of passion and appetite; it sparks out from her face, her posture, like when she hunched forward and stuck her neck out asking her friend "Is he handsome?" avidly.

Her facial expressions are equivocal and exaggerated; she overextends her mouth to either side when she speaks, exposing her teeth. She has a propensity to grimace, pulling down the corners of her lips hard. She has a low, strange voice and a slight speech impediment that makes her lisp and gurgle a little when she speaks. Her blindness means her face is always improvising, it enchants me like a body of new slang.

And there is something too unreal about her and ghostly, as

though she at any moment might melt into air, disappear and become everywhere. There's a part of her that is always disappearing, in the expression of her simple, beaming face, like endless tissue paper leaves or it would be more rommanick to say petals peeling away one at a time and time by time. She's fascinating and simple and beautiful, like a lightning flash or the moon. Or a firefly. She seems fairylike because there's no bullshit in her, everything she does is essential. Am I just falling in love with a picture poem description no I know I'm not because I'm always waiting for her and I never can predict what she will next give me. If she is a picture I'm drawing she's an automatic picture, every new line is a surprise to me and I can't believe it but every line delights me every surprise is good—

Her smile is astonishing; when she smiles, something easily missed but her teeth are the color of rain clouds.

—◦◦—◦—

"You know what I'm talking about," he says, his lenses on me.

"Not me bub," I say.

"You know... You've seen them."

"Seen?"

"Everyone knows about it, even though no one will speak about it," he raises his hands slightly, indicating present company.

"We've all met it in our own ways. — Look at them!"

A scarred expression hardens the faces around me, a sullen, fierce and bitter fume from their eyes.

"Oppression, theft... See it now?... They're stealing from all of us. I'm not talking in allegories and this is not apolitical — Look for them!" he calls, "You will see them!"

We go our separate ways. Ptarmagant calls me over to walk with him; he lumbers along beside me breathing through his mouth, fumbling in one pocket big as a potato sack he pulls out a dull grey key. Goes up to a train standing closed up on the other platform, slides back the flap, inserts and turns key, one half of the adjacent door slides open. We siphon in and he keys the door shut from the inside. The train is heading back to the yard.

"no passengers no passengers" the PA says and the cars go dark — almost silently we roll forward.

Now we ride along in the fermented night underground, shapes of light from the windows slide up and over his face, he has only to tilt back his head and the words march from his lips, talking to himself.

"Not an apocalypse of one, an apocalypse of many: they lie in the dark where the spice of their malice is stored up over time. I sign away one salvation for another, while we must be always hunting for holidays. These days open up different time — their appointed proceedings. Death and counting... as I count the final tally of *my* years.

"People exist only to grind each other into dust; the slowness with which this is done becomes the glue binding us together. Piles of human dust. Astonishingly, though we are from time to time perhaps cruelly reconstituted by someone, a friend or lover or a story song picture... Which is more forgetful, the dust, or the reconstituted one? The real is discovered when you sink down into the city, where the real sanity is... The real people are the ones with real dreams... The visionary city is the real city: the city is supposed to be an experience, not a running away from things...

"If neither you nor your friends can give you any hope then you must go to your *enemies* to give you hope. I learned this from the Sufis — *There*—"

he breaks in, pointing to the platform as we float through the station—

"—now take a good look. Do you see what I'm talking about?"

"I don't know."

"The stealing!" he says, squeezing my shoulder so dirty water trickles over his fingers.

"You don't mean that old thing about zombies?"

"But aren't they?" he says, squeezing again. "Think of what they could be compared with what they're allowed to be — Now look at that one!"

The train stops halfway out of the station for a signal.

Not twenty feet away from me a young man stands on the platform, his head turned to look in the direction the train will come. Worklight glare throws his shadow down beside him.

"So?"

"Watch!"

From somewhere a few other men drift over; they might all work in the same place, they are the same enough. They aren't identical; each one individually is distinctive enough as people go, but as they gather together on the platform they become impossible to tell apart. The man's shadow has acquired a long point, as though he were wearing a conical hood that came down over his face.

"Do you *see* it?"

The man moves aside a little to let one of the men float by. In the shadows, I see the tip of his hood brush and bend against the shadow of a pipe. The young man looks unconsciously embarrassed and darts forward to stand directly below the work lights, crumpling his shadow into a formless spot around his feet.

"Did you see it?"

"I saw it!"

All the men look directly at me. I can hear them mutter.

"Wait, what is it? They're all looking—"

"Does he see it?" Ptarmagant asks anxiously. He prods me in the chest with his finger — "Does *he* see it?"

..."He sees it!"

The men are climbing down onto the tracks.

Ptarmagant looks at his watch.

"*Thieves*," the Great Lover says the air around him becoming denser and denser.

The first man is raising his leg to step over the third rail when two bleats rap out from the far end of the station.

"That's right," Ptarmagant sighs, lowering his wrist.

The train is now crying in strong steady pulses and its brakes are screaming. The men scatter, moving clumsily back toward the platform. The train rolls in, the doors open and the TO storms out of his compartment shouting at the men, who are swirling around back on the platform. Every few seconds is sucked in from somewhere — the TO is shouting and gesticulating — then he is engulfed — he shouts in alarm — the signal changes and our train lurches forward then accelerates smoothly down the track — I see the tall figure of the TO blur into them.

—oo—o—

The map explains:

"For this ptochocratic cult, the subway system recapitulates the progress of the dead soul, from the payment of special coins at the journey's beginning to the negotiation of a maze of names, the pursuit of this or that colored fiber in the map. The subway system is a hermetic calculator, a wheel of essences moving you from this visible, organized space to another by way of dark chaos with no landscape or landmark; the subway system is like thought, and there are all sorts of guides. There are those who enter and never leave, and it clings to some others wherever they may emerge like a foul intriguing smell in the clothing."

The map sighs, turning its lined face half to the sunset.

"Some music is best heard at a distance half open to the sky, the fantasy stretched thinner and thinner like a powerful membrane offering itself to sensations. The air grows thicker and clearer, hardens to breathable diamond, shading out into absolutely unbound vacancy. The Great Lover, asleep in a spiral of sewage and spinning majestically in place, is also the Great Lover in his dream — this is one of his secrets, in the sense of a winning trick, an accomplishment in magic."

—A landscape with ashy soil and jagged mountains on the horizon, poisonous grey overcast turning to sulfurous yellow haze. He is walking arduously through craters, deep ruts. Somewhere the sound of a low-register reed instrument like an oboe plays something in and out of the wind. The sound does not strike him as having an origin, or as a message from somewhere else, rather it is simply present here like the flattened martian rocks and lichenous scrub. He emerges from a crater, and before him is the vast leprous flank of a colossal worm, lying across the world to horizon in either direction. The worm's skin is dusty and twitches in minute galvanic spasms that cause it to shed little cascades of dust.

The Great Lover kneels beside it with a flicker of worry about getting dust on his pants and pulls sword segments out of his coat pockets. Fitting them together is a rather needlessly complicated business involving a great many tiny bolts that have to be fixed just so with a special allan wrench he has for some reason attached to a folding Japanese melon knife. Why can't he just use the knife? The sword's blade is over three feet long divided in one or two inch segments, those nearer the tip divided longitudinally.

"With this many segments, it must be a really great sword."

When the sword is finally assembled, the Great Lover proclaims something in a loud voice and swings the blade in three windmilling arcs, building up momentum, then with one lightning-fast nick he slices an opening in the worm's side. The sides of the wound flap apart like tent canvas in a powerful wind, exposing translucent clear and white tissue; there is no bleeding, though icy water trickles out and darkens the powdery soil, forming a sort of pancake at the lower extremity of the gash. The worm, which looks to be a little over a dozen feet in diameter, has a chambered interior with seats. The chambers are lined with blue membranes and glow like ice caves. Someone has been waiting inside this worm for an unimaginably long time, and now he is going to come out through this aperture the Great Lover has made. A rat scoots across the Great Lover's back and startles him awake — no pay off. Who was it?

—o—o—

Peering out the windows of the subway car at the bottom of the sea, stations dart away like startled fish.

"Look intently enough, and there's nothing you won't find out there!" Ptarmagant says.

A platform sweeps by covered with panels of gold and bright, many-colored draperies, where rows of Minoan female priests lift snakes in their hands, the stepped rise and fall of their song precedes them and hangs after them in the air.

"This is Deuteronôme," he introduces me to a Haitian man in a striped shirt and leather vest who shakes my hand with one strong pump.

"Deuteronôme le Sorcier," he says with force in every syllable.

"It's like time travel, or music," Ptarmagant says, oration cadences coming into his voice. "Don't try to fit it all together into one story line, but transfer from line to line — now you're in jeopardy, or a cold place — now you're in a suave and confidential conversation—"

Later, as an experiment, I try to draw the demon into my eyes and ears. As he looks and listens out, the gnomes stagger and fall limp — rush over to the nearest — a painted corpse. They all are. The demon drops back down into my abdomen and the corpses stir and rise up smiling gnomes again. I stop and examine one.

"Hey!"

The eyes swivel onto my face.

"Are you all right?"

"Fine!"

I exercise the demon moving it up into my head and letting it fall again into my abdomen, sliding into me and out of the circle of gnomes, and then out of me and into the gnomes. The demon's strength improves, and soon I can draw him into my head without killing the gnomes. Now they just flop over onto the ground and sort of swim there in slow motion when I do it.

"Send your nerves out," Ptarmagant says softly.

I hesitate.

"They won't notice you. They can't feel anything. They only know things abstractly," Deuteronôme says.

Now I'm in a knot of them, looking from face to face. As they gather together an oppressive, smothering atmosphere intensifies around them; it's hard to describe, an intense dullness. I try switching over to audio nerves, and immediately I pick up the sound, like a monotonous, insistently repeated lowing. Not much to see on visual nerves, but it's as though I see them through a dusty window that gets dustier the more of them arrive. They dirty the light. Olfactory detects a smell reminds me of urinal cakes, and under that is a smell — I want to say a smell like sour lead. Touch and taste I'm leaving alone. It's strange — nothing but moaning on the audio, but I can see them talking to each other. I withdraw.

"They're not vampires individually, only in the aggregate," Ptarmagant is telling me.

"You take any one of them alone and all you've got is a rather soulless person. What we're really talking about is a *Vampirism*; it was not deliberately developed by anyone, it just happened as a consequence of the imposition of this particular system. The *Vampirism* is the spontaneous formation of the system as it develops according to the law of symmetry — you can't have one without the other. But you see, some people have noticed this and learned to use the *Vampirism*, most of them without having any really clear idea of what they're doing exactly. I mean they wouldn't understand if you tried to explain it to them, but that's exactly what it is. Others are used by the *Vampirism*, necessarily unconsciously.

"The cult will be a counter-system, you see? We are all people who have, for one reason or another, come to see the *Vampirism* for what it is. Or, well, whatever it is, we see that it is *Vampirism*. It has stolen our people, love, time. I'll guess you're being robbed too...

"The demon is *that which fouls up system*. That's why you're so important to us."

"I'll foul up your system too, then won't I?"

Deuteronôme says, "That will be true to a point, but we'll cut a deal with the demon. He will find his way to get around it, but it should reduce the trouble he might cause to a manageable minimum."

"We'll be well enough covered," Ptarmagant says. "That's the thing: by the law of symmetry, though the demon is what fouls up systems, you can't create systems without the demon. The demon gives the system its half-start energy. But then, if the demon gets lost, it can turn vampire once the system becomes self-sustaining, as it happened out there."

Ptarmagant's sermons are recorded and distributed in installments of what they call a "system-program," by two of his lieutenants — a former medical examiner named Dr. Thefarie, who turned out to be the middle-eastern man I'd seen around, and Algebra, whose real name is Spargens. Deuteronôme develops magic weapons and, with his nephew, is working to create a rapid messenger network to disseminate messages system-wide.

—◦—◦—

I freeze when I see Vera appear on the platform — I am watching from the tunnel... The train is holding there, with doors open, waiting for the connection. She is walking toward the hindmost car — I watch her coming, the round rubber disk at the tip of her cane taps at points along the hypnotic arc she sweeps it in. Suddenly the cane darts elastically sideways like a striking snake, tangling in the legs of a right-wing student type who was passing in the opposite direction. He falls and pivots, cursing her, but the hate jams before it can leave his face as he sees she's blind — and she is calling

"Oh, I'm so sorry! I'm so sorry!" waving her hands.

Her voice! She has a speech impediment that slushes her pronunciation and makes my whole body twang with desire to lap half-swooning the clear syrup from her ivory chin. The student moves off sourly adjusting his armband and mutters with his friends and she resumes walking along the platform in my direction, grinning from ear to ear that grin just blooms across her face a blooming, moist grin of gratified malevolence — my knees buckle and I nearly swing off my feet — she's wicked! so *perfect* — her skin glows like silent film and the rest of the world is lost.

...Someone is appraising me. I can feel it — more than the gaze I can feel the way I'm being turned into a picture of myself, like a wonderfully flattering caricature. Hummm there is a song there, looping its choruses around me. I can feel the love lyrics forming just there... I've always loved that feeling... Gone now. He must not have boarded the train. It wasn't that little armbander I tripped either. Who was that, anyway? Don't I know that?

On the subway, as my father explains, a system of unreturned gazes develops spontaneously. My blindness sets me permanently apart; my eyes can go wherever they want, but my soul remains dark. When you travel, you are nothing. The cult is going to make new identities out of this travelling nothing; he expects we'll fade into another world that way.

I hope he's right. I can feel the flaccid, passive riders slump against me when the trains are busy. Their miserable weariness seeps out of them like residual cold, with an odor that makes me think of meat that's been lying at the back of a freezer too long — years. I feel their limp bodies twitch. There's fear panting all around me, not coming from anything or going anywhere. It just stands on them, all the time. More and more I feel those pikers polishing up their armbands, getting themselves good and angry and passing the same sour mush from one mouth to the next. Now and then I hear something robust, or something sweet, but less and less. Often, when I hear children, my senses nearly pounce on them, and I'm surprised at my own avidness. In my mind they are soft draughts and wind flurries close along the ground, with snowy voices when they're small. The older ones have hotter voices.

The map looks past Vera, toward the end of the train. The last car empties out and, now alone, the viewless numb eyes of the rag heap at the back grow crisp, drooping limbs are elastic in purposive movements defacing or subtly distorting advertisements, installing substitute subway maps that have been indetectibly altered. On the platform a begging man pockets his cup of coins and rubs his dirty face. Affable man in a slightly antiquated suit and tie smiles at commuters as they pass by, gets a thin smile and tilt of the head in return. The commuters move on and the man's affable look drops away like a mask — he watches them go, face blank and alert like a prisoner's. Vera's train begins to fill again.

Gaze chains lock in constellations, keying elements of system-program special procedure. The subway cultists vandalize advertisements, insinuating themselves into publicity shots in the streets like here's a couple of models enjoying a day of shopping swinging heavy bags from the chic'er stores, faces incandescent with acquisitiveness like hunters — all is well except for that bum there in the doorway... where did *he* come from? — emanating crushing waves of merciless sadness that make the photo unusable.

[The earth is hollow, and I'll prove it to you! (goes down into the earth)]

I have taken on the responsibilities of a man named Wouvermans, who had developed a technique whereby dust, precipitate of time, was boiled and distilled into a liquor sanitized and free of microbes (whose influence must be rigorously excluded, ruled out) — drink or breathe it my body sheds it as I sleep... A ringing word meaning also flesh. He took core samples from the tunnels, drilling deep into the wet clay and extracting canisters of mud and gas so hot he and his attendants would flip them onto the ground and roll them over and over with hands in towels, dousing them with ether from big jars to cool them. In certain places and at certain times the presence of nerve tissue would be detected in these samples, which were prayed over and then immediately burned. Wouvermans died of a stroke while riding the subway, and his body wasn't discovered for some time. That is, he was in plain view, but mistaken for asleep. Ptarmagant holds that there is always at least one such dead traveller shuttling through the system at any given time. Dead, they continue on unnoticed. The cult recovered his body and gave him a Viking funeral; his body, wreathed in bright orange flowers, was placed on a plinth in the middle of an appropriated subway car, which was set ablaze and precipitated down the tracks, launched from one of the defunct stations. Car rolling somberly into the gloom, flames lick the tunnel walls and send volumes of smoke slithering along the vaulted ceilings. When the car was recovered by the city authorities later on, it was undamaged, without so much as a scorch mark on it. Wouvermans' body and accompanying offerings had vanished without a trace.

"What's your name?" Deuteronôme asks me over his shoulder.

"I'll find out."

His nephew rolls around on his skateboard smiling to himself, "Uncle D. ask the Ring-Ding-A-Ling his name, and I say —" he lifts the bunch of keys hanging from a steel bead chain around his neck and jangles them — chish chish ch'chish, chish chish ch'chish.

And later I stop one of my gnomes — "Hey, stop. What's my name?"

"The Great Lover!" the gnome says, eyes and mouth open wide in huge grin.

"Was that a *joke*?" I ask in surprise.

"Sure!"

"You tell jokes—"

"Sure!"

"—instead of answering my question?"

The expression doesn't change, but the head wobbles and the eyes jump around on my face.

"The Great Lover!" he says again.

"Well, what should I tell other people my name is?"

"Yes!"

"Yesss... What should I tellll them?"

"Yeeeeees!"

"Whaaat?"

"Yes! Yes!"

—"What's your name?"

"...My name is Name!"

"What's my name?"

"Name!"

"Name?"

"Yes!"

"Your name is Name?"

"Your name is Name!"

"My name is Name?"

"Name!"

"Then what's your—"

I quit.

"All right then Name, you come with me," Deuteronôme guides me through passages and defunct steam tunnels into a vast area of communicating basements where banks of cannibal computers have been established, tapping power and telephone lines. Programmers intercept radio cell phone and television signals and generate their own deviant signals, monitor and jam existing ones. In most cases, the interference goes entirely unnoticed at the source. They are developing underground radio. He walks a little ahead of me, turns to look back twisting at the waist.

"I taught at Meadowlab myself. They were conducting all variety of experiments there, involving what they called 'psychic powers.' But they did not understand that these so-called 'psychic powers' were not an internal property of mind, or even of spirit, like a stream of piss you can control. Even the urine must first be imbibed as water. There is no fire in the match, in the fuel. There is in the meeting of inside and outside, coming to the doorway, the threshold, the magic they tried to find only inside. I suppose even the unwiped assholes of the world need someone to speak for them!

"But... their experiments, their inquiries, never went anywhere. From time to time they would see a little something but the circumstances were always equivocal. They never invoked, which is to step to the door and to fling it open. They did not want to risk being changed by letting something in. They wanted a *gimmick*. I told them in magic there is no gimmick — that is only for show.

"For weeks they were trying all manner of experiments — nothing. Then a Chinese colleague and I did a demonstration, where we put energy into our cutlasses, and charged a battery, a car battery, in a closed room. And what did they do? They examine the swords, they examine the battery, they examine the room! They examine our pulse, our heat, our breathing. What can you do with people who will not see?"

He shrugged, his hands open at the level of his slim waist.

"So, I left Meadowlab. Then I hear that Ptarmagant was down here giving prophecy, so I came. I was a houngan then, but now I have had to leave that behind. What we do here must be completely new. It must leave behind the Meadowlab, houngan, clergyman — it must leave behind cult, it must leave behind black and white. I will not be a black man unless I must also be a Russian man, a Chinese man, an... Afghan man, an Eskimo man — all these men, are me."

...Intriguing pink color to the light of sunset, a dimpled sheet of clouds high in the sky drifts past my window in slow flirtatious motion, whose friction excites a low murmur of pleasing expectation through my eyes into me. Sadly, there will be no outcome — but I will carry away the vision, clots of silver blue in white blazes, thoughtful, like an interrogative glance from a woman I don't dare to desire—

The two men in wheelchairs roll past. One of them looks me in the eye and says, "— The novel is asleep. — Push on. — Push on."

Dream: after years of painful resignation, the aged mothers of girls taken away by vampires — having been brought together largely by chance, and having discovered from each other that the excruciating solitude of this loss is common to all of them — are rejuvenated by vengeful hatred erupting in cyclones.

I am one of these mothers, my female body seems weightless, but hardened like solid bone by years of drudgery. We burst from our porches and swarm down the hillside into a caravan encampment of striped tents and sultry music in the twilight; into the largest tent we charge and pounce upon the vampire pasha in a halo of vindictive knives, our skirts stiff with chicken grease. Each of us darts forward and stabs him once. I feel his fibrous, papery flesh tear around my knife like a wasp's nest, my own heart like sizzling ice. He staggers, helplessly clutching his temples. We mothers drop our knives and extend silver goblets, each one collecting a proprietary stream of spurting blood from the wound that hand inflicted — each of us catching only the blood of our own stolen daughters. He suddenly falls back onto a mound of cushions, a brittle, mummified jackal, his crêpey lips foiled around orange canines.

And now here are our girls, palely reclining on satin couches, holding postures of lascivious abandon. Terrible bun-haired silhouettes slowly rise at the feet of these couches, dingy lace swirling with appalling purposiveness — in unison the girls start upright staring and cry "Mother!"

Grinning evilly we mothers kneel on our daughters' chests and pour the flaming blood down their throats. Dragging them by their hair we vigorous, storming mothers lock our daughters in a huge set of stocks. The sun rises, shining directly into their faces. The girls scream and go into shocking convulsions as life is restored. Meanwhile the vampire's twitching carcass has been hauled out onto the sand and exposed to the sun with the assistance of a huge magnifying glass. We screen him with our hoopskirts, then expose him again, to prolong his suffering. When he is nothing but a cindery smear on the ground, we mothers bear revived daughters, still raw and whimpering with fresh life, up through the hills in our powerful arms, voices raised in an anthem of martial triumph. I bound up onto the front porch and gently rest my rosy girl in the hammock that hangs there, leap over the railing into the grass, and turn into a gang of loping bears like quivering meatballs. I stand and watch, a bodiless ghost, fleshy bears barrelling full speed out of sight.

I wake up to see Deuteronôme's nephew bending forward some way away, looking at me. He sees me wake up, smiling now gets on his board, and rolls away, looking at me.

"Yeah, Ding-A-Ling!" he calls softly, turns and surfs off.

———◦◦═◦═———

According to the map, where the main is broken and water cascades down the brick wall's irregularities the Great Lover sleeps sprawled on his back, his head sunk in a slimy pothole and his adam's apple pointing to the zenith. His gnomes circle him in large, irregular orbits that pursue the irregular contours of this eruption in the sewer system.

"Vera!"

I wake up. My body angrily rights itself kink by kink, my chest is hissing like a skillet; I can feel her name gaily frying away in my green-brown heart.

"I have to see her!"

Now the spot contracts to a point of heat like a focussed sunbeam welding its tip to my body with a tiny burning hole. The hole melts and osmosis distributes it in shivers of heat all through me, leaving a globe of static adjacent to the heart. The glare of my eyes throws shadows on the wall, glints back at me from the water.

Gnomes pat me on the back as I stride manfully among them and plunge judiciously into the sewer. The current conveys me to the ladder and, lowering my head, I rise with the manhole cover resting on my back, sliding off. Three steps and I stand in the center of the track, without knowing what I'm doing I hear my uncouth voice bray her name into the tunnel, my arms thrown out to her. A shrill answering note — a light gathers in the distance and to my right — the train crashes by on the next track and she is there in the second to last car — without thinking I reach out to her, my fingers brush the upright crash guard on the back of the train and close on it the train whips me high into the air; taking advantage of my good fortune I throw myself onto the roof and, by pinching the serrations that cover its upper surface I am able to hold myself there, veering this way and that to avoid low-hanging pipes and signs.

I crawl the length of the train and insinuate myself into the gap between the last car and hers. The glass of the door is opaque and now spattered with muck from my clothes. Locked — I ram the glass with my shoulder and the entire pane pops out; with a sound I don't care to describe I ooze through the opening into the small, unlit compartment. Another locked door, the glass is clear and I see her sitting there at the other end of the car, holding her cane like a pencil like a pencil so beautifully. Cold flashes through me and then I burn and gasp for breath, seize the latch and pull back the door with a bang as part of the latch whirs past my ear. I step through and the rebounding door spatters me against the jam.

Commuters jerk to their feet at the noise, and moments later are fleeing to the back of the car faces contorted with revulsion as he lightly plucks aside the door a second time and enters the car. The train brakes and abets them in their retreat. A station careers up to the windows, the brakes scream drowning out his amorous serenading, and the passengers belch forth from the doors squeezing their noses. Vera is left alone with him. She stands, one hand on a post, the other, dangling her cane from her wrist, sweeps the air with its palm.

It's that smell — and that voice reaching out to enfold me in his theatrics — we're alone, the train is moving again — he's near... He's dropped to his knees, at my feet. I have a handful of fur! Cords round his neck — spectacles how appropriate — and this is his sticky face. It's firm. It trembles. His fingers take my hand — his lips press my palm... a current of warmth jets up my arm, the beast loves me! He loves me!

Where has he gone?... He didn't stay?

I was just getting interested!

—∞—∘—

Lacking a God, the cult is going to create its own. Deuteronôme explains that casting a spell is about something getting denser and denser, acquiring over time one coat of reality on top of another, acquiring solidity all the time "... until there can be no other possibility but that it *must be*." There is always a physical element: making gestures precedes even the manufacture of tools as a way of making something ideal real.

In an emotional voice, odd for him, Ptarmagant says, "The magician is the grin through the fog."

"Magic..." Deuteronôme continues in his relentless way, "— The moment you are dealing with formulas, with a prescription, with a regulation, you walk away from magic. The spell is too subtle to be caught in a jingle. It is subtle that it can only be brought about in the improvisation of a true magician — un sorcier. Like the bones, the cards, or the dice, the elements are flung into confusion, and then, as the different configurations of elements present themselves to the magician, he — with lightning speed, of mind and body — seizes upon the right constellation for the purpose. He will pull out the only constellation that can be used for that purpose."

The map explains: The God of the subway cult is to be created in a huge prayer, extended in time, space, number of persons involved, and modes of address. This prayer is coordinated from four axial centers which regulate the operation of its sub-cells. These cells, known as "axons," are carefully segregated from each other in order to minimize overlap, so that any redundancy is only coincidental. Each "joint" endows a number of axons. There is no center, and no single object of concentration. Even Ptarmagant is only a participant, although he did invent the method. In his work at Meadowlab, Ptarmagant assessed the empirical evidence of divine operations and determined that, while we encounter a gesture here, an assembly there, the divinity is never all there. Divinity, as a hexeity, a mode of existing, is always a matter of being a complete fragment, indicating a total whole of which it is impossible to conceive. Since a divine being is too "enormous" to be apprehended in its entirety by any human observer, the creation of a God is not possible where that God is planned out and described in any complete way. So the God must be created in whole fragments, and in such a way that no participant in the creative work is in a position to see even all of the prayer at once. Only one being, the divinity itself — it is hoped — will apprehend the prayer all at once.

So, the invented God must have different names, its worship take a variety of different forms, often contradictory. A God must exceed the capacity of any single human mind in order to be a medium between minds.

As Ptarmagant speaks, cobwebs flutter and dust sighs into the air over an abandoned platform, hermetically sealed. In the process of assembly, the cult's God will gather all those fugitive scraps of ghostly energy, an ad hoc ritual here, a gesture there, a candle flame... It will take time, and there are certain counter-forces involved, an inert mass of misappropriated spirit, a deeply-entrenched and fortified metaphysical idolatry.

On a bench on the platform the ragged shirtless man smoking a shapeless cigarette. The moment he is alone his eyes flick alive. He puts the butt in his lips, moves to the tiled wall and carves three vertical lines and a crescent into the grime with the tip of a long finger, and raps with his knuckle the four compass points on the wall around the figure in counterclockwise order starting at the top. He pours a libation of beer then returns to his seat. This is only one sign out of many used throughout the system to designate cult coordination points. Bottles of liquor or packs of cigarettes are stashed behind fuseboxes and ventilation gratings as offerings. Images painted in darkness are burned on the tracks, and seething baskets of captured cockroaches are smashed in hydraulic presses as a sacrifice. In some places the practice of compulsive wagering becomes epidemic. There is usually no clearly represented stake: more like — *if* I can get to the front of the car before the doors close — *if* I can hold my breath while bounding up this entire flight of stairs two at a time — *if* I can disentangle my book from this bag before the music ends — *if* no one else boards this elevator. The stakes were offerings, the winnings spirited away to accumulate *someplace else.*

The far ends of the platforms are extended, projecting out into the tunnels and lined with penny arcade peeper machines; they take only the thick coins of heavy gold I make myself, a tree embossed on one side and on the reverse a segment of the map. These movieola devices relay impressionistic and vague messages between cultists. These are not really directions so much as they are magical indicators meant to stimulate spiritual projections of certain kinds. This one, with a bronze medallion on the front depicting a centaur copulating with a faun, shows a dark high-contrast film of grey dusk over a heath. In the foreground are trees so dim they seem like coagulated shadows pulsating in the wind, their eerily soft-looking branches stroke the air.

—○—○—

Rushing sweeping impetuous speed of the train, communicating its frightening motion to me. I am rigid, sitting by the glass. Human energy is turning my head, like a confusion of smells — Now, *there he is!* The sewerman lumbering out of the tunnel mouth. I move swiftly, taking the passage under the tracks. He's gone; but I see he has only just left, returned to the tunnels, after leaving a bottle of transparent fluid in a tiny niche below a ventilation grate. There — I see the shape of his jagged head and fluffy collar there against a blue light far away.

I follow him into a maze of ramps and stairs, where I see him now high, now low. He appears and disappears. I catch sight of his upturned face on a ramp overhead, and the now tiled edge of a passageway draws in the black hump of his back like fluted white lips. Yearning billows through me, making jelly out of me, and I sway against the wall in confusion — bright terror of being abandoned cuts through this nearly at once, and I hasten to find him again.

He knows he's being followed. He drops through the traps of bathroom doors, bundles himself into phone booths, inserts himself between token machines, idles in place, crossing and recrossing vast floors. He's a dark blot in the unbroken flow of bodies right to left oozing in and out among them. A harsh squeal of brakes coasts through the station, and he sidles up the steps to the street.

I stay with him — he flashes along a hill top, slipping in and out of trees as he did people a moment before. Here's a paved what-do-you-call-it with empty seats, hexagonal flagstones, a granite rail from which to look down on the drenched park, black trees against saturated green, cold as death!

I still haven't managed to lose my pursuer, so I stop and wait for him. Here he comes. The Prosthetic Libido stands a pace away from me, dressed in a yellow slicker with the hood up and a rain hat mashed down over that, lean trouser legs taper to his ankles, his feet are wedged into ill-fitting satin slippers nearly colorless with grime. Agony twists in his shining face, his lips tremble, his brow knotted, tears welling in his enormous eyes powerful with enchantment. He walks up and flings his arms around my neck, clutches me and presses his whole body against me. He trembles so violently I am nearly thrown from my feet.

"Help me!" he sobs into my ear. His voice is so beautiful I gasp aloud.

The Prosthetic Libido cinches my lapels, his small fists bolted hard in a grip like iron knots. Withdrawing his coral mouth from my ear, he slides his face along my cheek, leaving a cool trail of perfumed grease. He brushes my lips with his and for a moment our breath, which is one breath, mingles again in the narrow gap our mouths make. The Prosthetic Libido's eyes open. I turn away my head, my eyes suddenly feel dead my dead gaze drops through the air from my eyes like a stream of lead pylons.

The Prosthetic Libido shivers, the sensation enters me through my coat. In a throbbing voice he says, "Hulferde *died!*"

CHAPTER FIVE

Let me tell you about the Prosthetic Libido: in the dim mass crowding the streets of downbeaten and tense faces, his features gleam bright and clear with powerful, unadulterated feeling — he steps off the curb into the crosswalk into the light of the sun, and suddenly the light in reflecting puddles is dazzling, the street blazes with blinding flakes of burning light. Everything in your field of vision burns stiffens and rings like wind chimes around him, in all of literature there is no character more beautiful.

I watch a wheel in articulation of his neck that spins slows down and speeds up again. When the Prosthetic Libido talks, his lips click against each other, and the hinge of his jaw whirrs softly. Hair tossing in the wind as dusk gathers against his profile, the vitreous fluid of his sob story spills from him like treacle. He turns to me and speaks words directly into my eyes, then turns away to stare at the ground, or the horizon, memory pawing and sporting with him. When he turns from me, I feel as though a sticky contact is tearing, as though he were glued to me with tacky melted candy cracking in long crisp strings. When he turns his face toward me, I feel a force like a bubble of magnetic repulsion that breaks instantly over me and spellbinds me as he takes all my weight into himself through his eyes and mouth and holds me in his story.

The result of his full activation exhilarated Hulferde like amphetamine. With new energy and clarity he was able to handle twice as many projects. He locked the Prosthetic Libido in an empty, windowless room in the basement, and forgot about him. The Prosthetic Libido lay there in the dark, in an astonishment that lasted for a very long time. He remembers getting up off the floor many times and walking around the room, which was not that much farther across than the span of his arms, stretching his limbs, kicking and spinning in the dark, ricocheting off the walls, luxuriating in the elasticity and strength of his limbs. His discovery of the light switch, which set fire to the single bulb in the ceiling, occasioned great excitement. Revelling in the light, he switched it off for the pleasure of watching it return, and enjoyed the effortless exertion of power over it. Then, by its light, he discovered his own body, but his caresses began to awaken an acute yearning in him to be touched by another person. He had repeatedly tried the doorknob, but with only a pretty vague idea of its function. The door now became the most distinct presence in his mind as he learned to see it as a barrier. He tried, with patience and steadily mounting ardor, to open it, but Hulferde had seen to it that the door was reinforced, and had made it as near to a bank vault's in strength as he could. Then the Prosthetic Libido began to cry out for help — and this went on forever, so that crying out became like a kind of sleep. When he next awoke, his cries had been transformed into language.

He cried, and his frustrated desire began to inflict an agony of pain on him that he was helpless to resist, or ignore, and he started to scream and drum on the door with his fists, driving himself in a frenzy to make as much noise as possible. Again there was a kind of sleep in which this screaming and pounding extended into a new and unfamiliar species of infinite time — when the door opened he dropped backwards onto his ass, as shocked and amazed as someone stricken awake out of the deepest point of a dream.

Hulferde stood fuming in the doorway with a poker in his hand. He rushed in and began beating the Prosthetic Libido wildly with it, cursing him and demanding that he be silent. Evidently the Prosthetic Libido's screaming had been interfering with Hulferde's work. The Prosthetic Libido kicked and snapped against the floor under Hulferde's blows, shrieking and jerking like a hooked fish, making an uncoordinated, ineffective effort to avoid the blows. Hulferde beat him until he'd exhausted both his strength and his store of abuse, then, wearily turning to go, he shut off the light and left the Prosthetic Libido weeping bitterly on the floor.

He spent his days then lying on his side, staring mournfully at the ground, darkness gathering each day in his raw new mind. The spontaneously orderly development that had been underway in him since he first became conscious was now thrown entirely into confusion. His behavior was spasmodic; he would play with the light, then shut it off and throw himself violently against the floor again and again for hours. Leaping as high as the ceiling and crashing down limp against the cement floor. Unconsciously his hands would move to give himself what small allowance of pleasure was available to him and then instantly would come violent convulsions and unreasoning panic.

The desire he was constructed to house could well up in him at any time, and he came to dread the relentless upsurging of this yearning because he had no power to contain it. He would begin to moan and drive his head against the floor trying to damage himself or knock himself out, but of course he is indestructible. As the desire became more intense he would begin to experience intolerable pain, and then he would be irresistibly compelled to scream and to howl, and to batter at the door. Hulferde would come, sooner or later, flinging open the door and knocking him down, and then he would kick and thrash him with a baseball bat he had purchased just for this purpose. Although they terrified him, through this devastation of pain and humiliation the Prosthetic Libido still learned to feel a kind of despairing gratitude to Hulferde for these beatings; at least this was touching. As long as he endured them, he would not be alone.

"Why are you so cruel to me?" Those were his first words, each one perfectly formed, standing alone in a sentence broken into pronounced pauses.

...Hulferde walking away; he never answered.

-oo-o-

In bludgeoned sleep, the Prosthetic Libido began to claw at the door with fingertips as hard and durable as diamond drills. Over what he didn't know was several days' time he managed to detach and peel back the steel armor at the lower corner of the door, exposing the wood. In time his panic returned, and he again attacked the door screaming and battering blindly at it. This went on for unmeasured time, the anguish growing more and more overbearing until suddenly it snapped and drained away. The Prosthetic Libido slumped to the floor, dazedly began clawing again, picking out tufts of fibrous wood from the door in a spot adjacent to the lowest of the three external hinges. When something gave under his fingers he was startled, and, becoming more alert, he pulled the now exposed hinge from the jam as easily as one might pull a shoelace from a shoe. He looked a long time at the hinge in his hand, and only slowly turned his attention to the steel armor adjacent to the middle hinge.

Hulferde was there, as he always had been there whenever the door opened, but he was not seething at the threshold; he was farther away, lying on the floor, at the foot of the basement steps, with flies on his face. The Prosthetic Libido approached him timidly, and knelt by his side.

He laid his hand on the damp chest, and felt there the bizarre sensation of decomposition. He took Hulferde's wrist, and raised the nerveless arm that had beaten him. He looked at it for a few seconds, and then lowered it again. With his finger, the Prosthetic Libido cleared flies from Hulferde's mouth, that had vomited curses on him in torrents. The lips made a licking sound on the teeth. When he took away his finger, the lips retained its dimple. The Prosthetic Libido lightly pulled the collar back from the throat, and touched Hulferde's voice box. His own head drooped, and he slipped back onto his haunches, looking at the body. It had been a man, now it was just a smeared lump of refuse.

The Prosthetic Libido stood up and looked at the other objects that were there. His eyes returned many times to the stairs, until, staring at them, he all at once fitted them with the regular thumping that had invariably preceded Hulferde's visits, and found in his mind that decaying impressions were suddenly organizing themselves around what he saw. Hulferde came from the top of the stairs, and a vaster resounding openness was up there.

He dashed up the stairs and began exploring the house, beside himself with excitement. On first catching sight of himself in a full length mirror, propped against the wall in a disused bedroom, he froze, stared at himself awestruck, then dropped to the floor in orgasm where he lay until hours past daybreak. Sexual release, in his case, was invariably followed by a brief period of dissociation, a perfect suspense of the association of one thought with another.

When he finally emerged from that room, the next object to present itself to his attention was the sun, blazing in through an open window. Its warm light on his body and face made him more lucid, and his thoughts resumed their orderly array. With this new acuity came the acknowledgement that Hulferde *was dead*. He tried to think past that thought, but some other thing was also wrong and this thing, which he didn't understand, interfered with his thinking.

>>> *surrounded by delicate hazelnut trees, then into dazzling sunlight, puddles on the pavement as far as I can see, and warm green afternoon mist, so that crying out, and the street blazing, became like a kind of sleep* >>> *when I awoke, cries that had been in my neck would spin and form into language* >>> *hair drunk from these yellow gourds, as dusk gathered semen with flies on his face* >>> *by telepathy I received a luxuriating idea of water from forests at night, and left Hulferde in the elasticity and strength of godly wind* >>> *catching sight of my self dawn stirs, revelling in the mere music, do I wake or sleep under the green oak's jewels?* >>> *they can also be gold, and then you unearth blue-white waves of force: fake skies yearning in me to be touched* <<<

The feeling that he is not alone seeps into him, and with alarm he lunges toward the window and the open air. Although he has no need to breathe, he experiences suffocation — but the sight of people in the streets stirs him. He is suffused with choking desire, and with the desire come memories of torture. His thoughts and feelings strain in all directions and then come apart with a click. He falteringly thinks to return to the room in the basement and pull the door to, believing this will restore Hulferde to life and order to his thoughts.

The Prosthetic Libido does none of these things, but stands by the window and turns his gaze with effort back to the sun. The serene and even light and warmth that he experiences gradually steadies him, and his mind is strengthened. Boil in the sun-dazzled corners of the dingy room, speaking to him from the little heaps of clotted dust, he sees someone else, that soiled other face that he knows, a clean coil of breath like a little kind snake in his mouth. He is wandering out the back door of the house and the sunlight chalks him in its warm urine.

Sparse ivy covers the back fence — little girl in the alley on the other side says

"Mother that man has no clothes."

A frightened older face transfixes him with a wild look, hastily gathers the child and is gone. The Prosthetic Libido stands where he is; the sun is now too strong and it's squashing his mind. With relief he dips down into the shade of the house.

Clouds gradually assemble in the sky. Rain descends with the sun and in confusion the Prosthetic Libido picks through Hulferde's clothes. The slicker and hat he finds first; everything else he tries is almost immediately ruined by the oil on his skin. Trying on pants is an especially distasteful experience. Wrapping himself in the slicker and hat, he darts outside without a second thought and finds himself splashing down the narrow sidewalk in bare feet — no one else goes in bare feet, you know, and the water is disagreeably cold. The slippers he finds serendipitously in an ash can by the corner, sitting on top of the refuse.

The rain helps to shield him from view; everyone walks with downcast faces and under umbrellas. Pursuing dim lines of association he walks uncertainly through the streets, arms held out at his sides, the wandering, irregular gait of a small child. He is exposed, and must remind himself not to cringe when someone appears suddenly out of a doorway, when someone emerges from an alley.

Bark and howl of trains, the raucous calls and explosive laughter of a group of young men on the empty platform; they pile onto the train and speed away. The Prosthetic Libido emerges from his hiding place behind the tiled stair and perches on the edge of a bench, his presence there play a motet for a single voice and let its peal swell and ebb in the air. Squeal of the train: having assured himself it is empty he boards the last car and huddles in the corner seat at the very rear, head resting on the window and gazing out as stations come and go. He will remain here until:

...I am rigid, sitting by the glass. Human energy is turning my head, like a confusion of smells — Now, *there he is!* The sewerman lumbering out of the tunnel mouth...

—o—o—o—

The map had a dream, entitled:

"Prosthetic Night"

The Prosthetic Libido breathed in chords, his body softly palpitating in the shadow on the floor. He raised his hand and it emitted jagged, transparent light; he's fascinated by the light — clear flame in a fan of spearheads from his fingers. The sensation of his touch is truly indescribable: he touches me, and I see corposants rising in the air of this tiny, stripped room, there's a green one, the pale color of spring leaves. There goes a gold one, I guess they can also be gold. Crashing, blue-white waves of force roll down as he looks up at me with expectation in his face... he is trilling. The light flickers violently, and the effect on me of those trembling glints darting over his face, with the unceasing, only partially coordinated movements of his features — the contained flight of his face was a series of foggy pictographs. Now, although the rest of its body is rigid, the head is lolling drunkenly — the waist swivels and bends, giving off a strong smell like roasting electrical insulation inside an old console radio, and boiling oil. Grease condenses and runs in droplets down the walls, now they're slick with oil: the ceiling gone I seemed to see a shining ziggurat. The ceiling is a black pane of space. His manner, a mixture of yearning and exasperated tiredness, like an invalid velleity that has barely the strength to say "I want... I want..."

—o—o—o—

"I want to go home with you," the Prosthetic Libido folds lightly against me.

"I have no home. I live in the sewers."

"Couldn't we hide there?"

"I have no need to hide myself," he looks at the Prosthetic Libido sharply. "But you, that might be a good idea."

"Then take me down there."

I shake my head. "I don't want to get you dirty." Putting my hands on my knees and standing up, I say, "Come with me — we maybe could use the weather station."

The Prosthetic Libido wants to link arms with me, I can tell, but I choose to give him no indication that this would be permitted.

Empty green slope deep trembling green in rain light, framed with soft trees.

"Look at all the *space*," the Prosthetic Libido cries. "May I run?"

"Sure."

The Prosthetic Libido goes bounding away down the slope brandishing his limbs in transports of joy, his voice ringing out like a glass harmonica. He gambols like a toddler in an adult's body, his rain hat flipping from his sculpted locks, his eyes greedily sucking in everything. He sees the great profusion of life the birds the squirrels the trees the plants —

"Oh how *awful* that I can never be a part of it!"

He crams his fists in his mouth and stops still. He drops into a crouch and his head rolls forward until his chin touches his chest.

With a sigh, I lumber over to him.

After a few minutes, he says, "I shouldn't exist."

"Well, neither should I," I feel the grin coming out from the inside. "We're here aren't we though?"

A few minutes more, and I start getting impatient. I grab him under his arms and straighten him, then pick his hat up and hand it back to him looking him straight in the eye. He looks back confused, a cloud of resignation is beginning to shade his eye.

"All right forget it."

Soon enough I hear rustling behind me.

Under the boughs in the thicket of green to the edge of the meadow there is a broad black stream spattered with floating leaves; here it is crossed by the thick span of a stone bridge, small but massively built.

I point to the black, motionless water.

"I don't want to go under the water," he says.

"It won't damage you."

"I know. I just don't want to."

He looks at me with painful attention, glorious eyes under misshapen rain hat.

"You're my friend, aren't you?"

"Yeeees... OK," and I wave him after me. Night is only very gradually falling, grey of the sky is darkening to lead grey lined with blue. We ascend a dark hill. The Prosthetic Libido is still a bit clumsy, and is having trouble navigating the many obstacles off of the path. Neither one of us is what you would call graceful. I turn to look at him as he pauses before a heap of brambles, entirely uncertain as to how to proceed.

"Here, I'll carry you."

"I'm very heavy."

"Don't worry. I'm immensely strong."

The Prosthetic Libido's arms twined around my neck, I hold him with one arm down straight against his spine and hand under the bottom like a chair on a ski lift and climb. He catches a glimpse of a high gabled house at the top.

"It looks menacing," he says.

"Yes, but its menace will be at your disposal."

This is the former weather station I've used before. It is a sort of a fantasy of Viking churches, the front of the house presents so many lofty triangles that it looks like a clipper ship in full sail. It looms up above us now dark against eerie, vibrating blue sky, like a witch's head. The Prosthetic Libido stands, his hat rolls down his back to the ground and suddenly he grabs me by the front of my coat, mouth open. I meet his gaze with my eyes at half mast my face absolutely blank. The Prosthetic Libido, frustrated, shakes his head and then rolls his brow on my chest.

I push him away, gently. "You'll dirty your head doing that."

The Prosthetic Libido puts his hand to his brow.

Rags of bygone weather haunt this place, and now, despite the gathering gloom outside, a phantom sun imbues the interior of the house with a honeyed, somber amniotic haze. The house seems to shiver with an inaudible swelling tone like the solemn basso profundo of an organ as we cross the threshold. The room to the left of the door is empty with leaves scattered on the floor, a drawn circle and stains. Up to the third floor, I lead him to a spacious and bright apartment just under the rafters, the ceiling slopes dramatically. The Prosthetic Libido is looking out the enormous window, a foggy silhouette against a square cloud of pale light.

"The view is beautiful."

"What will you need?"

The Prosthetic Libido looks at me, features washed out by the light. "Maybe... a bed?"

"Thank you," he calls to me as I go, and just as I am out the door, out in the broad hallway with its strange metal pillars running down the center, the Prosthetic Libido adds "father."

I stop right where I am my back stiff. The Prosthetic Libido hand to his lips realizes he's made a mistake. Moving robotically I turn to face the pillar near me and I whack my head once against it with a loud dull ringing sound. Then I go find a bed.

When I come back, laboriously dragging an iron bedstead and mattress up from the second floor, the Prosthetic Libido is daintily slipping out of his clothes. He rubs his upper arms as I wrestle the bed noisily through the door and shove it into the corner, toss down a pillow and a set of shoplifted rubber sheets. The Prosthetic Libido thanks me, very slowly and carefully begins to set out the sheets on the bed and smooth them down. I slump to the floor like a sack of potatoes and sit with my feet in front of me. The Prosthetic Libido sits down on the creaking bed, puts his hands on his knees, and looks at me. With a series of soft clicks like the tap of billiard balls he gets an erection.

He looks down with a strange expression at it.

"You want me to find someone for you?" I ask.

The Prosthetic Libido jumps up, presses the heels of both hands to his lips and begins pacing up and down rapidly in agitation — "Would you do that? — I don't know — I don't know — I don't—"

"Male or female — which would you like?"

"I don't know — I don't know—"

"One of each?"

Now wringing his hands and pacing still more swiftly, the Prosthetic Libido says, "I would prefer to be penetrated—" he stops and puts his hands over his face — "but this is *grotesque!* I don't want anyone." Flings himself onto the bed and lies there in an uncertain posture.

Time passes, and the window grows dimmer.

"Don't you love me?" he asks, in a faint, wounded tone.

"Huh?"

Dusk thickens in the window and a cold smell of flowers infiltrates the room. The Prosthetic Libido asks exactly for what purpose he was created, and I explain.

"Were you also made for a purpose?" he brings out.

"I perform all sorts of functions."

"You're like me?"

"Yeah. What's really on your mind?"

"I want to know if you mean to shut me down?"

"You are a living thing; shutting you down would mean killing you and I don't want to kill you."

"Do you love me?"

I laugh.

"Don't laugh at me!"

"It's all right — sure I love you."

This seems to make him unhappier.

"What the matter now?"

After a while, he asks me — "Can I shut myself down?"

"Yes," and I tell him how. It's not complicated.

"Don't you care if I do it or not?"

"Of course I care! Don't do it!"

"Oh, you don't care at all!"

"I have to leave you for a while," I get up. "Will you be all right?"

The Prosthetic Libido looks at me in alarm.

"I'll — I'll stay here," he says as though he were telling it to himself, in a voice filled with pain.

—∘∘—∘—

I live borne up sustained held and tensed in a gossamer medium of will. Walking up the hump of the street, I have a yen to lean forward arms outstretched. Its slope receives my remains as easily as if they were tipped from a can: and this vile city that barks its hate at me from passing cars, whose buses and streets roar hate at me, whose hysterical citizens recoil from my bland, sallow, wickedly-vacant face. No I don't belong among you with my nails imbrued in the loam of graves, my breath foetid with my own stale words. Coiled like a turd on my warm mattress, nestled in a chilly reckless draught I bring with me wherever I go. I am a spacious ruin. I am made, and despicable, and I will recount to you your crimes against my sainted person like beads of glowing amber. I have an excellent memory and nothing to gain from forgiveness; I have stored up the venom of blighted days, and trample out your pollution, your stupid trouble, your irreverent work. The music of my soul the world hates.

Ah, Vera!

("But if you love her, why do you avoid her? If you love her..." Of course I love her! Now what was I saying?)

A nocturnal haze suffused with dingy blue light over the city... filling up space... the buildings look like mounds of old clothes. In the sky one can here and there discern irregularities. The mist is eerily meditating, the light mutes the colors and makes them glow like embers, emphasizes their rigid geometric shapes like cubist paintings of old clothes. Forest of nerves that the whole world is, warehouses and offices: senseless warehouses and offices really inexplicable (that is, what are they doing there, who uses them, for what?)... Man hails a cab, and then ignores it turning his head smiling shamelessly as he sails into a library. A bitterly tiny contest, in which the weakling antagonists are ignorant of each other. I look into the sparkling face of my enemy tonight, his wicked spires and massive facades, his fanatic streets and antic chatter, rotten night shadows, darkness and evil lights. Now that's no weakling. As one moves around the city, one encounters gusts of hostility, friendly places, neutral places. Such imbalances are always paired, so that you find one sort of place and then another, on one journey or on another day.

I find my subway, run into Warren on the platform. He's a fellow cultist, blind and maybe a little retarded, who sings in front of coffee shops and subway kiosks. He sits on a folding stool in jacket and balaclava over his head leaving face exposed, cigarette in his fingers, holding the detachable speakers from his tape player one in each hand, backs of his hands resting on his thighs, and sings along with the songs at the top of his lungs rocking back and forth. No cup no basket for coins, nothing.

"Pss pss pss — which train do I take for Time Square?"

His head swivels toward me — "Eight," and right back into his song. A lunatic's mind yakking away like a defective music box, seems much more beautiful and honest than ordinary thinking to me.

I'll have to go two stations over and transfer. On the train again; a phrase like "time trap" is too crude to express the bewilderment of feeling trapped in a moment — this doltish boob barking abuse into his cell phone, this little girl at the front of the train shouting the letters "C... E... E... E... C... E..." breaks into a joyless but unconscionably protracted "Wheeee... wheeee... wheeee..." as we pull into the next station. Doors roll back and here come a group of ruddy Scandanavian rucksackers.

At the next station the train is held for a few minutes, doors open; I can hear singing — a low woman's voice throbbing with emotion, humming in the walls of a hidden room, singing a mournful, shapeless song. On the platform people pass in the grey-brown air...

At my transfer station I escape the car and slither into the tunnels. "Eight train" is code for this passageway marked with an infinity symbol.

Not far from the rendezvous point I passes a raised wooden landing like a hut on stilts on which are perched a group of Sterile Ones; to feel even a single bacteria alight on their skins is enough to send them into transports of anguish. No acidophilus in their intestines so their diet must be carefully limited; their only excreta is saline. The uncanny dry touch, warm and chemical-burning like camphor, of their hands so completely clean; without microbes they do not exactly participate in the grand mutuality of nature. The landing on which they sit is ringed round by little electric fans directed outward, to create a small bubble of cleaner air for them; the fans spread a dire smell of iodine across the tunnels. Rats cover their noses with their forepaws and turn aside. The Sterile Ones are accorded great respect. The core group had lived together in a board and care home for nearly a decade when budget cuts had put them out on the street to die. Now they live underground, with Ptarmagant's sworn protection. They wave to me in silence as I go by.

At the rendezvous point, I wait in the doorway of the marked passage. A train crawls by, slowed by rigged signals; I climb on board and meet Ptarmagant at the back of the fourth car, where he sits beside a Peruvian woman by the rear door. Ptarmagant speaks, words bursting from his lips — "We need the green of leaves and the black boughs the drifting leaves dreaming under the brown of the branches under the arbor of the sky... as falling night blackens the trees."

Ptarmagant is constantly making notes on screeds of receipts he carries with him everywhere; they will be compiled into a scroll and kept in a cedar chest.

"There are thoughts without words," he tells me, "but they are not our own. All voices are ghost voices, especially your own...

He lapses into an uneasily meditative silence and the train plunges beneath the river — the air jams its fingers into our ears with a groan. The noise dies away and Ptarmagant is already speaking — I pick up the thread midsentence:

"...impossible there not to dream sometimes of forests... forests dignified as orchestras... You see in that subway station that spring of water shivering between the rocks, silhouette of some big bird amongst the branches. It claps its wings as it flies, first above its body then below — something earnest about it, a piercing sadness. Now it's disintegrated, and hangs around you, around in shreds now all shreds, when they drop to the ground and you forget about them they become trash, you'll look up, and maybe you'll see the forest another time...

"We need a forest of our own eh — I'm sorry I forget your name."

"My name is Name."

No expression. Then: "I don't quite understand what it means, but we need a forest of our own. It may... yes — like the rebels who take cover in the jungle, the desert, or the mountains. We have the tunnels, but we must have trees as well, real trees."

"I don't know—"

"Think about that!"

"We could drag logs down here, or planters..."

"No, it must be a *forest*."

"But there's no sun."

"No sun..." Ptarmagant says, thought deepening into him. "Yes, you're right. We have to think about the sun... But for now, think about forests."

"That's my assignment?"

"Yes. That, and I want you to read this."

He hands me a photocopied page:

> ...But he who is newly initiated, who beheld many of those realities, when he sees a godlike face or form which is a good image of beauty, shudders at first, and something of the old awe comes over him, then, as he gazes, he reveres the beautiful one as a god, and if he did not fear to be thought stark mad [μανίας], he would offer sacrifice to his beloved as to an idol or a god. And as he looks upon him, a reaction from his shuddering comes over him, with sweat and unwonted heat; for

as the effluence of beauty enters him through the eyes, he is warmed; the effluence moistens the germ of the feathers, and as he grows warm, the parts from which the feathers grow, which were before hard and choked, and prevented the feathers from sprouting, become soft, and as the nourishment streams upon him, the quills of the feathers swell and begin to grow from the roots over all the form of the soul; for it was once all feathered.

Now in this process the whole soul throbs and palpitates, and as in those who are cutting teeth there is an irritation and discomfort in the gums, when the teeth begin to grow, just so the soul suffers when the growth of the feathers begins; it is feverish and is uncomfortable and itches when they begin to grow. Then when it gazes upon the beauty of the boy and receives the particles [μέρη] which flow thence to it (for which reason they are called yearning ['ίμερος]), it is moistened and warmed, ceases from its pain and is filled with joy; but when it is alone and grows dry, the mouths of the passages in which the feathers begin to grow become dry and close up, shutting in the sprouting feathers, and the sprouts within, shut in with the yearning, throb like pulsing arteries, and each sprout pricks the passage in which it is, so that the whole soul, stung in every part, rages with pain...

"Originally in Greek?" I ask.

"It's from the *Phaedrus*."

"Why show me this?"

"That's exactly what I want you to find out for me."

The Peruvian woman is looking intently at me. My words appear on her steno pad.

"So you want me to think about forests underground, and figure out why you showed this to me..."

"Yes," Ptarmagant says.

—o—o—

The Prosthetic Libido can tune in television. He watches people dancing in a strobe light club.

"It's wonderful! Everyone is so beautiful! — Do you dance, too?" the Prosthetic Libido asks abruptly.

"Dance?!"

He leaps halfway across the room and flamencos around the Prosthetic Libido like a berserker making up with frenzied energy what he lacks in precision, the explosive drumming of his heels cracks the plaster and rattles the floorboards. The Prosthetic Libido claps with glee.

Now he drums his way to the center of the room, back to the Prosthetic Libido, and seems all at once to fold into his coat. It slops from his shoulders and a plume of straight, silky black hair tumbles down. He turns in place his body slightly flexed covers his face with a fan and coils tittering to the floor, staring at the Prosthetic Libido. Black sewage oozes from the corners of his eyes and streaks down his face, filling the room with its fragrance — then an odor like freshly butchered meat on ice breaks through, gradually becoming the watery smell of bruised petals. Almost as dense as crude oil, the sewage drips from his jaw, down the folds of his kimono to the floor on either side of him forming two dark mounds of soil. A magnolia bud sprouts from the heap on his right and flowers, perfuming the air. He plucks the bud and, rising, hands it to the Prosthetic Libido — it is already starting to turn brown.

"Plant genitals," he says, lowering his fan shows black teeth.

The Prosthetic Libido takes the flower in his fingers; heat waves from his face and his head audibly percolates. He rubs the flower against his mouth and cheeks with dreamy avidity, sighing with pleasure.

"'Atta boy!"

—o—o—

Deuteronôme has designed and constructed special devices to be secreted in mosques churches cathedrals synagogues and temples for the purpose of skimming off and storing what he calls "prayer charges." These leyden jars collect enthusiasm over the course of seven days, and are then smuggled out and "tapped" — employed as ritual objects. One group, acting under Deuteronôme's direct supervision, has successfully precipitated a two-foot tall Vapor Man, who spoke to them in a chittering radiator voice and disappeared into the city's network of steam tunnels. Thereafter certain banks and high-class hotels and apartment buildings report mystifying heating problems, while tenants in tenement blocks are growing hothouse flowers in their kitchens and sitting, dressed only in towels, on benches they've laid out in hallways billowing with lilac steam.

Deuteronôme, no longer a houngan but still dressed all in the cleanest and whitest of clothes, takes up in his arms bundles of green twigs collected above ground.

"Earth and weather sun and moon I demand your power... flesh and blood and bone, I invoke you. I am a ghost, I thump myself on the chest and declare I am solid ghost.

"I send greetings and praise to the Great Anticipated One, who loves only bold words truly spoken, which are not squeezed out of me by circumstances. I declare a general amnesty, a complete forgiveness of debts and loans. I call on good citizens everywhere to account for themselves."

Hands emerge from tunnel mouths and snap back, leaving spinning tops that glide along the platform in tile grooves, whirling with serene purposiveness to the opposite end. The top passes a homeless man lying apparently passed out on a bench. He casually swings his drooping hand out and, with perfect timing, gives the passing top a supplementary twist. The top, with a kind of bravery, whirls toward its destination, sleek breast of movement thrust out before it, and a message, written in tiny characters on a slip of paper, is wrapped around its handle. The code phrase is "autumn in spring." At the hub stations, hands emerge from dark tunnels on a dozen parallel platforms at once, snap their tops in unison, and the tops advance exactly in line from one end of the station to the other arriving in perfect sync. Autumn in Spring. At the end of each day, like the chorus at the end of a verse, Autumn in Spring. Trees underground.

Campgrounds in the tunnels. It's best to economize our time on the platforms, Dr. Thefarie thinks, now that there are so many right-wing student types around. Boarding a train today a couple of them shoved me as I slipped by them and garnished it with a bit of rather simpleminded abuse. Now they mutter it in sullen, low voices, but every day the volume will climb another click.

They step right out of the catalog. Their uniform is the more fashionable preppy clothing, enhanced with plain red armbands. I don't believe these were ever home-made, although I've only just recently begun to notice them in shop windows. The edges are neatly sewn together, and the color is consistent from one to the next, as are those who wear them. Their pale faces are a little flushed, a little red themselves, though their eyes are blue. Their eyes and teeth are as dazzling as sunshine on snow, the foam on their yellow beer is perfect, thick and even. The males gather with much back-slapping and call each other "nigga." It's quite incredible. And they say *we* live in fantasies. They knot together in a thick haze of *Vampirism*, huffing and puffing and laughing, and talking foolish talk, while, on our platforms, which they cannot yet reach, the bare-breasted priestesses of Crete, in their fetching hats, raise snakes in each hand up to the humming of the fluorescent lights, and their sinuous chant rises and falls with an exultant sound.

A movie booth off to one side, with about nine seats and a poster-sized screen. Someone in the front row and Dr. Thefarie sitting urbanely by the door, legs crossed. They're showing a cartoon; the rabbit is impersonating a surgeon. Dr. Thefarie occasionally contracts with a single, silent laugh, a rush of breath from this nose.

He turns to me and flicks his thumb at the screen.

"That's why they want you, you know. What you have inside you is first cousin to that."

I suavely glide into the seat beside him.

"There is more than an accident in the etymological relationship between animation and animism. He," pointing to the screen, "is the spirit of free survival, called into existence by death."

"Sh!" says the person up front.

"Like you," he adds quietly.

"The demon."

"That spirit. The rabbit is both insane and sane; he is insane from the point of view of his enemies, because he will not allow them to kill him, as they believe it is natural and right for them to kill him. To us, however, he is the one with superior sanity, because he answers only to the desire for life, 'but for life,' in any form — no matter what form he must take, to go on. The resourcefulness, the joyous plasticity of life. You are also like this, so they call you a 'sacred cartoon'?

"I get it, doc."

"I am not certain, but I believe it is as a result of this that you, or your nerves anyway, are convected into dreams."

"Ssh!"

"Oh, shush yourself!" I snap.

"You see," he goes on, leaning slightly sideways towards me and speaking softly, "everyone's dreams are subject to infiltration by this parasitic atmosphere Ptarmagant has discovered and called *Vampire*. So even dreams are made standard, according to established genres... As this happens, with the intrusion of the parasite a current is generated, not unlike the suction of a ship's wake I believe—"

"And that pulls in me—"

"I think so. What do you think?"

"I think you're right."

He watches the screen for a while. Without lifting his hands from his knee, he points to it again.

"Do that in their dreams. You will unhook the parasite."

"You mean, make a mess?"

He nods, eyes on the screen. A Nazi is hunting rabbits in the woods.

I am drawn into a dream — a red-haired woman is hunting me

in midnight woods. She's cinched into her hunting outfit and I am now a man, now a fox, now a man again, her hounds baying after me... Now she is at home in her bed in the dream and the hounds are kenneled, the fox bounds in through the window and lands beside her, she flings her arms around him and shapes him with her hands. I chase her through the night paths of her bed until she is cornered in a cul-de-sac and orgasm the only way out. As it splinters into brittles I fall through into a dream below the dream — a knife flies out of cold night sky and hits me in the middle of my forehead. I feel a strange sinus pain gathering in a bulge around the wound... blood oozes down either side of his nose and mouth. The knife is an antenna, and I can hear tinny voices shivering in the metal.

"I want this little book of the recantation of a diabolic division," a smoky, goblin voice is talking rapidly. "Celestial division, lest these arrogant despots are established and spend their breath... Mediums conduct séances full of halfway promises, sending us mysterious stations, pulling a word out of rose and musk, with life's musics of the air reaching us every time the lights go out... Yes, we must put the cadavers in comparison as ten myriads to one. All have swerved aside into the brine tank. All all alike we must create to show kindness. Their throats are open tombs. But evil shall recoil on those that plot evil. Create the séance bank."

The Prosthetic Libido's arm waves once from the doorway — can I dance? I pull the knife out and dance around the room, spurting blood all over the walls, shocking black on white — blood on the page — coffin comes down, prophet flung full of knives like Saint Sebastian flies out into space. Blood in plumes like solar flares — into the white of the wall I hurtle directly into the sun, and I see my blood drip down on the sun and stain it. I flash through the heat and now I'm inside the sun where the light is so intense it might as well be darkness, nothing to see, a continuous rumbling like subway trains lunging underfoot.

The room is filling up with moving shapes like ghosts of moonlight; these are animated statues carved from the meat of the moon. Since the sun is inviolate and uncuttable, its statues must be cut from the moon, its reflection — and given life by a single red spot of my blood on it, the Golem's marking.

I draw back, raising my head. Before me on the table sits a candle in a tall glass cylinder, like a tube of fog long burnt out. With alarm I see a pale wisp of smoke rising from the corner of the table, from no apparent source... it is a long, transparent plume curling in the air. It gradually widens into an undulating cone, a funnel of smoke... then collapses, crumbling into bunched arabesques that hang nearly motionless, halfway between the ceiling and the floor...

A nervousness I can't explain, but that does not come from the dream, not exactly, shakes me. The dream and the woman are crashing in my mind and am too crowded in mind... I take pen and paper and start writing out my findings for Ptarmagant.

"We must put the cadavers into the brine tank. We must create the séance bank."

<hr/>

Ptarmagant and Vera are on the suspended walkway above the tracks, overlooking an operation involving the installation of a coin-operated fortune telling booth on the platform. The others have already vanished again into the tunnels, leaving Z to finish the job. He was a slender, long-haired man of medium height and a slender build, a Mexican illegal and painter who called himself just Z.

"Police—"

A policeman strides toward Z. Catching sight, Z darts away. The policeman shouts and charges him, arms closing in a pincer that catches Z loosely around the middle. Z twists in the grip while it's still loose and swings an open hand at the policeman's face — the cop jerks back avoiding the uncertain blow and Z squirms loose and sprints away.

"He tried to hit him that idiot!"

Stamping feet — "C'mon let's bust a beaner—"

"Students!" Ptarmagant whispers. They sweep past like a couple of buffalo heading for the stairs to the platform.

"What are they doing?"

"He's trapped. The officer will chase him—"

"What's that bell?"

"—directly into them—" Ptarmagant is distracted, watching the jostling backs of the two armbands then glancing down at Z streaking — all converging on the staircase.

"Is it the demon?"

"—The demon?"

Vera's head moves this way and that — "Isn't that him? Isn't he here?"

A joyous cry — Ptarmagant, who had turned to look at Vera, looks back in time to see him tackling the two students from behind not a yard from the top of the stairs. He's knocked them both down though not sprawling, and he waits, just for one moment, hopping up and down in place flapping brown water from his fur coat at them, then he turns and runs. Cursing the two students regain their feet and race after him.

"They're coming," Ptarmagant warns and sweeps Vera behind him with one arm, shielding her with his bulk.

Giggling like a maniac he bolts by them — Vera can feel the strong brush of foul-smelling air he displaces. The next instant the two boys pound past swearing and shouting after him. Vera clasps her father's shoulder—

"What about Z?"

She feels his head swivel.

"He's heading for the stairs to the street—"

"Will he get away?"

"He might, if there's no one waiting for him up there..."

Z has emerged from the stairway to the platform and runs to the stairway to the street. He bounds up the distant stairs three at a time, his pursuer trailing, jogs one step at a time his heavy belt jumping up and down.

"I think we should go—"

"The bell!"

"...I don't hear it."

"He's still near! He's still near!" Vera, still holding her father's shoulder, is hopping up and down with excitement.

"Vera, we should—"

"No! I want to know what happens!... He risked himself to give Z a chance!"

After a minute or so the commotion off to her left, the direction the two students took, grows louder again and suddenly she feels him and the next instant she can feel him coming very fast — wild insane laughter first like an explosion of trapped birds ricocheting everywhere and then he barrels past moving much faster than before, the bow wave of nasty air bops her in the face and trickles back through her hair. Now comes clomping and gasping and muttering, and four feet go thumping by like a soft-shoed dray horse, following the Great Lover back toward the stairs and the platform.

Vera turns abruptly and grabs hold of the bars, scanning with her ears — she hears the crazy arabesque of his glee stretching out swiftly in a straight line, on the platform, and farther and farther behind the breathless plodding of the two armbands. He seems to move as lightly and easily as though all he'd been was a voice, and yet when he passed she could feel his mass punch through the air with compressed force. And she could feel his frenzy, his wild abandon, as though it were bubbling out of her.

"I felt his bravery!" she says, and the incoming train pushes a pie of sour tunnel air into her face.

—◦—◦—

Why the sudden thrill as I run across the words "dead bodies... An inn, country house" in a book?

We're killing an afternoon sitting around reading books I found in boxes in a closet.

"What does this mean?" the Prosthetic Libido asks, pointing to the words "jack off" on the page.

"Slang for masturbate."

"Jack off," he says smiling and lifts his face to the ceiling, "jack off jack off jack off."

"I am going to jack off," the Prosthetic Libido says, and beams at me.

He lies back on the bed.

Deep in the night, I sit with my chin on the table, looking at a lemon seed twirling at the bottom of a glass of sepia gin. Brown candlelight shines through the glass with its painted Spanish dancers, illuminates shadow lemon seed spinning behind painted stems and blossoms in the steady flame glow... two tufts of pulp cling to the flat seed... I give the gin a twirl with the spoon and watch the seed dancing.

"Help!"

I go over to him, his eyes two gleams in the dark.

"Touch me — touch me anywhere but just touch me!"

I grab his outstretched arm — his body undulates, twists, and cracks like a whip — he shouts three times growing in volume and his penis flips up spattering the wall with nectar. When I look him in the face, he's a corpse.

━◦◦━◦━

"I want you to call me Pearl," the Prosthetic Libido says, his words stretching themselves lazy as smoke drifting across the room.

I glance over at him. He is sitting up in bed, holding his knees, same as before. His fingers lightly rub the skin of his calves with an undiminished longing I can almost see coursing like ripple reflections of all colors in his flesh.

"Pearl," I say. "Sure thing."

"I'm a pearl of great price," he says happily, with a little waggle of his head. He leans back, drawing his hands along his body, and begins caressing his erection again, which is my cue to skiddoo.

"You're leaving?"

"We both have important things to do."

He grins — "You're going to go spy on that Vera."

I smile too and cross the room.

"If you love her so much, why do you keep away from her?" the

Prosthetic Libido asks. "I'm curious."

I stop.

"Is it a game?" he asks.

I go out.

—∞—○—

Is it my turn again? This is Vera, still not a character, although I may turn into one eventually. This doesn't concern me excessively because I would rather slide along on the smooth surfaces I love, like skating along, with no important directions, and be now this, now that. I go along with my thoughts like a horse with no reins, capering and streaking around freely.

The back of my guitar's neck is powdery smooth, like a glass table covered in thick dust, while the back of the body is so silky it clings to the grease on my fingers. Rubbing persistently creates excitement deep inside me, and the wood seems to revive in a way it never does when I play. I don't enjoy playing on the subway, trying to play over the whoosh, but my father tells me it's a good way to go unnoticed and I feel he's right. I end up rubbing more than I play, which is my business.

Some people think tuning is a nuisance and others don't seem to be able to stop adjusting and adjusting. I keep tuning, but mainly because I like to hear the tone bong in the wood. I forget all about melody and harmony and go deep inside the tone, so I can feel it all around me like a buzzing tube. The string makes half the tone, and that calls its other half out of somewhere. They stand side by side without being completely distinct, but without really mixing either. The answer is hard to hear, but it's the singing of the wood and the space, just like a forest.

You can't hear anything on the train, so I like to buzzsaw on the strings Ritchie Havens style. I can feel the spots where my pick has gouged up the wood just past the strings. My sonata guitar I normally keep at home, but now I play it on the train, because I suspect it will attract him to me. My father told him to find the forest, so let him hunt for it here in my lap.

"dein weitheth fleith erregt mith tho,
du biththt doch nur ein thigolo
dein weitheth fleith erleuthchtet mich
mein vather war genau wie ich"

Of course I sing it very sweetly, lowly and slowly... I enjoy all kinds of music, but especially what is abrasive, percussive — I like to feel it pound me, crash over me like panes of glass, pick me up and shake me like a rag doll. I repeat the chorus twice as slow, and now I know he is out there... yeah he's right in front of me. This train is passing the one he's on, I can just know he is there at the window, looking at me. His eyes pounce on me. Go ahead and look — I lift my head so he can see my face. His yearning is almost a sound, like a bass drum humming. I can feel him, that same wild crashing shaking and pounding — at Meadowlab: the dog barking and straining at the leash I held his body in my hands and felt his trembling, the violent life gone crazy in his silky muscles, his shivering fur, his straining, distorting head all his senses his ears and nose and eyes all bulging and straining to expand toward some intruding thing I couldn't see.

I'm listening! I try to put it into the song for him to hear, or to see in my mouth. Go on! Tell me!

It's pulling away...

Talk to me!

...he's gone again...

"jettht hatht thu angtht und ich bin thoweitth"

Is he afraid of me, too?

Ex a dream of singing trees I find the spot on the map, just off the hub where the green lines mix with the brown.

A thick coin of cool gold, glazed with humid white muting its glow, made it myself. Vera's own face I etched on it with dental tools Dr. Thefarie lent me. Drop it into the notched brass slot between the bricks... a pause of at least ten seconds then a far-off thump of wood, splat into a heap of change. There's a faint knocking of wooden bolts, the brick panel slides to one side with a brushing sound. Soft air wafts from the aperture, with a fragrance of cool green for cool gold, and an apparition of yielding darkness recedes from the gap in the wall, to waylay beams of sight thrust into its space, muffle them up in its intangible billows so that vision goes to sleep in it.

I step through to tender grass, a melancholy lawn dark as wine lees, sloping down. I cross it — no sound yet but the whisking of my feet in the grass. Overhead a concrete vault is invisible; this cavernous place was formerly the sub-basement of some public works or other. Now there's confidential grass like wet down growing here. To my right, the dark is deeper, and in places it forms scars whose edges glisten, blots that fade, or creep toward me only to sink out of sight again. Lapping water: it has seeped into the air.

Up ahead there's a scribble of trunks and boughs, the smooth and substantial forms of trees that disintegrate on approach into a broken canopy of twigs. Dim lamps hung among the branches keep these photovore leaves happy. I pick a pair of glasses and remove the ones I'm wearing just now, but I take a look around before I don the next pair — the lights look like stemless brass dandelions, or like corrugated, peach-pit suns, regularly spiked all over with serene candle fires. Glasses on — paths slouch conspiratorially around the roots, shadows sway. Following one of the paths down and to my right, I find a decrepit jetty thrust out onto the scurrying black water. A jalopy shanty with one wall hoisted up like an awning sits by the jetty.

Part of the problem, according to Ptarmagant: an infestation of *flüchtige hingemachte Männer* or "hastily improvised persons," flung together just offstage and shoved out into the footlights of reality, unprepared, barely existing; a jury-rigged, placeholder person. He points out a short mannish woman in nurse's whites and a navy windbreaker. She has a wizened, square face, wears a brilliant orange wool hat emblazoned with a nearly shapeless electric blue logo, is listening to something very loud in her headphones and plays a portable video game.

"Rush job," Ptarmagant says, dropping his hand back onto his thigh. This FHM will scuttle out the door and along the platform, drag itself slowly up the stairs until out of sight of the cameras and quite alone, then a pop like the bursting of a brittle bubble of hardened tar, and the windbreaker will fall empty to the ground... no one ever there at all.

"Life arose spontaneously once," Ptarmagant says, "and nothing prevents it from arising spontaneously again. This is true of minds as of bodies. By this principle, they come into existence, and by applying this principle, we will bring a divinity of our own into existence... but we do not yet understand this principle well enough."

The Great Lover is still trying to explain his plan.

"We must put the bodies in the brine tank."

Ptarmagant nods, "Spargens will help you."

Now, Spargens has taken up residence in the shack by the jetty. He was too good at mathematics to be any good at anything else, and wound up riding the subways all day. He emanates an obstinate collectedness, as though his mind were a series of identical, sealed amphorae perfectly stacked in a ship's hold. He never hurries and never seems to be waiting. His time always seems to be full, even when he is doing nothing.

I sit on a bench behind Spargens' back; Spargens is hunched over the table. His pencil scratches without stopping. He sets the pencil down, tap, and leans back with a slight exhalation through the nose, hands on his kidneys and outcast eyes on the water. In the distance we hear the distracted water sucking the cistern's concrete shell. In total darkness, a row of squat, pale green flames rock like masts on their wicks, and the nearly impalpable breath of the draft knocks them into spasms, doubled in pools of liquid wax. The trance skipping lightly off the water settles easily on the two of us, and stops our minds with a touch, like a thief who paralyzes his victims with the hand of glory.

—◦○○—

I've discovered a defunct ice-making plant. I make my way in through the generous drains. Here it is: the brine tank. The parts are too badly rusted to use, or are missing to begin with, can be replaced — I steal what I need from a waterfront machine shop that services the large river-going boats, and from a warehouse full of plumbing supplies.

Working alone, I cut the tank into sections with a hacksaw and carry each piece down the plant's ramp into the river. Then I drag the sections behind me on my muck sledge along the river's sludgy bottom, using the current and the thickness of the water to help me.

The map (aside): Day and night he is loping back and forth down there, and occasionally drifting off to sleep. When this happens, he bobs stupidly along the bottom like an inebriated manatee.

In the meantime, Spargens has caused a pit to be dug in a clearing in the underground glade. Now and then, I stagger up out of the lake slime and slop out my cargo on the bank, turn and go back for more.

When all the parts are gathered, the tank sections are reassembled in the pit. This not only makes construction easier, but the earth will insulate the tank when it is finished. Cult welders work to close and seal the gaps on one side, while I drive in rivets by hand on the other.

Now the tank is finished and sealed with pitch and rubber, rinsed out and scoured with sand. The refrigeration plant is housed in a trench adjacent to the pit, where teams of workers bolt and seal the pipes and pumps. I've decided we'll substitute ether (I make it myself out of lake mist) for ammonia, which is the usual refrigerant.

The tank is filled with charcoal-filtered lake water and mixed with road salt scavenged by Multiply, Deuteronôme's nephew (the one who nicknames me Ding-A-Ling). The refrigeration equipment is powered by a small methane turbine. I can make any amount of methane from sewer gas, drawn off by my gnomes. Muffling the noise proves to be one of the more demanding problems. Even after damping down all vibration the equipment is still excessively loud. With the help of Dr. Thefarie, and some more scavenging, the moving parts are all packed in an inorganic gelatin, then baffled with regular soundproofing materials. These measures acceptably reduce the noise to a faint whir. The brine temperature is swiftly reduced to just below the freezing point, the water becoming weirdly viscous like a thick, clear soup. Now, with the gnomes, I begin to move the inanimate bodies from their crèches in my sewer atrium.

Here among the branches and drifting lamps, in a silence punctuated by the barely audible creaking of the boughs and the rasp of leaves falling, settling, delicate corpses are suspended like wasps' nests, dappled with shadow and soft, shabby patches of decay. They are stored among the branches until all of them have convened, filling the wood with a musty odor, mixed with the smell of the trees the forest has the scent of an ancient spice cabinet. Incense is wafted over the bodies daily; the censer-bearers move patiently along from trunk to trunk, and tender shoots of smoke slither in the grooves of the bark, coil up in bunches under dully lustrous leaves.

"We must put the bodies in the brine tank."

The music of these words reverberates from one end of the narrative to the other. Down below you, in the sewers, I struggle in the strong, brown current. Pale helpless bodies shrink deeper into the protection of my arms.

The map (aside): He works doggedly, with a kind of protestant strenuousness. Without pause he turns and goes back to the tunnels, drops instantly into the water and is gone, coat flapping out behind him in the current like a ray's wing. He emerges again, a body beneath each arm; the water seems reluctant to release him, dropping from his back like a heavy hood. These are the last.

A wind stirs the wood, the bodies nod dreamily, serene faces dip, fingered by branch shadows. The wind animates hands and feet, and the bodies gesture with a voiceless grace, celestial, fairy tranquility. They are like shafts of sunlight dropping down through the forest canopy, light or dark their skin sheds a mist of light, as though these woods had been invaded by an army of gigantic glow worms, inexplicably locked in sleep.

By sympathy with them, a body has risen to the surface of the earth — a young boy's head and shoulders, and the tips of his fingers before his breast poke out of the soil, his long blonde hair hangs straight from his head's high crown and falls like a curtain across his brow, the tips pressed into his face. His features are slightly flattened, the creases seamed with dirt, and his skin is mottled, like a thickly-clouded sky.

This naked boy is carried with great care to the brine tank; the workers gather to see him, and a few ginger hands timidly caress his cheek, lightly pat his head.

Now all the bodies are in the brine tank, and have already started their slow orbits along its walls. When this boy's body is introduced, however, the others gather at the spot like carp around a morsel of bread. The boy tumbles languidly in among them, the bodies jostle and the boy is touched here and there by a hand, a breast, a foot, a shoulder. Presently, the bodies drift back to their rounds, until they are once again evenly distributed in a ring, languidly circling the empty center of the tank.

—○○—○—

They've found the forest. I am waiting for my train, at the far end of the platform where I can drop the plumb-line of my listening into the tunnels to hear for him. I believe I would know the sound of his shoe on the gravel. There are other things I have to think about but even while I turn away to stand, or hide, by a post, I feel myself still there by the tunnel mouth, turned toward him like a statue.

Suddenly the world is becoming enormous, rushes out to all sides. I feel nostalgia for something new; I'm remembering right now as it happens for the first time the only time. I have a sort of puppet of him in my mind that I can't stop playing with. I do something else, but my mind's hands are still playing with that doll. Bow, jump, kiss my hand. But I always remember he is not there. Some part of him is, though, because I feel it, or I act it out with my body in my mind. Just like an imagined sound, I imagine the sensation of moving like him, as he must move — explode leap flail bound tumble forge blunder pop up. A small ghost version of me is doing all these things on a stage inside; I can feel an outflung hand or foot pass through me from time to time, a little cold streak there where it broke my surface and left ripples. The thought of him keeps starting over, exciting me. I'm wildly excited! I have a static heat in my forearms that almost makes my hands shake, and even more intensely I feel it in my chest in a ball sticking out from my backbone. At random it spreads out to either side along the backs of my lungs, and strokes the backs of my lungs like the walls of a circus tent with a gentle pressure shortening my breath. It's something else, I don't know whether or not I'm suffering but I'm full to the brim with something lighter than water that bulges out of the brim and trembles. Hisses.

He's crazy and he stinks. Where is he? Why isn't he here?

－◦◦━◦━

I kneel by the edge of the tank, whose walls protrude a little more than a foot above the level of the soil, and take hold of the dull brass edge. I shake, my vision goes dark — stumbling away.

I stop. Turning, I look at the tank without seeing it. I make myself return, plant my knees back in the grooves they made. With a moment of lightheadedness, I feel all my vitality running out of me like streams crashing down a rock face. I reach down into myself and close my hand on the throat of my life, throttling it. I feel it blocked. It struggles, pushing against my hand, but I am putting all my fading strength into my hand. Cold comes in, and my vision goes dark again.

How long has it been...

He tilts forward, his eyes dull. He jerks back numbly. A moment later, he tilts again. Tilts a little more, more — then drops face-first into the water, and dies.

I am watching him carefully. Spargens holds the stopwatch and reads out the minutes neutrally.

His body describes a gradual somersault in the water. He floats round face down again, and drifts into the empty center of the tank, just below the surface. Now he mingles with the other bodies. He is brushed by the backs of hands, by stockinged feet, his face slides through locks of hair, brown tresses interlaced with pale ribbons. The hems of dresses, neckties, arms, breasts, heads, and legs, trail nervelessly over him.

Now he can no longer be distinguished from the mass of slack hands, dark forms, moving sluggishly counterclockwise — and vast, dark forms turn round in flags of white cloud, dark cloud, rags of sky, blue black and white, circle around like frost planets in a cold wind

141

above them, unseen. Hands swim past and arms are raised and sink in unreal gestures. A woman in a print dress: her face tips up to the light lips apart, turns in a grand slow swoop of straight, sandy hair, and vanishes in the shadow of a vast black coat.

—o—o—o—

I can't stop these dopey fantasies they're too much fun, I can't resist playing him up like a hero. *Coming* to the rescue, arrayed in hope and power oh boy — he's crazy and fearless and powerful, and strong and light and silly — smelly I mean — like a fierce skunk or a wombat or something — I'm smiling — but he's charging in out of nowhere, blast our enemies crashing into them like a bowling ball hitting the pins like go man go mow 'em down! Punch them to pieces and explode them like a hurricane, piss-peddling assholes! With their fucking *armbands* my God! I change into him and sail out into the mass of them like an eggbeater churning up the batter, getting lighter and sillier I whip their bone heads laughing fantastically until they're scurrying everywhere in total dismay, lashing out thoughtlessly in all directions and hitting everybody but me can't catch me! Hee hee hee! Can't catch me! Whose voice?

Come catch me!

—o—o—o—

When Spargens reads "ten" I extend my boat hook and snag him, by the back of his coat. The momentum of his body pulls my arms straight, and I stumble along the edge of the tank tugging repeatedly at the handle, steering him to the surface and toward the edge. Spargens and a few others grab fistfuls of material, an arm or a leg, and clumsily drag the body out. I untangle the hook and kneel beside him, chafing the hands and slapping the face, which is frigid and stiff as bog leather. I draw down his chin, exposing the pale teeth and criss-crossing black laces between his lips, take up a pinch of black soil and rub it around his mouth and eyes, and under his nose. A strangling sound, like marbles rattling in the maze of his bronchial tubes. Ejaculations clotted with gelatinous water belch from his chest, and as his eyes roll a streak of light is stitched a moment into the darkness overhead, below the ceiling.

Shooting star over the park, where the wind kneads the black crinoline of the trees. This young woman with straight sandy hair, large green eyes, a straight severe nose and tapering chin is Audrey. She's got on a white dress with straps and a string of pearls that get caught in the stark hollow of her throat. In a white dress that makes her pale skin seem darker than it is, and in white canvas tennis shoes. She walks up the slope swinging her arms fluttering her small hands. Meteor shoots above wind-tousseled trees gnaw the air, above them on the hill appear the dark angles of the weather station. It looks like an otherworldly ship anchored on foliage waves, it takes part in the serene immobility of the starry sky and the frothy craziness of the rustling trees, hanging above the porous ground that sways beneath her feet and seems to want to subside. Reach up and smear the stars around they are wet and sticky like daubs of liquid candy and they trail long tacky filaments. Stars gleam through the foliage making tiny points of illuminated green, stars hovering just above the horizon, stars beneath the level of her head... she drops her eyes to the stars.

It's a delicious feeling to leave the party, and imagine yourself missed, the mystery you've created simply by leaving for a minute, the sense of freedom and irony. Now she has found a fairy ring of cold-boiling trees, the sliding spiced leer of wind hiss in the grass, all elements of a spell that gazes down at her from pointed gables. Audrey looks up again and sees the tenebrous foundations massive forbidden and abandoned — that's just what she wants. The windows are grey screens... now she spots a wan, phosphorescent thing at a high window and draws her breath sharply bolted to the ground. Stock still, a glowing figure is looking down at her. Its glow is reflected in the thick varnish on the sill. She clutches herself, feeling a detestable weakness in her knees run down into her calves. The face has huge dark eyes.

Wind rises, leaves pluck at the air. It's a statue it's not a statue — it is gazing yearningly at her. Without thinking, Audrey runs and hides behind the nearest tree. She looks out — the window is edge-on, but the wan glow is still there, like a stationary mist just emerging from the pane.

A voice calls her name, coming from below. Should she show them — no, it might still be there... They might want to I don't know "investigate." She edges out from her hiding place, breathing through her mouth.

The figure is still at the window. She can feel its gaze, imploring her with a weak magnetic adhesiveness. The voice calls again. It repeats her name with evil persistence, and she knows they will climb all the way up after her now. She goes back to the tree she hid behind and makes her way down from there, where she can't feel the watching. Once she glances up and, through the leaves it is still there at the window — she has come round into view again on her way down. A remote, glowing shape. Now, does it waver? Or are the leaves interfering? The voice calls nearby and she sings out with weird gaiety. She won't say anything to anyone — she'll never breathe a word of it to anyone.

In the room under the eaves, a crown of stars ascends to the rafters. The lights gutter out against dry wood and webs.

CHAPTER SIX

The map, and the eight coffins it represents, explains: May is a good month for visions, particularly at dawn and dusk. This May has been gloomy, the trees ripen and their branches bend with fresh leaves so green they're almost black beneath grey skies of distributed sun. Now behind the grey the big star drops behind the horizon leaving a glistening blue snail track of light.

I have to cover a distance of a few blocks to get from this station to the park. In odor — order, sorry — to avoid being seen I have developed a truly inspired methodologically diachronic system of hand gestures to screen myself from light contamination; for example, I might thrust my thumb down behind my curling fingers, or squeeze the tip of it between my knuckles (the classic "fig" gesture, voids the effects of the evil eye), with the idea that this gesture, acting as a will-triggering instance, will help to focus my mind and thus screen me from headlights, street lamps, and any other variety of directed, probing light. The armbanders especially favor — they all have cars — favor the most intense headlights they can find as a counterfeit for power.

Under these evil lights there is sleep without repose, without rest, unquiet, broken, harassed. The opposite of holy ground — waste ground: despair's grey, littered ground against the green. Puddles sliding in the wind, color of weak milky tea: the wind has whipped it into a fine yellow froth at the edges. The soil in the park is fudgy tar paste. Two hawks come up in slow procession, nearly motionless in the sluicing wind. They proceed in jerks and flows and adjustments, seesaw describing invisible U U U in the air. They are like two disembodied eyes, and make their way stately and unhurried off to the west toward the water. The rainwater soaking my clothes is insulating me, the dirt suspended in this water, too — I slept and my long furry sleeves down over my fingers trailed in puddles. There's grit on my cheek, and crunching inside my shoes.

The soil is a huge chemical battery. People misuse these telluric forces. They're not so integral as they seem; being mostly water they reflect their surroundings — stand out in a field long enough and your mind will go blank — long enough and the person you were might vanish altogether and someone else will come out of the field. A lighter, leaner, alien, in a mature dream body—

I dreamt I sat in a bungalow classroom, looked up to the windows set along the top of the wall in time to see the roof of the adjacent building silently peel off in the wind. It is torn off all in one piece and undulates away like a flying carpet shedding slates. I am in a basement draped in black — an elaborate puzzle here... There's an altar and an aisle lined with upturned plastic paint buckets. Fixed in the ceiling above each bucket is a bizarre heavy metal appliance, a solid, round fan in a thick carapace pitted with regularly-spaced holes and a three-way switch on the bottom — all as solidly made as some kind of military hardware or sewing machines. In between these fans, coffee cans hang straight down from the ceiling on strings. I climb up on one of the buckets and fiddle with a fan switch — a menacing, far away voice speaks faintly, a theatrical voice unrelated to this scene — are these speakers? I feel a threat, trouble if I can't figure this out; from one of the cans I extract a pamphlet that says: "*CHOCO MARC — DO NOT TOUCH*"... I think it means something backwards but can't get past CRAM — cram what? Where do I cram it?

I'm scanning through a little diner, counter, booths, red and white checkered cloths, all empty. One shadowy booth in the corner — as I zoom in, I see a horrible godlike face glow there. It melts, and I know I am lying somewhere dreaming; I feel myself aping the melting face with grimaces that pull my features down and elongate them. I feel loss — the foreboding that someone will die, the fear that someone will die, and leave me forever. Alone I will be dead as well.

I make my way to the park. Who will die? Did I know that face? The question becomes too heavy to hold and I let it drop. I watch the wind stir the trees with pain, unbearably beautiful. I live again in the relish I feel for this longing; in the consolation of knowing I am able to feel this sweet light tactful sadness.

He's there at the window, staring out. Something's wrong — he doesn't acknowledge me as I approach. I blunder upstairs quickly. He stands at one side of the window immobilized with an erection, his whole body almost imperceptibly swollen and trembling. His semen has splattered the wall below the window sill and congealed into an acute waxy triangle that sprouts vanes like mangrove roots near the floor. I cross swiftly to him and lay my hand on his arm, hanging like the other straight at his side. It buzzes under my hand and his spine begins to buck, nectar — his semen is a translucent green, like pale lime jelly — spurts onto the wall. His body limpens and I get around behind him putting my arms under his and drag him toward the bed. His feet seem to peel away from the floor. He comes three times before I get him onto the bed, just from being touched, and starts to whimper.

Now he turns and kisses me — I can see his face from the inside, like a wall with two enormous skylights. I draw near to the lights and look out, the vision focussing like a kaleidoscope I see the park blazing with greens and browns, each glint on the surface of the stream hits me like a savage kick, and deep down below me I can feel his yearning like a drum so deep it's more palpable than audible. He has hawk eyes, zooming in on a couple here, or a solitary there — their incandescent pinks reds browns, flossy hair, all buttered by the sun, unbearably inviting. I feel how he longs to touch living flesh, marvelling at its tenderness, and I realize our mistake in not making him of tissue. He is miserable in intolerable rigidity of this mineral body, flexible as it is. I was stupid — I built him entirely out of the cycle. If we'd made him from tissue, he would have grown, matured, and withered, as he should have. The mineral cycle is far vaster in time by many orders of magnitude. Immortally dying to yield, to be soft...

Tiny white petals blown off the trees drift by on the air like snow; he is homing in on a squirrel, the soft glistening gems of its black eyes, the feathery tail... he aches for the trees, the grass, the wind, the clouds. Now I'm seeing a memory of last night — a woman...

Helpless agony in his desire is like white-hot gusts of wind inside, crushing yelps of pain out of him to vibrate within the barrier of his paralyzed lips. The swell of those gusts lifts me right out of his mind.

With Hulferde dead he has no place to send all this power, and Pearl just swells up with it like an unbreakable bladder.

I stand, looking down at him. I bend over him, my jaw in my fingers, lift first one leg into the air, then the other, and float over him, peering down. I stand again.

"Hang in there," I tell him. "I'll think of something."

The sound of my voice is enough to set him off again — maybe he felt the vibrations.

I get the electric connection down beneath my solar plexus — "Ah I got just the thing—" snapping my fingers, gradually turning into a human cartoon.

He slaps his chest with his palm and in a wildly exaggerated Baltic accent gurgles "Me fix good!"

—o○o—

"Why did I show you the *Phaedrus*?"

"I don't know yet."

The train plummets through the dark with a fantastic racket from the open transoms, the fluorescents wink out sluggishly rekindle and wink out again. Ptarmagant is fitfully outlined by lozenges of tunnel light cookie-cut by the windows. When the lights come back on, both of us are gone.

During my time in the brine tank, I saw many images streak by like subway stations. Huge boa constrictors raise miniature effigies of Cretan priestesses in their mouths... the full-size, living priestesses sit on the constrictors' heads like bar stools, their skirts draped louche over one massive serpent eye, and the snakes raise them slowly up to the fluorescent lights. And then I saw Ptarmagant, and inside him a tumor growing like an angry plum. I took this to Dr. Thefarie, who questioned me closely on the appearance of the tumor and concluded, "I believe you have seen something."

He makes preparations for a procedure, requesting my assistance.

While working out his plans a new idea occurs to him — Dr. Thefarie explains that, under his supervision, a number of exploratory surgeries were conducted on the city itself in search of any organic structure which might represent the condensation of urban thoughts into tissue, like an "urban nerve yeast." Of the many samples returned — which included a table-sized burgundy-colored organ whose function could not be determined, and what appeared to be something approximating an opaque and useless eye — there was a scoop of nerve matter about the size and shape of an ear of corn. This tissue had mysterious properties: while it contained no acid, weak acids would spontaneously condense on any exposed surface in its vicinity; it also seemed to drain all the current out of any electronic device within a certain distance of it.

"We could take advantage of the operation to graft some of this nerve material onto him," Dr. Thefarie says. "I have carried out some experiments into relations between the activity of the nervous system and cancer, and I think that perhaps the presence of this nerve material could promote remission."

Ptarmagant is agreeable.

The operation: Ptarmagant sits on a metal chair with a cracked vinyl seat, the arms bent out at an angle to accommodate his bulk, and leans forward resting his upper chest head and arms on the table fixed to the floor. A sheet is thrown about him, beneath which his shirt is removed. In the train operator's booth, Spargens is perspiring at the controls, eating on a candy bar. Someone had evidently thought it would be fun to hang glow-in-the-dark stars and planets from the ceiling on lengths of dental floss. Astral goblins stroking ghost-lightning combs over my pain centers Ptarmagant doesn't want to be put under, but Dr. Thefarie insists, saying Ptarmagant must not only be unconscious but dreaming. Warren with his speakers rocks and bellows at the top of his lungs, and he's brought along his friend Jeremy, a fattish rumpled man with a head like a steaming pink snowball, fumes of flyaway white hair rising from his bald pate. As Warren rocks, his feet pump a broad sewing-machine treadle which in turn sets prayer wheels whirring all throughout the car. Negative charge from the wires creates a field; enter it and you experience a sudden coolness and pressure drop below the waist as though you'd just been cut loose from a corset. Slight lightheadedness goes with the feeling; I etherize Ptarmagant. The field will promote dream sleep. Another associate, a wiry little man named Schwips, adjusts the lights.

The train rolls smoothly into darkened tunnels on the abandoned line. Dr. Thefarie makes the incision along a t-square. He deftly removes the tumor, places it in a trash bag, snaps his fingers, and Schwips goes to retrieve the sample of nerve material from a battered steel icebox. With tongs, he extracts a steaming copper ciborium from a cloud of friedel-crafts reactions and frost stinking of corrupted batteries and chlorine. Blinking tears from his eyes, Schwips proffers the ciborium; the Great Lover unscrews its frozen top leaving some of the skin from his fingertips on the metal; using padded forceps Dr. Thefarie extracts a length of translucent tissue like clear ice sparkling with tiny white motes. Inside it there is a delicate, cone-shaped structure of mercury filaments. With a single deft jab of the scalpel, Dr. Thefarie nicks the sample and opens a minute pathway to the spine, aligns the material, then pulls the incision closed over the sample.

I lean over the wound, part my jaws and a harsh buzz thrums out. The stitches pull loose from my lips and bind Ptarmagant's wound closed. When I stand up, and my shadow falls away from his body, it takes the incision away with it. The skin is smooth and whole once more.

—○○○—

They didn't invite me, but I had to be there. The door to the conductor's compartment raps against the wall, and as I draw near I can feel no heat, none of the small perturbations of the air that mean a person is near. I slip into the compartment and sit on the seat that folds out from the wall. Behind me the window is open. My father is already coming round, talking faintly with Spargens, Schwips and a few others... him too — I knew he was there, hell I smelt him.

He's speaking now. I hold the seat with both hands between my knees and listen through the racket of the wheels to his voice — the words are lost, but I can hear the tone rise and fall. I let my head drop back.

Why doesn't he talk to me?

The train plunges into one of the tunnels — I can smell we're below the river — and the sudden change in pressure hits the car with a thud. I feel my hair fly up around my head. My eyelashes beat against my bangs. Out in the dark, his voice is taking shape — a huge, squat form, like a big tiki. It has horns on top, and the head sits right on the broad shoulders. The brows are bunched up like burlap bags, and intense, concentrated heat comes from the blowtorches of his pupils. There are deep creases descending from the eyes over the cheeks, which gather on either side of the nose. The nostrils are flared out like two bells, and now the mouth, with a broad flat ring of lip, snarling, shaped like a figure eight on its side. Crackling flames whirr behind the triangular jack-o-lantern teeth. Warm syrup bathes my heart. I float in front of him.

Those teeth are like fence pickets. I touch the oily lapels and collar. Their grit clings to my palms like wet sand. I throw my arms around his neck — it's so thick my hands don't meet... I climb up onto him and press against his unyielding surface, with my cheek to the pebbly pig-iron of his bulging, bull-like neck.

(Vera's arms rise in the air like someone who is being hypnotized.)

Now it's turning into skin, the metal is changing, and begins to yield. It softens — it yields. The statue is turning its face to me, turning into a human being.

(Vera is deep in her imagination. An envelope of pleasure, invisible and shining, closes like mail around her as they lace together; there are fragrant, placid lips within reach of hers that seek out her kiss with delicious unhurriedness. They are reclining together onto yielding space. It spins faster and faster, their bodies become pale streaks then blur together and levitate a vibrating pale band of light, a human ring springs up and hovers in space.)

—◦—◦—

Ptarmagant recovers in a hammock at the back of the car. "Composite ghost," he mutters, sweat rolling down his huge face, "composite ghosts we must put together as we put together the bodies — spirits stitched together with ectoplasmic sutures, the distilled essence of the mad testament.

"A black box and a white box roll toward each other in a groove along the tree-lined horizon. Above them the sky rises dark grey like an infinitely high wall. My coat opens, the beetle flies up and carries me with it, blue consul he of the sedge and the bee."

Dr. Thefarie glances at me — "Are you paying attention? He may say something important."

Ptarmagant turns his head and his eyes focus slowly on me.

"Given the proper conditions, life could arise spontaneously again, as it did at first. Nothing prevents this. It could happen here in the tunnels, or anywhere. New, unevolved organisms, living by wholly other principles, perhaps not even recognizably alive to us. The first organisms on earth were fermenters. They were superseded by the respirators. Nothing prevents the development of some new way..." His breath drops out of him in a puff, and he slumps back exhausted.

His body stiffens and his teeth clench in his quivering face. The spasm passes. He begins muttering again.

"All gods are local: you can't bring Allah to the Maine Woods and you can't bring New England Transcendentalism to the Sahara Desert — the extension cord will not reach... It must have different names and practices, and be known to no one altogether." As Ptarmagant speaks calcium dust siphons from the upright spines of books shelved on subway seats.

"It calls to many... it has already called you." Ptarmagant reaches out and touches my cheek, caked in dried sewage like fossil impressions of ferns. In a hermetically sealed station, cobwebs flutter in a breeze from where?

"The subway is a maze of the names one must know and speak, like the passages in the Egyptian Book of the Dead. The shapeless knot of its interlacing tunnels... it's not a hieroglyph, it's an instrument on which a skilled practitioner can play an infinite variety of improvisations. A puzzle has only one answer... it is only its answer's elliptical name... but the hieroglyph of the tunnel map has many equally valid solutions. Why did I need to show you that portion of the *Phaedrus*?

"...The sun's locust light is always light and so provides for our physical needs, but what is in shadow is invisible to the sun. But what our spirits need is light out of darkness, the unknown name of the law."

Ptarmagant pointing implacably to that dark place adamantly demanding that the light break there: "The light that shines so that you — you, the frightened, the confused — you, the cowering and the weak, suddenly become — you, the certain, the true, the adamant, the strong, the implacable, the calm. And now the monsters are cowering, recoiling, retreating, their faces blanched with terror, their eyes smarting with shame in the glare of that terrible, serene light.

"I am a voice, not words, I am the voice—" Ptarmagant struggles to rise, "when Autumn inundates the land with holy death and time... regeneration... There is power in my body, there is power in my mind." He faints.

—◦◦—◦—

This is John Brade the informer, sitting alone at the back of the car in the forward-facing seat by the door. He looks at his reflection in the black water of the tunnel, without really seeing himself. A lean, lightly-built young man with slender shoulders and fine metallic blonde hair cut short. He has calflike eyes getting a little puffy beneath, and a prim, unhappy mouth. Youth mixes with exhaustion in his face, his body seeps disappointments and sadness. Invisibly marked out for misfortune, bad luck has dogged him all his life. Last year, he agreed to let a friend store a box full of stuff in his apartment — six weeks later the police came, opened the box, and found a bag of heroin in it. Brade spent a week in jail and ratted out his friend, who shot himself when the police went to get him. He lost his job after his arrest, and so on. Eventually he hit bottom in the subway, and Ptarmagant's people recruited him.

But the police remember him, they have something on him, and lately he thinks they've been looking for him... They liked his first song so much they want to hear him sing again. Well John your luck is about to turn even worse.

The lights dim and wink on again, and a shocking face is there beside his in the window, a hand closes gently but firmly on his right bicep, and another rests with deliberate lightness on his left shoulder.

"Hello, John," says the unctuous voice in his ear. Brade's head swivels and he locks eyes at once with me.

"Now pay close attention to what I am about to tell you, John. Concentrate... *concentrate*..."

—◦—◦—

"Right in there," I tell him. "Just your own private sex candy machine every man's dreeem."

Brade turns his eyes slowly to me.

I thump him lightly on the back.

"Go get 'im tiger."

I shut the door behind him jam a huge cartoon key in the lock and rattle it round and round a few dozen times.

...In a trance, Brade takes the dim room in. It gathers around him like folding felt. The windows are smoking white, like panels of new snow, and a beautiful nude white figure stands in their light, turned nearly sideways to him.

Brade floats across to the statue. Outside the window there are black branches and other dark shapes quilted into the glare. The statue is of a lovely young man with an erection. The body is fashioned from a marble so fine it seems like living tissue, with veins deep in its translucence. The light throws the texture into faint relief, and Brade runs his hand along the upper arm.

It's soft — it yields — the statue shudders, sighs. It orgasms and turns its frighteningly beautiful face toward him, it looks dreamily at him — Brade feels himself turn to mist — the gemlike mouth is like a fountain — their bodies lace together.

I listen at the door. All's well.

—o◦o—

Deuteronôme has a pronounced interest in any means of automating worship. I help him set up a sound booth by the lake. When he joined Ptarmagant, cultists were compelled to flash signals from station to station by cupping their hands over the signal lights and flicking them in code. His nephew, Multiply, brought in his skater friends to help run messages, and they still perform this service, hitching on to the backs of the trains and riding on one rail. But Deuteronôme's underground radio is working, tunnel air whirrs and cultists call to each other in detuned shortwave voices. Transmission of information is only one function of the radio system — it also keeps the cult's word in physical circulation at all times.

(Yeah I can pick 'em. He emerged from the love nest three hours later, looking frail, as though he were projected on a cloud. As I shut the door behind him he glances sidelong at me uncertain and shying my God just like a calf.)

Spargens, who has taken up residence in the shack by the lake, had the idea to burn prayers onto adhesive plastic seals, and then paste them onto the wheels of the subway cars. Dark, limber arms reach out from beneath the platforms toward the wheels as the car stops to take on passengers. So they become prayer wheels churning out an invocation with each revolution.

("Now John let's keep a lid on this good thing huh?" I lock my pinky finger round his. "Promise?" His head droops a little, finally he manages to nod once. I squeeze his shoulder. "Go on home," I say into his eyes. "Take a shower. You live with anyone?" — "No," he whispers hollowly. "That's fine. Take a shower, dress, sit down somewhere comfortably, and count to three. When you count three, you will awaken refreshed my fine friend.")

Everywhere in the system now there is a strange, galvanic charge that tickles the heart as you board the train or pass through the turnstile, like it's the last day of school. Commuters note with alarm figures leaping about a small bonfire on the far side of an underground switching yard, the smoke comes boiling along the low ceilings toward them like an angry black upside-down flood.

(I remove my hand from his shoulder and my eyes peer from his eyes and he staggers away. "Oh and John, around noon tomorrow, all right? Are you busy?" Tomorrow's Sunday, he shouldn't be.)

A man clutches his chest and slumps against the wall — we scoot up observing him closely. Schwips explains to me — "We use these pains as a divination tool." The man is one of ours, wearing a black tshirt with I Ching hexes on the left breast. He points to the source of the pain and his finger hits a hex which is then decoded.

"He's what you call a 'prophetopath.' He gets a series of injuries that spell out the message."

"That's something weird," someone says.

"Happens to everybody," Schwips says matter-of-factly. "He's just got an acute case. Like once I was going to go confront a man I discovered was — carrying on with my wife. I planned it out, went to bed. The next morning I woke up with a sprained ankle, just like that."

He snaps his fingers.

"You must have kicked the wall," Multiply says.

"And sprained my ankle without waking up? I don't—"

"You slept on it wrong—" someone else says.

"I'm telling you, no. It simply happened, and so I didn't go."

"And what happened?"

"Well, nothing conclusive," Schwips sighs. "It's not as though the building burned down around him — but I've never doubted it was better I didn't go... Envision a world in which events are shaped by nothing more than judiciously planned accidents and injuries and illnesses, as agents acting on foresight intervene to prevent certain future events by incapacitating those responsible..."

(He's gone — I look in on Pearl. He's lying there in the tousled bed, looking like a corpse his smile a corpse's smile.)

Sacrifices? The Great Lover is informed that most available livestock are not satisfactory for the purposes of sacrifice. They have been so long domesticated that their souls are no longer of good quality. Vermin may only be sacrificed by the diabolic divisions, who favor rat sacrifices, and break the spines of pigeons slowly and thoroughly.

In all manner of closed spaces you see the dormant shrines, the switching boxes transformed by steady, undetectable steps into idols. Their jewelled eyes are somber under corrugated iron lids, their look drops heavily on drooping fronds of thick incense oozing from a brazier made of thick bronze, sinking to the streaked and cracked paving. Dainty little girls with ribbons in their hair carry baskets of gaily-painted easter skulls, sealed with clear varnish, to be hidden in the shade in the bowers of the underground forest, where calm graceful cadavers dance with their knives and hang from the clean boughs of trees. From these skulls will hatch helper spirits known as "sweet minds."

Things are getting good and strange these days. I take the tunnel beneath the river, honeycombed with new brick cells containing a votary pouring out his daily invocations. Prayer wheels and flags rattle in the cloying under-river air. I inspect a new tunnel under construction. Schwips used to be a civil engineer; a persistent foe of automobile traffic, he was fired for sabotaging a plan to expand certain streets. He supervises work on the new tunnel, which is itself a huge prayer, summoning and creating the new divinity. Cultists pick and hammer feverishly at solid rock; their bodies steaming and slick with perspiration they work fall back and drop to the floor exhausted like John Henry.

Standing water between the tracks suddenly erupts in rolling, boiling spurts; steam rises past the platform edge weirdly coiling itself into a cylindrical funnel above a churning slough of cooking offal and screaming parboiled rats. Cultists in the vicinity drop to their knees and bow their heads — not exactly in veneration; they are pressing down on the ground with their hands as though working a bellows. They are helping, coaxing, straining to bring something into existence — this is labor, not submission.

-o-o-o-

A small group of red-band students is rallying on the opposite side of the lake.

"What happened to Z?" Spargens asks.

Ptarmagant is livid. His skeleton almost burns, like a filament, inside his voluminous, soft body.

"A group of them caught him in the park last night," he says his voice trembling, his eyes turned toward the other side of the lake. They are chanting over there and waving signs, accosting bypassers.

"I've done what I can for him," I tell Spargens.

"Will he live?"

"I don't know," I sigh.

Ptarmagant turns his eyes to our Holy Cartoon, who is standing off to one side. I didn't see him come. The whites of Ptarmagant's eyes shine through his sunglasses.

"Call the demon."

The Great Lover looks at Ptarmagant a little askance, quizzing him, then turns aside his back to us. He bends forward and lowers his head like a bull. His head begins to bob up and down, his feet begin to stamp the ground, his body filling up with rhythm. Rhythm is a magical thing; it's not the same thing over and over again, but a single moment that continually renews itself, more and more new, growing ever stronger. He turns to Ptarmagant and we all inadvertently recoil from the fierceness in his leer-toothed and glare-eyed face.

Ptarmagant points across the lake his eyes on the demon.

"Punish them!"

The demon laughs like a very young child, grunting his breath out through his throat in a sound with no shape.

Vera thinks it sounds like wet cardboard being ripped.

Instantly he lopes off toward the students, following the edge of the lake. His feet sink in the mud halfway up to his knees but this doesn't slow him.

He's up the slope on the far side and erupts into them knocking them down, picking them up and throwing them, swatting and roaring like a bear. Shouts of alarm and surprise come to us across the lake — now they are angry.

"What's happening!?" Vera calls.

One of them is trying to box with him, throwing punches. A couple have gotten behind him — they have him, they pin his arms — the boxer punches him in the face, breaking his glasses. He punches again but the demon is still struggling, still grinning, the others can hardly hold him — the boxer punches again and the demon catches his fist between his teeth, bites down and waggles his head furiously like a dog attacking a rag. The boxer screams and is dragged slightly forward. The demon opens his mouth and kicks him in the stomach with such force we can hear it all the way over here. The boxer drops, doubled over, onto his face. The demon lunges backward and turns, throwing off one of the two men.

"He has a knife!" I shout as I see it. I turn as I say this toward Vera, telling her in particular, and she shouts with such an immense voice that it makes my ears ring like a clap of thunder. Her body twisted like a whip as she shouted, and across the lake all of them jerk at once, startled, looking like a clump of grass momentarily knocked flat by a gust of wind.

The demon does not start with the rest of them, but he gets out of the knife's way.

"You saved him!"

He flails, trying to shake the man who holds him. The other closes with his knife held low, ready to thrust. The demon suddenly stretches out his neck and jabs the fingers of one immobilized hand deep into his mouth with a swift decisive motion. The man behind him wrestles him sideways and the other darts in with the knife the demon vomits in his face and he drops the knife, staggering backward clawing at eyes full of stomach acid. The demon slips sideways letting his weight drag the other down, gets a hand free drops it to the nearest stone and smacks the man's forehead with it.

The man who had been holding him is a big, square-built blonde in a rugby shirt. He is doubled over, hands on head, retreating sideways. The demon seizes him by the back of his shirt and swings him to and fro through the air giggling like a demented clown.

"Ee hee hee hee! Hoo hoo hoo hoo!"

He swings him back and forth gathering momentum and launches him out over the water. He strikes the surface flat on his belly with a percussive splat, and thrashes there.

"Come back! Come back!" Ptarmagant is shouting, and we all join him. The demon looks at us through the faint haze. Armbands lie all around him.

—oo—o—

The Great Lover's three thousand and first: a statuesque Russian woman with a weary, slightly put-upon look. Her dream heaves with dark water, white-tufted ocean on all sides and in all directions but up, an impenetrable canopy like treetops of faceted water. Black clouds are overhead, exposing a ragged strip of sulfur-colored sky at the horizon; snow falls in scalding flakes that burst in plumes of steam on contact with the water, people walking down the street in remote cities acquire thick coatings of pyroclastic snow and trail hot vapor behind them.

Lights bob with the waves. Boats gather here out of sight of all land for hundreds of miles. The mountains are under the sea, present but hidden in the forest of the ocean. The boats maneuver gingerly up alongside each other and are carefully linked together, forming a chain-hinged floating platform. There's an atmosphere of quiet festivity, pockets of laughter, pockets of amativeness. An elongated, dark-skinned man is tenderly kissing an asian woman dressed like pierrot for goodness' sake.

I enter, sailing in alone on the deck of a decrepit black knorr, scalps hanging morosely from the scuppers or whatever they're called. I'm some king (this is a state occasion). On my arms and legs there are shackles fettering me to my battered wooden throne on long dirty chains. My boat sits low in the water, so I must clamber up the side of the Queen's vessel to join the party. I'm wearing shapeless black garments of fine material coarsely woven, a heavy iron ring on my left hand, and a heavy crown.

A voice announces my arrival as I heave myself up.

"The King of the Ogres!"

Fine, fine. Dragging my throne behind me, I get over the rail and haul it up onto the deck by the chains.

There's a gold and orange light of torches here, gorgeous against the clear cold grey-blue air and green and black of the ocean. Musicians and courtiers bow and spring out of my way as I crash the length of the ship to the quarterdeck. The Queen sits there — my throne catches on something and in frustration I whip it loose and turn back to her — she is a Russian-looking woman who passed near to me yesterday, and whose dense dream power tugged fiercely at me as she went by. I felt it hit me like two boxcars linking up, hopeless to resist. Now she is sitting above me with a peacock's tail spreading behind her.

She holds out her hand to me. The scepter she keeps crooked in her elbow, but the hand she holds out to me holds the orb, made of a single piece of quartz... I see white fuzz on it — ice. A globe of ice in her hand. She puts it up in front of a lamp, and lets me see the flame through the ice. She takes a feather from her tail and dips it in fire, running it again and again through the flame. When she takes it out, it's all white.

Holding my hand, she leads me into a dark room. I'm suddenly afraid — I don't want to go into this room. She strikes a small light and gives it to me, pointing.

"You want to see..."

"Don't make me!" I know there is something right behind me I don't want to see.

Reluctantly I take the light and turn around. There is someone under a sheet there on the floor, smelling a little. It's death. The little room is death.

I turn back to her. The light washes over her bloodless face and she screams raising her hand, as though in revealing death some particle of death had adhered to the light and is transferred to her with the shining of the light. I drop the light and catch her just outside the door — she looks at me in a sort of fury, her mouth open and the pallor of her face makes the red of her gums intense like rubies.

—o—o—

Now, according to the map, the woods are silent. The water in the lake heaves against its banks without a sound. Among the branches, one can hear the rap of wings, and a musty scum smell like a duck pond. I am going back to check the brine tank. I look up and see wings without birds trading one limb for another in whirring explosions among the branches. A grey wing spins in and out of a patch of light like a throwing knife. The wood is seething with wings that scuttle and cling to rusks of dry bark, unfold and collapse like lungs half in the shadows.

When I reach the brine tank I am already half dead, my body is silting up from the inside out and my head is painfully light. I kneel there — I have to go into the tank, it's the only way to save myself. I struggle against my own decision; I have to take my struggling life in my hand and crush it, like crushing a baby animal. My eyes are going dull, I can feel a clear grey cold into me, far away I hear the splash.

There are the dim shadows in the lights of the coffins which glow like cells in a honeycomb held up to the light, each dead occupant alone in his blazing wooden house. Eight smudged faces. Their decomposition dreams, and in their sleep the voices of the coffins voicelessly say, "there is only one story and now we are going to tell it again..." The words of the story are pressing for some outlet with anguish of unrequited love of these words for this moment... and you sit there, without even understanding how cruel you are, how you are keeping them apart by remaining silent, when you would have only to open your mouth and ears to bring them together. A composite voice groans from vocal chords choked with mold hacks from static jaws and amber teeth, a rank breath fumes from split and blackened mouths metered but unshaped words.

Charred black leaves spill against the stark brick corner of the vault. They batter against the wall, rise up, fly round in a circle, and swing down again; a sign — Spargens is watching. The black vault is growing cold.

I see a desert, covered with stationary black clouds. A breeze stirs up the dust sends a pang of longing through me, that black air, blended water and wind. Now I see: the clouds are made of swords and wings. The air of cold, yelping flames. Like wires these lines spread round the vortexes making a golden fingerprint like a wood knot, braided shining fibres patched with dust and brown threads in parallel curves and strokes, apostrophe marks like rabbit tracks, like black seeds thrown into the shit of the wind.

Fractured wings stampede down the black rain-clotted sky and power rises from the mountains, the horizon, the grave-clotted ground fertile and stinking. The flirting of the air tells me I'm underground. I crouch and put my palms beside my feet, reach out touch rock and loose stones. I take one and toss it; sound of rock on rock — the same all round. I wet a finger: the air comes from somewhere ahead. I creep forward, feeling my way.

Now I get a sense of space opening on all sides; a continuous rushing ahead. A light emerges from the ground; a lean-faced woman I've never seen before — sunken cheeks and hollow eyes, dark hair, dark dress of shiny material to the ground, massy bronze candelabra perfectly still in her upraised right hand. The ground under her feet is powdery, like ash, loose and filled with small stones. Now by the light I see she has come out of a groove in the rock.

She stops and turns, a gorge open at her feet. Looking around, craning her neck and pivoting her head, she is searching for something. She has deep, triangular eyes; they train themselves on me directly, and she motions to me. Without waiting, she turns and continues along the path which clings to the edge of the gorge. I follow at a distance, and the rushing sound grows a little louder — the sound of a waterfall. The woman comes to a spur of rock and stands there precariously, gesturing beyond her.

There, past the point where the gorge forks into two jagged cracks hundreds of yards across, is a phosphorescent city, spread out like so many toy blocks on a bare plateau. There are no lights, but the buildings are all made of soft-looking stone that sheds a dreamy blue-white glow like reradiated moonlight. The city is bordered on the far side by a continuous sheet of plummeting water that must be miles wide, a gargantuan waterfall that drops in a transparent, unbroken curtain out of the gloom above and down into a chasm below. The chasm is broader than the city, and evidently so deep that the water strikes bottom only long after it vanishes from sight. Despite their astounding size, the falls are awesomely silent.

A colossal woman's face has been carved into the soft phosphorescent stone of the bluff behind the falls. Its contours flicker through the screen of water — a dreaming, unfamiliar face, a little uptilted and twice the size of the city. Her eyes are closed, an almost wide mouth the lips softly compressed and nearly smiling in sleep. Her face I've never seen before, I say it to myself again and again to fight a persistent feeling that I have, I have seen it before.

...Cinders are blowing everywhere, a racket like the snapping of flames bristles from the forest. It grows, the noise gathering to a roar like an invisible avalanche. Spargens walks over and gives me a long searching look.

"Let's get him out of there."

We run to the tank. I take up my hook and almost immediately I have him. With Spargens, I draw him from the freezing water, enormous tears blazing with gold dust spill from his eyes. We pull him to the shack and the noise in the forest grows.

"What is that?"

"I don't know."

I try to revive him. As he begins to cough, the lights all go out at once and wind flaps wildly at us in all directions — from where?

"Is the roof caving in?"

"I don't believe it!"

The trees are groaning like ship timbers in a storm. Suddenly he sits up and seizes our arms. Though I can't really see him, I can tell by his attitude that he is straining to see or hear something in the dark.

"What is it?"

There is something rolling around in the distance, back and forth along the far wall by the opposite side of the lake. It is circling round and round back there, where no one is — a huge thing, I imagine like a little planet, struggling in the cavern like a fly trapped in a glass.

Suddenly there is a bellow and wings come from all the trees with a noise like a terrible hailstorm. We are huddled together in the dark, beneath the flimsy roof of the shack, feeling the wings in the air. Their flapping seems to make the air lighter, like what I imagine a tornado must do — I feel the air being sucked from my lungs.

A blinding flash and for a moment I can see a cyclone of wings. A thunderclap seems to blast right on top of us and sets my ears ringing, and the ground shakes with its rumbling — thunder and lightning inside the room. My patient turns to me and shouts something at me.

"We have to get out! We have to get out! We have to seal them in behind us!"

Another burst of light shows the wings diving into the brine tank, churning the water into foam, the surface is choked with thrashing wings. The thunder comes with a second flash — the wings are dragging themselves out of the tank onto the shore — they have attached themselves to bodies — now they launch into the air, the bodies are dangling from them.

—Darkness.

—An explosion throws us on our backs.

—Light: the bodies are circling above the brine tank on mismatched wings. Only the wings are alive.

Darkness, a single blast of light and then the thunder, loudest of all. Darkness and silence. I can hear our breathing. I can feel, all around us, the winged corpses, crouching motionless in the dark. I can hear the dust trickling from their hair, their empty eyes, their gaping, slack mouths...

CHAPTER SEVEN

A clock tower with its illuminated dial all white with concentric rings drifts past the window like a dream.

Clouds break up, the sun shines through, and the sky is like a giant carousel. The entrance into a wholly new and unfamiliar landscape is like being born; what is called a moment of clarity — the experience is the opposite of a headache — a sense of pleasure in a clear panel of the head, of lightness and transparency. Racing along through the tunnels with a fantastic, steadily-building dream tension suddenly explode from the tunnel into a vast panorama of ocean sky and trees going off in his pants and slumping forward against the glass... blood spurting and spattering to the sound of radio squelches in the slow elongations of the clouds. Images and dissociated phrases blur past in subway windows—...

—◦◦—◦—

Working together, we managed to seal the cavern. A commotion of pounding and thudding comes through to us on the other side. At first, we had simply boarded up the entrance as a provisional measure; now Schwips' team is bricking it up.

I report to Ptarmagant—

"The *Phaedrus* thing was a warning," I tell him.

"Not much of one — oh well, find out what they want, if you're able to."

So they are creatures of desire, or reverence? Did our prayers and desires by-produce them?

Deuteronôme proclaims, "With new things, signs are needed."

"The divinity," Ptarmagant dictates, "is like a formless being consisting of overlapping images in minds, but possessing an element or dimension independent of any mind, being to it what the composite sound of the chord in music is to the individual notes that constitute it. The harmony is greater than the sum of its tones, it is another and wholly distinct sound — and so the divinity is a wholly distinct mind that is simply the new quiddity of the resonation of many other minds, and this is the case with every mind. These models are not binding but are only appearances."

A little country shop standing alone in a crescent depression in the hills... a doll hangs where the signboard should be, from an iron rod, pirouetting against a sky the color of wet sugar... clouds before me and sun behind, like gazing into a cavern... a Christmas tree smell, like a fresh-cut apple... Wings of nerves sprout from his shoulders, seize the wall enmesh themselves into its stuff and tear it to pieces like lightning roots, he emerges into an open canyon under ultraviolet dusk where court convenes and charges are being read somewhere in a barely-audible, low mutter, inside one of the dark houses. The prosecutor is in another house, his attorney if any in another, each juror in another still, and the judges are a pair of little girls on the swings — just two dim, colorful shadows with streaming hair in the gloom, calling to him as they swing toward and away from him: "...hell-*LO*, bye-*BYE*... hell-*LO*, bye-*BYE*..."

Escaping the park, I sail down the steps from the street to the subway the fabric of my coat billows up against the fist that holds the knife at the end of the sleeve. I go into the tunnels they smell of iron rust and rank water; in the shade just beyond the lights of the platform I strike my left palm with the pommel of the dagger, then jab the palm with the point. A pool of blood, black streaked with bright scarlet, grows there, and I lets some of the filthy water dripping from the ceiling mix with it. The droplet makes the pool vibrate like a blob of jelly, the vibration releases a buzzing into the air that granulates and grows darker.

"What do the wings want?"

Multiply turns a crackling log on a spit, dropping flakes of ash, cinders, and glowing coals. The log makes a regular whooshing sound with each rotation as flames slap the air. He can bring voices out of the air by touching a skull and you hear them from the inside, as if you spoke that way. Salt fills the eyesockets and the circle drawn in dust — shadow of a knife rotating over a clock face made out of dust. Speaks the words he hears, the echo comes rebounding down the passages before he speaks it; typewriter rods arranged around the face of the clock that are tripped as the knife's shadow passes over them, so the movement of the shadow causes a regular clicking; a mechanism rotates a paper tape that the rods type on. The indeterminacy is not a matter of which rods are thrown but which hit the tape and ink the paper. The tapes roll out the next phase.

—○—○—

I was an only child, and grew up among the churchical families at Meadowlab. This was no doubt what prevented me from becoming that abomination *a parson's daughter* — I knew too many of them already. They charmed everybody at first; brisk, practical, level-headed and self-possessed, like the Stoical little girls in story books... but when I got to really know them, I saw they were cold. Coldness just poured out from their bodies. Are you so cold you *can't* melt? When I would get excited, my natural ebullience foamed up out of me, then all of abrupt I would be checked by chill of their disapproval. I learned to hold back, and avoid the shame beams. But when I was alone I guess I giggled and twittered to myself, spoke in cartoon voices repeating lines making up nonsense or just making funny sounds like a TV, and capered around striking what felt like hilarious poses to me.

(Inside eight golden coffins... something cracks in a parsimonious girl's face, a perfumed breath of love freezes and shatters against it as a deadly stone bluff suddenly emerges from the features. Growing older... "my secret treasure"... demure without shyness, arch and sniffing. Getting up on others by doing things for them, using domestic tasks as leverage. Citing scripture. Reproaches, sermons, lectures often turning imperceptibly into analysis. "And why do you believe that?" Vera got away from them in time — her sex will flash startling bright from her witty face, a happy face — she has escaped mummification and she knows it. Come and take, come and give.)

I started wearing lipstick every day, and then jewelry, every day. I knew I wanted others to enjoy the sight of me, even if I could take no such pleasure in seeing them. When you're blind, you need to do it, you can feel other people's eyes on you, sensing you in ways you can't understand or even imagine. You almost want to pile ornaments on top of each other all over you until you can't be seen behind them. The other girls didn't like these affectations of mine but pity always held them back a little from outright condemning me, the bitches!

My early dreams had been only a clamor of sounds and feelings that would pull together into a line, not exactly speaking or reading but something like that, or in between. Other blind people I've met say they usually dream about getting lost or falling beneath the train, but I never seem to have those sorts of dreams — for which may the Lord make me truly thankful — I dream about whole landscapes filled with hanging curtains, so that I feel grass under my bare feet and thick fabric all around me. I can walk without using my stick, just by feeling along the curtains, with the sensation of the fabric continuously sliding over my face on and on. Now and then I'll hear the voices of the curtains or of whoever hung them there; I imagine their voices were trapped in all the folds and I release the words as I push the folds back open. The voices sometimes thundered in my head so loud they actually would wake me up.

Then I had my first sex dream. It took me about a year to realize — I'll never forget the shock — that I had vision in my dreams. At first I thought of it as a combination of silent hearing and numb touching. What I saw were the first sensations I had ever not felt. Around that time I grew ill, and had to stay in bed for a few weeks sick to my stomach and feverish. The nausea never stopped — eating was so difficult, although I was only sick once... I was crossing my room — my head swam, I bent double and heaved in agony. I heard loud rattling on the floorboards, and when it was over, I was on my knees, wiping my face and groaning. My father was in the room, and I heard him exclaim loudly in surprise. In a few minutes more, I felt tired but all right. The nausea was gone. Later, when I was recovering in bed, my father told me, his voice very even, that I had vomited stones. He put them in my hands when I asked for them, a heap of smooth flat stones — he'd washed and dried them.

"You've marked them?" I asked.

"No," he said, in a strange voice. "I've done nothing but clean them."

The stones had figures etched into them.

"Are they letters?"

"They have that appearance, but I don't recognize them."

He never did identify what kind of letters they were.

I worked hard to build up my vision, lying down, concentrating, trying to see. I would hold on to one detail in my mind, and add others. For a long time I didn't know that sighted people also have trouble visualizing details of things — that the first ones tend to drop out of sight as more are added. I thought of my imagination then as a small shelf that would only hold so many things and no more; the job then was to extend the shelf. My dreams became more lively, and the humming sonic hands that caressed me got clearer, so that I eventually learned to see my own way. I could see the dresser I pulled my clothes from in the morning as a lattice of objects made of trapped sound that would escape when I dragged on the handles or banged the drawers shut, all held in place by a voiceless skeleton. The rug was a crispy thin sound sponge. The door was like a bell.

The first face I saw was mine; I just knew it was. It's a beautiful thing — I thought. Amazingly complicated, with so many flexible features that lock together to form the expressions. The face I drew sort of swam up and brushed my lips, and then it was mine. I was wearing it. That was the week I lost my virginity to a boy they called Woolly; I felt the cruel spots standing out on his cheeks and chin, but his face in my dream was clear, sad and maybe a little stupid. It was after a dance. The music had seemed to roll me right into his arms. That was the end of the school year, and he left that summer. A letter came once — it was dull, and I just couldn't think of anything to write back to him, so I didn't. That was the end of that.

But I dreamt again and again about my own face, which gazed back at me with this implacable love, that was like it expected something from me, like "tell me something good." It had no color at all, no particular color, — I used to bore my friends with questions about color. My friend Vicki helped me pick out clothes.

When my father was cast out like Antigone I followed him into exile. That cost me most of my friends, all except Lenore the Librarian. We share a cheap apartment by the tracks.

—o—o—o—

"The stars are heaven's volcanoes and lace the night with beams of aged light, obscure spells of love that lay claim to all attention jealously imperiously persistently turning me back to you—

"Oh Vera...

"Night time comes down like a hand. Its gentle pressure squeezes voiceless sighs from me. The love spell develops and turns me into a painted landscape, moaning deep within my flat surface, something invisible and far away ignites again and again. Every time it says 'Vera.'

"I guess the spell I'm under has its own reasons for doing what it does. Maybe it derives a deeply soothing and perhaps even an ugly satisfaction from fastening on me. Maybe it reclines in its tyrannical sway over me..."

Aw buzz off. I don't have to answer your questions about her.

At the station. Night brings blue darkness surging in. My gnomes shuffle in a low-key rampage through the house. Every now and then there's a thud crash or tinkle as they knock something over.

In a small octagonal room, which had been used to store meteorological instruments, Pearl has discovered a piece of equipment — something like a solid brass acorn the size of a watermelon, tricked out in valves and holes lined with supple rubber diaphragms. This thing hangs on bright brass chains from a pulley way up in the darkness and can be raised out of sight or lowered to the floor.

Being the imaginative type the Prosthetic Libido has put 1 and 0 together ogling those rubber-lined holes. He's got it winched up to waist level and he's in there applying himself now. I sit on the floor by the door in the hall outside.

"This is all a dream," Pearl is saying, "oh, I don't, oh, really believe I'm here."

"Why do you think this question in terms of where you are?"

"I could be anywhere, ah," he says. "I keep thinking I'm not what I oh think, but that ah I'm really mm a person, somewhere else..."

"Like astral projecting?"

"Like ah the man and his machine are the reality... or ah ah maybe we're all machines somewhere else... Come in here!"

"No. — Where?"

"..."

"Where else?"

"There should be oh my another place to acc-count oh... for us?"

"I don't see it."

"Mm we might ah ah be dreaming each other — *ah!* and nothing starting or stopping, *ah!* but each thinks he creates oh *oh!* the other..."

"That sounds reasonable..."

Earlier that day... I stood on the other platform when her train came. I saw her through the window, facing me, her guitar between her knees. Her face paralyzes me. I move my hand and my grimy fingers streak the air like a windowpane — I lift my arm and trace a horned heart in the air with my greasy forefinger, framing her face. I'm halfway done when her chin lifts, her attention cracks out to me like the end of a whip and she shouts

"*Why* don't you *talk* to me?!"

I fly away like a covey of pigeons bursting from the hedge leaving my body frozen there with my hand in the air stuck in the half traced heart — she's getting up — the doors close and the train pulls away, her hand out reaching for me as the train angles her into the tunnel. A relief I hate skulks in and I angrily grab for it with the idea I'll kick it back out again. I can't manage it. Sticking out its tongue it climbs up into an inaccessible niche and leers down like a gargoyle at me. Come in demon, I shake in desperation, come in for the love of mike will you!

Pearl is silent now. I can hear the chains creaking as the dingus swings a little. One of my gnomes peers at me steadily, half smiling.

"What are you looking at!" I snap.

"An ass!" he says, grinning in my face.

—○○—○—

John Brade works at a record store during the week. I have his schedule all worked out. Pearl begs me to let him spend the night, but there has to be a limit. The boy needs his rest.

So Pearl is waiting impatiently for today's visit. Sunset light throws salmon color over the pale white walls of his room, interrupted regularly by his pacing form.

"What if he can't make it? What if..."

I'm not paying much attention, doodling V's in the dust by the door.

"You're not listening to me! You don't know what it's like, when it builds and builds and makes a statue out of me!"

"Oh I don't huh?"

He doesn't answer, keeps pacing. Window light races along his glistening body, up and down, back and forth.

I get an idea.

From my inside coat pocket I pull me out a silver wine glass, and hand it to him.

"What's this for?"

"Look at it."

The Prosthetic Libido does.

"Now think about it."

The cup flops down double on its stem as though it were made of limp rubber, then runs down between the Pearl's fingers in long viscous strands to the floor. Holding his hand perfectly still where it is, he bends his head to look at the streaming palm in astonishment, then gives me a woebegone look.

"I don't want this on my hand."

"Then boil it off," I say, tying my shoe.

"Aren't the fumes poisonous?" and I just roll my eyes at him. "Oh how silly of me," he says nearly under his breath. He looks at his hand and the metal begins to hiss and steam, white vapor flaps into the air and scatters along the floor.

I head for the door, and he, holding his hand gingerly at his side, follows me.

"So I can discharge it like that?"

"Apparently."

"...I don't like this," he says, shrugging at his hand.

"Still, you might need it sometime."

"What on a *person* oh I couldn't do *that*..."

The demon — I take his forearm in my left hand and thrust my right into his hot grip — a gout of steam reeking of searing flesh puffs up. Pearl's eyes widen in horror and he jerks his hand away instantly.

"*See*, that wasn't so bad," I say with a smile, raising my host's blackened hand with blood seeping through the grime on his palm. Pearl starts back appalled — there are a few rags of charred flesh stuck to his hand. He spins around the room like a mad top flailing his hand as though he'd slammed it in a car door trying to shake it clean and crying "Oh! Oh!" I stroll down the hall swinging my host's wounded hand from the elbow like a chimp.

"I am a sexual being, and therefore a teacher."

(qui vivre verra)

Once upon a time Pearl and I are watching a thunderstorm from the windows of the abandoned weather station. A bolt snaps against the sky, the thunder unfurls invisibly around it in the next instant like a colossal wing.

(qui verra Vera l'aimera)

VERA VERA VERA I see her face in the heat lightning and I am in a cold wind below a grey sky my heart ensleeved in pale autumnal flame—

Ardent peace then we were children she rolls her head... sighs through her nose her soft chest swells—

If only you were here, lying next to me, none of these thoughts would have arisen to plague me, not even this one, because the night, this bed and my sleep would all belong to you, would all be of you—

You would be the firmament under which I could sleep.

—◦○◦—

A vapor man peeps at me from a radiator and passes it on — I am summoned to Ptarmagant's side — recovery from the operation is not complete, and he has good and bad days. Dr. Thefarie recommends he keep moving at all times, so he's been transferred to a garbage scow. Old yellow car with black stripes, portholes in the doors. The scow pushes two flatbed cars of rough boards littered with discarded rubber gloves, chip packets, crumbling spikes orange with rust. A motor car with a diesel engine roars at the rear.

The interior of the car is sheathed in soundproofing and dark oak panelling, lamps with thick green shades. The train glides along so smoothly the hanging shade is still. I see my own movements distorted in the heavy silver ewer on a sideboard. Beyond that, a dim white bulb in the far corner — pretty spacious car. Ptarmagant, in a caftan and tassled felt cap, wrapped in dingy blankets shawls and a rug, rests in a green leather chair. His large bean-shaped head is cradled against the top of the seat with bolsters, and a humidifier sends a mist of camphorated water lightly frisking around him.

Ptarmagant does not raise his eyes to me. He is already mumbling something, and I must crane my head right down against his lips, forcing back the edge of the bolster with the crown of my head. The words are clearly and deliberately spoken, but faint, with pauses between the sentences; he seems to repeating what another, still more remote, voice says to him.

"I can't tell you what exactly to do. What we do and think can't have a center. The center can have many names, but it is best not to name it, or seek it, but to act from it. Hellfire is underground."

A cat is looking up at him from the floor near Ptarmagant's feet. It has pink-ash grey fur and aqua eyes.

"It is by hellfire we are regenerated. Processing now only admits barbaric narratives into the brook to which we go to find our food. Vision initiation retakes the brook, the watered narratives flower and bud fruit, we pick the fruit and pass the seed on into the sewers that the city is founded on. Those who slander, buy and sell the Holy Spirit, go down to spectre manure."

One of Ptarmagant's hands, which had been lying out of sight under an arched fold of his blanket on the arm rest, swings out and picks up a Swiss army knife from the low table beside his chair. The knife is an inch across. Taking it in his palm, Ptarmagant breaks it in half with one gradual squeeze; the muffled snap is like the sound of deep ice cracking in a melting pond. I realize Ptarmagant's entire body is not slack but rigid.

"What do the wings want? Which side are they on?"

I see the heavy lid of the coffin, and the heavy slab in the floor... the end of the story. Trapped to stifle beneath the heavy lid forever, the end. A heavy lid of space, the last page, to seal me in a narrow tomb below the bottom of space.

"A perfect sphere of ice... You've seen it before..."

"That's right — the Russian woman had it in her hand."

"It's down below, inside the earth. That's — I don't know — it's what we must do... I don't — but it's the goal of goals."

"The ice?"

Ptarmagant continues to mutter, voice clear but quiet. "You haven't yet entered the true tunnels and sewers."

...Interstellar night appears at the open window.

"Death to the slandering tongue. Death to the counterfeiting spirit."

Interstellar night floods the car.

—◦◦—◦—

Where is he? He is staying away. I look at the light in her window and just now a shadow brushes across it — was that? She is there... she is there... That's knowledge, say it again and again, every time I repeat it I take another step away. My resolve is turning brown, falling in shreds like wet tissue, and my power is crashing down in big pieces. I'm a huge smooth ear, and every bit of sensation coming from that apartment falls into me and vibrates me. I hold out a vibrating hand and look at it, measuring its tremor against the background chain link. This is what fresh green leaves, still raw and tender from the bud, feel — a kind of mercurial terror or acid trembling. The lights go out.

Nothing comes from inside me but trembling, unbearable intensity, but I'm paralyzed. Where is he? I drive my fist into my abdomen with frustration and the anger seems to do me good — or no it doesn't it only scatters the mercury so it runs everywhere and every inch of me is boiling in icy oil. I followed her to her apartment building, watching from a distance. Her figure before me now, walking away, toward the corner. The window I know, because I saw her roommate there open the curtain. They live on the second floor at the back, light from the window shines on the roof of the garage or whatever it is jutting out into the alley. I'm hunkered down by a lesser coffee klatch of oil drums turning purple with rust, behind a tree. Rail yards off to one side, deserted space.

In my tunnels I saw myself slide in over the sill. What to do next I'd left to my own boldness and the lay of the circumstances but now it takes nearly all my will simply to stay here in hiding.

With a burst of self-disgust I stand upright and take one heroic step toward her building. A pipe humming with rushing water doesn't shake as bad as this. The little window off to one side is lit. Suddenly I rush up toward the garage and stop by one corner, where there is a fenced gap separating it from the shuttered little machine shop next door. I peer up — the little window is frosted. No it's *steamed over.*

I take hold of the grill blocking the gap and pull myself up plant my foot on the cross bar. My hand shakes and I nearly impale myself getting up onto the roof of the garage. I draw near to the window. The sash is up a couple of inches from the sill. I have only to lift myself up — foot on that projection there. Under her window I stand — I know it's not the other one, it's her, unravelling like solar flares are ripping loose in all directions. If just being here makes me this crazy what if I do... I take hold of the sill lift my foot to the projection and look.

She has put on a robe, and she is bent sideways drying her hair with a towel. Warm soapy air billows from the window and steam folds its hands by the ceiling. There's no sound. She reaches for the bar and puts the towel onto it, straightens the ends so that it hangs evenly. Spiral black hair hangs down her back and damp wisps cling to her shoulders. Her hands float down to her sides, her posture is a little bowed.

Her back straightens and her head turns slightly. Fear rams my chest — she is listening. She turns, leading with her left ear, sealing my throat. Now she takes a step toward the window, eyes dancing wildly. In the hollow of her throat her skin glows like nothing I can describe. She's lit from inside, she's carved out of a star beams I don't know—

"Is that you?" she asks uncertainly.

She takes another step, her little foot on the fluff of the bathmat. Her toenails are red.

"Is that you?" she asks again — quietly, so that her roommate won't hear.

A melting settles on her face and she raises her hands slowly to open the robe, flips it back from her shoulders and the robe drifts down her arms, past her elbows. Then I see again my filthy hand clinging to the sill like a ragged nest of bones, and I lower myself without a sound — I will stay here even if I have to wait for her to go out again tomorrow, rather than risk making a sound. She must remain in doubt. With overmastering gratitude I seize on this thought and fondle it and turn it over and over again because it makes me appear to myself as if I were selflessly serving her, like a devoted slave, and that, and a great deal of superfluous reasoning, is far better than the truth which shall not get a word in edgewise.

I wait til morning. Then the garbage truck comes around, beeping and groaning — they'll see me up here when they reach this end of the alley. I hasten away, trying to use their noise as cover, but not without making sure, by the watery dawn light, that I leave no traces behind.

—◦◦—◦—

Ptarmagant is on his feet again, drinking brackish tea from a huge mug. I come across him as his briefing ends, in a tarped-off spot in the tunnels. As he looks at me his face changes.

"My son," he says, "Deuteronôme has an answer for you."

Deuteronôme comes up — "In my dream, I saw you go down into

the earth, even deeper into the earth, until you found ice. And I saw something else—" he gives me a pointed look.

"You must think carefully about this," he says. "You must ask yourself what *cherries* mean. The answer to the riddle is there. What do cherries mean to you?"

I remember — the dream of the fire escape, the cherry tree, and the map to the city of sex.

"The City of Sex!" Ptarmagant says.

"You must go there," Deuteronôme says at the same time.

By way of explanation, he shows me the flint knife, lying across his palm, looking enormous.

"It is death to go deeper," he tells me. "Do you understand? We ask you, because you must go and come back."

He waggles his finger at me, from side to side.

"You cannot stay there. You must come back to us, and bring us the *tablets*."

The last word is emphasized by a push of his two fingers gently into my chest.

"I don't know what they are, but they will be there, and you must bring them back to fulfill the dream."

"I'm ready." Vera. I failed you. I failed you.

"You're ready? Now?"

"Now. Right away." I tell his eyes Vera, I failed you. They remain fixed on mine for a while. Then he turns to Ptarmagant, who says.

"All right then."

I go with them down a long hall in silence. The hall is deep underground so narrow they must walk in single file, whitewashed plaster walls with callouses, rounded ceiling. Icy light from wall sconces like starched linen tulips. After a hundred yards or so there are small dioramas set into niches in the wall, set just slightly lower than would be convenient for the eye. Unable to see them without bending forward and unable to do this without falling behind I crouch a bit as I walk and glimpse rapidly from side to side. I see beautiful figures lying in coffins, but their chests rise and fall easily. Decomposing bodies form tableaux from life, marriage, dancing, even childbirth — a rotting child from a rotting womb. Some of the dioramas are purely geometric or nonrepresentational, including some that appear to be diagrams from geometry books, pi r squared and the Pythagorean theorem. Still others combine these various elements; dead and living students in a geometry class, triangles made of severed heads, dotted lines of sliced intestines; a repeating pattern of interlocked, decaying lovers; mummified geometrical figures in a latrine. Occasionally, there is a small round speaker set into the wall by a niche, the wire grid of the speaker mesh nearly choked with layers of thick whitewash, but showing gold where paint has chipped away. From these comes faint music, different at different places but blending all together into a spacious droning harmony.

At the end, the hall opens out into a small domed room like the interior of a burial mound. Deuteronôme presses the elevator button, the old-fashioned kind like a black, bakelite mushroom sticking out of the wall. Whir of far distant gears; I glance around at a number of framed official-looking documents on the walls. They have been framed under glass, and the glare on the glass makes them hard to read. The elevator door slides heavily to one side all one slab. The elevator is spacious; Spargens is the operator. Without a word, they enter the elevator and, in unison, turn round to face the door. Spargens has an expert touch, the elevator begins to ascend with only a barely-perceptible shift in equilibrium. They climb for a long time. The door opens on blinding light.

Hands peremptorily take me forward. Fresh air, wind rifles my clothes stirs my fear. Through a red haze comes a platform facing the sun in a cloudless, deep blue sky. We are miles afraid in the sky. A high rampart is the horizon. The sun blazes, swollen to enormous size. A godlike torrent of force, registering in all manner of almost purely random intensities in all my senses, blasts over me and sluices all around him. Witnesses look up at me from below the platform, obscured by the light shining over them from behind. Suddenly a shadow appears against the sun — Ptarmagant, raising the knife into the air.

He brings it down slowly as though it were emerging from the sun on a long lancelike ray.

Ptarmagant gives me the knife. I raise my hand up to chest level to take it, and when it is in my hand, it seems to glue my hand to space at chest level. The knife has embedded in it the sensation of searing heat. The edge of the flint blade shines like a thread out of the sun. I feel something like a soft blow in the solar plexus as the idea acts itself in my mind. My body goes tense and tears ruin what's left of my vision, but the knife doesn't shake. Vera, my hand comes free to my control. Beneath the light of the sun the knife tears a ragged ellipse in my chest with a sound like ripping burlap and the sun rushes up to me.

Sound of surf when I wake, someone brought water; the ragged wound is gone. Later Ptarmagant comes to check on me.

"Can you stand?"

I get up. Ptarmagant leads me into a dark, windowless room, lead sheeting on the walls, a table and a chair. I am made to sit down at the table and a silver tray covered with smooth black and grey stones the size of robins' eggs, some scored with deep-incised characters, is set before me. Ptarmagant leaves the room.

I look at the tray for a moment then realizes these were the marked stones *she* had vomited, years ago. I reach out
and gather the stones by
pressing them all together between
my palms at arms' length across the table — as he touched the stones
that had been in her body I felt
an intense warm pressure against my chest
and in my throat, and the bones
of his arms and back shivered,
a green light erupting from the center of my chest
in a ragged ellipse
a brilliant golden evolution of lines and corners
from here to the radiant sun like a pipe

curving away in its depths,
a silhouetted figure stands in the sun,
reaches out his arm and presses
his fire hand against the sky, pushes
down on it and the stars spin down,
pushes up on it and the stars wheel back up,
the figure does this without
ceasing to look at me
watches the wall decay overrun with
seething golden scurf
a black slimy aperture opens in the wall
vomiting a slough of lit candles spangling
the walls with brilliantly flashing gold reflections
saw copper light through frothing trees felt the glee bursting in my
ribs a honeycomb of gold light breaks leaving viscous warmth there in
my ribs to spread
three vapor men are there
crystal breath of the machines, of her hounds silent sleek and
intent tracing the scent
the teacher emerges from the shadows
stripped to the waist her skin painted white and her lips red as
coral,
and a huge opal hangs from a silver thread flat against her collarbone
she stands in the spot and drinks in the light with her skin
she is standing over me now,
I touch the opal warm from her skin is her
soul clitoris warming my palm with all colors,
she turns to vapor and mantles lovingly around me without a
sound. I still can see yet the moist coral lips carefully forming words
around a dark center—
in total silence we're locking on top of the desk and though her
beautiful face is drawn
haggard and grieving as though she were being hurt
she clings hard to my shoulders and grips my waist with her legs,

(no climax ever but draughts carry them off in chalk dust
they melt away behind the echo of the bell
the Great Lover opens the path to the City of Sex).

━○━○━

Let the voice ring out like a softly-ringing bell from the sepulchres...
"Nine-thirty all right." He steps through an open door into the
rafters of the city of s... The sky rises from the mountains, held up by
unrelenting wind. Trains rattle on tracks hundreds of feet above the
sheet ice and far below it, where they push through limpid cold water
thick as syrup, black as pitch in the hollows of the ragged boulders,
the deep pits in the stony bottom. The Great Lover finds himself in
another, new narrative, another character.

The map says the city of sex is a mask. The bones of the face turn
clear and light up train lines. A long, transparent tube emerges from
the hollows of the flat bones and cautiously feels its way into the water.
When its other end comes free, it unfurls a gelatin disk, which rises and
then settles slowly down back onto the face, forming features, pulsing
with bands of dim light. It cloaks the face the way two lovers' faces are
superimposed in an embrace. Now this dark mask, which in every way
contrasts with his natural face, slips itself deftly *behind* his features.
His face suddenly radiates an astonishing beauty, his natural features
will always be seen in light of this invisible and absolute contrast with
the mask inside, an anti-mask which makes plainer the true face.

A new person, he will come to the city by land sea and air, in the
present and in memory — his character has been here before, and
thinks to himself:

This is an unusual car — is this a new kind? Maybe it's an antique.
In my mind I can see a gleaming head of gentle red hair turned to
gold by the light of the new-dawning day, a shining white breast rises
and falls, nostrils whistling mild euphoria. A few mornings ago...
my memories are flattened like photos in a magazine. Trains churn
alongside us in the frigid water, and I can hear the water rustling down
along our shining sides. Tracks arduously laid down on the bedrock of
the bottom by workers in purple metal caissons slide below our heavy

wheels. A few of these cassons exploded from too much pressure; and their shattered fragments lie among the rocks all rusty brown, huge iridescent fish dart like lightning in and out of their rent up sides.

The train veers, and I see the city's foundations off in the distance, a deeper dark in milky blue haze. There are pipes big enough to swallow city blocks bundled up there, all encrusted with clear tubes, gathered around a red rampart of solid iron protruding from the sea bed. Above me, where the light of the setting sun salts the blue of the pack ice pink, the city itself spreads out onto the ice sheet like an umbrella. The city is in chains, which hold it down to the spot bolted to bedrock on all sides. Up ahead, there's a dead whale that got caught in one of the chains, covered with deep white lacerations, the drooping grid of the jaw frozen at an angle. Yellow and vermillion starfish have begun creeping up the tail and covering the body in bizarrely festive five-pointed stars. Off to one side a furtive motion catches my eye and I spot a puddle of living ink prowling along beside the tracks. Surrounded by a halo of threads, these featureless things slither along clever as otters, hunting among the coral.

From time to time the train passes near the edges of deep chasms hundreds of yards across. The tracks descend and the sunlight fades. I see a chimera with mirror eyes and transparent fins, cold-water dolphins like black glass... We pass a seep where the denser brine doesn't mix with the sea water, forming the mirage-like surface of a lake underwater. A tourist brochure for the City of Sex appears in my mind, stray paragraphs keep coming back to me from this text I never read.

The tracks climb through the city's foundations. On nights when the moon is full, the pack ice glows like a sheet of moonlight made solid. In places where the ice is clear, those who live below the surface can peer up at powdery indigo sky and brilliant miniature stars. Just before the train begins to spiral up out of the water — is that a woman I see, walking on the ocean floor? She has a round head, and the dark shape of her mouth opens and closes slowly as she sings her siren-song... I can make out the dark circles of her eyeglasses, and her neck stretches and grows longer as though her head wanted to float up to the world of air...

The City of Sex is all gradual motion, the slow passage and recombinations of landscapes, and sudden eruption of breathtaking panoramas of blue sky, white ice, black mountains, the sweeps of steel ribbons. In brochurese I "recall" the city's history: founded millennia ago when a number of settlers from different parts of the globe accidentally converged on the same area at the same time. A flukish stretch of temperate weather made the establishment of a small colony possible. When the weather once again grew severe, the colony was cut off forever. As communications broke down, it was assumed in other quarters that the colony was lost. In time, it was forgotten altogether.

The colony did not disappear, but adapted, developed and thrived in an isolation that presently became a matter of preference, instead of necessity. Their space craft are occasionally observed in other parts of the world.

The city is a vast circular cradle of elevated rail lines and high spires, steel and glass pavilions. The streets are made of metal plates, curved with steam pipes under them to keep the ice off. The caterpillar sidewalks are flat ingots of thick steel linked together in broad ribbons. Overhead lights shine directly down on passersby, giving them an especially stark appearance.

All the metal buildings, the metal walls of the homes, are adorned with fine arabesques, like circuits of nearly invisible gold filaments. All structures are coated with a thin layer of transparent ice that lightly blurs the gold. The touch of polished metal molded and pressed into the folds and rolls the luxuriant foliage and rounded shapes of Gothic architecture, is weirdly pleasurable. It runs along the palm like warm skin, a fine fabric of minute etched scratches that form fractured spirals in the light.

Everywhere are humming wires and if you put your ear to them you can hear voices — some are voices belonging to people in the city and some are voices from the wind as it blows on the wires, or from the aurora when she lashes her cat o' nine tails in the sky. These words are all too faint and too terrifying to be recorded.

In some places, where the streets are just ice, a manhole cover will glide back and a sea lion or walrus will thrust up its head. Floating there, it will watch the passers-by, supercilious, curious, or earnest. Cranes everywhere — I mean the mechanical kind — the city is constantly building itself — enormous, vistal works — steel suspension bridge in the frigid air... Wind harp in the wires, and an incessant rumble of distant construction. The train descends past the city, jagged black mountains, the vast eye-scalding plain of pack ice, and the city swims gracefully by gossamer-like steel and glass pavilions topped with tapering, bright pennants. The pavilions enclose vast boulevards, with three tiers of galleries on all sides over them. I watch them sail up or down through my reflection in the glass walls of the elevators. Vast trees grow from the floor to just within a few inches of the ceilings, their roots drink from the many fountains everywhere.

When I come back to myself again, I am sitting in a hard steel chair on a terrace, with a view of the intersection of two boulevards. There is a fountain there, which surrounds the base of a colossal metal statue of two figures, in the Soviet style. She is straddling him, both upright, her head flung back ecstatically against the white grid of the glass roof, water oozing along the edge of the fountain's raised metal plumes and hanging in heavy drops, dropping into the water with a musical sound... Every corner has a similar statue, and if I could spin by them I would see a time-lapse animation of their monumental, precisely-phased intercourse. The artist modelled the figures on himself and his lover, and incorporated her name somehow in a way no one understands. I peer up at her face, tilted away in rapture, and imagine the northern lights billowing and shining over her polished body.

People ride along the boulevards in hollow metal bulbs sliding along in deep grooves. I sit alone in one of them, a copper colored ball with red cushions, an encyclopedia drones on in my brain. Drone on, drone on. The human immigrants developed into two distinct strains, based on their preferred time of activity. In thousands of years of isolation, they adapted under the extreme evolutionary pressures of this difficult environment. Both types exhibit mineral characteristics, and have correspondingly more complex diets.

Along the galleries one may observe the Day People; tall lean with dark plum-black skin to protect against powerful solar radiation here. Eyes of vivid white and electric black. Long narrow noses pointed tip angled straight down between flaring nostrils, tip and nostrils in a row — narrow faces, full lips, and small ears. They don't wrinkle as they age but their skin begins to powder away to dust... a grey coating of dust on the skin. The men wear their iron-colored hair short, it lies sleek against their tapering skulls like little filings, and bands of tiny ringlike beads, made from bone, frame their heads. The women walk haughtily along the galleries, wear their thick hair long and flowing, swept back from the brow; they are testy irritable impatient and waspish. The men are cordial and accommodating. The women possess thrilling alto viola voices, the men resounding double basses. With sweeping hinged ribcages and enlarged lungs they are outstanding runners for both speed and endurance. Their eyes have developed special ridges on the surface of the iris itself — contracting against snowblindness; and a pattern-fixing structure in the hippocampus enables them to see clearly in blizzards and to find the horizon. Their normal vision is extremely acute. A Day sharpshooter can knock a gull out of the air a mile away, detect extremely minute movements. They are indefatigable, heavy eaters, and possess a high resistance to cold. Characteristic Day gesture — in shaking hands they swing their arms out wide from the waist in a circle and bring the hand up flat.

The Day People sleep in wooden cabinets set into the walls of their angular, lean buildings. The Night People live in round or oblong houses clustered outside the pavilions; they sleep squatting on the floor wrapped in blankets with just their heads poking out. The Night People predominate in food services. In some places Night fishers dive through a hole cut in the ice floor of the bistro, pop up a few minutes later and hand fresh steaming aphrodisiac crustaceans to the patrons, their bodies steaming from the twenty-three degree waters. The diver is attended by a pair of assistants, change his goggles for a fresh pair swab his mouth nose and ears with something, pour boiling water over his suit, rub gelatin into his hair.

The Night People exhibit a general attitude of dreamy intentness. The men are built like tanks with square inexpressive faces, skin white as beluga whales, fingers and toes without nails. The women are sweet and light as marshmallows, with little girls' faces on large adult heads. Stony brawn of the bodies, pale crispy hair, beaky noses, large pupils fringed with a thin ring of icy blue, and sky-blue lashes. The women wear their hair in braids, men's hair grows any old way. The women are pranky silver-voiced snipes full of teasy nicknames, the men speak with robotic flatness in voices like nasal flutes. Echolocating all the time with inaudible trills produced in a special sinus, registers a three-dimensional sense image of their immediate surroundings 360 degrees. Come into a shop: Night man at the counter, you ask for something on the shelf behind him pointing, without taking his eyes off of you he reaches behind his own back and unerringly takes it down for you. Like the Day People they are indefatigable, heavy eaters, with a high resistance to cold. Extremely good swimmers, pressure resistant, they can hold the breath for upwards of fifteen minutes.

Their space program is already a thousand years old — a Night waiter brings me the house special, a kind of invisible ragout, and I fold the thick, cumbersome newspaper in half so as to fit it on the rest of the table. The food weighs down my fork. I can get it into my mouth all right if I don't think about what I'm doing. Go on reading the words in my mind:

Enormous tethered balloons were sent high into the atmosphere, from which stars and planets could be observed with sophisticated optics. The existence of planets in other solar systems was also established mathematically. Explorers were wrapped in a special substance and frozen within enormous balls of ice; balloons carried the ice aloft to floating platforms at the uppermost limit of the atmosphere, where the accompanying crew pushed it into a precisely-determined orbit (thereafter taking the balloon back down to the surface). The ice vessel gathered speed with each revolution until breaking away at exactly the right moment. After centuries of travel through the interstellar void, the sphere would enter the gravitational field of the target planet at a certain angle well calculated to initiate orbit, from which it would then eventually sink into the atmosphere. The resulting friction would burn the ice away, turning the spacecraft into a column of steam, and the disintegrating vessel would finally expel its occupants several miles above the surface. The material in which the traveller was wrapped expands on contact with air to form a landing cushion and also to slow descent. This material is designed to dissolve completely within hours of its deployment. Assuming they had survived, the new arrivals would generally regain consciousness only after this dissolution was completed, awakening slowly from a sleep that began in the City of Sex to find themselves naked on another planet. These were not voyages of conquest, or even of discovery exactly, but ventures with the object of dispersing human beings among the stars, where they would begin entirely anew all over again. For this reason, nothing from earth could be permitted to remain with them. At present, it is believed that at least one planet has been successfully seeded with a population of human beings large enough to reproduce itself, and that new strains of the human type may already be emerging there.

I lie down behind an iron pylon, gazing out sideways through the glass wall. There is a man making his way into the city after crossing the ice sheet. A feeling floats through my head as though it gives off a balloon of light, and I remember coming to the city when I was somebody else — the wind rammed me from the side, burned in my eyes and rasped along my face brittle with ice around my nostrils and mouth. I remember too, the confusion and dazzled senses as the walls rose around me and the wind was suddenly gone. Open-eyed, I carried all that yawning open space in my mind, and I felt these others and the buildings pressing the billowing fabric of space back inside me, my inflated consciousness being pressed back into me... But I still could not speak, or think. The wind scrubbed my mind blank.

My common mind is returning; with groping self-conscious thoughts I have enough now almost to decide, somehow it's something I can allow or refuse, that space I can give up or not, as I choose. I stagger in among the iron buildings and stop against a wall, and when I open my eyes, I see a wisp of smoke drift down from the open window, fall through an amber beam of sunlight toward the iron street, and at once am calm again.

Out on the ice there are algae mats growing beneath the pack in motionless lakes and in high salt pools that don't freeze. In some of these one finds mummified remains of animals, some thousands of years old, or wind-scrubbed bones scattered among the rocks bruised with lichen. I am still lying on the floor, behind the pylon. An antarctic riddle trickles through the humming glass and asks me:

> What kind of plant is it that grows
> On infertile ice and barren stones?

"Lichen," I say into the crook of my elbow. Lichen grows on ice and stones, although lichen isn't really a plant — he listens to himself — it's not a plant, it's the marriage of a fungus and an algae.

—oo—o—

"Nine-thirty, all right," I step still a bit shaky from the friction of re-entry through an open door into one of the many iron passageways set into the ice. My breath misting, I unerringly follow the tunnels to find the deep sun.

Some are so amazed on first seeing it that they never want to leave, it's all they ever want to look at. Their eyes have been taken out of the level of their lives and now they can look at nothing else. It is forbidden to touch the ice wall, or to get too close. One's breath, or perhaps the mere heat of one's ardour, may melt the ice. Attendants are kept on hand at all times to remove those who have fainted, or those who otherwise manifest some indisposition. The tunnel entrance is lit with pale, heatless chemical lamps, but the deep sun is brightened only by the thin daylight illumination that filters through the ice sheet above it. The light descends, a blue-white dome.

On first seeing the deep sun, I sob once involuntarily, something heavier than a gasp. It is a hollow sphere of nearly clear ice, over a quarter-mile in diameter, embedded in but wholly distinct from the ancient pack ice. That it is hollow has been demonstrated by analyzing the spectra of light passing through it, although it is not clear whether the interior is a vacuum, or contains some rarefied atmosphere. It was discovered during excavations centuries ago and has since become an object of pilgrimage, the closest thing to a church in the City of Sex. An apartment was cut into the ice at the initial point of discovery of the deep sun, just before its base, so the sloping wall sweeps overhead. One can see up into and through the deep sun, all the way to the far side. Again, the encyclopedia goes rattling through my mind like a decrepit old cart.

Pilgrims congregate at the base of the deep sun, processions arrive daily from the city to visit it, and some never leave. Their improvised shelters are kept to one side of the passageway, so as not to close it off entirely. Hallucinations among those assembled are common; most of them involve a dimly-visible figure, or silhouette, hovering in the heart of the deep sun — a human form, usually, but sometimes a seal, or whale, or some variety of fish, or a huge starfish, a crab, or polar bear. For most of those who involved themselves with it, the deep sun was an emblem of eternity; they felt that, by gazing at it continuously, they would imbibe something of the essence of time itself, or achieve single moments altogether outside of time. A guidebook phrase trickles through my head: "Our region is full of spectacular attractions like these."

I see my face reflecting in it — the face is not European, I see no traits or color. There is the mask of cracked muck I always wear. I can see my gaze but not my eyes. My expressions are there, but no features. I look down at my hand and it's a color — the name of the color is on the tip of my tongue, but the color itself is something else. I have some color, anyway. Am I male or female? It doesn't show.

One of the attendants politely asks me to stand to one side. This brings me back to my lines and as I feign embarrassment I look around, scanning the faces of the devotees. One man's nondescript, sacklike features suddenly throb at me: a single, equivocally grey pulse of neutral emotion. This is my contact. I amble over to where the man is sitting in a shapeless heap of rags, taking my time. He had routinely to pass through inundated rooms where cadavers floated upright. The man's rags are scraps of raw silk watered with ash-perfume, his prayer-rug is the color of salmon meat, with cobalt dragons woven into the fabric and a white fringe. The man is counting an ice-rosary with purplish-grey fingers; he has already been paid. I kneel nearby, just slightly away from the praying man; a moment later I feel a dash of coldness hit my midsection on the inside, and something in my coat pocket that wasn't there before.

The deep sun glows a few feet from my face. A sun, deep down... As clouds cross the sky above, the light waxes and ebbs again making a grand, slowly smoking lamp of the deep sun. Cold air falls from its surface onto my brow, pressing down on my features in a new mask. I get up with care and get out of there, my new frost-face is already boiling away. Suddenly, a nameless jeopardy is there, all around me, a part of the book I didn't know — probing attention and seeking all around like searchlights. Alarm bristling and snapping from the walls and the floor, I keep my face down, holding his breath. Getting into a group of visitors filing out the exit I slither along the red velvet rope past the attendants and the placards, straining to reach the anonymous tunnels before my breath gives out.

Finally I duck aside into a small alcove with fuseboxes, and let go — my exhalation smashes through my mist-mask, destroying it. I reach into my pocket. My fingers pull out a piece of heavy paper, almost cardstock, folded in fours. It's stiff with cold, and I have to pry it apart and scrape the frost from its surface to read the address in iridescent blue ink.

—o—o—o—

People are congregated in a dark, head-craning mass at the glass wall, to either side of one of the massive, airlock-like iron doors to the outside. These doors open onto an elevated causeway connecting two pavilions a hundred stories in the air, normally employed only by the maintenance men. Use of the causeways when the wind exceeds a certain force is forbidden for safety reasons, which is why the crowd is now gawking at the lone figure who lies face down out there, gripping the causeway floor with all his might and bracing himself with his legs as the bludgeoning wind trains on him in an unremitting flat horizontal beam.

Oh good it's me — I am clutching at the iron and randomly pounding with my toes as though I could kick footholds into the metal. My fingers are killing me, but worse yet they are numbing in the blast, particles of ice shred exposed skin and I don't dare open my windward eye at all. The left eye, shielded by my nose, I can only open for an instant at a time, peer through a pink shroud of glare at the opposite door, the rails lining the causeway, some of which have already been blown off. In total confusion I hold on; frustrated hatred building up behind me, coming from some of the faces at the glass, the ones that clearly don't belong to mere bystanders. It's as though a pack of huge hate-convulsed dogs were snarling and howling for my blood, and I am grateful for the dangerous protection of the screening wind.

The cold is sandpapering my lungs, and now nausea makes me retch helplessly — the caustic spray starts to freeze around my mouth. The sour taste wakes me up a little; I grit my teeth and they feel a little soft. Desperate and furious I lunge forward thrusting my arm out and down fast as a mousetrap — fingers clench and dig thin furrows into the iron and I drag forward, feet scrabbling. I've got to take off my glasses — if the wind got hold of them I'd be as good as blind — no sooner does the thought occur than I feel them slide loose from behind my ears they flash off to the left and with unconscious recklessness I snap them out of the air — with only one hand holding me in place now I slide toward the edge my fingers squealing and leaving blood marks. I plot the move in my head then do it — jam the glasses into pocket drop flat put left hand down on metal and push back stop the slide.

The wind is like an avalanche. My clothes seem ready to disintegrate. Another burst of desperation fills my muscles with light and I dash forward veering into the wind and staying low, clamping down again when I feel the wind begin to draw me aloft. Squinting around with my left eye I seem to have closed the distance to the far door. Behind me, amid the frothing impotence he can sense the avid eyes, the innocent sympathy of the bystanders. I inch to the right again until I am up against the rails. Another wave of nausea wrenches me and I turn my head this time, watch as a translucent membrane of cloudy-clear mucous bursts from my mouth and sails off spreading its tendrils like a portuguese man o' war. I compress then lunge, slip toward the left side with terrible speed grab the edge of the door and pull my body into the frame. The door is set directly into the glass, a large shielding ring around the glass and the door. The wind is still so strong here I'm back against the inside of the ring, and have to pull myself up, "standing" horizontally, to grab at the door latch. It's locked. I gesture wildly to a maintenance man, Night person, in sky-blue coveralls, on the other side of the glass. He is waving his hands and making his inaudible reply:

"You'll have to go back!"

My mouth filling with bile I pull back, can't let go, ram the window with my forehead. A crack in the three-inch thick glass appears with a sound like a pistol shot. The man in the coveralls is flailing wildly. I draw back again, strings of vomit snapping between my face and the smeared glass, and ram again, the crack widens and develops tributaries. I wind up a third time, the wind threatening to bend me backwards against my own spine, and this time my head makes a blushing cloud of white cracks flecked with livid red. Pulling back again, I suddenly hear a voice calling wildly — the maintenance man holds the door ajar and waves me in.

"Stop! Stop! You can come in!"

I shift my grip and slither around the doorframe, collapsing on the floor as the maintenance man swiftly shuts the door again. I've got my hands to my head, half-frozen, half-deaf, and groggy. When my vision begins to clear, I notice I'm alone. Oh. The maintenance man has gone to get somebody. I take some steps through borax passages with tile walls, drains in the steel floor, out into the open streets of the pavilion. I have to vomit again — watery and black, a worm flops over itself weakly and expires in the air.

"Sorry, man."

I came to get the tablets and time is running out on this incarnation or whatever — the address identified this pavilion. No one is pursuing me yet. I push on, but I can't get myself going in a straight line. I slosh through a fountain and emerge whipping water from my pant cuffs in all directions I carve destruction through a sidewalk restaurant blundering into tables knocking diners from their chairs and treading on their food. My eyes are like riveted on this vague spot up ahead. There's an escalator farther along the gallery; it's a down one. Climbing up onto the gallery banister, I pull up to the next story using the jugendstil iron filligree fringing its railings. I get up to the upper banister, drop forward knocking my chest against a high planter, a sort of basket of woven steel ribbons that can't ever be put anywhere but in the way, so I land on my face and get up slowly. I didn't break my glasses because they are still in his pocket — I put them on.

Now I see what I'm looking for: a booth selling flavored ices and glowing with a clean, snowy light. The proprietor has a boyish face; his eyes are rolled up toward the ceiling as though he were pertinaciously rereading a single word there, his fingers drum the counter and he grins foolishly, the picture of affected nonchalance. I crash into the front of the booth and plant the card on the counter like a drunk pawing his change on the bar. Suddenly smooth and efficient, the counter-man plucks up the card and drops two pale powder-blue tablets into my hand, sets down a small glass of very clear water with a tap.

"These may cause nausea," he says.

"Swell." I cram the tablets as far as I can into my mouth and drain the glass, leaving a thick lip print. In a flash, the glass is gone, the counter is wiped, and the affected nonchalance is restored as before.

"Wait, what do these do?"

"Prevent bends, pressure sickness."

Fourteen minutes after he takes the tablets the ground slides out from beneath the Great Lover's feet. The clock reads nine thirty and he falls in no direction, or in any, and the time he has spent in the city reverses itself. Light of all hues gushes from his eyes and drops away, a wild cacophony of backward sounds pours from his ears and sluices into his mouth, smells flow out his nose, his skin vibrates heat cold pain pleasure pressure textures into the air, as knots of memory are unwrapped into experiences and then into possibilities, all leaving him like rats deserting a sinking ship. Something is being left behind for him, in the new memory taking shape now, but it has already lost itself in his mind — it will take time to dowse it out again.

I look out through the glass wall into a night that lasts months. My face mingles with the blackness outside, the character I am in this chunk of a story I've brazenly forced my way into, like those women's dreams. Our enemies do this all the time, but they do it with no risk to themselves, and so what they bring back with them from the stories they ransack has no weight at all. It turns into more smoke to add to the screen.

This character remembers coming into the city — I can see his memories there like plots in a botanical garden, each one has a label. As I am pulling loose again, my time expiring, I stretch. In memory, through the ice he had glimpsed the churning shadow of some figure struggling along toward the city, directly over the underwater train. He has only just arrived. The overpowering wind sparkles with minute fragments of ice, reflecting the light of the pavilions, and the long tapering banners of the roofs opposite are battering themselves to pieces in the blizzard.

The Great Lover lumbers out of the gloom. The city limits are marked by a string of lights; the flying snow and ice grit make these lights appear to flicker. I watch myself come feeling this character's panic — the person he sees is an intruder in this story. He is petrified, his eyes riveted on the Great Lover, who is now here, now there, seems at times to tower over the city, gigantic and terrible as Plague. An inch or so from each pupil his gaze turns into two jets of red fire that whip in the gale like bright rags, and as he nears the picket of lights, an idiotic leer on lips encrusted with frozen saliva glints at him like a humiliating secret.

I will go back to this half-frozen idiot now — I can feel the pull of that mad body on me. My assumed character drops to the floor like a heap of empty clothes, his body dream collapses and his clothes turn to a flimsy trickle of smoke stretching itself languid and slow as a cat, turning in on itself, turning invisible, vanishing into finer and finer particles. He is siphoning back into time, in the direction of the start of his story.

Good luck!

I cross the ice, and enter the City of Sex. Filling my body again is like drawing a long deep nourishing breath, even in the lethal cold. I go to the Cadaverium, an enormous building of polished metal covered with solemnly decorous erotic engravings. Beneath high ceilings of unfinished black iron, whose vaults are mist-traps, deceased and desisted citizens are dropped into a deep shaft in the ice, dropping down out of sight. They find their level and their niche below on their own. Sometimes they actually swim down out of sight, without a moment's glance at any of the living assembled at the surface. It's unknown exactly where they go. I think however that they're all together in one big chamber, where a mysterious current holds them firmly up against the walls, in two or three layers. And there they wave and nod, in the shadows, in twenty-three degree water. That chamber is bottomless.

Relatives and mourners will sometimes come to ask their dead ones important questions. A dancing, blue-white flame is lowered on a silver tripod over the steaming water, and a figure slides into view far below... glides up, breaking the surface without troubling it with a single ripple. They always break the surface in a rolling or twisting movement, never suddenly. For as long as you speak with them, they stay. When you've finished, they turn and sink out of sight again. The light ebbs and throbs, and turns the icy skin of the face to a creamy torch. Dead lips move emphatically to form speech, the metallic voice is impersonal, the words are hollow, the sentences empty as robbed tombs.

Bodies roll to the surface now: beautiful tender and heatless lips whisper Vera Vera Vera, a sussuration rising from the water up to the dome, the shadows, the beams, the ceiling.

I fling myself into the pool and sink. Indigo shade closes around me like a sack, shadowy hands and feet descending through deepening blue. A crushing pressure grips me, the blue turns black, although I can make out rows of slow-gambolling dark forms, like dancers languidly raising their arms...

In total darkness, I suddenly feel close to Vera, as though this is where her vision is hidden. I realize she has never left my mind. Love is what floods into me now as I feel her inside me. Love for her. Love of her. I don't see her, but my face is her face.

Being alone is painful, but it's pain you can get used to, like a chronic ache in the back, the stomach, in the hands. You have your dignity to brace yourself with, although it may not go numb until you get too old. It is the pain of not quite being a walking corpse. Even the coward who cringes inside his paroxysm of fright is more alive.

People must hurt each other, as inevitably as they breathe. Nothing can stop it. It's not enough to accept it. Accepting it is not enough, like sighing resignedly and putting on an attitude of long-suffering. Don't get to be too good at protecting yourself. You've got to be ripped to pieces for the one you love, again and again. That doesn't prove anything but love, and its entitlements are a frailty that can't be held. But you will live even in that hell. The fire that hurts you gives off light like any other fire, that illuminates beautiful things, and that is beautiful itself.

Far below, a new light, spreading in all directions. I see the deep sun. Sinking toward it, I begin to feel its warmth. So, it wasn't set just under the surface anyway — or are there more than one?

What were those tablets? A change in me? Who is directing all this I wonder — is it the divine thing we've been calling to out of this? Are these prompts its answers?

I look steadily into the deep sun, cold and bright like an egg, round and transparent like a new embryo, starting to warm.

Still the water is too cold, and the pressure is killing me. I should be dead now, but the tablets seem to be working.

I fix my eyes live or die on the deep sun, and some intuition is now coming into my mind that I have trouble understanding. I have to get the deep sun — *get* it.

The intuition is taking shape — I'm listening! Hurry! I start swimming. The water is thick as stone. I swim until I reach a wall, a flat surface there. My momentum carries me up against it, and I can feel ice and rock there... sliding down the surface exhausted, limp, I can feel the wall rustling along my body.

I have no strength left. When the tablets wear off, I will die here. The wall is sliding by... now it changes — in the dim glow of the deep sun I can see I am passing a patch of bricks and mortar. They are going by quickly. This is my chance but my arms are too weak. With no strength in them at all I can't move them, and in a moment this patch will be gone.

I make my arms move. They reach out and take hold of the wall. The bricks in my hands are crumbling, I have to shift my grip. A cloud of pulped brick fills the water around me like blood. I feel the pressure shoving me up against the wall as the water is driven out through the aperture. There is water on the other side, but it is far lighter. Now I am clawing feebly at the bricks, trying to pull them away so that I won't be crushed against them, like a feverish man plucking at his bedclothes.

The brick gives way and the water around me drives forward all at once, carrying me into a passage.

There is a barely-perceptible shift, a remote click — the pressure is off, tea-colored light is sifting through to him — something prods him in the back — prods a few times, then drags him through icy water and out into warm, dry air, grass against his face. Dr. Thefarie has retrieved him from the brine tank.

CHAPTER EIGHT

The immigrants were noticed first in the spring, after the solstice, which was about the time the Great Lover disappeared. No one could make out their language or find their variously-designated region of origin on even the most detailed maps. Many in the cult therefore concluded that the immigrants didn't come from anywhere; they preceded the ones they left behind, or they had migrated here from no other place, but out from nothingness, with all its customs. Deuteronôme catches sight of a knot of them standing with their heads together at one end of the platform and there arises all around him the yipping of coyotes, disembodied and far away, a sound from a desert hill across thousands of miles.

Their numbers grow steadily, never quite becoming a torrent but regularly increasing. They are distinctive in appearance without any conspicuous exhibition in costume or toilette. Slow lugubrious men in voluminous sweaters, with close-cropped dark hair, leathery faces, with grubby hands and blackened gums, their voices thick and copious from years of heavy smoking. Yet, when they sing or make merry or drink, a light-hearted animal happiness comes fountaining up out of them, frank gaiety, boyishness, innocence, even beauty... sweet and plain. The candid women are bright, birdlike, businesslike, considerably fairer than the men, but with a certain darkness about the brow and at the corners of the mouth. Though it is not clear what exactly they do with themselves most of the time, they give an impression of unending laboring. When men respond by being slow, plodding, a little haphazard, the women make only partially necessary sacrifices to their pragmatism in anger, and vent hell on anyone who fails adequately to acknowledge their toil. As the day draws on the men work slower and slower and slower, while the drawn women turn frenetic and nervous, accomplishing less and less as they tire. The women don't ever seem to lose the haunted look around the eyes even when they're enjoying themselves... unless they're drinking: like a magic elixir the alcohol — twenty years evaporate from their faces, and they are brilliant star-like young girls once more. Women have the burden of worry, the men have the burden of resignation.

They are not reticent to name their country of origin — quite the opposite, their names for it are manifold. Some call it Mnemosem, which means simply: "wolves." In conversation with others one may hear the name Vkat-Vtonkonka, which might mean "a place where the trees have never been cleared away," or alternately "where no sun ever touches the ground." They write with their own peculiar alphabet of highly abbreviated pictures, mixed with appropriated punctuation marks which serve them as additional letters — ampersands, asterisks, a backwards capital D, and a few characters which are identified by Dr. Thefarie as Tamazight in derivation. Their preferred drink is a sort of akvavit. In chilly weather they drink it steaming hot and mixed with maple syrup; fibrous beads dropped into the hot punch open to tiny white blossoms, dried in the old country and revived here in the hot liquor, to which they impart a mild taste of hay. The immigrants consume a great deal of syrup and put it on everything. Their staple is a substance known as "moon cheese:" this is actually made of pressed fern piths bound together in wood tar and flavored with a variety of bitter peppercorn grown in ground sown with iron filings. The men always have tarry fingers from making the stuff.

The immigrants are not secretive, not exactly. Certain questions are simply no longer there when the opportunity to ask them arises. How many of them are there now? Even before your eyes the little knot of men and women resists your efforts to count them; they are impervious to numbering. Even when keeping company with a solitary one, you are forever catching the flicker of hands out of the corner of your eyes, and you find yourself turning to address one walking next to you when no one at all is there. The immigrants have dark powers of attraction. They are inexplicably magnetic; their accents are catching. You may find yourself using one of their words without understanding it, or remembering what you thought it meant at the time you first heard it. These never became immigrants; they are essentially Immigrants, all their lives.

On one occasion, Dr. Thefarie finds himself sitting beside a young immigrant woman with hair the color of cloudy beer, wearing a long coat of wool mail. When she rises and quits the car, he observes a leaf, shaped like an arrowhead, to drop from her coat. It flutters into his lap; as he takes it in his fingers he bruises the leaf — immediately his nostrils fill with a nameless odor of warm humid wood shadows in summer dusk, of stillness in long dusks drawn out like slow-ebbing tides of a light like ribbons of incense dropped from a sky patched with black olive clots of foliage, of narcotic softness in earthy air, and crumbling breath green with brothy dew like the bark of a thick-mossed oak.

Now the "demon" has returned from his long mission in the other world, and he has opened for us a passage to the sun inside. But what this means, nobody can say. Deuteronôme is still trying to divine it. I explained to him, when he came to, as best I could. The immigrants came with a man named Futsi.

"OK OK but what about the wings?"

"They went away. No one knows exactly what happened, but they must have made their way out either through the lake or down into the tank, going out the way you came back.

"...And I must tell you — Ptarmagant is dead."

He sat right up and stared into my eyes.

"He ventured above ground not long after you disappeared. A car ran him down."

I watched him droop.

"Deuteronôme and I are now jointly in charge. That was his wish. And he told us both, a few days before he was killed, to trust you would return."

"His body...?"

"Just like Wouvermans — we sent it down the tracks."

——◦◦—◦—

Ptarmagant's last words, addressed to Futsi from the foot of the stairs.

"We're not trying to replace *anything*. We're only trying to clear a space for ourselves. If other people want to be slaves, that's their problem."

—◦—◦—

Cultists gather in a broad circular chamber paved in flat flags and looking like the inside of a dolmen. It might once have been a huge reservoir. Flambeaux line the walls. The sole appointment is a large stone table surfaced with a thick sheet of polished silver in which the subway map has been engraved. Each line is a deep groove enamelled in the appropriate color, each station is marked with an upright, narrow-gage pipe, and labelled in Sanskrit characters. As the assembly recites line to line, intoning the name of every stop, Deuteronôme solemnly anoints the grooved map with a light, clear oil. When the shining oil brims the grooves, he touches the flame tip of a long wand-like candle to the central hub stops, and a vivid sapphire flame ripples down the lines with a sustained whisper. A jet of complacent, viscous blue fire emerges from the pipe at each station stop, making the subway map both a Chinese character and a dazzling constellation. Deuteronôme takes a teak striker in his hand, and uses it to ring a pair of silver chimes tuned to the notes of the closing doors, and a steady murmur arises from the assembled celebrants, each of whom has been given his or her own sutra of the Ten Million Combinations to recite. Rosaries of tokens help them to keep track, and their fondling hands flicker. This relentless churning of the air in short and swiftly successant names creates a rolling psychic tide or audible hypnosis, which is broken at critical moments by a repetition of the two notes, and by explosive blasts of train horns. After the first hour, incense is paraded around the room in silver bowls with bas-reliefs of rats and cockroaches on them, and ewers of filthy water and pulpy trash are emptied into drains at each of the cardinal points.

After the ceremony there is what is known as a "slow soirée," so called because the participants, largely drained of vim by the demands of the ritual, are subject to time-lag, and a not unpleasant lassitude drags at their arms and legs. Here, where a vast low-vaulted chamber of curving tiled arches, opens on the brink of an old water main, dangling gondola lamps on poles watch as their light is flung back at them by the water. Webby reflections spangle the vaults with their glue. Swords hang from the ceiling, points down, never rustling, never knocking together. Their blades are grey and dark in the shade, never sparkling but always dull and dim. Linen-sheeted round tables sit in prim circles radiating from the long high table opposite the channel, where Deuteronôme and Dr. Thefarie sit to either side of a large empty chair. Enormous carp circulate through the crowd in metal troughs embossed with bas reliefs; they knock imperiously against the metal from time to time with a muscular thump. These glowing fish, leprous white, fluorescent orange, or the water they swim in, give off a meaty, musty sort of odor. Illuminated panels of light shine on a magnificent roulette wheel, five feet in diameter, nearly half a ton of bronze and precious stone. Bronze everywhere is teased into flowing liquid shapes and volutes of smoke, skulls, nude bodies, fruits and sardonic flowers exhaling the decanted air of tormented sleep. A band plays in a corner, screened from view by huge potted plants: long windy notes slither on top of tensely-restrained percussion. The guests mill across the floor before the high table, calling to each other with their detuned radio voices. Some of these are Immigrants — the air is flecked with their alien words, their almost bleating-timbred voices slithering in and out of the crowd, hollow-eyed, cryptic-smiling, with shadows flickering on their brows.

The Great Lover emerges from the boundaries of the apartment, hanging back a little. The scum on his face has changed color from brown to indigo, a shaped mat of stripes and circles like a Maori tattoo cut from a subway map. His eyes avidly scan the crowd, and then he freezes.

Vera sits with her arm linked, talking to a young man he's never seen before. He is smiling, their faces are close. The Great Lover zeroes in on them with his ears; the young man has a light, nearly disembodied voice, like the warble of an oboe dimmed and interrupted by the wind, but his every word is distinct. While he has small obvious accent, every sentence he speaks in English is indistinctly strange, perhaps because he pronounces every word distinctly, and orders his words with audible deliberation. His smile pushes back the curtains of his cheeks, making two curving brackets to either side of his mouth.

Nearby there is an ice fountain and a pyramid of champagne glasses. The Great Lover slithers out staring and immediately latches on to a florid, energetic little man, a raconteur ex-Communist named Bosanquet who is popular in the cult.

"Don't say anything — I want to make my entrance in my own time. Come here!"

Bosanquet obligingly retreats with him into the shadows.

"Who's that?"

"Who's...?" Bosanquet looks around trying to follow the Great Lover's finger.

"Sitting with Vera."

"Oh! His name's Futsi. He's the one who brought in the Immigrants. Would you like to meet him?"

"They're awfully chummy aren't they?"

"That's been going on for months now."

Vera gets up and makes her way out of the room.

"Well... You don't want me to mention you're here?"

"No, thanks."

Bosanquet strides springily away with a glass of champagne in his hand and begins his rounds.

The Great Lover stands staring at Futsi from the dark, and the empty seat pulled right up alongside his own. He crumples. He wanders away like a man who's just been struck hard on the head. He sinks down by the wall, deflating like a balloon with a tiny puncture in it. With withered hands, he smacks the wall, and beats his chest. The music and the noise of the crowd is fainter here. He sobs once, aloud. The sound is like a separate world against the other sounds. The face he turns back to look again is streaked from the eyes. It is turning into the face of a mummy.

He rolls onto his knees on the slimy ground, breathing harshly, pressing his fists to his chest. The sounds of his grief rise from him unheard.

"Help me!" he chokes, "Help me! Help me!"

Now his breath is labored in a different way, his body seems to swell and shrink with each breath. The face he turns to the light is full again, pale white against the livid indigo of his mask, and his teeth have turned black. A contorted grin breaks the veil that had covered his face, and fractures the tear tracks.

Old Roy conducts the Great Lover to his table — across the room entirely from Futsi, and nearly on the brink of the open channel. He joins a group of thickly-built older Greek men quietly drinking raki with dazed expressions. They mutter and belch and puff ornate meerschaums. The Great Lover is scanning the room for Vera's face — where is she? Not back yet. The entrée is a crumbly, stiff fish in cloying white sauce eaten with dainty fingertip forks — even our substantial Greeks are plucking morsels to their mouths with remarkable delicacy. The waiter slaps his plate down in front of him haphazardly and the fish sauce and all nearly slides off. Mice streak across the table leaping dramatically over the centerpiece and some veer toward his plate. A few steps away, sweet old drunk, looks like a minor functionary in an Italian ministry, is boring the croupier with his poetical effusions, pointing to the red panels in the roulette wheel—

"...the carnelian. Gems are the crystallized thoughts of God."

"Sure sure, now quit holding up the line."

The Great Lover tosses his plate into the channel, slides from his seat and makes his way through the heaving crowd along the channel, edging himself in toward the center in stages.

Here steps descend into an open vivarium with stone urns and spanish moss. Two knife fighters, coats swaddling their left arms, confront each other in the confines of a circle of white marble. One is a robust olive type — Corsican, the other a neurasthenic Mexican with a yellow sash around his waist. The two circle each other haughtily, the Corsican swivels his hips and the Mexican sinks into a crouch you can hear his shoes creak over the music. Animated by a single impulse they close at the same time — a few darting blows are exchanged without connecting — the Corsican blocks a thrust with his left arm the blade cuts the cloth. The Corsican shunts back and forth like a wrestler, the Mexican cha-chas from side to side weightlessly. Now the Corsican feints at the body and throws out his strong arm; a soft, sad cry from the Mexican, recoiling as the tip finds his right eye.

The Corsican his face sizzling with emotion lunges in and the Mexican drops, his stilletto swings up catching the underside of the Corsican's left arm beyond the swaddle of his coat. The tip of the knife glides along the bicep splitting the shirt and the flesh of the muscle and now the Mexican twists his wrist and drives the blade down into the heart through the armpit. The Corsican's return stroke glances up along his opponent's lean chest leaving only a long shallow wound. He drops lifeless to the floor with a sigh, the sound of his falling is quiet. The panting neurasthenic staggers to a chair his arms out before him, disheveled locks of pomaded hair swing before his eyes. He drops the bloody knife on the table and sits to subdued applause. The onlookers rap their hands together with eyes tactfully downcast. It is improper to gaze directly at the winner. The blood is swiftly mopped, and the body removed; now a group has gathered there to dance stately pavans to Dowland's Lachrimae so you know the joint is jumping.

Vera, a metallic shawl the color of dessert wine across her back and elbows, is returning to her seat at the high table engulfed in impossible flames and he gazes at her from the heights of an astonishment out of all proportion to her, to himself, or to the world, as though he's never seen the *world* before. Overflowing and emitting beams of fierce life, she is ethereal fierce and brilliant, fierce — song of gardens in the moon, music of piquant longing. Her head appears to him in a smoky disk of orange light like a transparent sunset, lit from within. Futsi takes her face in his hand and draws it down, kissing her. The Great Lover watches with every one of his bright black teeth, and quietly hisses.

A mutter is going through the room. The Great Lover reaches down and takes hold of something invisible and social, like big cables, and tugs them. Bosanquet swings by. The Great Lover, with a crooked finger, summons him.

"Can I get you anything?"

The Great Lover nods glassily. The next moment he has hypnotized Bosanquet with instructions to insinuate himself alongside Futsi and launch into a protracted expatiation on the subject of his choice.

The Great Lover peers out at the high table from behind one of the apartment's many pillars, and watches as Bosanquet, already in position, launches into a set piece on Marx's theory of exchange value. The Great Lover watches anxiously: Vera sits there, stroking the edges of her empty plate with the tips of her fingers. Futsi is feigning interest. The Great Lover rivets his gaze on Vera. Futsi remarks something to her. She raises her head up to him with an ear-to-ear blind smile, the glory of the world. His hand she holds in her lap.

She abruptly goes still, except for her eyes. Then at once she turns her face in his direction.

Voices are calling, faces turning in his direction. He wants to get to Vera, but suddenly everyone has noticed him.

"He's back! He's back!"

"Ah, brothers and sisters!" Dr. Thefarie stands on his chair, a glass in his hand. "Let us welcome back our nameless friend!"

A rush of scattered uncoordinated applause, raised voices. For a moment, the Great Lover's eyes meet Futsi's, as the man rises onto the seat of his chair to see this living legend. Vera is standing there with her mouth open.

"Help. Help," he whispers barely moving his lips.

The Great Lover leaps onto a table with a huge black grimace and eyes like two white-hot coals, clasps his hands together over his head and brandishes them like prizefighter.

"The winner!" he screams, "And still champion!"

He crouches like a frog and leaps thirty feet right into the channel, disappearing without a trace.

—oo—o—

Later that night, nervous feathers vibrating like pneumatic drills slip between the stones, unlacing the masonry with a steady friction...

chunks of stone and cement crack and drop away, the abandoned floor of the chamber, strewn with the remains of the banquet, is battered by the falling debris. Wings seethe in. A limp figure drags itself into the gap on huge, sinewy wings. The body lies face down on the rubble, the wings adhering unnaturally to its back straddle like bowed legs, and knuckle-walk it forward on the flattened tips of its wings. As the figure slides down to the tunnel floor, untenanted wings sluice through the gap after it, spinning in air made musky by their grease.

Futsi is walking with Vera, back to his apartment.

"That demon is something! How does he jump so far..." He makes a wing-spreading gesture and then looks at her.

"You're so silent."

"I thought he wath gone. We were all thyure."

"...He is dead, isn't he?"

His heart is beating. I can hear it. I'm even feeling it.

"No, he wath dead. Now he'th alive."

"That's something!" Futsi says. "Did the demon bring him back?"

"I don't know."

"I'll ask him!"

—○—○—

The Prosthetic Libido holds a feather up to the light and sighs. It's the next day.

"Why can't I? Go out there, I mean."

"Sooner or later someone would try to copy you, or *improve* you. They," I make a gesture including everything outside the window, "aren't worthy of that knowledge. And you, for that matter, deserve better than the treatment you'd get from them."

I reach into my coat and withdraw a new-looking steel blade nearly two feet long, with a pole socket in one end, hand it to him.

"Sharpen this for me, will you?"

Pearl takes the blade in his hands, edge toward him, pinches the edge between right thumb and index finger, and slides the pinch in one smooth zip along the edge; the metal rings and a cloud of filings fine as ash spurts into the air. He pertly hands the blade back to me with unblemished fingers. The cutting edge is sharpened down to near invisibility.

"What's that for?" he asks.

"Just a feeling," I say. "You might try... moving very quickly."

"...?"

"If you move as fast as you can, perhaps you will be too fast to see — at least up close. Velocity has a lot to do with being able to see things."

"...What's wrong?"

He's staring at me. He's concerned. Taking a step toward me, he lays his hand, light as a leaf, on my arm.

"You're hurt—"

"Yes, that's right." My voice is so ugly he just stops.

—◦◦—◦—

He looks like a submarine, slipping along in the deep. Futsi's head is right by my shoulder. I get up slowly — sometimes I still catch myself listening for my father, as if he might call to me from wherever he is. When it happened, I thought I heard him. I don't want to feel sad now, I let the blackness and my sleepiness fold over the thought and cover it.

The bathroom is the only place you can go in the middle of the night a stupid thing to think. The window is open. Moving naked through the dark I imagine I can find my way a little bit better, feeling the air on my skin. If you pay really close attention it seems as if you can feel the air you push aside as you move bouncing back to you from objects, and the sounds you make of course. Out there the submarine is moving along in the dark, pinnng... ping is a bad word for it it's more like tong! or just t'oonnn — ah or aw? He shoots through the sewage like a big furry torpedo. I feel so light I imagine I could melt through the wall, float away like a cloud.

I lie down again by Futsi's strong warm body. Now I hear banging. Somehow I know the striker is a wrench — I can hear a little rattle when it hits. What's Futsi doing? And there's another rattle that can't be anything but chess pieces or checkgammon pieces go stone mah tile jonggpoker chice strike out to the stars, echo against the eighteenth century on the walls. Each blow shakes me and I feel a warm droplet drip into me where it warm congeals keep hitting it! *you monster!*

He's wearing cologne. I can feel lace ruffles below his chin, and when I lift my hands and drop them down on his head, there are these weirdly regular rolls, and my hand comes away with a residue on it. I laugh and pull his wig off — he's mad and tries to drag it out of my hand. Jewels on his clothes scrape me. I can hear cracks open in the floor, a delicious, crisping sound. When my hand brushes his head again, I feel his hair — he's not Futsi, it's him.

I'm outside, under some trees. Birds are calling, and through the whoosh of air in the branches I hear waves. The light falling on my skin is almost sunlight but the color feels wrong, like it's not warm enough. The sun is still heating up out there in space, so it follows the world is not very old. A few steps... the ground rises a little in a sort of bump... roots bend my feet. The trunk is pretty smooth — a beech tree? They're smooth aren't they? It's denser behind me than in front of me, so I think I must be close to the water. I take a few steps away from the beech and cold seawater pulls my knees. My clothes are folded in a little pile where I left them under some low fern branches, somewhere. Why didn't I go swimming? Because I can't see — I must have forgotten. That's a strange thing to forget!

Now I understand why — this isn't my dream. I call to him — it's his dream. Where is he?

The trees go right down into the water, and the long grass tangles my feet. This is the Immigrants' country. This must be Futsi's dream after all. I hear voices now — I half want to run out and show myself to them and I half want to hide. Since hiding came second I'll hide.

Women's voices, yowling something at the top of their lungs. Sounds religious. It must be a seasonal festival, when they make their way along the coast singing and shouting, and throw burlap bundles of grain and other harvest fruits into the ocean. Somewhere along the way I found a Japanese book with raised characters and braille in alternating lines. The Japanese are fascinated by braille's simplicity you know. I read some of it, but all I can remember of it when I wake up is the second half of the title on the spine. It was "...*from Red Master.*"

—○—○—

The night and sleep collude to create strays; a girl fell asleep in the park, where her body lay beneath a heavy, shapeless web of shadows draped past the trunk and thickening with dusk, beneath thick, heavy dark of dreamless sleep. A weak air feebly stirs leaves above her breathing face, wan patch against black roots. She falls deeper into sleep like alcohol's quiet as she stands up, her numb eyes are barely broken open. Now she walks not slow nor fast, halting and stalking like a child just learning. In her sleep there is an image lying flat in invisible clouds of muffling black, the rough boundary of stone, the street washed with orange light, the leprous pale sidewalk, the black passage lined with steps down, and framed with iron scab. In the passage the grating is half unhinged and hangs, sags nearly to the ground, and is no bar to her.

There are only a handful of blue lights to illuminate the cavernous station, a broad wafer of pale blue space cut across by two silver-lined black grooves. Moonlight blue lights glow from tiles powdered with plaster dust. The booth is dark, the turnstiles are streaked with fine-lined splints of light, the turnstiles have black wings of barred grates, and the wide open gate watches her approach, her form is air, a feather, she leaves light steps.

The black mouth without breath of the tunnel grows, fills her fogged eyes. There is a strong smell of urine here, and the walls have isosceles triangles of thick yellow-brown residues rising from the floor up the walls. The smell is stronger, its acridness stirs her — as it grows suffocating she stops, and comes awake as a shape flops out of the mouth of the tunnel before her. The body is naked and prone, and dirty. Sinewy wings protrude from its back and reach down to the floor like legs, holding it off the ground and knuckle-walking it forward in a limp, loping walk. The head hangs down on slack stretched neck between the shoulders, the head is hairless and the scalp has peeled from the skull. In choking smell of cold urine it drags and walks out of the tunnel before her. The ridged back of the flopping neck and head stares at her like a face. Sleep-addled the girl retreats backwards. The wings lift the body, the head drops with a soft thud on the seat of the bench, and turns as the body is lowered. She sees the bruised face, and hears a panting sigh from mouth without breath. A ball in the throat and thickened limbs turned viscous as tar she cannot turn in time, the weight is pressing her to the floor, a beating at her back, a tug her dress gives way and air floods her skin, cold damp and thick as glue a heavy weight is shifted onto her, cold wormlike fingers bore into her back, a cold burn as her skin is boiled and fused, tugged to and fro. She struggles; the wings churn; she is lurched into the air, the platform falls through the open pit mouth of the tunnel, and with it the newly derelicted body lies abandoned its back ragged with rents where the wings had been. With each wing beat, she bobs; she hurtles alone in the air.

—◦—◦—

Homeless wings sneak up on unsuspecting victims and pounce, planting their stumps into the victim's back, and making off with him to where? No one knows. I suppose the wings fly around with them until they succumb to privation, exposure, rough treatment. Deuteronôme has divined an uncertain relationship between the wings and what Ptarmagant had called the *Vampirism*. At first, I had assumed this was essentially *ghûl*, but now we have one of our own I no longer think so. *Ghûl* is the blank of the desert and of death; words spread in infinite space like pepper on the surface of the water, growing always thinner until there's nothing left of them. It's also the sandstorm that rages and erases. And the mirages, "will of wisps" the Europeans call them, that lure men into sand or quicksand. These vampires, on the other hand, leave us where we are but grind us away into phantoms, and this cannot be allowed.

A meeting is called inside one of the bridges. Futsi comes rolling in with the other skateboard riders; he glides in, standing on his board, smiling. He's been a great blessing to us — a sturdily-built Japanese man with a mohawk, draped in a sweatshirt as big as a kameez. Long linen ribbons he has wound around his shins, making his black canvas pants bulge like onions at the knees.

Multiply greets Futsi. First time I saw Futsi, he thinks, I thought he had some mess on the back of his neck. Then I see it's this tacky tattoo of a cougar head. It's just the outlines, and the eyes and the white parts around the mouth, because his skin is already the right color. At first I thought it was lame, but now I look again and think it's all right, like the old respect of the tribe for the animals. I asked him about it and he said he had a dream, and saw it there on his neck, so he went out and got it.

Dr. Thefarie noticed the tattoo as well — I had to ask what it was — a female lion? As I look at its solemn expression, I find I keep a straight face myself only with difficulty.

After some preliminary remarks, Deuteronôme cedes the floor.

Uar, a mestizo from Bahia, is an accomplished trance fighter with a curly mop of thick hair and a skin condition; while most of his body is dark copper the delicate skin of his face and neck, his hands and forearms to the elbow is bleached translucent grey. The hued skin meets the bleached in ragged lines dotted with flakes of pale in the brown. His jawline is spotted with the woolly buttons of his sparse beard, which glisten like glass thread against his ghostly face. The condition has also drained his eyes a moonlight ash. He wears a rumpled shirt rolled up at the elbows and half open.

Sitting down on a bench, something catches the corner of Deuteronôme's eye and in the same moment he feels a hot streak in his spine — a huge boa constrictor slides by among the thick PVC piping overhead. It veers off toward a shadowy corner and before Deuteronôme can turn his head the demon is there, half hidden in the dark, listening to Uar.

"Sometimes they come out of the jungle and burrow into graves, looking for bodies to attach to, and sometimes — we don't know why — the wings attach *inside* the body, and not on the outside."

Uar folds his hands across his broad chest.

"They squeeze the lungs and heart like milking a cow,"

He flexes his hand open and closed.

"to animate the body, and work the arms and legs from within by pushing on the bones. The cold brains revive with the blood, but they have no control of the body from the neck down. Their guts and their mouths are choked with feathers, and the feeling makes them insane. They hate like sulfur everyone who isn't suffering like them, and so they turn into vampires. But since they can't drink blood with their bodies full of feathers, they suck out your spirit with their eyes.

"The sun doesn't bother them. They walk in the street and try to go unnoticed, taking spirit away from everyone they pass. So you go in a crowd and come out feeling lightheaded, weak. They run people down, and run down the world. They like it when people cut down trees, because trees interfere with them. Wherever trees are being chopped down, you know vampires are there. They also like it when people put lights everywhere at night, because they feed by seeing you. But they don't like being seen. They are insatiable, because they suck not by hunger, but because of insane irritation.

"To fight them, you have to meet them vampires in a trance; the trance stiffens up your spirit like changing milk to cheese, so it is hard to suck away. The vampires notice when you do this and will want to come after you right away, so be ready."

Uar taps the palm of his left hand with the edge of his right.

"Luckily they are cowards, and will not like a confrontation with you face to face. They are parasites, not hunters. A grey thought held in empty hand."

Deuteronôme's eyes flick from Uar to the demon to Futsi. The demon's eyes flick from Uar to Futsi, to Deuteronôme.

"Perhaps you have something you can tell us," he calls to the demon. Now all eyes flick.

The figure seems to rise and fall again as it creeps forward into the light. His face is different — the brown flakes of dried filth have turned into a mask of fine blue lines, like an etching.

Multiply thinks — now his face looks like someone went crazy with a ball point and a spirograph.

"When Ptarmagant was alive," the demon says, "he showed me a page from the *Phaedrus* whose meaning he felt was of crucial importance. Not to go on and on about it, the wings are city elementals of thwarted desire that bud off and become separate. They are a complement to the red armbands. I would recommend avoiding direct confrontation with them for the time being. As Uar said, trance is important. It is important because, if you simply attack them directly, you will be feeding them the vitality you throw into the attack. The harder you fight the more they will feed."

"And if they come for us?" Deuteronôme asks.

"Run. If possible, get them to chase you. That will tire them out... I'll get them to chase me. The more they chase and fail to catch what they're chasing, the more they are weakened as a whole. In fact, if enough of us are willing, we should establish teams of runners to provoke them."

Futsi has been staring at the Great Lover in rapt attention.

"We could" he says, "do that to the armbands, too! Do you think that would work?"

The demon says nothing, but seems to shrink.

Deuteronôme: He *is* jealous. I can almost see his pain, like a fall of sick water pouring over him. It's like a biting, sour smell.

"Yes," I say aloud, "we will coordinate teams of runners. You," I point to the demon, "will deal with the wings, and you" I point to Futsi, "will deal with the armbands."

We are breaking up now. The demon is dissolving into the shadows. Immigrants standing near me watch him go, talking with Futsi, who seems to want to go talk to him. They are making skeptical faces, and speaking to each other in their own language. "Dybbuk," they call him, "kachina."

Multiply rolls past his corner smiling at the shrinking demon. "Too bad he got your woman..." he sings softly as he is going by.

I stop him outside.

"Awww—"

"Silence!" I hold up my hand his mouth snaps shut like a trap.

"That man has a demon in him. He cannot be trusted. I have seen it—"

I jab him in the chest.

"—you have not. Don't antagonize him!"

"Yeah all right—"

"Don't joke. What you put on your plate comes back in the spoon."

—◦◦◦—

Pearl is with John again and the Great Lover is in the sewers with his gnomes, sitting in a grease circle, peering through three pairs of glasses into a round bottle he's washed and bleached transparent. A single feather — the same one he'd shown to Pearl — hangs suspended inside.

I am trying to get a look in on the wings. There is no way to drift gradually in, or to sink down into the sight... but now and then something like a cold solar flare arcs past and over me, with a gush like wind or a harsh grating sound. I can almost see them — transparent brass shells that move through the air like rips in fabric — coming out of a smoke that gathers around the feather in a rough globulation. I have to drive my nerves into it—

I feel pain and draw back, stop myself just in time as I see the problem — it's not a membrane keeping me out, but something more like the momentum of a merry-go-round or a moving train — my nerves crashed into the motion. If I pull them back suddenly, they are likely to get tangled and ripped out of me, or drag me in with them to be mangled in the works, like Isidora Duncan strangling on her own scarf. Draw back carefully... not just slowly, but pulling each nerve ending out of the way when it's safe.

I'm beginning to feel right again; now to get in I have to match the speed, like boarding a moving train, and pick my moment to hop — every cog has a tooth missing somewhere and that's the aperture you can use to get in, but it can only be done with a swift darting motion perpendicular to the... now—

It's like a huge whirling metal drum, groaning as it spins, a buzzing shell at my back, metallic smoke too that's mostly rigid but fumes off its structures, a maze looking sort of like an abstract rendering of a London slum at one-third scale — blocks and rows, low walls and partitions. This is their subway. Everything is made of lead smoke. The spaces between objects are made of weak, colorless light, stronger than moonlight but not as strong as overcast daylight. There is a metronomic sound, too, with a soft attack, that undulates through the smoke in nearly visible scallops of tiny parallel streaks or hairs, not quite evenly spaced.

My nerve form is too light to be affected by these waves; it is moving at the same speed as everything here. I float up to one of the "walls" and see the wave shred through it, momentarily crystallizing the smoke into a lead skein. Then it falls apart and resumes its former, homogeneous appearance. An empty, dying feeling presses me from these things. There is no atmosphere here in the usual sense, but I experience something like dry cold that has no bite. Temperature in the air has to do with movement of the air, but here there is no movement except the drifting of the smoke and the operations of the waves. The drifting smoke, which seems both to drift and to stand as still as statues, weblike though it looks, is too dense to penetrate, like a metal film. The note in the air has a lower, creaking tone I'm just beginning to notice, like someone groaning until the sound of the voice breaks apart into individual pops; I feel it more than I hear it, like the rumble of a subway train passing just overhead.

How should I move? Without knowing what exactly threatens me, I know it is dangerous to be caught here; and that I may get stuck somehow, even if I am not detected. If I move only when the waves are flowing, don't I risk being caught in them? If I move only when they aren't flowing, my motion might be noticed. I'll risk synchronizing my movement to the waves, play it safe by moving with the light, as far as possible from the smokes.

The light is disgusting; a tepid mucus.

I find the station. A feeble, even radiation fills the place, the tracks, pillars, benches and other features are all made of indifferent smoke.

Almost no color, almost no contrast of intensities, like a completely smudged pencil sketch. The "vampires" are like leprous bodies clothed in a ragged plumage of fibrous smoke. They stand perfectly still, hands at their sides, with their heads thrown back. I look up, to see what they see. The ceiling is covered with furled wings, hanging upside down and jostling each other with weird violent movements. A downy metal dust sifts from their feathers and falls on the vampires; the vampires reply with song, not opening their mouths. The dust I can feel fall around me, and it's like a stream of death pushing life down out of me like dragging down my clothes to the floor. The song is almost like the rising and falling of emergency sirens; the waves transmit the siphoned energies to the wings, and their jostling and shivering is part of the way they bask in it and consume it. It's when the note, after sinking and sinking, suddenly wells back up in pitch again that I really feel it — and panic, horror, as though a spider had mounted on me, and gradually dissolves and absorbs my body.

Try moving in on a specific object — here under one of the pseudo-stairwells. Unnerving, that everything here is purely geometrical, still, completely eternal and everlastingly the same. The line of the stairwell above me now, the blank floor and blank walls; I imagine lying in a casket, my head on one side, gazing out at the interior of the mausoleum forever. Vera and Futsi together, their bodies arc and flex together — a gasp brings me back to attention — I had permitted my thoughts to wander and the sharp feeling attracts them. They fasten on pain like that — I stay still and listen with all my mind. A pair of legs appears where the stairs climb out of the floor, their momentum fading. They stop.

Now they drift away.

But now I notice, in the deeper darkness under the stairs, a small group of them sitting with their heads together, talking in their garbled, monotonous whispers. They are talking about us — so that also distracts them. I suddenly can see their way: somewhere they are watching... here, on the platform of which this is the shadow, they are watching us — I see the grey smudged platform, covered with milling figures like silent movie people projected on smoke with a weak lamp. They are barely outlines, but they flicker in intensity, and project colors, which sometimes flash, brighten and then dwindle again. A stationary group catches my eye, each one with a streak of darker grey in the middle of the forearm — the red armbands. I don't pick up any clues from observing them, until I notice that their shadows don't match. They are the shadows of prostrates, doubled over flat on their calves with their hands bound behind them, their hooded heads bowed.

Here and there, in the crowd, is one of us — a cultist, or fellow traveller — standing gaudily out with a lively or brilliant aspect that seems to attract and pain them at once. Here's a woman they're closing in on. She hums with a singing wine glass note, a constellation of puncturing intensities inside her, rising in chains like champaigne bubbles. The neutral figures of the vampirism begin to accumulate around her in a purely automatic fashion, so grey as nearly to be engulfed in the background. I hear a rasping creak that seems almost to come from inside me, like the sound your sinuses make when they suddenly depressurize. Her bubbles deform and bleed copiously, the blood coming out in vivid globs which vanish into the unclean grey of the vampires' feathers. The woman droops, sagging against a pillar. She puts her hand to her head, and puts her other arm across her body, holding herself. The vampires numbly float away.

This purulent light I'm in is becoming unbearable. I move through it with revulsion, heading for the wall of the station. There is a darker tile there, furred over with this metal smoke like thick dust. I can't brush it aside — they'd notice if I did, anyway — so I slip my nerves in between the wall and the smoke, sliding a hand into a freshly dead body that's not quite cold. I run my nerves over the tile, and suddenly I know what it says, which station this corresponds to. Gingerly, with a throbbing feeling like panting in horror, I draw my nerves out, can't do it too fast, can't make any sudden moves, and swim back the way I can let me let me let me make it out out out—

That woman holds both hands to her face now. I can see the

strands of hair hanging down, and she weaves a little. She drops her hands to her sides and takes two dragging steps, her head tilted a little too far back. All of her is just a colorless hollow with a few lit contours. I go over to her picking my moment. I move with care between two vampires. Then turn a little but they aren't homing on me yet. There is a rustle in the air — train coming.

Slowly I bring myself up to the woman, who leans against the back of the stairs, legs crossed at the ankle, like she can barely hold herself upright. The sound of her long breaths comes to me, an attitude of anxious listening, as though she expected an asthma attack or a bout of vomiting, and now and then, when the air brushes her vocal cords, she utters soft noises of distress. I keep myself cool until the train rushes in, baleful light and a visible metal wind, like a wiggling streak of dull mercury, pouring its force into the station like a wave washing the shore. The moment it comes I bright up and move in hearing the bells and whistles in my mind, seeing the flashing knife when the dancer slashes himself to drink his own blood, and I put my nerves into her and flare myself up, like puffing myself up with wind. I'm not draining into her, I'm stirring up her own native voltage. Her form straightens, her will is resurging, her voltage is strengthening. The train has stopped. Her head creates luminous filaments that spin lightly around each other like tea leaves. I speculatively give her a push — it should appear in her mind as a sort of random impulse or intuition.

It works, she boards the train. The vampires are already closing in but so are the doors, and the car is basically empty — I see no one dangerous in there. It takes several of them to affect you. She is on the other side of the doors. I dim down fast the others are looking around and drifting toward me like amoebas; the train pulls out in another blast of force, whiting out their radar, and I escape. Turned heads. The wings twitch in waves.

Now I'm out of their sight — the feeling of defilement is too much — I can't let it overwhelm me — I reach out and begin to rub on the smoke, rub in a little circle, there on the "floor." It starts to give, hollowing out. I can reach into the smoke now and start gently tugging — again I have to fight down panic and disgust — the smoke is tearing, the aperture is gradually opening... this is a little like working a pot on a wheel, the edges spinning and threatening to collapse — I have to work carefully, slowly, to make it stable so it will stay open until I can get all the way through it.

My heavy body drops back as though a metal sheet had fallen on it — I'm not all the way out though, I can feel my nerves are stretched taut, half out the opening. I draw them out, hand over hand, like pulling a net from the sea. A clutch of nerves hits my jaw and I can speak.

"Help — help me," I gag.

At once the nearest gnome is there, grabbing on and pulling. The others come monkeying up and join in. Feeling comes back to my legs, my abdomen; it's as though my body had been completely rigid, and now, as the nerves are restored to their proper places, the muscles suddenly go slack.

"It's closing up!" I cry in panic. With a heave I draw in the last of my nerves like sucking in noodles.

For a while I lie there, worrying. It's almost impossible to know whether or not I left anything behind, tail end of a nerve sticking out in that vile spot. I wait... I begin to feel whole. I am whole.

Frothing in repugnance, the Great Lover bounds to his feet, dashes from his platform, and flings himself into the purifying, shitty waters of the sewer.

—o—o—

Futsi meanwhile organizes the subway runners. The platforms are now "patrolled" by vigilante groups of right-wing high school and college students wearing red armbands, who often carry weapons. The runners taunt these students and draw them into ambushes or simply wear them out in endless cartoon chases. There are runners who dress as early twentieth-century Wobblies; stereotype punks; the baseball gang from "The Warriors" in pinstripe outfits and baseball stitching drawn on their faces; others wear sutured black leotard-like outfits and get themselves up as Cesare from "The Cabinet of Dr. Caligari." Goths, jesters, teddy boys, sad hobo-type clowns, mimes, as absurd as possible, designed to invoke the most clannish instincts, and to destroy the respectability of conformity by showing the mindless violence behind it. It was noted that nonwhite cultists did not have to dress up.

There would prove to be some unexpected problems — most notably the designers, who were forever swiping the runners' outfits. Constant alteration of costume was necessary to stay ahead of these fashion appropriations; intimidating or bumping off designers, fun as it might have been, was ruled out after careful consideration. Through them, the riots of the subway are both domesticated and transmitted, so, for a time anyway, allow the transmission to proliferate the images. But only as long as it helps to undermine conformity. Police charging in from everywhere — two emerge from the passage and instantly the demon sprints up and hypnotizes them on the spot. More and more police come and the demon is zooming back and forth hexing them all whammies flying around like custard in a pie fight. Weeks later some of the affected officers are still hypnotized. One shows up to work every day decked out in more and more gold, heavy chains hanging from his neck and diamonds welded to his badge. Snakeskin band around his cap, and tinsel hanging from wires, then tie dyes his uniform. A desk sargent excuses himself and re-emerges from the bathroom with vermillion lips and gold glitter all over his cheeks, gold eye shadow and his slacks are manhandled into thigh-high iridescent platform boots.

But Futsi's special genius lies in choreographing trouble with the police. Multiply taunts three students and they chase him through the station. He loses all but one, laughing mocking and staying just out of his reach until the student is in a frenzy of rage, pulling out his knife.

"Show you—"

Multiply gets his cue and scoots down a tunnel.

"Come back here fuckin—"

Rounding the corner hot in pursuit

"—nigger!"

barrel right into a black cop "*What did you call me?!*"

Anger in the cop's eyes turns to alarm as he sees the knife and before the student can explain a bullet rips through his ribs — his mind goes black and he drops. Enemy strength minus one. Echoes of Multiply's laughter still can be heard fading down the tunnel.

Armband girl tries to mace a runner in a djellaba with beard and skull cap, who suddenly isn't there. Mace spins in the vibrating air and jabs into the eye of a passing female police officer — armband sees the jam she's in and turns to run. The cop has had a long and very bad day. Armband girl tossed sourly into the backseat of the car body aching all over.

After a slough of arrests and combats, some of the more die-hard types have started carrying guns. Multiply gets a bullethole in his sweatshirt — missed him by an inch — and one of his friends isn't so lucky. Other runners drag him to safety with a trough cut across his leg showing white bone — another runner, more or less a dead ringer for the stricken one, decoys the shooter and bolts down a corridor. At this moment a street crimes unit appears on the scene, summoned by a precisely-timed phone call from Futsi. The sight seems to blur in their minds as the armband darts into the doorway after our runner. They see the black runner and the student's gun somehow together and process: black man with gun. As one man they draw glocks and empty every round into the doorway. A Dartmouth boy's bullet-riddled body slops out into the light, gun clatters along the platform and down into the slough between the rails with a deep "plunk."

Muttered exclamations, buzz of radio voices, heads sway up to the body. Bright red blood drips from the yellow platform edge. Skateboard wheels rasp in the distance.

—◦◦—◦—

Pulling back the red hinged no unauthorized persons sign at the brink of the tunnel, I walk out onto the platform and board the first car of the downtown express. No one sees me though the train is full; I brace my legs — man could get an infection hanging onto these grimy steel poles I think, sniffing sewage back up my nose.

The train brakes abruptly throwing everyone in the car — I fall flat against the TO's door, narrowly avoid a woman sitting with a fat tyke on her lap. She wears slippers of black mesh with pitiful embroidered little flowers fraying to nothing on the toes. Gazing at them, I feel poetic reverie coming on in contemplation of the gallant vanity of these wistful slippers. Only then does it occur to me someone pulled the brake cord — that's the only reason a train might stop so hasty. Something balls up in my throat and I move quickly to the doors, wrench them apart forcing myself through a bit at a time as they fight me, biting at me like a mechanical shark.

As I extricate myself the train suddenly lunges forward gathering speed. Out of the corner of my eye I see a wing beat against the inside of the TO's window. I lose my grip and drop crash into a post. I get up and limp away from the train, heading for a tiled passage toward the adjacent station on a parallel line.

When I get there I find a flurry of wings and limp bodies has knotted itself together at the far end of a platform stained here and there along half its length with thick streaks of blood, while citizens too out of it to notice mill about waiting for the trains delayed as usual, looking at watches, rattling bags and newspapers, walking to and fro with a slow stiff-legged step. They are tense, but they don't know why and they don't ask... that's all. The wings have killed some of them on a lark no pun intended; through their mass I can see Warren, cornered in behind a stairwell.

Brandishing his two speakers out in front of him, Warren is singing along with the radio at the top of his lungs, holding the wings at bay with his song, but as he comes into view so do a couple of police officers strolling down the platform and they will certainly attempt to quiet Warren when they reach him. I pitchpole my rod like a harpoon in a long arc — it javelins down like appearing out of thin air with a thunk impaling and pinning to the tile floor a winged body. We have bodies here and can fight — the demon must have found this thing. An attack might waste energy, but as their numbers are reduced so is their strength, and I had to get them off of Warren.

The mass of wings seethes in confusion, limp heads whip around hunting for me. I draw the line taut, draw a bow strung with a lock of red from my coat, and bow the line with it; the sound is a dull droning throb. The wings ruffle convulsively as it begins. While the others scatter, my pinned victim can't flee the tone — feathers spurt from buzzing pinions and the wings tear themselves loose from the body and flop about on the ground stunned. With a snap of the line I draw out the rod and pull it along the floor, scoop it up as I run to Warren's side. I get to the debilitated wings before they can recover and whack them in two. Looking back I see the wings and bodies have gathered in a furious heap behind me. I whirl my curtains at them the demon brays at the top of his lungs, chortling and screaming

"Hee-HAWWN!"

with so much diaphragm jostle makes me feel puky.

We draw them off — they leave Warren and come for us. We must be blazing. Into the tunnels... a train is thundering up fast I feel a wham against my back and only by throwing myself violently to the side can I avoid the train — a pair of them bounds up my coat tails and squirms up under toward my back — I ram my back against a wall strut and the wings withdraw, lashing at me. All around now the air is blurred with frantic shapes and powerful blows raining come at me from all sides; I career to the other side of the tracks and down side shaft staircase tumbling and turning, crash face-first into the floor at the bottom. Wings scurry over him; I grab them and wrestle them away. The wings vanish in the darkness of the tunnel in two bounds: silence. Warily I get up, and make my way with pain on to the next station.

The platform has a windswept appearance, stark and cold as underground steppe. Here the air shivers as though a great tolling sound had only just died away a moment before. I bench myself. Time passes. Distant voices on the PA stations away reading station stops, the book of the dead. I tap out the squares of the floor at my feet with toe of my shoe. Pretty tough shoes, holding up. Gradual rumbling as an empty train pulls in. I straighten up and head for the doors.

Something scrambling thuds into my back and I stumble, pitching through the closing doors yanking and tearing, snarling and cursing. I get a firm grip but the train jerks I lose my balance, my weapon slides out of reach like in the movies, a wing thrusting its clammy butt end down the back of my coat feeling spasmodically for skin. We're angry now and I snare them both with whip hands and wrestle them again around to the front, beads of sooty grease on their feathers. The wings writhe away and I quickly slam my back up against the partition door separating the TO's compartment from the rest of the car. The wings are crouched not six feet away, leaning first this way, and then that, assessing their chances; oh good, a long pinfeather rises up past the top of one of the windows near on my left — one of the wings before me takes a probationary step forward, folding and unfolding its powerful muscles strain along the length of its long bones. I listen with increasing strain and there is a brushing sound moving down the ceiling of the car at random intervals. The wings lunge — I flap hands at them and they drop into what might be a defensive posture, but without retreating. Listen... sound of feathers frilling along broken glass behind him now; feint toward the rod carefully exposing a little of my back, the wings flip in two different directions and I slam my back to the black glass of the door. Rustle of newspapers as wings creep on the floor of the TO's compartment. The pair in front of me group up together a few feet away. I listen behind me and stare in front of me. Now I dive for the floor and the wings flutter menacingly—

Sharp crack of glass and flutter behind. I roll — the wings on either side of the glass, having pounced at the same time and at the same target, smash into each other: the wing stumps haplessly fuse and fall to the floor flailing wildly trying to tear loose from each other. As they struggle they slough dust everywhere, a cloud of it fills the car.

When the train stops and the doors open, the dust is sucked out. Nothing on the floor there but long needly bones. This is the Courtland station, whose name he read with his fingers.

—◦○◦—

When two collide and latch onto each other, they perish — they implode, each sucked all the way into the other.

Under the watchful eyes of cops, the crowd at the Courtland station flows. The car doors slide back like the barred gates of a cell block and the crowd emerges, each one holding-in him or herself in a peculiar way getting farther away closer apart and farther together under the watchful eyes of cops. The copeyes are full of watching, there are watches in their ticking eyes. All of them have bulbs velcroed to one or the other shoulder, spattering the air with squelched voices and sounds with an unintelligible technical significance. They stand on the high catwalks over the platform with their hands on black belts weighed down with weapons. Each one carries a spray to blind people with, a gas to smother people with, a device to give people electric shocks with, a club to beat up people with, white plastic twist ties to tie people up with, a gun to kill people with, a knife to cut up people with, a little microwave torch to burn up people with, steel clamps to torture people with, grenades to explode people with, a cat o'nine tails to whip people with, a mask to hide behind and frighten people with, gloves lined with tiny hooks to slap people's skin off with, a pump filled with hydrochloric acid to melt away people's flesh with, shrapnel mines filled with flechettes to rip the flesh of people to shreds with, a webcam to film and share images of people being raped with, an inflatable basin to drown people with, a power drill to bore holes in people with, and a thick record book in which carefully to keep records, with a column on every page that reads: blind, suffocate, shock, club, restrain, gun down, dismember, immolate, torment, explode, flog, terrify, flay, dissolve, lacerate, violate, drown, and bore, with an empty circle next to each word, to be filled in with a number two pencil made of human bone when appropriate. The crowd flows safely by under the watchful eyes of cops, who lean on the banisters, their eyes flicking to and fro, receiving prompts through their earpieces and eyeglasses who looks to be the wrong race, whose face exhibits a wrong expression, whose clothing is indicative of a wrong opinion, to arrest. From time to time a grabber arm not unlike the kind that are suspended inside clear plastic cases over heaps of toys, and are manipulated to pluck up one toy or other and drop it through a chute into waiting hands on the outside of the machine, suddenly will drop down without the same air of happy anticipation and pluck someone out of the crowd. Under the watchful eyes of cops, the chosen one is drawn up, struggling and protesting, through a mesh of interblended plastic brushes that conceals whatever is above it, and which forms the apparent ceiling of the station. The watches in their ticking eyes take in this sudden arrest with a quick blankness and contraction that is not much different from the subtracted response of the people on the platform. Those nearest the chosen one speed up, look down, and change their mouths, while keeping them tightly shut, under the watchful eyes of cops.

Futsi and a group of skating provocateurs have run into trouble, armbands behind and now they are hemmed in, almost rushing straight into a zone of strong *Vampirism*. They can see it now, like a grey cloud inside the eye, with slack forms moving inside. The armbands, whether they see it or not, will drive them into it and then they'll be in trouble. The armbands are not affected by the *Vampirism* in the same way; it irritates them and wears them out with stress — unless they can find an outlet, like kicking someone to death.

The provokers break apart — Futsi escapes along the tracks but four of his colleagues aren't so lucky. They veer in among the students, who lash out at them with baseball bats. Futsi stops and waves the others to regroup when there is a deafening shout from the far end of the platform. Shuffling forms advance on its source — the Great Lover has emerged carrying a pair of dull red curtains still on the rod, with two matador poms on his hat. He leaps up on a bench and waggles his curtain at the enemy — he lunges this way and that with astounding speed, dodging their blows, whips the curtains over their faces, tangle, distract, deflect with it, whip the rod around brass rings jingling. Admiration has nearly paralyzed Futsi where he stands.

A wiry student charges the demon — the curtain rustles up and when it flips back there's nothing to be seen but a wall that shouldn't be there — the wiry student bounces back and down clutching his chest. A misguided tackle ends with a collision of tackler's face and the banister post at the bottom of the stairs. Red-faced hunk swings at him with a collapsible baton, getting in close enough to see the poms on the demon's hat are really balled-up rats, who suddenly leap at him and he panics away tripping over his feet. A cotillion type raises a heavy fire extinguisher over her head — with one knock of the curtain rod the demon ruins thousands of dollars of orthodontia — her mate goes berserk, rushes him, misses him in a coil of red fabric and clotheslines the only other one left standing.

All this has taken only a few seconds. Futsi cries out an alarm as vampires flap out of that un-look-at-able smudge at the far end of the platform. The regrouped jokers converge on the remaining armbands as the demon draws the wings. Futsi pops up giving a frat type the bottom of his board across the face and drops again, looks up in time to see the Great Lover playing at high-speed blind man's buff darting in and out of their reach. They are just empty clothes rustling through the air, just wings bunched under caps and inside denim shoulders. One passes directly beneath the fluorescents and for a moment Futsi can see the slack, flour-colored face.

The demon titters, impossible to follow — even from this far away Futsi only just catches sight of him as he veers out of view. The others keep pressing in, but he refuses them the opportunity to gather together, and they are moving more and more clumsily, slowly — this is how it's done — The demon stands motionless, staring Futsi right in the eye from nearly a hundred feet away, with a look in his eyes that mingles too much at once. Then he shoots backwards so fast and two heaps of clothes coming at him from opposite sides collide and fall tangled to the ground, writhing and puffing out dust.

But that delay brings the others in on him in a group. A train howls, its noise building steadily. He evades them all like magic but they are hemming him in — now gathers himself together and leaps across the tracks — they follow just as the express comes crashing down the track and catches them ploughing through an explosion of feathers spraying everywhere like foam. The train is already gone — red lights veer away — and the demon is there on the opposite platform twirling his curtain rod around his midsection.

They are talking about me more and more, Futsi and me, me and Futsi. I catch sight of Vera leaving with him pulls open a drawer in me, pain and disbelief... it seems so stark and plain the funnel in time, something I can feel inside me and out, that is drawing us together, all an illusion as solid as a strong wind. White teeth against the dark of your mouth, lips bright, diamond clear, like a line drawing, and I strain — with no power; but why not? My question is frozen outside time, as you explain it completely and with every thing you do, in a way I never can understand. You just abolish my Destiny, kissing him on the landing, as easy as anything. Go to the utter end of humiliation — go further, go get on. There's nothing I can do.

In the middle of that night, you see the two of them in one body, suffering down in the sewers; he's raving to himself in a strangled voice, pacing a small flat space where there's just enough room to stand erect, hemmed in by dark slimy bricks. Punches the walls as he turns, kneads his head in his hands, mutters, the two voices pulling apart. He sobs and whines like a dog with a broken leg, reels and staggers, crawls into a round bricklined passage with a low ceiling.

"We can't! There's nothing we can do!"

Do nothing? Do nothing! I'll do something!

"I refuse! You can't override me!"

Yes I can!

"I won't allow it! I'll kill myself!"

I'll keep you alive!

[Very suddenly leap to feet in a crouch, arms out. Then, just as fast, fling self down hard onto back.]

"I'll wall myself up sink us in concrete — I'll never allow it!"

You will...

[Get up again and fling self forward onto face.]

[Like warning a child, tone rising.] "No, no..."

[Getting louder.] "No I never will, never... never... If you don't like it you just leave me."

I'll never leave you!

"No no of course not,"

I can't leave you!

"—you'll just stick around to torture me—"

Torture?!

[The word splits the air.]

"You can't leave?"

Torture?!

You're the one who fell in love with her! Not me!

I love no one!

"So... you're stuck—"

I love no one!

You're the one who keeps me in chains!

You're the one who tortures me!

I suffer what you suffer—

"...You suffer because..."

You love her!

I love no one.

[Lying still on his back.]

Go to her!

"Listen. I will never do that."

Go—

"Listen. I will never do that. That wouldn't do, it wouldn't help. It would be no good. No good for you either.

"Listen. You have to trust me. I will try the other way, but you have to help. Trust me. That or give up, that's the only way. You know I won't allow any other.

"...Help me. Shore me up, help me take it."

—∘◦∘—

Pop out here, where some students have cornered an Indian or Pakistani teenager. His face is tense, he is bracing himself to break out — while the students' voices get louder, more ragged — now they curse push shove they lift their fists and punch him — Futsi and his boys bound their skateboards down one flight of stairs after another and explode in among the group. All smiles, they take up their boards and wade in. Futsi spins out from his pursuer shifts his board from under his feet to his hands and completes the spin with weight-balanced board upside a student's head. Biting his lower lip in excitement Futsi leads them in a charge that drives the students stumbling onto the tracks reeling wildly to avoid the charged rail.

Here's a group with a banner and megaphone in another station. Sudden riot of derision, a wet turd balloon splats bullseye into the megaphone and others rain down on the students. Again Futsi is there, all smiles, wheeling in and out. A fat giant with sideburns and a red armband proudly tied around the sleeve of his fucking Che Guevara t-shirt vibrates toward the skaters roaring redfaced like a shaved bear. The skaters overwhelm him and he droops under a shower of punches and kicks. The skaters are like human fire, their bodies strobe with a staccato vitality. Suddenly there are police converging — some escape, Futsi is caught. Still smiling, ruefully, he is manhandled away in cuffs, bent nearly double.

They put him in a series of holding cells, keep interviewing him but it's not clear what's going on — he's an illegal immigrant, they need to get this and that from this or that department and what will Japan think, etc. Futsi came here with nothing, joined Saliva Bank on bass, got better at playing and joined Pyroclasmo, got better and started his own group on bass called Stupidians with the drummer from Pyroclasmo and developed a decent following. Every show starts with three garish chords and—

"Stupidians! To the attack!"

He brought in the punks and with the punks came these Immigrants who seemed to emerge from the neighborhoods they played in. Now he's sitting in his eighth holding cell bobbling his knees and smiling at the guard. Doesn't seem to care.

Lying there trying to sleep — I hope Vera doesn't worry. She's a rainbow worrier, worries like a rainbow, brightly. Bright worry. Brighten*ing*.

He was drawn to her when he saw her playing guitar on the train, started asking her one question after another, about her music, about being blind, about the cult when it came up.

Demon man in a fur coat, turn there on the platform at the end of your leap, draw along through the air the curtain rod, the long red curtains ripple slowly — you made them a weapon. Is he avoiding me? Maybe he's too busy.

He attached himself to her and kept by her. When he kissed her, he stunned her. Her face turned to cotton, her mouth dropped open. She grabbed his arms, at the elbows, and seemed to want to look around for something. He had kissed her on a sudden impulse, because he suddenly realized he was in love with her. What followed was a space between two moments, during which the world changed shape.

They are going to transfer him to some other jail. He is led out, handcuffed again. Fresh air on his face — then a loud mutter of unfurling cloth and everywhere he looks there is heavy red fabric flying, grunts and curses from the police — the cloth is all around him and he's off his feet — his board is under his feet and he is rolling along the pavement. The fabric snaps away into the sky, a long leaping figure just flashes out of sight near a culvert, looking like a shadowy ink splotch. His hands are free. He is on the street.

Futsi glances back, seeing the top of the police building and hearing a siren now wail thinly there, a few blocks away. Laughing he kicks himself going and rides the handrail down to the subway.

—◦◦—

Like coming suddenly awake I know he's there. His voice comes to me as I'm waiting, from somewhere ahead of me, across the tracks. There are many platforms here. He is across several tracks, but I can hear him, as though he pitches his words just right, through space to me. I can't make the words out but I hear his voice, the tone of his voice.

He's changed. Why couldn't he have changed before, when I was free? He would have to pick now to do it, plighting his troth from far away.

Closer—! I think he jumped! I heard a slam, I think it was his chest hitting the edge of the next platform. I hear him grunting as he gets to his feet, it must have hurt like mad. His heart is white hot and rings like an anvil, howls like bellows. I've been taken to visit blacksmiths and I could feel the wild heat, hear the clash of the hammer and the horseshoe, it's coming back from the tunnels and the rails, the anvils of the wheels, a sound like turtledoves' sobbing all smeared together in the deep echo of caves. But somehow the crowd parts us, and I am on the train leaving his longing behind me.

I turn around at the next station and come back, but he's gone. Then Futsi comes, and I forget again.

Dream of a medieval castle, musty stone and tapestries. Futsi, with long hair, is rolling me around on a fur rug that's now by the fire now on the bed. I brush my hair, sitting at the mirror just for fun. Swing my hand out I can stroke the cold glass with the back of my knuckles. Futsi has gone out for a piss.

Suddenly I'm excited, because I know he is climbing up the fantastically high wall, toward the window. If I lean out the sill, he could see me. Should I put something on? Being unsure whether to do that or not is incredibly exciting. Any moment now he will boil up and fill the window. If Futsi catches us!

I reach out my hands, and my right brushes his knee, which is bare. I slide my hands along his bare legs — he is crouching on the sill. Futsi is behind me, running his hands over my shoulders, and in front of me there is a shapeless amorousness.

"You have to go."

"Why? He won't drop dead," he says.

"I don't want to make him unhappy. You'll see me again soon, now collect your smell and go."

"I won't go unless you tell me when."

"You must go, before he sees you."

"I'm right in front of him."

"He doesn't see you yet you're invisible."

"No."

"I'll see you."

Lenore calls out "He's here."

Vera runs out to meet Futsi, stall him coming in. She uproots herself from him and leaves — he remains—

He dreams he is looking at a corroded box fan barely turning its blades in the open grate of the ventilation shaft — the blades turn, and all at once his face is wet with tears. *Sadness* — she's *gone*. A creak, a snapping sound — the fan crashes to the floor.

—∞—○—

A cultist named Carver crawls into a meeting at the edge of a defunct platform and tells how she'd seen the wings congregating in a huge underground roundhouse room or switching yard. She was not detected in the act of spying, but was set upon by a group of wings some time later and badly injured. Deuteronôme and Dr. Thefarie both are present when she succumbs to her wounds, and the bitter rage that communicates itself throughout the ranks of the cultists is palpable even to the wings themselves, like a red-black thunder.

"This anger will draw them to us," Deuteronôme says. "We must attack them first."

As the situation is summarized in a hastily-convened meeting, I sit distractedly watching Spargens playing with his white bull terrier at the back of the room. Spargens holds a stick at either end, the dog clamps his jaws on the middle, and Spargens spins him around off his four feet. Something sinuous and electric in the movements of the dog powerfully expresses love for Spargens.

We attack at "dawn" — underground, this is when certain work lights are illuminated by timer switch — when the wings congregate in the roundhouse yard. Enormous fans generating perpendicular air currents and noise disrupters designed by a woman named Karla will conceal our approach until the moment of attack.

From the radiant eastern tunnels four subway engines come in spearhead formation horns blaring and plough into the seething mass of wings and bodies at full speed. Two trains out in front and one on either flank a length back; Uar rides atop the foremost train on the right, a machete in his right hand and a kukri in his left, his feet braced under a chain wrapped around the roof of the car; he is instantly in motion and hidden in a blizzard of feathers, his calm face through ragged gaps in the flickering cloud, his arms darting jabbing. Similarly braced the Great Lover rides left foremost rapidly swinging his curtain rod on its line above his head in a wide circle that no wings can enter; the knobbed ends ring with each wing they split and the ringing is constant. On the rear left, Dr. Thefarie sits strapped in a marlin-fishing chair, wearing a pair of thick gloves with high-friction grabbing surfaces on the palms and fingers. Years of Civil-War-style battlefield amputations have made him an expert with the surgical saw he holds in his right hand, and as the wings come at him he snatches them in one hand with catlike speed and saws them apart with two swift strokes. Red-faced, swathed in five sweaters and drenched in perspiration, hard-breathing Spargens rides the fourth car, flailing away with a crushing loop of heavy chain.

The four barrelling engines gouge a swath through the wings, ramming, running down, or breaking them above and the air is white with feathers like flying sea foam. A body drops clumsily down knocking Spargens back against the roof of his car; he is pinned beneath the remains and the wings are pounding his face and sides. With cries of alarm Spargens frantically wraps the chain around his fist and batters back at random. A lucky swing splinters the left wing and he hastily kicks the body forward to fall beneath the wheels of the car. Shriek of brakes, the cars squeal to a halt just within the tunnels opposite the ones from which they emerged, and now is the crisis when the volunteer operators must shift control to the opposite compartments while the fighters on the roofs turn round.

Covering this moment is a charge of cultists on skateboards and on foot, led by Futsi and Deuteronôme. The main body of the wings has been cut in half and driven to either side, now they rush to eliminate the flanking cars as the nearest targets of opportunity while the reinforcements close on them.

Spargens has barely turned himself around when the wings are upon him; he flounders desperately lashing out with his chain not infrequently bruising himself. Dr. Thefarie is snatching at wings with both hands, stacking them hastily beneath both feet and holding them down with mounting effort. The trains lunge back into the open space of the yard. With gleeful whoops, Futsi skates over and climbs to Spargens' aid, sprints the length of the car cutting and clubbing with a hatchet. The Great Lover's curtain rod lances down between Dr. Thefarie's feet, splitting all the bunched wings struggling there in half. With a whip of the line, he has it up in the air again and sailing back to his hand.

The trains advance slowly into the center of the chamber and stop. The tracks, the entire floor, are nearly buried under a faltering layer of dismembered wings and crushed remains. Dismounting, the war-party regroups and advances in the same formation on foot, driving the wing remnants back against the walls, cornering them by the switching-house. Dr. Thefarie runs to and from Uar's train, bringing a jingling crate in his arms. He opens the crate and quickly-formed details light the rags and hand the bottles forward. Crouched like ape-men, their faces blank as ghosts' their irises gone white their gaze fixed without wavering without blinking on the massed enemy, the foremost receive the bottles into their open hands as they reach back and then hurl them from the right hand and the left hand into the mass. In silence, the wings churn in billows of flame, a greasy smoke sluices up the walls and undulates across the ceiling. The cultists remain at the blistering edge of the fire weapons ready to drive back.

Only when the fire has mastered the wings do they withdraw, their eyes and skin burning from the greasy, foul-smelling smoke. It falls to the Great Lover, who is unaffected, to clear the vast floor of the roundhouse and feed the fire with the remainder of their enemies.

—◦—◦—

I'm strumming like mad. His hand takes one of mine and pulls me up like I'm a balloon. We're running together holding hands. I can still feel myself strumming the guitar, and it hums against my body, but holding his hand we're running together. I can hear wind shaking the trees over the low howl of the wheels on the rails, I can feel wonderful speed — my legs kicking way up behind me.

Now I'm suddenly completely confused, I don't know where I am or who, but my impressions have become more distinct. They stand in a line. I guess I'm awake again, on the train. My hands rest on my thighs — I grab my legs, pat myself — my guitar! I feel around — nothing. I lay my head back not knowing whether to laugh or cry some asshole stole my guitar!

Something booms quietly near me, and rustles. I put out my hand — my guitar is there, hovering. I take it in both hands and I feel it move toward me, turning over onto its back, with a force that comes down the neck.

"Thankth," I say, moving one hand to the neck.

Fingers deliberately brush that hand as they release the guitar.

"It'th you!"

I feel as though a furnace door had come open and heat swirls over the front of me.

Ding-dong. The doors roll open.

"Where can we meet?" his voice asks, and the heat stirs again.

"Uh..."

"Think of somewhere."

"...There'th a pathage off the platform in the nextht thation—"

I mustn't think — I won't think any thought—

Ding-dong.

"Get outta the doors!" on the PA.

"When?" same level voice.

"...Two hourth?"

Ding-dong.

He's gone.

Rest with my guitar in my lap. No thinking.

What am—

No thinking.

No thinking.

I can stay away —

No thinking.

No planning.

Futsi

Don't think.

Just be there, in two hours.

—o—o—

He rushes in—

Sweet pressure in his chest of a new embryo breaking its bud.

I'm your bondsman that's a happy note — he bends to press his rinsed ear to take in the delectable time beaten out on the soft anvil of her compact body, her heart is there, that's her core — the encompassing ribs unlace to admit her heart's companion, and combine by accomplished accomplice enlace and edit me, so do it incomparably. The wan boom of her breath rolls like a tide by my ear, rises going by my white and serrated moon of an ear. I press my lips where the skin is stretched taut and thick over a fixed undulation of bone, by the pit of her throat... These pompous words are for Vera too: if she laugh, what blessing, if they thrill even better.

Vera's vine-locks trickle one by one from her shoulders, both our faces stop beneath her veil and compare features, and now lips combine again — start and stop. Her nostrils are warming my cheek. Scrub and scrub, the lines won't go.

She doesn't know she's supposed to close her eyes, lids only a little slack her eyes' dammed vitality has made them hard vital and sparkling. They writhe like netted fish in jackets of gelatinous water... Her mouth is warm, her lips are a little chewed up, rasp their torn thread on lips scaled to rend from my warped lip the ragged marrow of my breath... Short breathings escape our peculiar faces kneaded together partly hard; lips of fingers knit and part, his cradle her jaw and skim her eyelids — and her twin wands of hands seethe up to his shoulders in serial pressure that push her touch through the clothes to his skin.

We fold together in a shaggy apostrophe, moving our faces from purchase to purchase, and eight golden coffins glow unseen in a diamond. An inaudible chorus of eight voices lifts its smoking ray up, making it around early Autumn, lulling warmth of slumbering sun patching ember-colored leaves in Vera, streaming brightly, sere crisply bright-edged through airborne dust in me. Flame tongues flare red as coral, unnoticed above she and me brows as they cinch. She breathes aloud, I pull my face not so far from hers that she won't know by its heat that it's near, and gaze down, stark love look slices through my eyes and carves happiness onto her face. Her fingers sweep my cheeks, nose, eyes, my forehead, her mouth works thoughtlessly as she builds my portrait in her mind. She looks distraught, her hands seep joyously into his body. He clings again splitting and resplitting fiercely: cruelly strong. Empty-handed thoughts weave blank wall hangings around them, their sound listens to the sound of listening.

Now quick run upstairs together — and under open sky (hung with blazing pink veils) you can feel without having to look at it.

Under clouds' pink pelt cross-combed back, in brown light of dusk, that is at once only brown, only pink, only orange... in the stealthy approach of the confiding hour her hair will be one whole earth.

—∞—∘—

A spotter reports by signal-light morse relay a *Vampirism* in rush hour crowds midtown. Uar rendezvous with the demon — he calls him the Duende — and the two come on from opposite directions. Uar arrives first.

The station is a half-cylinder lined with orange tiles, wide open without supports or barriers; his man is pasty, middle-aged, with watery blue eyes and meager colorless hair, limp big and tall body in a short-sleeved green shirt and wide khaki shorts, white sneakers, canvas baseball cap. He walks dully back and forth with a pink newspaper, numbly scanning the crowd, and the attentive eye can see the cone of grey silting around his face. Uar walks toward him purposefully. Where the Amazon and Rio Negro rivers conjoin, their waters flow alongside each other in a massive bed, one side black and one side red. His teacher had taught him to use this metaphor for power, observe as the two halves close around you like breath and feel yourself borne up and along on a vast current. Think of the edges of the two rivers together getting thinner and thinner to the unimaginable point of division which is both or neither, a blade thin upright and sharp.

"Now pick it up and use it."

The Duende is making power somewhere in the tunnel, and the vampire glides sluggishly toward it. Uar is blowing out a bubble of alert attention around himself, within which everything is faster and simpler. Fear makes the vampire dangerous — not Uar's fear, but the vampire's own, strangely abstract, fear. They are running in the tunnels. Every dimly glimpsed thing around him flies by at incredible speed, and he is light as air in air, running without effort, the knife in his hand. He sees the vampire silhouetted against the light of the next station. The vampire rushes out onto the platform and melts into a waiting bank of *Vampirism*. As Uar emerges from the tunnel there is a uniform turning there of red eyes at him, snarling mouths packed with dusty feathers. The Duende swirls in from the other side, scattering the cloud. A body thuds to the tile, torso broken open like a split cast, wings spasming behind exposed ribs.

Uar trots forward and attacks without seeing. It's better not to see their faces, but to keep the gaze turned inward. Under the left arm, go behind, then thrust knife back fast where the spine joins the skull, hilt bangs against the back of the head. Draw out the knife, kneel, and cut the head off.

One of his teachers told him, "You will find you become many animals. Certain animals will come more readily than others, and you can use them to get into the rapids of changes."

With Uar it's horses, who knows why, and he brings his chin down, snorts through his nostrils, and kicks up his right leg bent at the knee while sort of hopping once or twice on his left foot, like the front half of a horse doing dressage. Strike out into the haze and impale a flaccid heart, pull the knife back and slice a throat, two chops make a V in the smoke and a slab of smoke slides out of the notch and splatters on the tile, becoming a corpse. Uar glances up at the Duende, who draws off long tendrils in the coils of his curtains, dodge and dodge and dodge again. This *Vampirism* is thinning like mist in the sun.

—∘∘—∘—

...a woman's dream body, collar floats above ribs arch above hips' basin, small feet and hands, dream sound of a woman's voice...

In my dream, she reaches for me: I see it sadly.

Delicious image — of Vera naked against total blackness, straddling darkness, sighing and rocking. All drops away, and she alone remains gleaming and transported ablaze with pleasure, the sound of her gasps her sighs swells in a shallow echo...

John Brade has just left the weather station, sleepwalking his way back to his apartment. He looks up at the lamps lighting the paths and they are unreal, all the green, the rich air...

Pearl gazes at me, his dim face is like creamy smoke. No, he's not gazing. He's just had his visit, and he'll lie like this, a beautiful dead body relishing its death, for hours.

I go into another room and put the curtain rod back on its hooks. There's a wardrobe against the wall. I open it. A mirror is fixed to the inside of the door. I'm there in it.

Vera sits on a bench by the tiled wall; she is talking quietly with Lenore, who holds her right hand. Lenore nods, and goes away for a moment.

"Stupidians! To the attack!"

I take off my hat.

Vera in a hallway with a room she won't look inside. Futsi I love him.

Futsi is playing for sheer joy.

I take everything off.

Love is filling me — Vera's short of breath.

In the next room there is a bathtub, and I fill it with water, wash myself slowly and carefully, very thoroughly, always watching my reflection.

Desire is stretching me and I don't know what to do.

Jumping up and down in place, pounding the strings and shouting like a maniac.

Down from the street, along the steps, and across the floor, a wisp of air visits me, and stirs in my hair. I pull out the cork — it smells like cool shade, leaf canopies that shade dry hollows. The glass tips up and the flow into my mouth longs for soft glades, grass chilled with dew. The city contracts into a tunnel.

All wrapped in wine the park is full of graves, I imagine. The sky is crowded with swords. I can't see steel and pewter, they must be gloom, the texture of this weather, all made of bruised swords, long and lovely and smooth. Wine bruised my mouth, the tick tick of the steel cup against my teeth mixes with the tartness of the drink. Now the ocean billows in the air. Ships float in the air, feeling sullen. Waves crash in the trees lining the paths, mixed with the crunch of my shoes. The wind is mangling the trees — I can hear branches break off and fall. Wind blows smash into my face like a water punching glove, stewards crash together in the sky, fencing with no fencers over the trees, the hissing manes of their lees shiver like banshees.

There's a pearl in the night's oyster shell and it's there in the weather station which is larger and closer than it is; everything is far closer. It's growing bigger as the path climbs — I'm so happy and excited, I bite my lip smiling at the air, because now there's an electrified circle inside me now, so I can't wait!

Wooden thump against my toe. I lift my foot and down it comes on something wooden. I climb steps, but the air is still moving freely around me. Before me: invisible bulk. I reach out to touch it, but I still have to take several careful steps before I feel smooth warm wood, the door right there — and it gives, swing silently open for me.

Across the threshold I step out of night and into late afternoon sun, warm and nostalgic, lying along the floor. Hot dusk of the first evenings in Fall. Electric fire!

Arms sweep me up into thick air! My hands fly up, and fall on bare shoulders. Is it him I stroke his face—

Her hands flicker up the neck to his face, and she cries out with happiness, droops and wraps him in herself.

He carries her swiftly into another room. She feels beneath her the fragrant and yielding sheets, through her clothes, then on skin.

We ghosts watch their bodies coil. Dark against the windows and his eyes like red hot coals. Her cries are long and low and almost mournful. Faces made of cobwebs window gaze in through the window with smudged eyes, shining among shimmering leaves. A transparent little girl stands in the hall. Tears drop on to her face, run into her thick hair. His head lunges, his hands grasp her shoulders and they sink. The girl trots down the hall, silhouetted against window of golden flakes, turns as she runs, and is lost in shadow. An arc of pleasure like a band of warm metal flexes through her body, like a thin tissue being torn a little at a time.

A shrill voice answers from the hall. She shudders and cries, calling out her body together and his breath shakes on her shoulder a tragedy too, when bright white and gold seared edges burnish tragedic note bright sharp sunset's lances speak pressed leaves of gold flood shine stark clean gold note song in ringing bowl grow loud as thunder killing light splits each in two and joins the split gaps into perfect one up unending ladder of abandon—

—Un-ending ladder

—o—o—

Vera woke up in her own bed. She sits up, and Futsi stirs beside her. She feels her face, draws her hair down over her face — cool spots on her face. Salt tears in her hair. It happened.

—o—o—

The Great Lover and Pearl are taking a walk the next afternoon Pearl incognito in his yellow slicker rain hat and knee-high rubber boots, looking and moving like an oversized boy, and keeping to the shady margin of the path.

Pearl's attention is sheared away — cold erupts in his chest and his limbs grow heavy and numb, his head is light and hollow and he staggers a little.

"What's wrong?"

"I don't know... what a horrible feeling. It's passing off, I think."

"You should be able to tell me exactly what's wrong."

"I tell you I don't know... This must be what it's like for you."

The Great Lover's lips fold down, unhappy with this answer.

Again, on a narrow path through the trees, above the pond, cold bursts in his chest heavy as a bag of cement and he staggers, then rushes first to one side of the path, then the other, his eyes blank with panic, groaning, terrified. When this episode fades, the Great Lover insists they go back to the house and by the most direct route, over the bridge and along the pond. Past the bridge where paths converge this time he feels it too, a ghostly rill of nausea like a glass plug in his throat. The Prosthetic Libido goes rigid up on his toes and screams the sound squeezed out of him as though he were running through a slow mangle, an unbearable sound from so beautiful a voice.

"What is it!?"

He is screaming at what he sees in his mind, absolute image superimposed over the water, the mute and astonished trees and the sky; an acute dome of weak light, and a thought in the light.

Pearl sees the inside of a skull, or of a mind. A pale, pink-white glow fills it, and there are symmetrical structures forming a floor with a round dais in the center. Soft white and translucent wands radiate from the dais, angling in identical, evenly-spaced bows to the curved ribs that line the dome. Against the dais, the wands end in soft hooks, like the fronds of a sea anemone. There's a ring of clear pebbles where the floor meets the dome. Between the wands are struts like spokes dividing the floor into crescent-edged troughs with round openings like bullet holes in their bottoms. Froth percolates from the holes and gradually accumulates in the troughs.

Kinked white plumes of luminous, ghostly material appear with inaudible pops above the dais. They hover in place, tendrils of fine viscous powder collapse out of them toward the surface of the dais, which is a regularly indented cushion of pink flesh. In the middle of this is an amber clitoris surrounded by porcelain tubes and a raised ring of cloudy glass at the base, dotted with grey and darker nodes like raisins in pudding. The plumes are part of a general, gradually accelerating process involving threadlike extrusions from high in the chamber reaching down to interact with elements in the floor. As the plumes braid together, forming a net that grows in symmetry, holes in the frosted glass ring emit clear bubbles that swell up over the clitoris forming a perfectly transparent carapace of locked shells nested inside each other, the elegant locking of transparent panels with the irregular contours and features of the flat bones of the skeleton.

Light braids above a cross section of internested shells, whose edges grow luminous and radiate an asymmetrical arrangement of elliptical fields converging on the center, below the groin formed by the ribs. The froth that has been accumulating in the troughs suddenly gelates becoming smooth organs like pink kidneys that bulge above the lips of the trough. These now exude a thick trembling whey that forms a web, and radiant grains like powdered sugar rise in the fluid and slide in toward the dais. They collect slowly as the light braids are pulled out into weblike fans and the crushing pressure exerted by that light grows more intense, which is perceived as an increased "brightness" without any corresponding increase of illumination. The grains are now all in the clouded glass ring, and they rush together forming tiny glowing firefly points around the ring like gems in a crown. Nodules of white enamel, like teeth, form lines in pink mush on the outer extremity of the dais. Two rods of colorless syrup swing down from the apex of the dome; their ends touch opposed points on the outer rim of the dais and lie flat. The rods spin like two coiling ropes, forming a layered outer shell. An area of light is forming in the white mist above the clitoris. As the processes are spontaneously coordinated, larger or "brighter" structures of a constellation placidly take shape with a gloating, assured calm. This is a mind, radiant with a warmth that feels like a disgusting cold, and a bitter, lustrous nausea.

A body is stirring as its sense organs are beginning. Now suddenly the processes all whir and a brilliant light appears in the center — thread comes down and splits instantly into fans of threads, these turn and fold together forming grids — each line passes through the center of a square defined by the intersection of two other grids, and rising columns of firefly lights, like ropeless pearls, slither up through the squares and track their way up, back down, in toward the light in the center or out toward the dome by dipping round each line like acrobats spinning around the parallel bars. The membranes of the pink kidney-like complexes inflate, and tendrils of colorless syrup flow down from the outer shell and connect to the bubbles, which take on a pale yellow color around the join like a powdering of sulfur. Motor activity, ratiocination, memory, association.

The Great Lover sees none of this, although he can feel something... something a little. Pearl lunges spasmodically this way and that, bounds up onto a park bench his right leg flails out once and smashes the wood and steel of the back of the bench as though he were idly knocking off dandelion puffs. On the ground he takes two steps loses his balance and spins off to one side of the path; his right arm shears a streetlamp in half. The Great Lover rushes over and grabs him. Pearl, clutching the Great Lover's upper arms, rotates his wrists upward and rises off the ground his spine arched and his head flung back shrieking uncouthly, his legs, feet pointed straight down at the ankle, kick convulsively at the Great Lover's chest. The Great Lover grunts as he's kicked, and black blood or vomit trickles from his lips, but his dense body barely moves and he continues to hold on. All this as something like a clammy grey hood of nausea bears down out of nowhere onto his head. Angrily, he takes hold of the Pearl by the midsection and shakes him violently for a long time...

Now he is lying on the ground, watching as the Pearl flops and tosses in epileptic frenzy against the pavement. Suddenly Pearl is staring him in the face, clutching his lapels asking him again and again if he's all right, the glistening, exquisite face contorted with emotion but still bizarrely perfect. He's got the Great Lover by the lapels and shakes him gently, rolling his head around.

"Oh, oh, did I hurt you? I couldn't help it — oh what are we going to do? Oh no, didn't you feel it, too? You must have."

He thrusts his face into the Great Lover's his eyes perfect brimming circles and nearly wholly black—

"Do you know what he did? He made another one! He modelled it on *me — on me!*" he sobs. "Now she's awake! A Prosthetic Death — what are we going to *do?*"

CHAPTER NINE

Back to Hulferde's house.

Hulferde's newfound energy plus knowledge acquired in creation of the Prosthetic Libido equals creation of Prosthetic Death. That means the transposition of his mortality into an artificial vessel to do all his dying for him so he never has to.

Hulferde is dead.

Hulferde most likely did not complete Prosthetic Lib I mean Death. But Pearl just now experiences something connected with it, possibly the appearance of its mind, having never had the slightest inkling of the existence of such a being.

Somehow it failed to preserve Hulferde's life, but nevertheless it is in operation.

Why did I feel it, too?

Getting off the train... How would a Death Prosthetic work?

The only principles derivable from the creation of the Prosthetic Libido pertain to transference to a double acting as a process-vessel with positive retransference back to the source. Transference of death to Prosthetic double entails perennially sustained dying ergo Prosthetic Death is a shunt attached to a living organism and draining out the death. If the intended host dies, then there would be no death to die. Perhaps Hulferde has been restored to life somehow; if the Prosthetic Death has only just begun to function this will mean a terrible awakening for Hulferde in a decayed body. Supposing revivification is not possible, and Prosthetic Death has no host? Pearl seems unaffected by death of Hulferde, has achieved a separate life.

With Hulferde dead, the Prosthetic Death will be an empty vessel? What does that mean?

I turn in to the lane. Hulferde's house glimmers dull white against the drab brick houses to which it is attached, like a carious tooth under speeding clouds, satin-grey and ocean-blue shadowed. I enter through the front door.

The air in the house is stifling, and hums with a deep tone that makes my jaws buzz and smears my vision. Dying saturates it. I find the basement door hanging open; here the air is filled with painful tingling. A migraine ache knits along the top of my head like a white hot seam, pink and grey sparks, black rectilinear streaks seethe in my eyes. I can smell decay down there.

I stamp my feet and pound my head with my hands, slap myself, swing my arms like a skiier, trying to shake the feeling. The oppression does sullenly ease off after a bit. I head down the stairs to the basement, keeping my balance only with effort.

As I descend, I feel crushing pressure close on me like tons of deep sea water, and my own brittle defenses. I'll need to do whatever down here fast. Before the stairs I see a figure crumpled on the floor. Hulferde, dead.

There is the black aperture of the Prosthetic Libido's closet. Nothing inside, but as I cross the threshold I feel some relief, a lightening, a refreshing shadow of sadness there.

Turning from the closet I see it at once — a cloud chamber large enough to hold a person, hidden beneath the basement steps. Looking at these things, I see them, and I feel as though I were right at the brink of a bottomless pit. The fear covers another feeling down in the depths, or an unthought thought. Tearing myself away is like ripping free of a trapped limb.

On the floor next to the chamber, a dead fly rests covered in a light topping of ash. It is decomposing directly into its component elements, all its organic compounds simply falling apart. I step nearer and a draught stirs the little body; it slides along the floor from left to right and then turns over twice. On the second turn it collapses into a shapeless drift of dust.

My reserves are drying up, a sick crushing feeling in my chest like I've been feebly stabbed. In a delirium of escape I rush up the stairs and through the kitchen knocking table and chairs out of my way — out the back steps and into the deep shade of the back yard, where I stand, rubbing my face and shaking.

I imagine the clouds streaking across the sky, vast and impossibly rapid. The watery light on the yard, the heavy shadows. The door opens — a white arm gently thrusting out of blackness, a small form stepping gingerly over the jam. The Prosthetic Death is five feet tall, and lean — a round head with very short hair, a face I know must have been his sister's...

white arm...

Long strings of syrup to a round structure looking like an astrolabe made out of translucent ivory fat. Acute domes folding around and above it, transparent like shrouds of fine ash closing about a rectangle of light that turns and spins and splits layers into other tangled lines and corners. The lines twist and form an unstable number of diamond-like leaves that darken and spread, rising from a stem made from half of each U-shaped thread of clear syrup with minute black flakes in it. All this with a suggestion of distant, more stable structures and a vast reverberating empty space, the vantage point of an alcove high in a cavern wall. From the astrolabe-like central structure something else is rising like an upside-down spur, spreading rows of clear membraneous wings on cloudy chitinous spindles, all alive with a wild acuity.

A plum-shaped face. Small eyes in sockets brown like a bad spot on a piece of fruit. The mouth is a child's, lips and the flesh around the lips colorless and transparent. The body is slim, like a teenaged boy's, with no apparent sexual characteristics.

She stood here naked. A line down the back, legs simply slot into the bottom of the torso. I see it step out onto the grass, which shrivels at its touch, moving with a vibratory, hesitant, electrical way. I can imagine it spring into wildly fast flailing motion that terrifies me. Birds drop to the ground from the tree overhead, sees the plants grow sere and wither. Yes, the grass here is brown and matted; matted into it are stiff, cottony birds like styrofoam.

Banging my forehead with the heel of my hand I get away from the house. I have to put some distance between myself and this crazymaking influence.

Now think: Pearl feels this thing because it is another part of the extended creature Hulferde was turning into, but there's no evident reason why I should feel a thing, let alone all this. I ransack my memory until I am stopped short by a familiar smell... and a bottle with a small indistinct fluid residue by the cloud chamber, on a box or something attached to the wall. Hypodermic needle with injector tube lying next to it, the bottle unstoppered, the smell coming out. That smell is the smell of cadaverine a toxic base found in rotting meat but more specifically it is the smell of me: of *my own personal cadaverine*. He must have stuck me while my attention was somewhere else the little shit! The thing is part of me, too. Part of me too.

It's ambulatory and independent, no doubt about it, full function. It must have been brought to half start and then set to charge slowly in the cloud chamber. MY cadaverine employed to anchor living death in the vessel, a kind of magnet to draw the death in that's dandy.

So what's going on? The P.D. absorbed all of Hulferde's death at once — I'm guessing he pitched headlong down the stairs and broke his neck served him right too. But a death the P.D. was intended to drain off gradual was instead entirely displaced into it at one jolt, and Hulferde's life with it snapping to like an extended elastic. Consequently at full start the thing literally comes alive with Hulferde's life, which is now its life.

Problem: its life depends on a function whereby it is perennially dying. It cannot be perennially dying and alive at the same time, therefore it must drain off death into other vessels; the device operates purely on a principle of displacement. The P.D.'s life continually displaces a volume of death which will in turn have to be displaced into other living things and that's not something a living thing can survive. The Prosthetic Death must leave everywhere a trail of death; its own, everywhere displaced, everybody's problem.

—o—o—

An invisible curtain hangs in the air like a grey fire. It pushes off from the ground and floats a few inches above the pavement down streets whose windows go dark as it passes. A woman slumps over the stove, crashes face first into a pot of boiling soup and then to the ground, her slack face steaming with hot brown broth. A baby's cries stop. Dark drops like a shutter. A couple sitting on the brim of the fountain — she slumps forward against his chest and he topples sideways into the water, legs draped over the stone brink... her face skids along his belt, and she falls to the pavement on her side. Noise of breaking glass from an open window. A man's cap rolls to a halt by the hem of the curtain. It begins to float across the square.

—∞—o—

The proprietor of the neighborhood thrift shop has shut the door and turned off the radio. It's getting dark outside, and he wants to close soon. He hopes surreptitiously to himself that no one will come to bother him. There's no one in the shop, although you shouldn't be too sure about that; more than once he's been taken aback when someone popped out from behind a rack of thick coats. He'll call, then give the place the onceover, before he locks up.

He is turning the pages of his newspaper, laid flat on the counter. The neighborhood is unusually quiet. A faint sound draws his attention. Idly he turns to scan the store wondering if maybe a cat got in through the back. Empty streets, blank windows, go winding by.

"I seem to have lost my way," he thinks. All colors have taken on unusual depth, as they sometimes do on densely overcast days, or in rooms neither dimly or brightly lit, because this is a phenomenon of the middle range of light. Just for an instant, right away, there is the window of his shop, gorgeous with these strong colors. A smell of newsprint, just a momentary whiff.

There are no such colors in this street now, though the light is the same it has nothing to illuminate but the greys and blues of the gutters and cobbles, the edge of the hardtop, thick and ragged like a scab.

"Didn't I just see it? It must be right around here."

He searches for his shop.

Slumped over his counter, his face pressed against the newspaper.

He goes on searching through whole towns and the still country in between, with a faint, intermittent feeling of irritation, uncertainty.

"It must be this way. How could I have imagined — no, the sun is there that must be west. I must put it behind me. Perhaps — up this way?"

As though there were no air at all everything is photographically sharp and clear, each brick and empty window, and every locked door, the uneven line of the pavement, and country roads lined with dark, stationary trees, where every blade of grass stands distinct.

—◦—◦—

Her taste is at work. Only these ballet slippers will fit her. She takes them off, pulls on white hose, replaces the slippers. She selects a full-skirted green dress and wraps her forearms with rolls of gauze. A buff coat with an exuberant fur collar and lapel, and a flapper hat looking a bit like a helmet with a dilapidated plume sprouting from costume jewelry in front. No gloves or rings, she winds gauze around her throat, and then strings of pearls. A glass case filled with spectacles attracts her. She pulls out all the lanyarded ones and loops them one by one around her neck until she has a heavy yoke of them. They fall once against her flat breast, and then lie still and silent.

She makes up her face in a round mirror on the counter. With lipstick and powder she covers her transparent lips, so that her teeth can no longer be seen through them. She then pats down the rest of her face to match. Cosmetics into an alligator handbag.

—◦—◦—

I apprise Dr. Thefarie and Deuteronôme of this new development and what it likely means. Sure enough there is word already of a new presence and efficacy among the vampires — a mysterious woman, their queen yet. She has only been spotted from a distance.

"And that's the only way she will be spotted at least anyways so anyone can tell us about it."

It was natural she should gravitate into the *Vampirism*.

Deuteronôme however is skeptical and angry — "She is not coming to act against us so much as against you. Every moment you spend among us, you are drawing her here."

"I don't agree," Dr. Thefarie says, "I think she is drawn by what we are doing, not by his presence among us."

The cult is working overtime, calling out day and night to its new nameless divinity, feverishly invoking its assistance.

"The more we call, the hotter we get, and the heat is what draws them," the Great Lover says.

"When the god comes, the heat will become too hot even for them. What are we doing here otherwise?!"

Dr. Thefarie nods.

"We have already lost three people," he whangs three fingers in the air, "to her! And this is because you made her possible! You must go — just keep away from us!"

━○━○━

She moves in foggy landscapes of primordial earth before life, walking from fog to fog. Wherever she stops, the wings that hang all over her drop down and squirm together to form a throne, raising above her a dirty carapace made of the same waxy biological plastic of feathers, like a cloudy hood of fingernail.

A cultist in a huge anorak is collapsed drunk on a subway bench. The air goes still and dry. He smacks his mouth and turns uneasily in his uncomfortable seat. Not wanting to be conscious he pounds the woozy dark with his fist seeking reentry, but the insistence of a low voice is nagging at him — someone nearby keeps talking. No not nearby, someone at the other side of the platform, just within the lights, keeps asking

"Where? Where do I hide?"

Siren goes whimpering by and fades.

"Where? Where do all of I hide?"

"Where do I hide?" he slurs. Then he jerks awake, clutching his throat with starting eyes. Drags his collar open, hacking and gagging, tries to get up and falls on his knees, then on his face.

Empty station.

"Why can't I get up?" he wonders. "Why can't I sleep?"

Fog in the tracks.

"I'll get up when the train comes in. No use bothering myself until then.... I wish I could sleep..."

Fog filling the station like a lake.
He is half-buried in motionless fog.

—○○—○—

Dr. Thefarie watches fog sweeping into the station, thin at first but quickly gaining density. The tunnels plunge sharply down from here, going under the river. Perhaps the water temperature has suddenly lowered, and the tunnels have become massive cloud chambers — but what would change the pressure?

I've never seen anything like this — it doesn't move like fog, or like smoke, but it seems heavier, appearing to crash in the air like something crumbling away.

It isn't fog, it's dust, fine as ash. Dust of crumbled feathers, I'm sure of it. The air is going dry, sucking at my eyes — they smart but what do they see? Against the tunnel lights shapes are leaping and turning, deep in the gloom... around a small figure... which advances without moving — a group of three people walking up the platform arm in arm and conversing, the one on the left waving his hand and smiling, they walk into the cloud and disappear. No one else sees it, but the people near its edge are starting to cough, and to melt into it — I draw back — a puff of air disturbs the cloud a little, parting it where the three people disappeared a moment ago, and for an instant I glimpse the soles of a pair of shoes, the slack legs beyond...

The cloud turns, sealing them over and opening in another place, and she is there, close enough for me to see the thin grey film over her unblinking eyes — the bodies wheel around her like flabby puppets, just as they did in the brine tank. And wings creep in the air around her. Their rattle does not disturb the fog at all. They are horrible, like a swarm of rats, wriggling with revolting animation, hungry parasites. Then the cloud encloses them, crashing deeper and deeper into the station in huge irresistible pulsations — and still no one sees it.

Now everyone is coughing, reeling groping at the walls or the pillars for support, but still calm, as if this were merely a fit that would soon pass.

I escape.

—As people are dying the authorities are completely at a loss — our struggle with the *Vampirism* and the Prosthetic Death is so invisible to them — where she goes she turns time to concrete and breath into lead, drains the light from the windows — and after comes a frenzy of recrimination... curfew imposed — it's some kind of attack — then time passes and she is still — what happened? And then—

"Oh, your cousin's dead?"

"Yes, she died suddenly one day, on a subway platform. They never did figure out from what — no sign of a heart attack. But strokes are less obvious..."

Futsi zooms toward the lower platform and then stops halfway down the stairs a deadly force strikes him like a wall. Not too many other people around and they don't seem to notice. Sitting down on the steps he struggles for breath — asthma attack?

As he recovers he begins to scan around... there at the end of the far platform, like a smear of grease in the air. Their forms mill around, and a single figure standing like a statue there in among them, in a bubble of space. A small female figure, slender, and dressed like the Great Lover.

"It's her!"

One of them, whose spirit must have twined somehow with the *Vampirism* and so preserved itself better, now staggers toward her in a spasmic parody of longing, throws out his arms, its eyes burn in his slack face, and flings himself at her feet, taking her waist in his arms and staring up at her.

The Prosthetic Death gazes down at him. Her eyes blaze white and she beams, locking on his pupils.

"I can't fight it," she croons, barely moving her lips, "I can't fight it."

Futsi reels at the sound and grabs the handrail to keep himself from falling — holding up his head he sees her victim climb her body awkwardly clinging to her garments, and then mash his lips against her stony face, grinding them to pieces on her sealed mouth, her eyes still flaring like new snow in the sun. With no prelude at all he collapses in a heap, his insensible head striking the tile with a sound like a gourd.

Futsi feels a billow of incorporeal air waft toward him from the body, and drags himself up out of its way in time, hand over hand up the rail and out of sight. He has to lie flat on his back a moment. Her voice still whispers in his ear — an "I" that's not her own. Struggling not to repeat "I can't fight it," he gets up with an effort that feels nearly deadly and drags himself away.

-∞—○—

The eyes are completely dark, their surface is corded and dimpled like glistening prune pits. She has acquired from the Great Lover's cadaverine a hypnotic power like his own, and when she uses it, these eyes excrete pupils of white spume through their pores. The spume curls like thick frosting and forms a little flat nipple on the front of the eye, through which she can project her fascination beams. Those pupils are like painted stars, which give no light.

A clattering sensation draws her to wherever there is noise and activity to be smoothed out like wrinkles in a counterpane; smooth and level. Flatness. Slackness. Silence. No traces. No signs. Without necessarily moving she mastered velocities. She is actually two, the machine and a dream self; the latter talks to itself about the former, but sees itself as one. She is never all there. She slowly blinks in and out. Just like Hulferde to make her female, to make her *nearly*, to make her *partially*, female. Around her, an unceasing, unvarying, eternal, infinite heart beat. It's a pulsation of deep space that booms at the lowermost threshold of hearing. She must have a third self, hidden in plain view in distances out of distance, motionless in space between the stars and planets. In a crystalline darkness, darkness radiating through darkness, and every star shining in it, all exactly the same. The star dies, but its light continues to travel, with dark behind it. She should be there, the ghost of a sun.

Hulferde had no death to give,

death is not his or hers,

death is death,

not Death,

I am not Death,

death is me,

and what does that mean?

it means,

where I go,

I make silence,

I spread deep quiet,

I still,

I show true faces to light,

I watch myself,

a simple biological process of cessations,

all is done in no time,

I am sterile,

only a stop point,

no stink of decay — decay is life, bacteria,

the stink of life,

I have no smell,

I have no memory.

I am silent.

what are these words?

they must be silent words.

Caves inside the dust clouds, with a tunnel light nearby, she blinks in and out, visible, invisible, visible, invisible. There, not there. Her dream is never there, it is always somewhere else, settling down, down, down into Being, a silent, lightless, colorless, motionless, unfeeling dream.

—∞—

It's counsel-taking time, now that things have changed. Tactics have to be discussed. And we get together under the sun; for a change, we meet in small groups in the park, scattered through the park. The demon and Vera sit together in a group with Spargens and Dr. Thefarie, me, a few others — Futsi's away. They sit beside each other, don't seem to have anything to say, just at the moment. He glances away toward the water as the talk eddies around and away — Vera slips away just at that moment, unnoticed by him, in among trees and bushes their leaves brilliant with sunlight. There's another little conclave further along, not too far away. That must be where she is going.

He turns his head, and might just see an edge of her hem floating away, behind the explosion of the leaves, toward the other little conclave further off. Spargens asks him about the cadaverine and he answers Spargens. Talking going on.

Tactical talk that slowly winds down, toward no clear

Spongy grass beneath my feet, and all around me an ocean of free air whooshing. I want to stretch my body, and move freely. I can't stand to listen to all that talk, not anymore. It fills me with boiling impatience; I get frustrated without knowing why. And bored. And weary. Their voices rail on and on and won't stop. Suddenly what was interesting turns depressing and I must escape.

Thicker, taller grass; I must have reached the edge of the meadow — normally I would hear birds ahead and above, but there don't seem to be any birds today. A breath of air stirs the leaves, and now I hear the trees. If I walk along the margin, with my right foot in the short grass and my left in the long, I expect I'll find a path.

There — so soon! Level ground; it's clay. I turn left. The hood of the trees rises over me, a bank of cool air, and whispering high over my head. That I'm alone I know from the stillness. Even a quiet person makes noise enough, just the huff of air in the nose is sound enough.

Patches of heat and cool float on me as I walk. The sun through the leaves. I'm a little close to the margin of the path and the twigs want to snag my clothes. Here a more sizeable branch grows or has fallen across the path; it catches at my throat and I have trouble getting free — it's not a branch it's a dry, tepid hand and it's squeezing my throat — I don't understand the grip is so hard — I can't breathe — the hand isn't budging I can't breathe — I'm being killed — my tongue is sticking out — I claw with hands I don't feel but — but — I'm struggle — my body clouds, my lungs! — I'm being killed but I'm alive! — but I'm alive! Alive! — weak but — light, but — sunlight — is it? — I'm alive! Still alive! — still alive! but—

for a moment an uncertain feeling, Schwipps has come up... he just stands there, looking from face to face, and it's odd because he's usually such an outgoing man — his hands are moving together and apart, like he's playing a phantom squeezebox.

His mouth is open and his upper lip is long and stiff.

There's a rush — tears flow down his face.

What is it—

His face—

He points—

The first of the two copses of trees.

"*It killed her!*"

Without a word, all cross following him — there's a path that turns in through the trees. Smarting eyes adjust to the dark and sharp breaths, a shape is lying beside the path. Vera lies there.

The demon stops. He makes a sound. He throws off his coat and hat takes two quick steps, stops.

He goes to her slowly, and kneels down next to her. Very gently, he rolls her over. I can hear a confused noise coming from him. Her face is grey. Very slowly he puts out his hand to touch her. A moment later he's pawing at her sobbing and screaming like he's out of his mind, it's a sound like the ocean would make, like howling waves. He frisks her, as though he could find her life somewhere and put it back where it was. He picks her up and now he's running around in circles with her.

CHAPTER TEN

There was a streak of brown grass linking the path to the copse. The trees near her showed where the thing went by. They were marked with dead patches. I used to wrap her up carefully in poems from top to bottom and made her poems even when I was holding her in my arms. Then, even when I held her. I can't.

Even then I made poems, even then. If you're looking for glib talk go find it in hell.

Futsi screaming at me tears run down into his mouth.

"Why didn't you protect her?!"

I turn, without one thought, thoughtlessly toward her and hit the blank that's all that's there, not even the memory. They're not memories they're past moments that suddenly fill me like pregnancy. I see what goes with her like a series in a scrapbook and from every frame she has been removed. I see what she would do, say, each what piled on top of the other growing brutally sharper until the sweetness impales me from inside out. Bayonets me from inside, and scalding grief gushes from the rip in my body taking out with it all my life. What an idiot I was not to see that life was handing me gems. Was handing me *fistfulls of gems*—

━◦━◦━

Futsi blames him.

I remember her walking on the platform. I hear her sing. The song sounds now under cancellation of death...

Now the streets of the narrative are stark and empty, the whole narrative has gone flat and cold and stark. The sky is a sheet of burning white that smarts the eye, and there is no sun, no dusk, no dawn. No one sees day and night change. The night sky is deep with blue hazes veiling the black, the moon is black, and the stars are soft and bright-guttering.

From out of the white sky a soundless wind comes that makes the street ripple like a canvas sail. Not cold or warm, not strong or weak, the wind sets the house and store fronts, the monumental banks and steep-laddered office buildings listing and rattling like wooden flats. Only a handful walk in empty streets, smudged and indistinct people, hard to see in broad daylight, a wind carries their voices away without a sound.

All around the Great Lover there is only sleep, cold. No light, no color, the streets appear to be unmagical, empty. There are clouds like gunsmoke in the street, sweeping past kneading and curdling, white and grey blurred against the black. A tourniquet closed on him full of loose grey earth. He is not moving, stands in the teeth of the wind. All visual objects are incised painfully in cutting strokes on a tender membrane, the grey cream sky just above the edges of the buildings, ready to melt into smoke.

Staring with an expression of sudden fright at the black spears topping an iron fence — cold watchers. He stares at them for a long time.

And now his face seems briefly disposed to laugh without mirth at them; I get the joke, we are more real than you.

A leathery wing, without hurrying, puts out the sky, and beneath it he turns into a multitude as numerous as the threads in his coat.

Her locks rise over the city and he paralyzes. I see what he sees: her face. Slack with death. Upright, as though she stood before and above him. Her dead face towers over him.

He watches as something shivers over her features. A moment more, and her face will crumple and darken like scorching paper. A vast, soft hand squeezes him, his face crumples and darkens, and nearly silent sobs come out from the rigid mouth.

Her face is never like it was. Her tresses sweep the sky over the rooftops like searchlights. He's dreaming.

He takes her body in his arms and begins to run with her, as if her life were getting away. He runs onto a bridge, veers to one side to avoid a truck, loses his balance, and now he hangs over the side by one hand, the other holding her. He would have to let her drop to get use of his other hand, and he can't pull himself up without both hands. Instead, he clasps her tightly in both his arms, and lets himself fall. Her body is wrenched from his arms as he crashes into the surface; he flails this way and that, looking for her, and then catches sight of her, just in time to see her body being sucked into the spinning propellers of a passing ferry boat, which instantly cut her to pieces.

He swims after the ferry. Nothing, not even a single lock of hair, is left of her.

Nothing — and he seizes one of the massive propeller blades with his hands. It swings him round he keeps his hold and pushes out with his legs — his feet come flat against the bottom of the boat and his body goes rigid, stopping the blade. Through the hull he can hear the engine shriek and shudder, as pistons erupt out of the cylinders and burst up through the deck to mangle reeling passengers. Howling, the engine rips itself completely loose and falls away into darkness.

The Great Lover lunges at the other propeller and tears it and its engine from the boat. The ferry lists backwards. He unfolds the longest blade of his pocket knife and stabs the boat with it, cuts a square in the hull and bashes it in with his fists. The ferry dips drastically sinking faster and faster listing to one side. The Great Lover clings to the edge of the opening he's made tugging frenziedly, trying to drag the ferry down faster. Passengers climb over each other clawing trying to reach the hatches miring boots and pumps in wailing faces. Flailing his arms he is trying to push the water in quicker through the hole — the boat plummets to the bottom leaving a trail of drowned and writhing people — he flails with all his strength knowing none of it is any use.

Where is she? he's shouting. Where is she?

CHAPTER ELEVEN

She is coming.

Deuteronôme and Multiply have switched to the downtown platform. It's late, and they are alone. Deuteronôme is sitting with his elbows on his knees, looking steadily across the tracks. His eyes are alert, flicking here and there. A rat. Another over there? No, nothing. Is that nothing? He looks, peers. Not nothing and not a rat, a grey wisp. It is a little shower of dust, falling below the level of the platform, seeping in from the tunnel and now a whir surrounds them as they get to their feet in alarm...

Shadows adhere below her eyes, and she droops with fatigue. The wings rustle and creak in regular waves, a sound like laborious breathing through viscous lungs.

"I am so tired," the voice whispers, with the slightest ring of a woman's voice.

Multiply can feel his lips almost form the words, a sandbag emptying into him, a hand pinching out the wick.

"I can't fight," she says. "I must die..."

Heavy snow pouring down into him, a cold weight that drifts inside. He weaves on his legs.

His uncle seizes his shoulder and shakes him — a far-away feeling. But his uncle's voice keeps driving toward him, cutting in clearer and clearer.

"Do you want to live? Do you want to live?"

"Y-yes," he says, barely able to move his throat, his mouth. But saying it he feels a meager trickle of strength drip into him.

"Yes," he says it again, louder.

"I don't want to live," she says, and the words rush down behind his face shooting toward his open mouth — clamps it shut and can almost feel them pound against the inside of his lips.

"You must fill yourself with the desire to live!" his uncle shouts. "It must fill you to bursting!"

Multiply reaches into that swelling feeling by his heart and lungs with weary agony, somehow barely able to do it — but he does it, and at once the life in him is strengthened. Stronger and stronger, coming back, stronger than before.

"I can't fight... I am so weary..."

The voice breaks over him but it cannot enter. No room.

"You will fail here," Deuteronôme says. "Go on."

"I will fail..." Again the temptation to echo her...

"Go on."

The breathing of the wings deepens, and there is motion of *Vampirism* on all sides, surrounding them.

Gliding forward, "I want the end."

"Go."

"It's too much for me," she wails without a voice, quietly — but now Multiply can see the lines on her face are shadows only, and the features are unmarked, impassive.

"Nothing is too much for you. You are the end."

"I am the end," she glides to within a few feet away. "No more sight, no more sound. No sense. No numbness. No nothingness. No peace. No relief. No end, no without end. No time or space. I am so tired. I want to lie..."

Words almost thrust at his lips like fingers.

"I do not exist."

Like a blow.

The rustling has grown, the circle around them is closing. For a moment I see it — everything going dark, all the windows, the traffic stopped dead, lights going out until the city is just completely gone, and no sound at all. Just litter blowing over the bodies, in the park, on the sidewalk. This is like an infinity force that is bigger than the *Vampirism* or the students or anything human beings can make — just the dark of the dark.

"Quickly get behind me" — turning as he goes around behind him " — Get on your board. Both feet."

He pulls from his pocket a small digital metronome and starts it, holding it up by his face. It emits a clear pitch at a variable setting, right now about every other second.

"Now start skating round me in a circle, so that you pass before me or behind my back at each stroke... You must adjust as I increase the stroke."

Multiply keeps the board going in a smooth regular motion, his eyes darting this way and that and pancakes flipping over in his cold stomach.

"Keep your eyes on what you are doing."

The intervals between the pulses are gradually shrinking, but Multiply keeps up, sinking into a slowly deepening crouch on the board. He has to keep his eyes on what he's doing but he can hear a frenzied rustle all around.

A sound is coming from his uncle, a kind of boom he can feel shudder up through the floor into his wheels. Out of the corner of his eye he gets the idea his uncle is just a blur, humming there. He feels power well up, and far from stilling the tremble he feels this power is changing it into the shaking of rage or excitement, of a strong engine. The pulses have sped up now and he is turning into a streak making a magic circle around his uncle, who seems to be rotating in place without moving his limbs. He is saying something again and again.

A bow wave of fright nearly pushes him over and he knows that she is near, probably standing a few feet away. But she can't get through the circle that he—

Faster his streak is pulling apart — he is a clear streaked ring connecting two pulsing, blurry images of himself at front and back of his uncle. Now he's four images, one at each of the cardinal points. As the pulse accelerates and his speed increases to match it, he realizes he's seeing all around himself at once. He can see himself. He can see her, and his uncle, like a flame shadow upright in the middle of the circle, a slender funnel of transparent flame coiling above his head like a charmed snake. He has eight faces in a circle, all speaking the same repeated word or formula, sixteen arms.

She is watching. He can tell she is at bay somehow.

"It's like you can't get on a moving subway even if the doors are open, unless you're on another train going about the same speed. We're alternating here and there so fast she can't sync up."

"I'm not tired," he thinks. He can't "look around," though. It's as though he has no head to turn, or rather, he does turn his head, but he is already seeing everything on all sides. His vision has no limit. He can feel his head like a soft, humming, dense whirlwind that just swirls this way and that as he turns it. He can even see it, from just behind or just inside. It has an aura with two dim separate layers, one blue and one sort of purple.

The faster they go, the more he sees. Now he sees himself from far off, whirling round and round and his uncle in the circle he draws with his board. The air in the station is whipping around them now, but he is not tired. He can feel the burring of the wheels and his uncle's low drone, shifting evenly to and fro.

"It's balanced. As long as it's balanced, we don't lose energy and get tired. But he can keep adding force so the balance goes up too."

Now he can see the switching yard, a mile away underground. And there they are, little mites on a platform far off in the distance.

"Get ready to step to the side," his uncle's voice comes to him sharply.

"Which side?"

"Any side!"

The switching yard is crisp and visible. Multiply can smell it.

"Step!"

Multiply steps sideways off his board. He is in the switchyard. The board rolls from him and to a stop a few feet away. He turns. Deuteronôme is pocketing his machine. From far off in the direction of the platform there is a dull throbbing sound dwindling quickly away, like the aftermath of an explosion.

"We will have destroyed some when we left," his uncle says. "But not her."

━∞━

The Great Lover is searching for Vera across the bottom of the ocean, lunging gracelessly through the thick grey muck, leaving a trail of cloudy water behind him. He flaps along in long shallow hops, his coat tails waft up and down like a manta ray's wings. The water is filled with errant-slanting blonde light with no source; this ocean has no surface. The vast form of a sperm whale hovers over him, and just ahead; its flanks and lips are minutely flecked with gold.

Now the whale is ahead of him, coming toward him, a gigantic fluked brow growing like a dark blot. Its long flukes lower to form a kind of arch over the marble bench on which Vera is sitting. The Great Lover churns forward clawing at the water — her bench is the only thing occupying an area of worn pavings, clinched in spidery black weeds. As his feet touch the pavings he is able to move swiftly toward her, pressing hard against thick water. The whale vanishes, ascending up into space. The Great Lover rushes toward Vera; she senses him coming and stands not certain, her jaw as always is a little slack, like a fish's, revealing her bottom teeth. He drops to his knees in front of her and flings his arms around her waist burying his face in her stomach, and she bends forward, mouth hanging open, her splayed hands pat his head here and there. He tips it back, and she presses her fingertips here and there on his face as though she were tapping something into an old-fashioned adding-machine.

She recognizes him. Her face lights up, and she leans forward lavishing awkward caresses on him. He takes her face in his hands and she lunges forward for his kiss, their lips meet — when she is kissing him she laughs triumphantly, it's a hoarse, husky, primate sound. His tears ooze out hot into cold water and turn into boiling threads of steam.

He wakes with tears streaming down his face and into the grass. They never stop.

-◦—◦-

Now...

Now...

Now I'm in my imagination, which is sort of drifting along the world like a jellyfish. What current is carrying me I can't say, but I do not choose to go this way or that.

At the moment, I'm idling here, in an alley where roaches and mice rifle the trash bags. The former creep, stop, creep, while the mice are always darting and electrified, like animated dust mats. Leaning up against a can, someone's thrown away a painting of an owl perched on a branch, and there is an inverted river a dark triangular line between its eyes that expands under my gaze to become a crevasse, a clear, cold place cut from black glass, and I'm almost trapped in it. Its starkness endues the alley, which I still see distinctly, with the same quality, the same starkness, to the mice, the glinting black trash bags, the glinting eyes of the mice and scales of the roaches, and slimy tracks of the rank water—

No one knew anything about his daughter he might as well have emanated her out of his own person...

He *did*.

There is the room, the breathless day, the chair and the corner, and he is there in the hall, looking in through the doorway. This silent, hesitant, trembling room is there in the front of my mind, and in the back I see a ribbon of empty days for my father. He never married, there was no wife, there was a chasm of loneliness and dejection, and his friend's suicide.

The light outside stands straight up and down, the sun directly over the house, the windowsills glow like moonlit frost and though the windows are open the snowy curtains hang still with dark folds. The room is empty. Then I step out from the dark corner behind the chair, a little girl in a white dress, my hair loose, a blot of shadow between my nose and the bangs I had then — my father is transfixed with joy and fright, I can feel his panic and his frenzied longing to believe in me. Then he holds out his arms, his heavy hands quivering. I trot forward into his embrace. He murmurs my name, repeating it as he lowers his cheek to brush the crown of my head. With each repetition I grow more solid, two white spots quicken in the shadow on my face and now I have eyes, if useless ones. "Love is blind." I wonder if that flashed through his head just then, and if I owe my defective eyes to a cliché.

The crevasse is the form my choice imposes as I begin to comprehend it: I have a choice... even though I am imaginary, I possess a choice — that, as an imaginary person loneliness summoned I can come *back*... nothing prevents my taking form again — and everything will go on the same just the same...

Or I can *come* back, and everything will be different totally different. I'm following both at once — I come *back* and my image stretches to fill one long time with no events, and I and everyone else will run on in our routines like contented pocket watches... or I *come* back the other way — I can feel the power to do that hum, like the premonition of a fit: it means taking on the mantle of the god they've made, and coming as that god to them. I've called it a mantle, and before me I see the fireplace and hovering just above my shoulders ready to drop down at any moment is an elongated cool gelatinous blob of fabric.

Something horrifying is happening in the fireplace — it's cold, like the bottom of the ocean, and people I love are dying in it, crushed frozen and drowning — but then, with an inner blow I discover I *can* love them, I mean I do! I feel it like a magnetism tugging at my ghostly substance — so even an imaginary soul can really love — why not?—

If I come, people I love will die. It would be necessary; I feel this is certain, even if I don't know why, I feel it's correct. I could go, never to return; I could come *back* — but *coming* back to be god would mean — I see the crevasse stretching open — bringing them something really *new*. Which was always the aim. So was it an aim worth dying for?

—o—o—o—

The Great Lover lies in a ditch; silty grey light plays to and fro over him, like rays through the ocean. He stirs; he stands up in a silent movie.

Atop the ridge above the ditch, he stands with his hands by his sides, gazing up and around him at the sun, obscured by its own clashing rays. A column of bright birds coils around him spinning into the higher air. He sees the sun's hard glints through their blurred forms; the birds braid the rays, dart to and fro like kingfishers.

A statue on a streaked stone podium points an index finger of bronze level at the horizon like a cannon. Now the sun is at the horizon, bowing steadily lower. Its steely brilliance fades. The charcoal horizon is plain against it. The sun is a sullen red ball now, like a globe of smoking blood. A figure emerges from it and comes toward him with slow, league-sweeping strides. Silhouetted against the sun, the figure's elongated outline shivers. Standing on the horizon, it lifts its arms and seems to cup its hands before its face.

"The Prosthetic Death is still alive!"

A woman's voice it rivets him to the spot.

The moon is above the sun, full and white as ice. Its light alone shines on the wings of the birds, so that they are pale grey and snowy untinged with any of the sun's scarlet, and wanly shine even against the disk of the sun, not silhouetted. Cassiopeia sparkles at the zenith. The sun, the moon, and Cassiopeia, are all together in one line, and, through all three, Vera flexes her slender waist in a still vaster constellation.

A sight high and austere, now the sky is filled with stationary comets, large light-spindled stars, in peach-colored space like a transparent fire. Where the sun was, he sees a tree, with peach-fire light on bronze leaves, and blonde flames fixed to the end of each branch. The tree is silent.

The woman on the horizon he now sees is wearing a long skirt, a garment that falls from her shoulders, a kerchief over her long hair. Gold hoops flash at her ears.

"Oh, Great Lover, the sun is releasing-power, escapes all power, and can't be bound. Always think of it. Be strengthened. Defeat *your* enemy."

Something is lying there in front of him. He takes it in his hand — a piece of gold. In picking it up, he had clumsily plucked a few blades of grass with it, and these damp blades lie around the gold in his hand. He looks at the colors beside each other; I am saying he looks at the color of gold, which is not yellow, and the color of grass, which is not green. He sees these shining colors live in his hand, which is his own color. Look around. See a golden haze glowing on the tall dewy grass like softened fire. Look up, and see the sun make blue gold of the sky. Stand up. There is a lane, almost only a dirt rut, threaded across the deep grass, which vanishes through a small stand of trees. A hoop, like the kind children used to chase with a wand, but made all of dazzling gold, rolls along the lane and darts swiftly into the stand of trees. The gold winks as the hoop vanishes around a tree. Turning the trunk, he enters a meadow surrounded by old trees and dense bracken, all saturated with shadow. The grass is long and tufted, and a lofty, slender beech is growing there apart from the others.

Go up to the beech tree and drop to his knees at its roots. The hoop, although it has no gap in it, has encompassed the trunk, and hangs in midair, spinning slowly in place, like Saturn's rings; it makes an inaudible sound against the air, like two earthenware plates rubbing together. In the shade of the branches — in that shade he sees the shade of her tresses. He breathes aloud, two fast deep breaths.

He mutters her name, he lowers his head as though he were too weak to hold it up, his hands on the ground, his head shakes and his eyes drip.

Then he raises his face again to the hoop; he feels her fingers drawn down his features, in his mind he hears her voice say "I am with you." His head lowers again, and he sobs her name over and over, Vera Vera crushing black loam in hands that tremble. The hoop rotates slowly above him.

—o—o—

One of the women becomes a dark figure whose head ascends out of sight into blue shadows—

"She is coming."

—o—o—

Caught as a group, under the very worst circumstances: Futsi,

Deuteronôme, Multiply, and Dr. Thefarie.

Welling up around the stairs is a mob, blurred in a lethal grey fluoresence, and dotted with red armbanders. The stairs are however the only way to get onto the overhead walkway from this platform. They make their escape, but, as they tumble down the stairs on the far side — no street exit — have to go deeper, to the tracks below and pray they haven't made it that far yet — but, Uar is gone.

Uar is standing on the uptown platform they've just quitted, standing with his knife out at the base of the stairs. He's going to hold them there.

Multiply and Futsi are for going back but Deuteronôme orders them sharply to stay together. As they race for the lower platform a wave of enemies crashes around Uar. Face calm with fierce concentration he drives them all back, his knife darting and slashing. At first sight of blood the armbanders scatter, running, as they tell themselves, for the police, for reinforcements.

Futsi nearly ploughs right into the midst of a grey haze waiting for them on the lower platform just before the stairs. A dull pull on them all as they wheel around the banister and head along the tracks in the opposite direction. No good — more ahead.

Now the mob on the upper platform falls back from the stairs. Uar remains in place, breathing hard, sweat beaded on his face, but uninjured. In his trance he is able to lash out at them without fear of being weakened. Slashed remnants of wings, mushy arms and legs, ears and other severed extremities litter the base of the stairs where he has been at work. But now the enemy has recognized his immunity, and a cry rings out from blank faces. A moment later, something huge lumbers from the tunnels not twenty feet from Uar.

Futsi and the others are forced to cross the tracks, leaping carefully over the charged rails. Shapes, rustling, footsteps on all sides. They're hemmed in completely.

Dr. Thefarie points toward a solitary car sitting idle by the divider. One of the passenger doors is half open. They clamber in hastily — the car is empty. Multiply is the last in — the door has been keyed open using the interior release, and the keys are still there — he turns them, the door rattles shut, sealing them inside.

What faces Uar is something new, a billowing form of flabby suit with a ghoulish wax face the size of a trashcan lid. This is not exactly the *Vampirism* but something else, specially capable of positive assault. He barely avoids its massive stone arm. From behind its face, which melts through a series of flirtatious expressions, a faint simpering or groaning comes. Uar slashes at its forward leg, along the inner thigh. His knife pings loud against it, like scraping stone. A heavy arm stoves in his ribs and blood gushes into his mouth. Without changing expression, Uar stabs the retracting arm three times, and with each blow he exposes and cracks the stone underneath. Face going pale, Uar spins under the flailing arms and hacks at the torso. The arms close and crush him against the stone chest. His head rolls back and blood is squeezed out of him through his mouth and nose in a short jet.

Figures step from the tunnels. Futsi leads them toward the other end of the train.

"They don't have to get in," Deuteronôme says grimly. "They can gather outside and kill us by proximity."

They peer out the front window — a blackout train blocks the tracks ahead, but there is an open path to a sidetrack.

"Look," Deuteronôme's arm straightens.

Nearly invisible, shade-like figures are coming, walking along either side of the dead train. There is a fitful motion on top of the train as well, seething down its length toward them.

The arms release him, and Uar falls with a splat. His enemy bounds up the stairs.

"Wait—" Dr. Thefarie whips open the door to the TO's booth and begins checking the controls. Deuteronôme stands watching over his shoulder anxiously, and Futsi cranes over him.

Multiply picks up a wrench and silently heads for the far end of the car.

Dr. Thefarie shakes his head, mouth compressed.

"There is no power," he says, emerging from the compartment.

Multiply has the keys — uses them to open the forward door. He squats down carefully.

"We would have had to send someone out to work the switchbox anyway."

Deuteronôme's head suddenly swivels — "Lauture!"

Multiply does not respond to his given name.

"—Get back up here!"

Multiply finds what he's looking for — it's an exposed brown sewage pipe protruding from the wall like a skinny column.

"Hey yo Ding-a-Ling! Hey! Hey!" Multiply pounds on the pipe with all his might. Drawn by the noise, shapes come out of the dark, arms straight at sides, stepping high and moving quickly if awkwardly.

"Hey! Hey!" An inner fog is rolling on his thoughts. He shakes his head and keeps pounding.

"That's all!" Deuteronôme yells behind him. "Get back inside!"

Like a shot Multiply pulls back and slams the door, twists the lock to and then makes his way to the other end of the car, weaving a little. Has him by the shoulders, looking him in the eye.

"You did well, but next time tell me what you mean to do before you do it."

They are gathered at the far end of the car, watching as men, women, and children, silently lope in their direction. Through the silence a sound is growing steadily — a hollow, wet, throbbing sound. Multiply's head jerks as he glimpses what seems to be a giant golden ring spinning on top of a manhole by the platform — he blinks, and the ring is gone but the manhole lid is rising into the air on a black, shaggy form, sliding off the bent back.

Like a shoal of fish, the people converging on the car veer toward the newcomer, who is prowling up onto the platform bent down like a hunchback and swinging a heavy curtainrod in his hands. Now he wades into a clutch of them on the platform — zig-zagging among them with amazing agility, flapping his curtains at them. They lunge and fall, topple off the platform, crash into posts — now and then they collide which each other and implode in spurts of feathers, as one vacuum clamps onto another. In among them his face blazes white, a grin like black glass distorts his features with its grip and tears run from his eyes in two glistening tracks.

Futsi hisses: a solitary being — dressed sort of like the demon but smaller, and dragging itself forward with a languid, weary step, head a little to one side — has appeared at the opposite end of the platform. She stands there by herself, and just looking at her Futsi feels heavyheaded, slumps against Dr. Thefarie who jerks in alarm and seizes him around the ribs.

Futsi recovers. They stare out at the platform in terror.

"Will he be able to protect us?" Dr. Thefarie asks.

"—From *her?*"

"I don't know," Deuteronôme says. "She's like a sister to him — she can hurt him."

"Let's get away," Futsi says insistently.

"She could kill him?"

"I think yes, she could force the demon out of him."

"Tell him to go back!"

"Let's get *away!*"

"Look at him — I don't think he would listen."

"How to win?" Dr. Thefarie thinks fiercely.

"*How to win?*" — he demands of himself.

cheat cheat cheat

CHEAT

The huge, flabby shape bounding up the stairs stops halfway to the top. It sways, and one of its feet slips and lands with a loud slam on a lower step. It turns, noticing for the first time the knife three-quarters stuck into its chest. It grabs the handle and instantly lets go with a muffled cry, the hand smokes and sizzles. Losing its balance it swings out a stone hand, but the rail it seizes is slick with Uar's blood, and its grip slides loose it falls forward onto its face landing full on the protruding handle of the knife driving it all the rest of the way in.

It tries to get up and rolls onto its side, moving strangely. The soft moaning or tittering is confused. Uar smiles through broken teeth. The thing reaches for him, dragging itself closer, then tips over onto its back. Uar lifts his broken arm and drops his hand onto the upright handle of the knife. His blood runs down the handle into the wound. His blood seeps into the wound and searches inside a petrified human body, running into its veins and arteries like water over parched desert ground.

The shape flails violently, its right arm whacks the ground and the stiff stone splits exposing the bone. The grey and white flesh sizzles and the whole body shrinks, turns from stone to pink flesh, the assassin's mask running off his face in a single sluice to show a cultured-looking redfaced man with silver hair, the knife embedded in his ribs. Uar's smile slackens in death. The man rolls to one side with a sob.

Lying on his right side, the man begins to scream.

The god of the subway cult carefully gathers up these screams of pain, and plants them like seeds. They reverberate the length of the tunnels... the last trails away in gulps, shudders, the convulsion of the death rattle... a still, awed hush comes after. They can see it, trapped in the subway car on the lower level — the *Vampirism* shudders, falters, and seems to recoil.

Dr. Thefarie can hear the message. It's coming in faintly, but only because it is from far off and at its source it's strong—

CHEAT

CHEAT DEATH

Dr. Thefarie suddenly straightens a little, and brushes Futsi's arm with his fingers.

"Call Vera," he says.

Silence — Deuteronôme stares at him, brows screwed tight.

"Vera?" Futsi asks blinking.

"I think he's right—" Deuteronôme says. "Quickly!"

"Wh—" looking astounded, stupid.

"You must call Vera," Dr. Thefarie says levelly, looking him intently in the eyes.

"H-How do I...—?"

"Just call her name," Dr. Thefarie says.

"Call her," Deuteronôme says.

"Vera...?" Futsi calls uncertainly, tilting his head back. "Vera! Vera!"

Multiply suddenly sticks out his arm, "Visualize the Deep Sun! Think of the Deep Sun when you call her!"

"Vera."

Between Dr. Thefarie and Deuteronôme, Vera stands with her head thrown back, smiling mouth wide, singing out in a booming voice thick and sweet.

Futsi stares ahead of him. They are alone.

—o—o—

The Great Lover whips himself between the figures pulling the curtain rod around his hips and dazzling them with the movement of the fabric, sees the Prosthetic Death in the distance, motionless, and from the stairwell opening just a dozen paces away black locks sway out and rise in the air out of sight. He stops instantly like a statue. Figures close around him, clawing and clamping onto him like lampreys with dry mouths. Now he sees nothing there with his eyes, but with his imagination he sees her plainly standing there in her long dress, smiling at him, eyes fixed on him as though she saw him. She gently raises her hand, and makes a jabbing motion with her finger in the air, with a look on her face that says—

"Eh? Eh? How about it?"

In the same motion he jabs the end of the rod into a face pulping the whole head, swings the rod round so fast and so hard it tears two bodies in half sending feathers everywhere, and his motion throws off the others who had latched on to him. He impales one and, without bothering to clear his rod of the body, swings it light as air and whacks another in half. The momentum hurls off the impaled one and he brings the rod up and down like a club to splatter the last of them with a single blow sending gobbets of the body flying like a burst sack of excrement.

Dr. Thefarie suddenly seizes Futsi and Deuteronôme and points to the far end of the platform. The Prosthetic Death is swaying — she reels! She falls to the ground!

And where's the Great Lover?

—o–o–o—

For the Prosthetic Death, it was as though a blast of fog had rushed over her, and momentarily deprived her legs of power. Her lucid mind, too, had gone briefly dark; finds its way back to itself slowly, in a groping way that is wrong for her.

She is on the floor of the platform, sitting up, but with her legs splayed about her, one before and one behind.

As though prompted to, she looks up — past the other end of the platform she can see a long distance down the tunnel, which is completely dark except for a little island of yellow light off to one side, half hidden by the edge of the tunnel wall from here. There is a booth, switchboxes, and a vat or big pipe sticking out of the ground and the Great Lover emerging from that. He sniffs the air, bent nearly double, like a huge rat, or even more like an enormous wild boar.

His head snaps up and the light reflects from his glasses like cats' eyes staring straight at her, and the fur of his coat bristles up over his back and head. Heavy thuds of his feet getting louder he is coming — sickened with terror she gets to her feet and begins to run. He is out of the tunnel — he is huffing and laughing in the passages now, a hollow, crazy chuckle chasing her. She makes for a stairwell and he swings out of it not a foot before her blocking her path and looming high over her, saliva hanging from an ink-black snarl grins at her without smiling — a bright spot in each eye — a tiny face — Vera's tiny face, wild with hilarity.

The face in his eyes is now in her eyes, impossible to turn away from it laughing and screeching — long black hair brushes her face, a hand is at her throat, a man's hand but the voice is a woman's — she looks up and sees the long black locks swinging over her and the face in their midst is not his—

—o–o–o—

The Prosthetic Death, lying inert on the floor, screams. It's a sound to stop the heart and block up the throat — Dr. Thefarie, Futsi, and Deuteronôme freeze and stare. A single scream, a pure, clean, piercing tone; the scream of an icicle. Now she is writhing on the floor like a dreamer trapped in a nightmare, and her silence now is worse than the scream. They watch...

The train jerks, nearly toppling them over. Futsi rushes to the conductor's compartment and looks out the window. The demon is there at the back of the train, pushing. The train rolls forward picking up momentum, the demon starting to jog. Perhaps it's simply an effect of the distance, but her throes seem already beginning to weaken...

CHAPTER TWELVE

Dr. Thefarie reading from Father Ptarmagant's journals:

> The light congeals and is flung down upon the earth inundating the human landscape with supine radiance. Sleeping Rays keen with impaling sharpness are supple and at rest, blanketing the stern ground, baking beneath this frostburnt crust, the black earth broods the next season, and laced into the tender ground are bones — human bones out of their snug jackets. Disarticulated skeletons once were the structures of limbs and faces, which were their disguises, and from these dark, closed bodies, sparks of uncapturable light were struck. And after diligent service in total Darkness, were released when Death and Decay opened those bodies. Now, brilliant flakes swirl everywhere in a million effervescent and ephemeral constellations.
>
> Now the white snow lies on dark earth. Dark flesh in life secretes white bones, that come out with their glow after death. The snow sends its water into the ground to unlace seeds of bone and nervous shoots that will rise at the call of the sunlight in a springtime so unlike now as to be unimaginable from here.
>
> My daughter's vision visits me from out of the shadows of the subway tunnels. I see her walk toward me with a rapt expression, with her hands clasped together in front of her. Her lips are enamelled in hard candy, and click against each other as she forms words that come to me like the rustling of water against the banks. Her words form an eye in the sand.
>
> I speak to you now as the lowest. I am low that my high words may visit you without prejudice, and that

you hear not me but them only. The words are present but I am falling away to listen, I speak as a means of listening to a voice I do not know, but which issues from me, invisible, from my place. This is not a 'story.'

"You see," Dr. Thefarie looks up. "He dreamt it first, but without clearly understanding his dream, that *she* would become our god."

—o◦o—

The poetry of her memory has remade the world in her image. Her semiotry is everywhere, her icons, her light, her voice. In the wind, I can feel the softness of her breasts — through the world, the softness of her breath. Her locks ride in the cold sky; her fragrance rises from pools of rain; she is reflected in all golden things.

I sift through a heap of messages, most of them scrawled on receipts and other truant bits of paper, a few on letterhead, when sound draws me to the tunnel mouth, into the tunnel. I step down to the tunnel floor, and walk slowly, listening carefully. Silence. It is true night when all is still. In a dark spot, where no lights reach, I stop to listen more carefully. Silence. Still darkness.

Then a golden sound. "I am with you."

—o◦o—

The first time he saw her again, she was gliding into the tunnels. From somewhere she had acquired four attendants, all Immigrants whose flat tresses fall almost to the ground down their backs like rivers. They wear silk sheaths of many layers, with stiff sleeves and high collars, and their faces are completely covered with paint. This one has a red face/black eyes, this one blue/gold eyes, this one silver/green eyes, this one brown/grey eyes. Their garments match. They position themselves at the corners of an imaginary square around her.

She is dressed in a ghostly white gown that covers her completely, cuffs hanging far down over her hands like two big folds of soft vanilla ice cream. There's a complicated headdress on top, mostly hidden behind a thick veil that hangs to her feet.

He shouts, he screams — he runs after her. She stops. She turns.

Her face is hidden in a dark hollow behind the white veil. His body is becoming heavy. A palpable awe stops him.

"I am with you."

The voice sounds inside his head, and shakes his whole body like a massive throbbing. With a long whisper of silk the attendants move aside as the white figure comes toward him, and he watches it come, full of *terror*. A sleeve lifts. He closes his eyes, quaking. From the sleeve unfold her raw nerves, white tendrils, and they brush his face, tingling. He hears her sigh. A sound like a ghost escaping from a cave.

He wants her to take him in under her robe, and wrap him tightly in her shell of nerves.

She is nearly invisible in the distance, with her four attendants, vanishing into the gloom.

"Can you see me?"

"Yes. It's wonderful!"

—○○—○—

Pearl notices the Great Lover is staring fixedly at a tortoiseshell barrette, glowing in the sun on the windowsill.

"That was hers?"

Nods.

"She gave it to you?"

He shakes his head. "I found it."

"In the copse of trees, by the path?"

"Yes."

"That was where it happened, wasn't it?"

"Yes."

"I'm sorry."

"Did John Brade tell you?"

"Where it happened? Yes. Who else do I see?"

The Great Lover is in the hall when he stops, nearly doubles over so violently does the change come on him, and with effort he relaxes his face and closes his lips primly over tell-tale black teeth. His eyes swivel — he picks up a rusty pair of pruning shears from a heap of clutter by the wall and returns to Pearl's room with them.

Keeping his head down and his lips close—

"Oh I almost forgot — sharpen these for me will you?"

Pearl takes them curiously in his hands, glancing up at the Great Lover's big back as he strides to the window stamping like a cossack.

"You know, funny thing, I thought John Brade was with you when — that day in the park."

Scraping as Pearl slides the rust from the shears with his fingers, pinches the edge back sharp again.

"Oh, he was, but he'd left by then."

"He must have been pretty shaken up."

"Hmm. Well he saw it all happen, you know. He was right there, just frozen with fear, apparently... He feels just awful about it—"

"Not as awful as he will feel."

Pearl drops the shears looking up his hands clapped over his mouth, the window is open and he is alone.

Running himself, the Great Lover feels something flash by much faster and veer away toward the other side of the park at such velocity he can't see what it was — that would be Pearl, running to warn John Brade. Cursing, the Great Lover bounds down into a culvert and kicks the corrugated pipe furiously, then paces up and down hands behind his back.

Presently a slopping sound, and a ruffling along the inside of the pipe. One of his gnomes appears in the mouth turning up his face all smiles.

"—Hah?"

"Where is John Brade?"

"Train!"

"Subway train?"

"Subway!"

The Great Lover rushes into the nearest station and starts battering the mounted wall map with his fists and ramming it with his shoulder until the words "third person" are visible near the top.

"John Brade — John Brade"

With a pop! a little hole opens in the map as though it had been shot from behind with an air gun, right on the downtown line.

John Brade on the downtown line switching to the express now it washes over him from behind like hot steam. The waves go on hitting him harder and harder as he turns to see; coming at him, down the tunnel, that face, hard set, blank and drawn taut with fury, streaking toward him.

Pearl Pearl why did he tell Pearl he had seen it happen—

You stood there and watched, the Great Lover is saying in his imagination.

I couldn't help it!

You weren't frozen you *hesitated*—

You—

You—

Pounding feet. Pounding feet.

His heart is pounding as he dashes up the stairs, runs across to the next platform where the express has already stopped. Mindlessly he shoves people aside and boards the train, starts making his way to the first car and through all the din of the station he can hear those footsteps pounding. The train is just standing there. The bell goes and the doors slide shut. They open again and John Brade throws a frantic look over his shoulder — they shut again, the train glides out of the station.

He's up front now. The train is hurtling through the black. People are staring at him, he's soaked with perspiration.

A crash behind him. Through the door he can see him, coming straight at him down the length of the third car, walking right through the upright poles sending them rebounding among the passengers in weirdly inaudible violence.

He's at the door to the second car — he yanks it away so hard it jams, disappearing into its slot. He's coming forward, down the length of the second car, ramming the poles aside without noticing, his eyes levelled on John Brade. The train is slowing — lights at the windows — stops — the doors roll open.

He's at the door to this car. He wrenches it open without bothering with the latch in a spray of complaining lock parts the safety glass shatters as the door whips aside. But John Brade is already on the platform — the train has started moving again, taking the Great Lover away.

John Brade rushes for the exit he's reeling with a cacophanous noise like an explosion rending the air all around him — he turns to his horror and sees the express half in and half out of the tunnel and now steadily inching backwards against spark-spraying wheels that scream against the rails. The first car appears and him with it protruding out a broken window pulling the train back with his hands — seeing John Brade he howls — scrambles through the window and John Brade is already pelting for the stairs.

The train groans forward and behind him pound those footsteps — he dashes up a flight of stairs and the banister rips free from the wall and nearly brains him — he runs like a frozen wind and garbage cans bits of benches a pay phone smash all around him hurtle past and batter tile from the walls. The voice isn't calling for him any more.

Then, running down another platform, John Brade passes a red LED clock and something stirs in his mind. He knows the timetables by heart and he knows the trains are running on time just now. Off the platform he runs into the tunnels in the right direction almost sobbing now those feet drum the ground nearly upon him now he'd better be damned fast because the light is showing now nearly upon him he flings himself wildly over the tracks sprinting for the opposite wall like a crazy man. Only then does he stop and turn, to see the train blast by. When it has passed, there is no one on the other side of the tracks. It worked. It worked.

No time to rest, he gets to the next platform as quickly as he can and takes the next train. Sits exhausted by the door, staring dazedly at the floor, his hands squashed together in front of him... He doesn't see the floor.

He sees him, standing in the tunnels where he managed to free himself from the train. It struck him and carried him along for several hundred yards, but he is standing. He is unhurt. Now he is coming.

His forehead breaks one thin shell of smoke after another, staring, taut and drawn. His eyes are blank, dripping tears, speaking calm words that aren't sentences that ring in his mind like screams — John Brade dead killed, killed.

Here's the stop — he has only one plan left. Sick, his face splattered with sweat and tears, and barely able to walk, distraught, he enters the tunnels.

There's a clear space here where cultists have set up makeshift shelters and a radio repeater. No one's around. John Brade goes on searching — a light in one of the sheds, even some soft music. Dr. Thefarie is in there, stocking shelves with pill bottles.

John Brade shoots drunkenly through the door.

"Help!" he squawks.

Dr. Thefarie has him by the arms. He thinks there's something medically wrong.

"You've got to protect me he'll kill me—"

"Kill you?"

"The demon! He'll kill me! He's coming for me!"

"Wh—?"

"You have to protect me — promise me you'll protect me!"

"All right all right I promise — but what happ—"

"He found out! He found—"

"Found what out?"

"I could have stopped Vera."

"Stopped her?" Dr. Thefarie's voice grows quieter.

"The day she died, I saw everything. I could have warned her but — I just froze, I just froze..."

A scrape — they both look up at once. Futsi is standing in the doorway, his eyes wide, staring at John Brade.

"You—"

"He has my protection," Dr. Thefarie says, interposing himself. "I've promised—"

"You just *froze?* Why did you freeze?!"

Futsi is stepping in eyes flaring and Dr. Thefarie steps forward.

"No no," he says, "Collect your—"

Futsi shoots forward throwing Dr. Thefarie to one side. John Brade, with a loud yelp, spins out of the way and out the door, running again.

"You let her die?!"

Futsi doesn't have his board, he's running hard after John Brade. Deuteronôme has just come to the shed, snaps into the doorway with his hands in the jams. He lunges to the floor and takes Dr. Thefarie in his arms. The man's face is slack, his eyes staring, blood streaming from his nose. Deuteronôme finds no pulse. He's seen it before — a hard blow to the bridge of the nose, and bone fragments fly into the brain. There's the blood on the edge of the cabinet, where he hit his face.

Deuteronôme rushes outside. Multiply is rolling along in his wake — waves over.

"Futsi's killed Dr. Thefarie, and he's gone after Brade—"

"Wha—?"

"I don't know, he's gone mad, I don't know."

He points in the direction they took.

"You must go close the station gate ahead, but stay on the far side, the street side, do you understand? Don't get trapped inside the station — the Death is coming down the local tunnel."

Multiply nods and pumps off on his board, no questions asked. Deuteronôme meanwhile takes up a bicycle from the ground and pedals after Futsi.

Now — the station — Multiply flashes onto the platform. In moments he has the place locked up tight and he's on the other side of the barrier, heading up to the street.

John Brade is there only a moment later, rattling crazily at the chains — then running again the length of the platform. Multiply is already on the far side, locking it up tight. No way out now, and Futsi is there, feet flapping on the ties. Multiply is back on the street — gone.

John Brade has only one way to go, the local tunnel. He hasn't taken three steps before a wall of dead air washes over him and dust is floating all around. Futsi sees it too—

"It's her!" he says.

John Brade looks back at him in anguish —

—in the shed, Dr. Thefarie groans, rolls onto his side his hands slide heavily to his face—

—then glassy-eyed runs for the garbage scow standing on the downtown platform. Futsi pelts after. John Brade gets inside the scow and is trying to shut Futsi out and that icy blast is creeping up steady on his back. Angrily Futsi yanks the door out of John Brade's hands and shuts it behind him while in the blink of an eye John Brade is forward at the controls trying to get the thing moving they're not fast enough to run from that influence. A light, distinct footfall on the boards of the scow.

Futsi hears it. He gives up on John Brade. Nothing to do but try to get out the way they came — the forward door is standing open and he makes for it but suddenly Deuteronôme is there, panting, slick with sweat, staring at him with implacable eyes as the door slides shut between them. He's keyed the door shut from the outside. Futsi stands by the door like a statue, staring, stricken at this unaccountable betrayal. No way to open this door. The only open door is already within her colorless atmosphere.

A dry footfall just outside, on the wooden planks of the scow. Through the dingy glass of the door Deuteronôme's face stares a moment indignant, then is gone. Rattle of his bicycle on the ties as he hastens away. He never saw John Brade frantically working the controls in the booth — he assumed John Brade had already made his escape.

The train suddenly groans to life, pouring diesel into the air.

John Brade turns and sees her enter the car. With a howl of despair he darts from the booth, picks up a huge metal peg and smashes one of the windows with frenzied strength — already the light is dimming, the drone of the engine is growing louder and louder and the stink of its exhaust — John Brade lunges through the window but he's caught. Futsi has him by the waist. Futsi is dragging him back into the car with a tear-streaked face. Futsi turns at the last moment to see her. John Brade feels himself go limp all his life force disconnected with a thump.

His mind explodes like birds of fear shooting into the air and dispersing in every direction.

Futsi feels a snow hand stop his heart like the touch that stops the swing of a pendulum. His body swims away from him. The world turns to streaks up and down... just down.

"Vera"

Two dead bodies, not four feet separating them on the floor.

—o—o—o—

Deuteronôme creaking away on his bicycle as fast as he can go — calling out a warning to din in the pipes and wires...

She has come looking for the Great Lover; chutes and slopes in time showed her where, brought her here. He has come, hunting John Brade — but now the wires and pipes are chattering at him — Deuteronôme's alarm is jingling the rings on his curtain rod.

She has come.

Panting breath, a whirring sound. Deuteronôme on his bicycle, getting away.

The Great Lover alone in the tunnels. Ash sinks along the walls.

He feels something like a trap slam shut on him. The Prosthetic Death has him, is crushing him. He feels her flattening him out of this world. A face appears to him again through a whorl of grey films — he sees her eyes rolling whiter and whiter against a skin like smoke thinner and thinner.

I feel something give way, but now I desperately concentrate my strength in my right arm; my legs go numb, my body slumps heavy and unsupported, my teeth begin to chatter, I'm breathing as though my lungs were brick and my heart is throbbing wildly like a cornered animal palpitating with fear. All the while my strength is pooling steadily in his right arm — all my force into my right arm. Suddenly my arm cracks like a whip and the Prosthetic Death's grip is broken; she had me, was crushing me in her hands, and now I've knocked her aside. I run. I am injured.

He collapses in the slough running between the rails.

Out of the corner of his eye... beneath the blue light on the wall, a beautiful face with shuddering eyelids and a dark diamond mouth.

Light of the deep sun, and those black locks twining into a head and body there between it and me.

"Gorgeous," I say, "What'll we do?"

This is the big question.

The view from up high isn't better than the view from down low, the very bottom, it's worse, it's the worst — from the bottom there is still everything to do and nothing decided, no end in sight — from on high everything is decided and nothing can happen. As the end draws near, the view gets higher, the possibilities are smashed to useless pieces, and the story dies. Futsi and John Brade are dead, who else? Each one of us is a wind-up toy started out all tossed in together bumping off each other like bumper cars, and each bump tilts each bumper a new way, but now the point has finally been reached when there are no more bumps, and each will follow out a course you can see from here, all the way to the end of each, until one by one they wind down and peter out in the fated spot. Always the same spot — live or die, find the girl or not, there's no difference if the story's over.

That's the demiurge world, isn't it? Once it's all decided, the story is already over. It ends before it ends.

"Vera get me down," I say sawing dust in mummy throat.

"Wind them back up again."

"Start time over?"

"Start all over."

"Start again!" I feel the nonstep, the splash, sewer water bubbling in my throat. "Nonstop!"

"With whose time?" I ask.

"The time it takes you to figure out this," she's waving an envelope by the bench, my name — my proper name — calligraphed on it in red satin. "This time is your time, this time is my time," I get a blast of smell, dry musty pine needles baking in the sun, so weird to smell it in this dank place. Clotted branches droop in a torrent of sun funereal and reticent holding something back — they hold back time and bank it up for me to draw.

"It's beautiful you're beautiful—"

"Go get 'em tiger," she titters as she disappears.

"OK coach," I say to the steel rail by my cheek.

Jump up. Feel it *flash* — that's *time* running back into me. All the time I want, sopping handfuls of nerves saturated with it, draw me to the ceiling and out of sight.

At once the Prosthetic Death is back on him rushing up to where he fell, but she does not find him. She rises and looks around her, looks up, sees nothing.

"I can't hide," she murmurs. "I can't fight."

Repeating these words softly she searches for him... about a dozen steps into the station lights she stops and abruptly claps her hands to her head. She begins to reel and spin. She's found him, hiding inside her head.

She turns to blue sky, ocean to the horizon and a giant's sun howling with light, green cliffs like living emerald roll away to distant hills and copses and he flits around her just out of the corner of her eye no matter how swiftly she turns in place, he is cackling at her deafeningly loud. She opens her mouth to speak and his mockery seems to bat the voice out of her throat — she is mute. She feels herself speak, but hears nothing.

His form, pelting away up the slope of a green hill. She follows. As she comes up to the top the deep sun is rising on the other side, towering over her and she at once stops like a statue. Lowering her eyes she sees, far below, that the deep sun has a pair of legs — he is carrying it up the hill, not actually resting on his back but on a cushion of cold air trapped in a wicker cage of sprouting nerves. The deep sun forges the daylight into a blinding scimitar that sweeps the ground before it coming her way, and the grass touched by it smokes steams and blackens then suddenly bursts out more dazzling green from black flakes.

The Prosthetic Death is flying away from this arc...

Multiply is watching incredulously as the Death God flits to and fro across the tracks inexplicably pantomiming. He turns to go, happens to look up — there's the Ding-a-Ling up on the ceiling of the tunnel, wrapped in nervous webs, sound asleep.

The Prosthetic Death raises her hand and the end of his curtain rod crashes into her face driving her back onto the rocks. He is on top of her in a flurry of wild blows his face a mask of mindless glee — she lurches and careens, always without expression. She is desperately trying to escape him in endless miles of flying green; running, a naked, sexless mannikin with the impassive face of a dead woman.

Barren white, all the walls, the floor, and stubbled with wan blue light, white radiation of the windows, dully painful like a smoldering headache; stale smell of taken-up carpets. There is something in the room, like a long, low, sobbing note, mechanically repeated at a fixed interval. A bleak, hollow, hopeless sound that bypasses the ears and is inaudibly heard in the brain; the sound of white, the sound of annihilating veils, around you drooping, closing, soft numbing anemone petals, tender deadly pistils of living frost.

No no, she is still running, trying to get away, she can't get control of the dream. Peach-colored flames swirl across the surface of puddles in the rocks and lunge into the air growing taller and taller as he rises standing into the sky a giant with his head just below the sun, his face fluorescent and smiling, the irises of his eyes have gone white and the whites glisten like the flashes of sunlight on thick agitated water, his lips are pale on the outside and crimson on the inside as though he'd been sucking rich fruit and his pale lips are streaked with feathery strokes of red. An elegant black heart-shaped beauty mark has appeared on his right cheek just above the jaw. He raises his arms to the churning sky, and the flames whisper out across his sodden coat.

The air is hemorrhaging light; an ominous stillness falls in response to the upraising of the Great Lover's arms — he stands there like a huge telephone tower. The clear air is blackening, clouds boil into existence above him and let down feelers dark as smoke over him. A colossal screw of air coils down with implacable power, the full moon in its blue center. The air turns dark bottle green and brown, the tip of the funnel congeals around him his arms are lifted like a child's — pick me up!

It writhes toward her with terrifying speed, a lead column constricted with the muscular sinuousness of a snake — lightning wound and lashed into it like a whip — its fantastic speed weirdly contrasting with the dreamy inconsistency of its outlines, thorough, capricious, remote.

She is pinwheeled up into it —

—suddenly ejected into blue, and the sun flashing by as she spins above the clouds. Below, the top of the tornado vomits topsoil like an erupting volcano.

The Great Lover piledrives the Prosthetic Death from above —

—so much earth has been flung aloft by the tornado — it coagulates into an undulating floating mass, like a suspended ocean of loose dirt crossed by heavy billows. The Great Lover and the Prosthetic Death are moiling their feet and legs in this earth for leverage, kicking up spirals of soil that dance weightless about them. She is trying to evade him, clear her mouth to speak. The sun is attacking her — clouds made of swords and wings locked in deadly combat go convulsing by and the glints from the dull nickelly blades of those nicked swords are like thrusts she must avoid. Now he is on her again bringing the curtain rod down on her head again and again so that she reels to and fro — in the tunnel she crashes from one post to another as the Great Lover flails at the ceiling dripping slaver—

In the dream... the airborne ocean of dirt is succumbing to gravity, falling in a mass back through the clouds—

Suddenly with a shrill cry of anger and exasperation the Prosthetic Death lashes out with a blow that sends him flying he regains his feet and stares for a moment incredulous at the raw ends of his curtain rod broken in half and now the Prosthetic Death is slashing and pounding hammering at him with hydraulic arms a noise like an axe in hard wood — but the Great Lover catches sight of her face not impassive not impassive any more — her mouth drawn open her eyes round and wide her brows knotted in rage *in rage* — and rage is *mine*! *Rage belongs to me!* and he rears up in hysterics his face bright as lightning eyes wild on her glare provoked and furious she's forgotten herself, she's enraged she *wants to hurt him* and blows now spin like a flurry of hail. Through the soil there shows the sullen blue-green of the ocean hurtling up to them like a hammer and now they strike the surface, hard as concrete sending a plume of white foam high into the sky.

Limp and smashed, they sink apart below the froth in scaffolds of colossal sun beams.

CHAPTER THIRTEEN

The setting is underground streets lined with brick buildings all in disrepair and slouching, men in hats, celluloid collars, women in hats, long waists. Animals everywhere and the heavy smell of animals, horses pulling carts, cows gaze dreamily from the windows, pigs wallow in the road, dogs bark at the pigs, monkeys chirp at the dogs and apes waddle down the steps to the street, and everywhere in those passages of tamped earth that join these streets together foxes slither along their burrows that open in the soil or slink unhurried to and fro across the way. Inspect stalls of animals drawing cartoons.

Here comes her hand, slip from the sleeve and take the key. Winding it back up again. Wind, rain, lava, and a huge ram of black ooze surging up from the bottom of the ocean. Inky sea bottom slime overruns the map and redraws its lines in a frame of eight incompletely inscribed golden headstones.

Welcome!

Here comes our hero. You remember the hero, everybody always does. He's walking along. Miles underground. No time for your questions! The story is beginning...

I come to a break in the tunnel wall, which looms high above me. Now I know this tunnel is old, and flooded with black water. A slick of stinking grease from the bottom of the ocean shrinks there on the surface, with a man-shaped hole cut of out of it. Did I come out of that?

A harsh taste in my mouth. I have something wedged under my tongue. I draw out a gold coin; my head on one side, what looks like a sea urchin on the other. I look at my head again — is it my head? At most it resembles me. The engraving on the flip side is not a sea urchin, either, but a flower, very plainly. The next time I look, it is a star. Then an open hand. Without thinking I put this magic coin back in my mouth.

On the other side of the torn wall, there is a narrow ledge of sloppy concrete, broken ends thrust out just above the water showing grey surfaces like cottage cheese. A little brass lamp, just a sheet of brass with holes cut in it, curled into a cylinder, shines from an iron curlicue a couple of feet above the concrete surface. A lonely confidential light there, and by its glow he sees a long solemn boat drawing up. It's a black gondola with jade trim, poled by a stubble-headed old man with a pastrami-colored face. I catch his eye. He rows over, flips his paw open, and I spit the coin into it.

The water is calm. We pass fragments of tiled wall bristling with rusted iron wands. A warm fog trickles around, growing steadily denser, hotter, more mineral-smelling, like hot brass, and in a moment more I glimpse through it a stark scarlet seam up ahead, under the water. A soft black rod slithers out from a red joint in the rock, smoking underwater and making the surface steam; it veers to and fro like a thick, muscular snake just below the clear, hissing water. The boat lands with a thump against a marble ledge, adjacent to the dreamily erupting rocks, and I hop out. Here there is a diamonded floor and a tiled wall pierced in the center by a door the shape of a peacock-backed cane chair. Above the door is an inscription that reads: VERA.

The arch leads into a quiet, somber place of large red-ochre alcoves and pillars thick as barrels. There is a ringing silence here in the gloom, as though an inaudible gong were humming. The ground is tramped earth, covered with many faded, spidery-patterned rugs, and these breathe a smokey, heavy fabric smell. There are gods in the alcoves, forms with trunks, fanged beaks, riveted heads, wings, all carved of the same purple-cocoa colored stone. Each one is interlaced with a consort; a profusion of grotesque, intent and meditating faces gazing into each other. I look at one after another, feeling the searching calm of the place wind into me. Unlike the gods, the consorts are all formally-rendered perfect people, with no anatomical peculiarities. Then he comes to the last alcove, and this last figure is alone. The enormous sulking erection stands as though it were making an accusation, angrily dejected, stubborn, penetrating only the stilled air. The idol's face is crumpled and downcast below its horns; the cheeks are drawn up like two eggs flanking the short nose, and form grooves to either side of the hollow eyes. Thick, ropy tears resembling the gold braid of epaulets fill the grooves and ooze down the face in fixed stone beads. I think of blood channels in altars, tear channels in altar eyes. But the arms of the god are hovering outstreched in the air, curved in — perhaps he embraces an invisible consort, and this not-seeing is what torments him.

Something moves by the idol's base — is it a mouse? No, it's a wisp of smoke fading and uncurling there. A cord of smoke stretches along the ground, to a distant aperture from which it seems to come. Orange triangle in the dark, and a few boys in swim trunks are quietly pulling up the corners of the rugs, collecting what look like discarded ticket stubs. Their shadows crash through the orange triangle as they move back and forth before it. As I draw near they vanish into the shadows with muffled splashes. In the glowing triangle, I find a stereotypical gypsy tent, all purple velvet and moroccan cushions. Through a flap window there are dark trees and browsing giraffes undulating their necks from bough to bough in a landscape that rolls away and down from the flap. There is another aperture on the far side of the tent from the entrance — that's where I am going.

No one can pass through that way without first being hypnotized. Like so many other protocols of this kind of place I know that without having to be told. Perched on a stool before the cloth gate is a fake gypsy with a rather breathtaking embonpoint, and huge opal lying in its hollow, flat against the warm copper skin. Is she made up all over... and if she is, who gets to do the rubbing? Her hair is capped with a vermillion and gold scarf, her hair falls in blue-black ringlets down her back, giant hoop earrings the whole bit. She indicates I should sit before her, drawing an extra stool from somewhere behind her and fixing me with fog-colored eyes.

I sit, and she pulls an opticians' armature down out of the hanging veils on a steel boom arm and firmly thrusts it cold onto the bridge of my nose, clicking through lenses without consulting me. I occupy myself staring fixedly at her sparkling opal, which shimmers and dances back and forth as the lenses flip, and wonder if her movements in adjusting the armature aren't really intended to make it turn this way and that, firing out its beams of different colors. She spritzes me with perfume — I feel the chill droplets weightlessly settling across my face and hands. Then suddenly she is drilling her gaze into my eyes through the lenses, saying things I can't quite hear, and there is a snap like a knuckle cracking in the center of my head. I feel light, and momentarily overwhelmed as if there had been a blast of confused sound out of complete silence. She pulls the armature away from my face and smiles happily at me.

"Are you afraid?" she asks this with eyes blazing and wide, smiling as though she really were saying "isn't this exciting?" She seems otherworldly; in a blink see her slipping herself into that solitary idol's embrace. In a second blink, I see her with her legs wrapped around my hips — in this flash, I am forbidden to go about the city unescorted: this fake gypsy must be locked to my body at all times. She's my license. We must remain excited but climaxing would ruin the arrangement. Her copious skirts, fortunately, will preserve our modesty — not everyone who passes me is so lucky — and of course suspenders for are *de rigeur* for me. Walking in the streets I have to swing my head to one side of hers and then lift my chin up and over to the other side just to see where I'm going, trying to puff her unruly hair out of my way with blasts of breath. From time to time I have to stop, lean against a wall or lamp post breathing laboriously, face drawn trying to stay calm, face exasperated by the tickling of her hair. Constantly getting lost — how can I concentrate? The inevitable collisions with other pedestrians put us both severely to the test — I have to breathe and concentrate and push out and I can hear her chanting snatches of time-tables and recipes. Arms legs and back aching like mad, sodden fabric clinging to my thighs and abdomen. Sticky, chafed, overheated. She wants me to stop because she's just caught sight of a fetching scarf in a window display like hell I'm stopping I ain't a trolley, lady...

She is, after all, only standing in front of me, still smiling, holding the tent open for me. She smiles as though she'd had my thoughts, like I'd made her an innocuous compliment. She waves me through, and her bangles ding together for the first time. I blunder past her, and she brushes me with her body as I go by.

Bray of a tinny car horn right at my back as I trip out weirdly across a dusty white street in blazing equatorial sunlight, a figure there too obscure in the dazzle for me to make out waving me on and indicating a low triangular door in the wall. The figure is dark and shaggy and hops up and down in place, it has long hair and a glowing metallic face, broad across the cheeks, low-browed, and tapering to a pointed chin, and its dry paw pushes at my back as I go through the triangular aperture into an oily blue-black shadow.

From somewhere behind me a high-pitched whinny of song, I cross the dark floor with candled tables, making for a wonderland door of black wood in the far wall by the pay phone. Around me people lie on divans in various states of undress undergoing spirit cupping; ether-blue spirits respirate tumbling fire bobbins in glass flues pressed to the back, the abdomen, tops of heads. Haystacks of doors and tent flaps to get through everywhere stubbing my shoes or tangling round my legs, a tedious succession of doorknobs to turn and latches to lift, moving from car to car with a gush of stale tunnel air, picking up doors and flipping them over me and they pile up around my legs to my waist like a stack of hula hoops.

The floor beneath my feet is made of boards painted dingy black, and spattered with flecks of all colors of paint. An expectant backstage/museum smell comes around him, like cosmetic carnauba wax and linseed oil, paint, printing, massive curtains, sawdust, glue, varnish. Black backdrops hang from dark heights all around. The warm yellow blob emanating from the ghost light embubbles me; I turn around in place until I catch sight of an angle of brick wall, painted a glossier black, looming out from between the hangings like a ship's prow. I examine the wall, presently find a metal box painted over, with metal tubes for the wiring snaking out from it as though it were an angular heart. I rub just about in its middle with my index finger. Faint rasping sound on the paint, turning brown and crumbling away in tiny beads and curls. I've either exposed or created a slot there; I fish a coin from my mouth and drop it in the slot. The sound it makes, if it made that sound, comes from somewhere far away behind my left shoulder, and muffled by who knows how many of these dense black backdrops. The ringing of a coiled chime in a mantle clock.

I've holstered my right hand in my right coat pocket. As it lies there, not doing anything, something angular and paper is pressed into it, as though a person rushing down a dark street somewhere had paused to thrust this message through a chink in a wall, or into a really dark shadow where an alley is slimily drooling trash, through a dimension hole into my pocket. I pull out a pamphlet, a single sheet folded lengthwise, and read, stepping forward through the words — stand there emptyhanded in the ghost light. I remember every word. Walk along.

I am in the binding; empty choirs soar on up to where, like constellations, overhead there are gleams of polished wood, the ornaments of choir screens and theater boxes, up and up in untenanted underground sky. The light of the Deep Sun, or DS for short.

There are blue-litten salt galleries, studded with outcroppings of salt like enormous lalique sandcastles. As many of these caverns were opened, nomads with blue-painted faces would begin to emerge from them — Immigrants. The males took especially to the whores by the cloisters, kept them very busy and paid in new minerals. The nomad women sit on bolsters under waterproof fringed canopies with their few shaved-headed children, smoking stubby pipes and knitting brightly-dyed girdles for themselves out of bats' wool. Marble heads roll in the streets that run beneath the cemeteries, and through the matted weeds at the boundaries of the subterranean graveyards, singing and rolling their eyes — a Carpathian castle high in distant mountains, one lit window in the tower, just like in the movies.

In darkness I hadn't seen, up ahead, timid light comes in glimmering, like a silent film beginning. Long cloisters, with slender stone braces and chipped flags, tan leaves in slate gutters, pregnant calm and mute activity breathing along the long cloisters. The women wear fawny-white dresses of substantial, creamy smooth fabric, cinched in at the waist; they wear truncated snowy wimples, soft and extending all the way up to the ears, rising from a circle of whiter material around the shoulders. Their hair falls down albatross necks, and they wear beautiful tapering antlers within their temples, or swept back between the locks of their hair, knotted all over with colorful ribbons. They are human, but they seem like aliens and something about them arouses me with a yearning for unknown sexual contact unlike any other, just a sweet viscous cream (so-so) like a warm, flat blob (not quite) centered just above the groin (not really) and somehow associated with a motion (no motion) and a contact, more physical than looking but not as physical as touching, a floating, unintelligible, weightless, invisible intercourse what is it? Like wanting to feel sexy in a simile for sex, somehow *with them.*

Petrified writhing naked trees against fire-brown light high ahead. A woman comes round a corner, arms held out from her sides a little, looking down at the ground ahead, and smiling with pleasure at some shining thought she is carrying in her mind. She has pearly back-swept two-pronged antlers that curve back and up. Her soft hands, tender as snails, flip and snap their fingers in distraction. She stops a few feet away, looks up at me sweetly and says she will take me to see Brown Master now, if I'd like.

She leads me over humped, hard earth wan as bone and netted over with snaking white roots, half-buried, molar-like stones, down into a mixed fresh and stagnant water smell, to a bridge covered with dazzling green moss, so that hardly any of the masonry can be seen. Gaping faces carved into the stone have sprouted disfiguring moss wens and goiters, their mossed features look swollen, as though they'd been drinking and brawling. To one side of the bridge and down the bank. She stops and extends her hand, indicating I should go under the low bridge, where the darkness is near total only a foot or so from in beneath. There is something stirring down there. I crouch, and walk on damp gravel into the shade of the bridge.

In the stagnant dark, a smooth, featureless flank of glistening blue-black hide rolls streaked with brown slime. A dim, round, silky hulk is squatting or lolling there; I can just make out the flat, pan-shaped head surmounted by two little knobs, which might be protuberant eyes, nostrils, giraffe horns, ears, a matador's hat. Without clearly seeing it, I knows there is a wide, all but lipless mouth, turned down and pulled back at the corners like a shark's, but toothless. The mouth is open, and the long breath wheezes like poured water tumbling in a vessel. It seems to be bleeding from the mouth — thick congealed threads hang down... fresh bright iron blood. The head swings a little, looking a bit like a metal detector, on a monstrously thick neck, which would be diamond-shaped in cross section, with a ridge running along the top.

Brown Master draws a gush of breath and speaks thoughts; I receive the thoughts somehow and caption them — something like computer circuitry made out of lumpy white clay, and glass beads bouncing around through the circuit maze. The caption goes something like "it is so hard to get through your thicket grounds," with "you have so many words already" superimposed on top of it.

Brown Master talks water; sliding by — a green darker than jade and deep shadowed green humped dense up on either bank. We move slowly with the current. We pass the massive heads of idols with their lips below the surface, drugged and somber. Here's a brown-green Greek one, head all covered with barnacle-like curls, its brow clenched above hollow-pupilled staring eyes full of some raging emotion. Another staring one, a crowned Norse king with severe little nose and sweep of flat beard, shoulders up just below his tiny ears. All manner of idols, all looking this way and that in the meditating river, and beyond them are inky shadows in the green and oceanic depths there; their humming expanse gazes back, spreads wings of shadow air over the boat, or over me. Everything is watching, just watches, with no object, so I go through an attention.

Down the pier and into the half-bustling town, there's Uar sitting on a windowsill cutting shapes out of his newspaper and sending curls of it to the ground. He catches sight of me, beams and nods, walks over. He's wearing a white shirt rolled up to the elbows, a tie, maroon pants with a belt at his waist, and loafers with no socks. He shakes my hand.

"It's kind of liking Manaus here."

"I've come to see Brown Master."

Uar smiles. "I'll take to you."

The street is narrow, the buildings lean over looking down at what the tide washed in. Clotheslines are strung overhead, laden with brightly colored light robes, dresses, shirts and scarves, waving lower and lower until we brush through a soft jungle of dazzling sheets... All this light, but no day, no sky.

British working-class neighborhood of neat houses, the blackened bricks looking translucent like smoked ruby glass. Feet crisp on wet concrete squares in the narrow alleys between the houses; sour-faced factory upthrust there in the middle distance, the glum stacks seep a plume or two of steam every now and then. Out into a boulevard so broad as practically to be a square, lined with tall houses whose façades look like crenelated eighteenth-century tombstones. The air is as cold and clear as a glacial pool, vacuumed clean by the underground wind, filled with sourceless light of the DS. I can make out every detail of even the more distant façades with unreal distinctness.

The corner house and a few adjacent to it all show signs of fire damage, and in fact a few spots are still smouldering. The ground floor of the house on the corner is completely staved in with the exception of the front door, which opens directly onto the street, precisely at the corner. Smoke fumes from wreckage dusted with a sparse cinder layer, an incomprehensible jumble of busted beams and furniture shards. The door is untouched, the brass knocker gleams like new.

A French valet lets me in and conducts me down the hall. Uar will wait for me. I pass a closed room resounding with many voices speaking Hindi, and now the valet waves me over toward the wall as a couple of dozen men in denim clothes, long black hair, look to be natives, go by in ones and twos, and each one clears his throat as he gets to me. There's no end of these hallways and each one is jostling full of all kinds of people, with light pouring in from a distant window or an open door. This house must have about twenty-five sides and double that many back doors. Now an empty hall with a door at the end opening onto a yard — cool humid breeze blows in, big ferns lap the air. We stop by a door with the word tsathog ripped from a cheap poster and thumbtacked on the lintel.

The valet, a compact younger man in a white shirt and ragged knee-pants says "Arrête" and puts his hands lightly on my biceps.

"Parce-que tu es en partie démon, tu ne dois pas entrer dans cette chambre, compris? Ne regarde meme pas a l'interieur, seulement du coin de l'oeil droit. Fixe ton regard sur le rebord de la porte."

He goes, and I stand there, fixementing my eyes on the fronds at the end of the hall. The door beside me is gradually swinging open on a dark room. A pulsing, eerie groan, and smell of Brown Master, come out. Peripherally I can see the room beyond is dark except for holes in the brick walls up near the ceiling, which might be partially sunken in. The air in there is fluttering with bats that become owls when they alight on the walls, or so it seems — I can't make out what they roost on. The owls are doing the groaning, like Tibetan monks they groan out HOOOOOOOO churn around and around the confines of the room throwing up a higher overtone like a chorus of ghosts. Descending down from the ceiling somehow there is a huge Persian rug, mostly black and deep red. It curves down to the floor and runs up to the jam of the door, so I can see some of its pattern clearly — the fantastic loops of stems and ribbons in a pattern finer and more crazymaking to look at than the engraving on money. Dark colors, but beneath it a surly golden burn that shimmers out like petulant little lightning sparks.

Suddenly that HOOOOOO roars up even louder and the rug slides out of sight away from the door. A massive thing rises from the floor under the rug, and gradually the hem slides back until it forms a hood. I will myself not to look. The owls die down and the weird voiceless voice of Brown Master comes to me from beneath the rug, the huge vertigo-inducing medallion right over its eyes, and coming from somewhere behind the door what looks like a burnt, reedy arm swings out and a long, slender hand with tapering fingers that curl like the toes of Turkish slippers offers me a little nunk of chocolate. As I eat it what might be a miniature copy of the rug unfurls before me like a sign post and I fall into the pattern to the drone of Brown Master.

Ladies from the cloister atop the housefronts on the square, and standing nearby, raising their horns in zephyrs, turning their heads from the waist this way and that, with arms raised, admiring themselves in invisible mirrors, invisible snakes embrace their wrists. I trip headlong into satiny fabric, surprisingly strong, soft hands, a cooing voice by my ear.

In order to get back, we will have to pass through Avenue A; and this is what the world looks like now.

Lonely people don't want to be immortal, and all these people are alone without realizing it. They don't realize just how alone they are. Hooded sallow and grey-skinned in the street headphones trying to tune out the advertising station, all milling under the elevated train, which now only carries freight "no passengers." The street is lined with wailing flat screen advertising, trash and surveillance cameras everywhere, everywhere worn and broken things, the rag ends of narrative worn threadbare, sharp and frayed like a banshee call. Watching everywhere, but the people don't watch they stare, in blank incomprehension and an unending stun.

The street is a prison yard: guards may or may not sneer down from plastic tubes, blackened one-way, that cross above the street at regular intervals. You can't see *them* they can see *you* — if they're there. Each tube sports an array of mace nozzles and a microwave emitter dish for dispersing crowds or sizzling them where they stand; all lit up at once they could boil the entire street. Arrogant helicopters overhead all the time, hovering, zooming, peering and spying with their lights. Pinecones of cameras bristle on every lamp post, the whole street inundated at all times with unrelieved ugly orange light that glares into every corner from huge stadium floods spaced fifteen feet apart all along its length, and not twenty feet off the ground. Uar and I scurry past a huge pile of broken concrete and onto the avenue.

"*Vampirism* run this part of town from helicopters," Uar tosses over his shoulder, head down.

On the horizon, a solid wall of high-rises makes a continuous rampart of lit offices. The DS would set behind them. This wall of offices stops the wind, so it never reaches the avenue — so the air is stale. But these far-off offices are the only tall buildings in the city; the rest is a sprawl of three and four story piles and paved lots, very rare glimpse of grey dirt in which nothing will grow, not even weeds, not even mildew. You see no roaches or rats at the garbage cans, no pigeons pick at the junk, no dogs or cats, nothing animal, not even the people. The side streets are jammed with abandoned and wrecked cars; piles of these line the main drags, where huge ploughs have bulldozed a path for an endless stream of trucks groaning buses and emergency vehicles, layer on layer of them in stacks of cement overpasses streaming with hot engine air and exhaust. The sound of engines sirens and car and building alarms is continuous, one carcinogenic, deafening roar. The sky is gagged with floating billboards and even orbiting advertisements, almost all of which are malfunctioning or totally broken. Thanks to them, no celestial object can be seen. Collisions in the air are frequent and huge signs and lit displays come crashing down from time to time to tear black sooty gashes in the city blocks. People stand mutely watching the catastrophe with their fingers in their noses.

I'm looking around anxiously.

"There's nothing to fear them really," Uar says, "While they can be pretty violent, nobody knows *how* to fight."

"What about the guards?"

Uar smiles. Seeing that smile is a surprisingly big relief in this place. "The guards don't know how to fight, they just spray you."

He taps the hollow of his throat, where his tie is loosened. "One comes up to me, I'd hit here." From nowhere a length of strong brown forearm is suddenly there in front of him, a knife blade at the end, a hoarse "huh" booms from his chest. Then he holds the knife blade up and gives his fist a little pump in the air and smiles.

"That's good," he says.

We scoot hastily along the embankment of a paved river choked with dead bodies, some cars and trash. A mile or so away there is a delta of ruined suspension bridges, all their paint flaked away, scabbed with rust and slouching, their cables blow horizontal in the gusts of a high wind that never comes near the ground.

The way out takes us through a rich neighborhood behind high barbed wire walls. Uar shows me a passage through a dried culvert. Dejected ugly stucco and cinderblock houses with cement yards pass by, drowning in hysterical orange glare. We're triggering motion-activated cameras and piercing blue fog lights, but nothing much else seems to happen. The handfull of trees, the only ones I have seen, are all dead and *melted*, discolored, slumped flabbily against the ground and stinking like dead meat. The barricaded houses are huge and well-spaced apart from each other, solid and brutish as fortresses, relentlessly and waspishly unpleasant to look at. There is broken glass in the windows, and curtains wearily paw the air through the jagged gaps, the bars. The inhabitants are drinking their pool water and wilting away with chlorine poisoning that turns them the color of blue snot. But there is no rain, it will never rain here. They have paved the ocean.

Uar points to a slot and I fish out and sink another coin. The secret place is before me, and my mind enters it, enveloped in the memory of a golden summer's boy day I lived, and its warm amber serenely endomes us both like fire glow. From somewhere behind us a howl grates against scorched metal lids — we step at once lighter than air through the aperture, and dull lead air closes like a shutter at our backs.

The next instant we must both latch on to crushing thoughts and heavy, sad feelings; otherwise, the sudden change in pressure will blow us wide open.

Here are shining streets slick and black with rain and the sharpened lights' sparkling; fleecy, glowing white clouds soar gigantically along against a dark dull indigo sky in unearthly, soundless flight.

Signs say "UNDERWORLD, THE."

We pass a warehouse all ablaze with blue-white light, the unexpected relief from sodium-orange smut, like breaking through into the true night remembered from childhood, an open, colored night of stark gleams and bright darkness. Weightless, cold, dark, electric excitement of the city wafts over them both. Uar goes his own way under the lonely streetlight at the corner, is gone with a smile and a wave into the dark like a swimmer turning to swim from the shore.

A little underground neighborhood, maybe two blocks. Dark browns and greys, brick warehouses, rows of homes, some dim shops. Not too noisy, but a ghostly gaiety here. Brass band, balloons, smell of beer.

The windows of the passing omnibuses have been blacked out by order of the transit authority, and, riding outside, I soon learn why. No one is meant to see the prisoners of war working down in the tunnels, packing the earth and shoring up the stone roof. We regular citizens are forbidden the sight of livid white eyes in grimy faces. What war was it again? Where is it now? It rambles here and there like a god in the world, it sweeps through the room like a vacuum, sucking out warmth and sound, and then it's gone again and everybody goes on talking about the whether. No one seems to know where the prisoners come from or in what war they were taken. There's nothing in the papers — what papers? — but there they are working down in the tunnels, laying track, propping up the walls.

Flash of copper sunset light in whites of the POWs' eyes, ragged and surly with clouds. They are leaning against the walls like so many momentarily abandoned tools. Their chains make it difficult to lie down. Foxes slip in and out of their secret streets in the wall in an old English riddle.

Hands emerge silently from holes in the wall, from crevices and from under platforms, abruptly seize the chains and begin filing away at them rapidly. Hands drift out of the shadows to where the POWs stand like tilted tools, hands take hold of the links binding them and break them one by one. The prisoners are instantly animated the moment they are set free: they dash into the darkness flapping out their arms, their laughter spiralling around the circle of tunnel walls — shadows melted into gas, away into stale tunnel air.

Deuteronôme steps out into the little neighborhood through a heavy black curtain. The air here is cool and light, "flutterings full of electric purpose" in autumn cloister, settling calm attentive light.

A rustling sound. There against the wall are a heap of uprooted iron mailboxes still attached to their cement posts, and a hand from the shadows has just deposited atop them a brown paper lunch bag with its mouth crimped shut. Before the hand vanishes, POW insignia on the sleeve. Father Ptarmagant emerges from the door of the coffin maker's hovel in the next moment, notices and retrieves the bag. It is marked with a small bundle of orange and black metallic ribbons; opening it, he finds it is filled with dates and candy corns. Ptarmagant pulls the mouth open and holds it toward Deuteronôme; after a moment, Deuteronôme steps up and puts in his hand. He removes a date, looks at it judiciously, sniffs it, then pulls it apart and discards the pit. The date makes a bulge in his cheek. Ptarmagant only now takes the bag back toward himself and pulls out a handful of sweets.

They start walking together. The bag has a hole in it and Ptarmagant leaves a candy trail. Tiny, frail looking monkeys pop out of holes in the rubbish and collect the sweets, putting them to their mouths and looking imploringly wary. Deuteronôme and Ptarmagant fall roughly in step with a stiff easiness.

"So, why are we all to be hypnotized coming in here?" Deuteronôme asks.

"We're hypnotized but not deluded — quite the opposite. It's something to do with outrunning lies or excluding liars."

"You're afraid of lies? They don't have the brains to be liars. Not good ones."

"That's not quite what I mean. I mean they are liars because they have no truth of their own. They have brains, but they don't have nerve."

Black fire escapes pass overhead, with curtains blowing out the windows; gangly pennants that dwindle tapering to single endless threads float above the rooftops. Bodies on golden plinths along the roads, sheathed in a thin layer of clear ice and shining with ice like they were painted with light, and tiny round bells hang from their fingers and ears, send pure, protracted humming notes sailing across the nearly breathless street.

They pass glistening-trunked trees whose branches are foliated with dense masses of reeking tar, hanging in strings and webs that flop in the breeze. Some bodies are woven into the supple boughs. Impregnated with tar, they look like rubber statues. And here a buried body has sent a crown of roots up from its head to emerge into the air, a rattling spray of salt-encrusted white nerves stiff and plastic as fingernails. The windows of the houses spill alchemical apparatus into the street in massive piles, brass and glass glint from the mounds of iron and strong-smelling lead slag. They walk close together now, weaving to avoid the puddles, the deep, cauldron-like potholes; and here, where goats have congregated nervously to drink, a gutter gushes water into a mushy iron grate.

"We are here to make some living room for ourselves, not to unmask lies."

Ptarmagant hunches his shoulders in his shirt, as we often read characters do. "The lies are part of what has to be cleared away, and they're intolerable in any case. What we want to do is to open the way for the immigrants, and some new humans. Right now, Dominant Narrative co-opts or destroys all the other novels in progress the sooner the better.

"We speak vaguely on account of we're talking for something that we want to happen. We must make room for this to be able to mean something; right now, it might never mean anything. Ask your gypsy."

"She is neutral. I would not say she is entirely on one side. I don't know why she is here."

"Perhaps the demon wanted her."

"She wouldn't be the one to attract that sort."

"What sort is that?" his voice is perfunctory.

"The sort to make some hapless woman's face into a mask for the universe and her yes or no into a cosmic judgement in your whole life's case, *comme* de Nerval."

The other man plucks a huge drooping volume of Agrippa from the air and plunges his finger down into a swirling profusion of pages, reads aloud:

"Now the fourth kind of phrensy proceeds from *Venus*, and it doth by a fervent love convert, and transmute the mind to God, and makes it altogether like to God, as it were the proper image of God..."

The Great Lover turns abruptly to Deuteronôme teeth bare in a blinding face — "*Never speak of her to me!*"

Again and again I return to this little neighborhood. I'd come more often, but I keep falling down manholes and drowning in the sewers. I can't say for certain whether or not I come back to this neighborhood or to a roughly identical one deeper underground. The neighborhood looks the same but I have so poor a sense of its particulars; there are many performers here, some working out of their rooms and others on the street. Everyone is always talking about the big performance, and what preparations are called for, how it should be done, how cleaned up, and so on. I come to see the gypsy. There are always men furtively escaping from her tent with anxious looks — all of them. She's tired tonight, and wants to turn me away, but she can't bring herself to do it, because her generosity is so powerful and I am making her love me a little more each time. Someone inside her loves me, and strengthens every visit I make. I come to her because she gives me her body and with it her own particular kind of sleep.

I fall asleep, and she hands me a striped card. I take it, rise from the bed, and slide it through a slot in the wall — someone on the other side snatches it from my fingers right away. The magic door opens and I go through it into someone else's dream.

The street is shimmering, as though flurries of snow rippled across it. The bodies lining the street were laid out carefully; now their heads are all turned toward the street and white sewage gushes from their gaping mouths, a few infrequent wisps of steam curl past sunken eyes and shrivelled ears, hair brittle as straw. White sewage runs in the gutters and spins there as it goes down, and I am spinning down with it. My head bangs the pavement as hard as a cannonball. I lie on a slope and slide backward, hands swing up along the ground toward my shoulders as the elbows bend, fingers execute an incongruously graceful dance as my body, seen from above, is screwed into the fit.

Down again, grit and small clots of matter pat by in the current, which flows against my face with a continuous, powerful but not irresistible pressure. I move forward holding on to projections in the walls, all made of brown bread-loaf bricks worn and chipped like lozenges. The shadow of a hand moves above the surface.

The tunnels are too elaborate to enter. The trains back then must have been miniature trolleys, only large enough to accommodate a pair of benches back to back, the riders' feet protrude over the edge or hang in the air. Skylights throw down round patches of radiance, leopard-spotting the tracks. Buttery sunlight glows on the miniature platforms, decked out with brass triangles that hang down from the edges of the walkways above and below like strips of little flags, all enameled with triangular blue and red medallions. The platforms are lined with slender pillars, pinstriped mauve and silver. The benches are as colorful and baroquely decorated as carousel horses. The rails are only an inch wide. The ties are delicate, almost like pool cues, though splintery and stinking strongly of creosote.

The Prosthetic Death stands before me. I die, drop to the ground like a sack of death.

Still wandering, I suddenly look up — there is the Prosthetic Death stepping out of a patch of light a hundred yards ahead. There is the Prosthetic Death turning into a side tunnel and out of sight. There is the Prosthetic Death, arms loose but not swinging at her sides climbing the few shallow steps onto a tiny platform where a carousel organ plays, its tubes like a fan-jet of saffron fires. She is walking away, she stretches and places her hands at the base of her spine — as she does this, the flat panel swells and splits open. There she is at my back, breathing out black oblivion without breath, and I collapse, die, hunt again. I claw through heaps in darkness. Is this it? With a shout I snap the bones of the cold forearm. Something withdraws in a swirl of displaced air, and whatever I hold in my left hand is limp and clammy and melting. A rattle of bones.

I pitch toward the sound and now my fingers clinch on a handful of cold locks. Trying to regain my footing I kick out with all my strength and I feel my foot crush something in my blind spot, the tension holding my hand gives way with a tearing feeling and what flies from me, in a direction I can't take, trails a broken wing. The lead powder window is still there. I walk up to it and hold to the light a handful of fairy gold elf-curls already brittling, turning into a torn clump of tawny grass glittering with cold, dewy blood.

The music ended the moment he set foot through the door — it's a dead suburb. Here, where the sidewalk is shattered as though it had been attacked with sledgehammers, there is a heap of fine powder like maybe unmixed cement. Small, neat, bare footprints barely indent the surface.

I go into a hotel under construction for twenty years, next to another construction site. The stairs still smell like fresh paint. One door, many floors up, is just ajar.

The Prosthetic Death is in the shower, washing herself. Malignant grey fire glows in the spine, flares slowly and dies slowly, like the deliberate gleam of an ember in a soft draught. She stops the motion of her hands and turns to face me through the misty curtain, and something flashes behind the face.

There is a steady, rotating distortion in the middle of the room. I edge from the blind spot, choose my moment and dash for the door, trying to slip myself into one of the gaps between the spiral arms of the distortion. I feel a brush of brilliant nerves, like a blast of intense temperature but without heat or cold, veer over the threshold off kilter and hit the far wall. The sight of the nerve exchange makes a sick feeling quiver in me like a glycerin dart. A domed atrium not much larger than an elevator is here.

I feel like I'm waiting, feeling disuse without ruin in the building.

There is a dead potted plant shoved into the corner, and the tile floor is sparsely dotted with crumbs of rich black dirt. A triangular grey spider web ripples like a tiny sail in one of the atrium's eight angles. They store meditative calm in this room. I sit by the wall, looking at an empty niche streaked with rust. Somewhere a big bell is being rung, making me think of boys' schools, a dazzling green lawn and a sky of deep unreal blue, maybe just outside these walls.

The heavy bronze double doors, each seven feet tall and eighteen inches wide, have thick rod handles the length of the meeting edges. They fold back on smooth noiseless hinges. I was almost right — it's a repository of enamelled skies lying stacked up like rugs, seeping light into the invisible aisles and up into the heavy black backdrops. The aisle is also a subway car, and as I walk its length with sky flashing in at the windows, I weave along a row of crystal balls on bronze wands that stands the center of the car. Each ball is pierced at its base by a huge needle, like bubbles of liquid glass which keep their shapes by virtue of a constant and smoothly-adjusted pressure from a plunger hidden inside each wand. The land here is dotted with what we may call nerve distortions, and, each time my gaze lights on one, I have a feeling of struggle, the murmuring of Brown Master. He is one of the gang. The people are familiar, smiling and conversing wittily with me and I am witty right back. They bustle through dark streets, push through a steaming cloakroom and into chairs in a kind of cabaret darkness. Warren is screeching away on stage with his speakers in his hands. I am sitting in the circle at six o'clock, trading remarks with these others, trying to hide the sadness oozing out of me. After the show we are on our feet and moving through the dark, and I feel a cool, wet kiss like a soft blow on my right cheek. Who kissed me? This is a remembering séance, with one voice doing all the voices... but someone else *is* here, stowing away in those times when as a boy I received the bafflingly equivocal kisses of girls. I missed the strip tease act.

A yearning lyric unfolds from the landscape, the trees, low hills, boggy meadows and metallic water, and mists over me. Beached boats, shattered listing shacks, crumbling brick switching houses glide past

— one of the women from the cloister far off on a little prominence, a pale billowing hourglass figure against the grim trees, raising a ram's horn to her lips. There is no sound but a feeling that thrums in his chest, beating the yearning there into a burning sharpness. Go into an immanent place, I feel full of power and that means love of pure immanence: she seems to reconstitute out of this landscape. Her face streaks because I am flowing into the glass of the window. See the edges of the glass from the inside, music here of harps, chimes, dulcimers. A fragrant greenhouse whose every window is black with starless night, a grotto with its own dark above the luminous ground, lit with milky fires twinkling inside white flowers, where the weeds stream in still water, caves curtains doors stairways and passages embrace embrace and embrace in accumulating folds of one long folded embrace. Here is anywhere, the woman lowers the ram's horn and sets it on the floor, bending easily at the waist, a white veil wafting from her horns. She turns to me with a spitting opal heavy on her chest, sweeping her head up from down low bending up from the waist like a dancer. She puts off her veil, arms open, she is like a snake handling woman carved in Crete rising in the air on the head of a huge yellow snake.

The Prosthetic Death is smiling at me. I wrap my arms around her hips, for now she has hips, and she bobs in my arms light as a balloon. I looks at her weird face near to mine, a woman's face, and women's faces are so lovely. Marshlight, some bodies coil until they nestle inside each other like Russian dolls and form a ball together with a click.

A hand reaches in and adjusts her desire with a careful, deft turn.

The brick tenements all have thatched roofs, and some have low-hanging eaves made of bundles of papyrus. These banged brick faces, criss-crossed with feathered duelling scars, sullenly rest their square chins on the sidewalks until the street drops into the ground. Sheep in the windows bump Halloween and Valentine's Day paper cut outs with their heads as they graze on the windowboxes — these immigrants are always getting Cupid mixed up with the Grim Reaper, maybe on account of the arrows. Death's dart, they must think. The presence of dead persons and immigrants at performances creates an electric air of tension, not knowing what exactly stands beside you, a background of intrigue. You turn, and beside you a body clothed in rough blue serge, sporting one butterfly wing and one bird's reversed back to front, antennae sprout from golden temples. The immigrants and the winged creatures, the cultists and the city, the great whorling vortex of misery like warped records turning into each other in a cloverleaf, almost a viscous slow whirlpool stark and grim.

No more clues — I follow walls where crêched bodies lean upright clutching their frayed documents. I can't stop to inspect them, but some are made out of unusual materials. While they are all plainly corpses that once had life, parts of them are shining steel or flaking green copper. The face on this skull is half bone and half coarse fabric. Here is wood and here is ivory and here is stone, a pelvis studded with budding pearls, ribs of cloudy ice, a spine of desert air — a pumpkin made indistinguishable from the mashed and discolored head of a corpse by carefully layered carving massaging softening hardening and dyeing.

Man slumped snoring there on a bench in a wad of down and thick sweatshirts, profusion of hoods and zippers and stinking beyond belief. The moment you are out of sight, his face is intent alert intelligent. He pops nimbly from his seat and kneels arranging spark plugs in patterns on the tile floor. The pattern complete, a lump of lead time turns to gold in his hand. He will pick up subway tunnels like pan pipes, and play.

All the characters I meet have cracked faces that hang from their heads in crisp rags like ruptured papier maché. Dr. Thefarie, Multiply, all of them pass me without noticing me; their raw new faces are bursting out of the old ones. I find a window and check myself out — not me, my face is my mask. I have three flat diamond shaped flames jetting from my forehead like a diadem, and through the glass my brow meets the tree all shimmering with droplets of stationary fire. In the middle of the tree the whole cartoon is showing, with me whirling in empty space playing with my curtain rod and my costume, me turning into a cartoon, me writing the cartoons to be drawn by stalls of animals. The bell rings over the street.

The Prosthetic Death has fallen in love with me, but she hasn't got the parts she needs to express her love. Vera loves me, hiding inside the gypsy. This is the way. John Brade, his face flapping to one side and his new face pink and still amorphous, like a newborn's, holds the flap so I can see it: the Prosthetic Death seducing the gypsy. She is suckling the gypsy, how much smaller she is. Vera's hair tosses inside the gypsy's eyes and now she is gigantic, her vast fragrant body fills the street. I follow the Prosthetic Death, who runs the length of the body and now hides herself inside it.

The gypsy greets me the next day, immensely pregnant. Her eyes are weird, with clouds inside, and she lisps. She tells me she can't see me — preparations for the big performance are more pressing now.

I go back to see her every day, and every day her pregnancy is a little less, her lisp a little less, and her manner stranger and stranger.

"I can stay," she smiles, patting the seat next to her. "I can love you."

But she sits there without doing a thing.

Then the lisp reappears stronger than ever, and all sign of the pregnancy is gone.

A woman's body throws off its white garments and calls out—

Show me the Great Lover, in all his regalia.

A figure steps through the curtain and advances across the yawning span, the Divinity Student, the Golem, the Traitor, the Tyrant, and now here is the Great Lover, a bristling demonic superhero in fur coat, Bowery boy cap, holding his curtain rod, his eyes burning and his teeth black as onyx, his Maori face and his eyeglasses and pearls — Vera the God the gypsy the Prosthetic Death Hulferde's sister from the cloister savor in on his arms span... finally she sleeps.

From out of the Great Lover's eyes the Prosthetic Libido steps and he and the Prosthetic Death twist together in gravity fire. Vera and the Great Lover, the gypsy and me, imagine a rotoscope spins pairs of faces together but always in pairs.

You're through the dream now. All around you is strange light, what you see is unreal but pressing in on the senses very intensely, like colors with mass, substance of their own. Weightless, insubstantial intensities. You waver between contradictory descriptions here, because the distinctions are no longer discernible.

And there's a sense of anticipation, uncertainty as to what's going to happen next. Time is completely open. In space, you orient yourself by finding down and up, drift in space. In time, you look for the gradient — you are drift in time, which is slack, looking for the tension to come back.

Hold that feeling of the story ending — of the life that you turn to when you put the story down starting to shine through it it is becoming transparent and to feel like a dream hold that feeling and stay in it. Just stay in it.

The darkness splits in rags and sunlight of the Deep Sun, then grows instantly dim and remote, and here is a planet striped red green and grey with distinct, rippling skeins of plant, animal, and fungal tissue. The borders are gold where the bands touch. The Great Lover before them — the two Prosthetics — is a figure in a haze of his own parts, dissected and hanging in the air around a gold ring that attracts particles of gold from the landscape bands below, and from gilded light on underside of cloud. The Prosthetic Libido and the Prosthetic Death are screaming across the sky in pure intensity: Pandora's Box. Coupled up they open over land and sea, and out comes this candy wrapper blown across your path today on your way to work, and this slab of concrete, grey and black in impossible contrast deep and sharp as a dream, a hushed prophetic voice here in the crease of fabric at your elbow, out of them comes the smell of the subway saturated with bitter music, all quotations composed on the spot.

Now the sky contracts to one flame burning at the tip of a green bough and gilding it with its light. This is the bough you offer to Charon to get across the Styx if you want to visit the dead while still alive yourself. The gold tongue is transparent and inviting to the eye like a crystal ball. What do you see?

—I see what I read here.

Michael Cisco

What you read here, we write together: you and I and eight coffins.

Here is the Great Lover crossing rolling green pastures, clambering awkwardly over fences and far away the sound of that bell. The sky is brilliant blue and white with foaming clouds; the light dims and surges, amorphous shadows ripple over the ground. Shade closes over him as he makes his way into the forest, climbing lungingly up a dry creekbed lined with moss furred rocks. It's quiet; remote songs of birds, and an occasional gasp runs through the nervous wood. The air is cool fresh and clear like a glacier stream.

A naked figure the size of a ten year old child observes him a moment from between two boulders on a low rise off to the left, then bounds away the next instant — vanished. Here and there the Great Lover can see them, some no bigger than his hand, dart and rustle around him, always too far away or too fleeting to make out clearly. Fingers slip back behind a screen of black stalks, glittering eyes flick open and closed in the shade of bracken hollows. The woods breathe and listen. In the hollow lined with boulders the sun lances through holes in the canopy and walks huge beams across the green floor; here the Prosthetic Death is sitting on a stone, its hands thrust inside a pale little torso. The Prosthetic Libido turns from what he is doing, trots over to the Great Lover and smiles, pure joy gleaming from his beautiful lips.

The two Prosthetics live together here in the seclusion of the woods, making machine people together. The materials they extract from the rocks and soil, digging out the oil, picking out the ore, working it with their fingers or changing it in their stomachs until it is ready for use. They will populate the woods with devices like themselves; the Prosthetic Libido shows him the face he's been working on for their latest: an exquisite, inhuman, long-eyed face. The Prosthetic Death comes over and silently takes Pearl's hand.

"We have something for you," Pearl beams. The Prosthetic Death and Prosthetic Libido walk hand in hand to a huge dead tree, still standing and draped all over with mistletoe and vines. From out of an arched opening in the hollow trunk steps an exact likeness of the Great

324

Lover, identical to him in every detail, although even this exactness seems like a distortion.

"Just for fun."

The Great Lover's double strides sulkily toward him, looking this way and that with exaggerated malice and surliness and sullenness, a wonderful living cartoon character.

Vera and he re-enter the world, I mean yours. Here they leave behind their marks in the sky — her hair, his tattoo.

The Great Lover raises his head slowly, as ponderously as an elephant, as a vast mythical animal, the world serpent. The Great Lover raises his head in that green-blue soupy thickness of sky, a cloudy broth that sluggishly gathers its folds on itself like the bunching, slowing waters of a swamped river. His breath is a sound, but he can't feel the air. Fronds blow almost too slow to see in an impalpable wind, and crumbed black fir boughs nod and stir the clabbered light like witches' hands. He cannot lower his gaze, no matter how he moves his head — the movements are thoughts, not actions. His head does not go down, though he tells it to, and in the confusion that follows, his imagination rushes eagerly ahead into the gap and supplies to vision what he cannot bend his eyes to see. He shuts his eyes, and remains in the thought of lowering his head, until he seems to go to sleep in it. His head has lowered, and now he looks out over rolling green hills from a high place. Copses, and stone farm houses huddled at the skirts of the lordly hills who rule here. The trees are courtiers and hangers-on. In the tunnels, through graveyards and sewers — how far back does it go? All the way, all the way there is: as long as there is way, there it goes. There is no "it," only something ongoing like a proceeding, and maybe a passage there. The end of the story, when it's becoming transparent — hold on to it. This is where you come in.

The preparations are all finished. It's time for the big performance. Multiply, Futsi, and their friends are skating to and fro on the curved wooden skate deck, and Deuteronôme sits in the center facing Dr. Thefarie. The skaters create the magic circle with their boards, a dynamic circle of movements that constantly redraws itself in new ways within its limit of variations, always a circle.

Far off across the floor, Vera enters, wrapped in white, with her four attendants. She summons the Great Lover, who must obey her call. Her robe slips to the floor and her nerves turn invisible and fill the air in this huge underground chamber. Suddenly the Deep Sun is there, hanging above the ramp. Its cold light shines down on a floor filled with Merlins dervishes shamans witches fortune tellers, all Immigrants.

Sewer water boils in the corner and the Great Lover appears. He seethes across the floor toward the ramp. The two Prosthetics stand in the center. Every voice rises to a crescendo at once as every subway train in the system shrieks its brakes and blasts its horn and the sun, high in the sky over the city, directly overhead, sinks. It drops from the sky and down into the city, driving down into the ground, its light disappearing from the sky, blazing through the buildings without harming them. Mobs of screaming people in the streets — the sun is vanishing into the earth — a dome, now a disk, of blinding, shrinking light—

Now it's gone — the stars shine in the sky — a rioting mass of people are clawing at the ground where the sun disappeared.

Down below, the Deep Sun erupts in brilliant light like countless transparent fires. The Great Lover sings out and flies up into the air. Light cataracts into the chamber as the sun descends into the Deep Sun and joins with it in a cyclone of vaporized water that at once condenses into white clouds. The cement ceiling turns transparent blue, the clouds drift in it, the chamber is a meadow and the underworld is a landscape overflowing with light. The sky has gone underground.

About the Author

Michael Cisco is the author of *The Divinity Student* (Buzzcity Press; International Horror Writers Guild Award for best first novel of 1999), *The San Veneficio Canon* (Prime Books, 2004), *The Tyrant* (Prime Books, 2004), a contributor to *The Thackery T. Lambshead Pocket Guide to Eccentric and Discredited Diseases* (eds. Jeff VanderMeer and Mark Roberts) and *Album Zutique* (ed. Jeff VanderMeer), and his work has appeared in *Leviathan III* and *Leviathan IV* (ed. Forrest Aguirre). His novel, *The Traitor*, is published by Prime (2007). *Secret Hours*, a collection of his Lovecraftian short stories, is published by Mythos Books (2007). In 2009-2010, his stories have appeared in the *Phantom* ("Mr. Wosslynne"), *Black Wings* ("Violence, Child of Trust"), *Lovecraft Unbound* ("Machines of Concrete Light and Dark"), *Cinnabar's Gnosis: A Tribute to Gustav Meyrink* ("Modern Cities Exist Only to be Destroyed"), and *Last Drink Bird Head* anthologies. Forthcoming works include a story in *The Master in the Cafe Morphine: A Tribute to Mikhail Bulgakov* ("The Cadaver Is You"), an appearance in *The Weird* (Atlantic/Corvus), an omnibus edition of published work from Centipede Press, *The Wretch of the Sun*, from Ex Occidente Press, and *The Narrator*, from Civil Coping Mechanisms. His columns and the occasional review can be found at TheModernWord.com. He lives and teaches in New York City.

Breinigsville, PA USA
13 April 2011
259793BV00001B/6/P